THE
SPIRIT
OF THE
DRAGON

ALSO BY WILLIAM ANDREWS

Daughters of the Dragon: A Comfort Woman's Story
The Dragon Queen
The Essential Truth
The Dirty Truth

THE
SPIRIT
OF THE
DRAGON

WILLIAM ANDREWS

LAKE UNION
PUBLISHING

Published by Lake Union Publishing, Seattle

www.apub.com

Amazon, the Amazon logo, and Lake Union Publishing are trademarks of Amazon.com, Inc., or its affiliates.

ISBN-13: 9781542004657
ISBN-10: 1542004659

Cover design by PEPE *nymi*, Milano

Printed in the United States of America

This book is dedicated to my amazing daughter, Elizabeth, who got me started learning about Korea

'Tis but thy name that is my enemy. Thou art thyself...

William Shakespeare, *Romeo and Juliet*

ONE

I can't say if having the comb with the two-headed dragon has been a blessing or a curse. Perhaps, like most things mystical, it's some of both. It's like Korea itself, the country where the comb came from, the country from where my American family adopted me. South Korea—the Miracle on the Han River; North Korea—the enigma on the Taedong River.

I'm at my bank in downtown LA to get it from my safe-deposit box. The ancient clerk looks like a ghost haunting the dark, dank basement of the seventy-year-old building. She has long white hair and wears a black skirt that reaches to her ankles. She's slow and deliberate as she rises from her chair and comes to me. I give her my driver's license and tell her my box number is 1257. She pulls out an index card from a wooden file drawer, verifies my ID, and then says, "Follow me, Ms. Carlson." I push through the counter's swinging doors and follow her into the vault.

It's dead quiet in here, and musty. The lighting is poor. Everything is cold hard metal, even the floor. There must be thousands of boxes in long rows with impressive hinges and brass numbers on the front. As I follow the clerk, I wonder what's hidden inside these boxes. Wills declaring who will be rewarded and who will be repudiated when the box's owner dies. Diamond jewelry and pearls stashed away until the next wedding or high-society affair. Valuable coins, gold bars, rare bills. Journals with the owner's confessions. Love letters. So many treasures, so many secrets, but none as precious or as significant as the one in the second row from the bottom, halfway down one of the narrow aisles, inside box 1257.

We're at my box and I'm surprised how nervous I am. I haven't seen the comb since I moved to LA. Back then, I put it inside the box, turned the key, and waited for the next adventure it would take me on. It came at exactly 9:55 this morning.

I was in my office reviewing a green-card petition for one of my clients. My assistant, Jon, knocked on my door and stuck his head in. "Anna," he said, looking worried behind his trendy black glasses, "sorry to bother you, but you have a call. It's a Detective Jackson with the LA police department."

"Seriously?" I said. "What does he want?"

Jon stepped inside my office and closed the door behind him. He raised his palm. "He says it's about a murder."

"A murder? Well, I guess I better take it."

Jon went to his desk and put the call through. I answered on the first ring. "This is Anna Carlson," I said.

"Detective Frank Jackson of the LAPD," a gruff voice replied. "You have a new client."

"I see," I said. "My assistant said you're calling about a murder. Well I'm an international law attorney, Detective, not a criminal lawyer."

"Yeah, I know," Jackson grunted. "Looked you up. But hear me out." The detective proceeded to tell me about a murder that happened early that morning at a nursing home near Koreatown. A ninety-nine-year-old woman named Suk-bo Yi apparently stabbed a hundred-and-one-year-old man in the stomach, killing him. They had the woman in custody at the police department and she said she had a story to tell. She said she would only tell it to me.

"That's terrible," I said, "but I'm afraid I have to decline. She probably heard about me because I represent a lot of Koreans with their immigration issues. But I'm an international lawyer. I don't know criminal law. I'd be no help to Ms. Yi. I'm sure the county can appoint a public defender for her."

"Yeah, she said you'd say that and that if you did, I should tell you that when you come, you should bring the comb with the two-headed dragon."

I took a full five seconds to absorb this. Then I said, "I'll be there in forty minutes." After I hung up, I told Jon to cancel all my appointments, rushed to my car, and headed to the bank.

From somewhere inside her dress, the clerk produces a large brass ring with a single skeleton key on it. She unlocks the door to box 1257 and steps aside. I take the metal container to a privacy room outside the vault. Inside is a faded brown cloth package tied closed with twine. I touch it and feel the spirit of the comb inside. I pull on the string and the cloth falls open.

The comb is the size of a woman's hand, made of tortoiseshell, gently bowed with long tines. Solid gold curves along the spine. The two-headed dragon is made of tiny pieces of ivory in the handle. I pick it up. I'm always surprised how heavy it is. I run a finger over the cool gold spine. The dragon's two heads, curled tongues, and claws seem to reach for me.

The first time my grandmother placed it in my hand, I never dreamed where it would take me. Quests, adventures, a search of my soul, great secrets in strange places. It has taught me a lot, too—what it means to be Korean, even though American parents raised me; the lessons of history; what justice is. It's part of me now. It's in my soul.

I know I'm lucky to have it, but there are times when I wonder what my life would have been like if it hadn't found its way to me.

Certainly it would have been more normal. Perhaps I'd be married by now. Maybe I'd have a child or two. I'd probably be a typical professional wife and mother, blissfully ignorant of the things the comb has taught me. But that isn't the way my life turned out. I'm the keeper of the comb with the two-headed dragon. I must go where it leads me. I must do what it says. It terrifies me sometimes. The responsibility of it. The dangers. What I might learn.

I wrap the comb in the cloth and slip the package inside my briefcase. I take the empty metal container to the clerk, and she locks it inside the vault. She gives me my key. As I drive to the police department, I wonder how a ninety-nine-year-old woman accused of murder in Koreatown knows about the comb.

TWO

When I arrive at the police station, there is a TV truck parked outside with an antenna on a pole pointing skyward. Another truck pulls into the parking lot and begins setting up. Technicians in jeans and reporters in suits huddle alongside the trucks. They're probably here for the nursing home murder. The reporters study me when I get out of my car, and I feel like I'm making a stage entrance. Since I'm Asian, wearing a business suit, and holding a briefcase, I must look like someone they should talk to. As I walk to the entrance, a wolfish-looking female reporter approaches me. I push past her and march into the police station.

Detective Frank Jackson meets me in the glass-and-steel lobby. He's an African American and is as tall and large as I am short and slender. His hair is close-cropped. He wears a gray suit that he should have donated to Goodwill years earlier, a gold badge clipped to his belt. He greets me with a look that says he thinks it's a bad idea that I'm here, a lawyer with no criminal experience.

"I assume those TV people are here for this case," I say.

"Yep," Jackson mutters. "Someone at the nursing home musta tipped them off. They have all kinds of murders they can cover in this city. But this one in a nursing home . . . Don't worry. My captain'll take care of 'em."

"Good."

"You need a pass," Jackson says, pointing a long finger at the reception desk. I sign in and the receptionist hands me a visitor's pass, which I clip to my lapel. Jackson leads me into a meeting room with a small table and chairs. A manila folder rests on the table. He takes the chair in front of the folder. "Sit," Jackson says, pointing to the chair across from him. His tone is cool, almost condescending. "Before you meet your client, you should know the facts of the case."

"That would be a good idea," I reply, wishing I knew if it really was or not.

Jackson rests his elbows on the table, and his large frame hovers over the folder. "Been a cop for twenty-five years," he says. "Last fifteen in homicide. Seen shit regular people can't even imagine. Then I come into work this mornin' and there's this. Victim was a hundred-one years old, for chrissake. Nursing home said his health was failing and he didn't have long to live. Suspect is ninety-nine. Doesn't make sense. 'Course, none of them do, really."

He shakes his head wearily and opens the folder. He hands me photos of the crime scene and explains what he's showing me. The murder happened at the Angels of Mercy nursing home, an upscale nursing facility in a nice neighborhood northeast of downtown. It happened in the morning. "About eight a.m., best as we can guess," Jackson says. He tells me the victim's name was George Adams. "He's Japanese, so it's probably not his real name."

I nod. "Sometimes immigrants change their names when they come to the US. I do that for clients from time to time. Some do it because they want to be like Americans. Some do it because they don't want to be found."

"Uh-huh," Jackson says. He hands me a photo showing an elderly Asian man sitting in a chair and leaning to one side in a nursing home room. The man's mouth is agape and he's clearly dead. He has thin gray hair, and his skin is blotched with age spots. He is so thin his ribs show through his shirt. A red silk scarf is tied around his head like a bandana.

There's an ugly open gash across his midsection and a pool of blood on the carpeting underneath him. I feel my stomach turn and hand the photo back to Jackson.

"Killed with this sword." Jackson hands me a close-up photo of a short sword covered with blood. There are Japanese characters on the handle. "Never seen a sword like that used in a murder," Jackson says. "Don't know what it says there on the handle. We sent a photo of it out to get it translated."

I examine the photo. "It says 'honor,'" I say. "And it's a knife, not a sword. It's what it's called—a *tanto* knife. It was used by samurai for *seppuku*." I look at Jackson. "Seppuku is also called hara-kiri. That's suicide, Detective."

Jackson returns my stare. "Is that so?" he says. I can't tell if he's genuinely impressed or if he's being sarcastic. "Well, Counselor, a sword like that . . . knife, whatever you call it . . . can be used for murder, too. Your client was in the room with the victim."

I give the photo back. "Did they know each other?"

He nods. "Yep. Staff says she visits him every day. Lives about a mile away. How exactly they're related, we don't know. We're looking into it."

Jackson points to the photo of the dead man. "He's got that scarf on his head. Nursing home staff say they never saw it before."

"When Japanese samurai committed honor-suicide, they would wear ceremonial clothing. It's strange that the scarf is Korean, though. I can tell by the design in it."

"Well, that *is* interesting," Jackson says. This time, I can tell he's sincere.

"Where's Ms. Yi now?" I ask, pushing away from the table. "I want to talk to her."

The detective stays seated and eyes me. "What's this thing about a dragon comb?" he asks. "What does a comb have to do with this?" I can see in Jackson's glare that he's good at his game and that he likes to win. He's been a homicide detective for fifteen years, he said, and I've never done this before. If I'm not careful, I could blow my client's case.

"Honestly, I don't know what it has to do with this," I answer. "But whatever it is, it's between me and my client."

"Okay," Jackson shrugs. He still doesn't move. After a few seconds he says, "Ms. Carlson, we don't want your client to claim she wasn't properly represented. So I gotta ask. Now that you've seen all this, doesn't it concern you that you're not a criminal lawyer?"

"It does concern me, Detective," I say, facing him straight on. "But Ms. Yi requested me and that makes me her lawyer for the time being. I assure you that when I need help with the criminal aspects of this case, I'll see that Ms. Yi gets proper representation. Now please, take me to my client."

Finally, Detective Jackson gets up and opens the door for me. "She's in the interrogation room. Can't exactly put an old woman like that in a holding cell. She asked for some sort of special tea. One of our counter clerks—she's Korean—happened to have some. Follow me."

She sits straight-backed at a metal table in a small windowless room. The fluorescent lights bathe her in white. She wears a buttonless purple blouse and plain gray slacks. Her gnarled hands curl around a teacup as if she's trying to keep them warm. Deep wrinkles crease her face, and her hair is pure white held in place with an elegant silver hairpin.

She lifts her chin when she sees me. "Hello, Anna," she says as if she knows me and knew I would come. With her contented expression, she looks like she could be at her great-granddaughter's birthday party.

I give her a polite bow and say in Korean, "*Anyohaseyo*, Ms. Yi. Have we met before?"

"I do not think so," she replies in Korean. "No." Her voice cracks with age, but her words are clear and direct.

"I'm pleased to meet you, ma'am," I say, keeping the conversation in Korean. "But I must ask, why do you want me here now? You should have a criminal lawyer."

"I do not want a criminal lawyer," she replies. "You are the one who must hear my story." She looks at me directly. Her eyes are watery but keen.

I remember that Detective Jackson followed me into the room and is standing behind me. I turn to him. "Detective, I'd like to be alone with my client."

"No," Ms. Yi says in English before Jackson can leave. "He should stay. I want to be on record."

"Ma'am," I say, "I don't think that's a good idea."

"That depends on what my objective is," Ms. Yi says. She speaks English well, but has an accent. "I am not concerned about their criminal charges. No. I want my story on record. He should stay."

"You know, Ms. Yi, they want to charge you with murder."

"Maybe they are right!" she says with a lilt in her voice. "Or maybe they will change their minds once they hear my story. Either way, I am ninety-nine years old." She gives an almost girlish smile. "What can they do to me?"

Without saying a word, Jackson goes to a cabinet and takes out a recording device. He sets it on the table and turns it on. The "record" light glows red. He sits in a chair off to the side and folds his arms across his chest. I shoot a disapproving glance at him but he doesn't move.

With Detective Jackson in the room and the recorder on, this is where I should call a criminal lawyer. Ms. Yi, my client, wants to talk on the record. I don't need to be a criminal lawyer to know it's a terrible idea. But when I look at her now, she seems lucid, intelligent, and perfectly capable of making her own decisions. She has a story to tell and somehow it has something to do with the comb with the two-headed dragon. My lawyer's instincts tell me I should back out. But as the protector of the comb, I must stay.

I sit alongside Ms. Yi. I make sure to sit straight and proper like a good Korean woman should. "Tell me, ma'am, what happened at the nursing home," I say, taking a notepad from my briefcase.

"You must hear my story to know what happened there," she replies. "May I have more tea, please?"

"Bori cha?" I ask.

She gives me a nod. "Of course!"

"Detective?" I say over my shoulder. "I'll have some, too." Without getting up from his chair, Jackson opens the door and says something to someone behind it. "It'll be here in a sec," he says.

"Thank you," Ms. Yi says. She points at the recorder. "Your recording device, Detective, how long does it go?"

"Two hours, I think."

"Two hours?" Ms. Yi says. "That is not long enough."

Jackson gives me a look. "We'll take care of it if necessary," he says.

There's a knock. Jackson opens the door and someone hands him a teapot and a teacup. He sets them on the table and folds his arms across his chest again. I reach over and pour the barley tea into Ms. Yi's cup, then fill the other one for myself. The sharp, earthy aroma fills the room, making me feel like I'm in Korea again. "In the Korean culture, Detective, you must show respect to your elders and pour their tea for them," I say. Jackson doesn't reply.

Ms. Yi takes her cup in both hands and gives me a knowing smile as if we are actors in some grand drama. It feels like it has many times before with the comb with the two-headed dragon—secrets, inside stories, mysteries. I set my pad and pen down. I take off my visitor's badge and lay it on the table in front of me. I take my teacup into my hands. "I'm ready, Ms. Yi," I say.

She nods almost imperceptibly. She takes a sip of tea and curls her hands around the teacup. She lifts her chin and closes her eyes. It is perfectly quiet in the room. With her eyes closed, her face softens and she looks years younger, almost like a girl from long before.

Then she begins in a faraway voice. "The Japanese administrator came to my father's house in a Ford Model T motorcar . . ."

THREE

Northern Korea, 1936

The Japanese administrator came to my father's house in a Ford Model
T motorcar. It was the type that had only two seats in the front and,
instead of back seats, a low trunk. A late spring rain had fallen the
previous day, and I was in the root garden along the side of our house
helping my mother pull the daikons we had planted the previous fall.
We already had a half basket of the long, white radishes when we heard
the car sputtering up the road. Mother stood and wiped her hands on
her skirt. My mother, like me, was small in height and build. In her face,
you could see that years earlier, she had been pretty. Her hair, worn in
a loose braid, was speckled with gray. She watched as the Ford's spoke
wheels churned up clods of mud fighting the ruts in the road. Yellow
splatters covered the sides of the car halfway to the windows.

We didn't often see cars on our road. Of course, I had seen many
cars in Sinuiju, the city closest to our village. I sometimes went there
with Mother to buy supplies when we had money. In Sinuiju, the
Japanese sat high in their cars looking down their noses at the Koreans.
Mother told me not to stare at the men in their cars, but I snuck a look
when she wasn't looking. Once, I saw a big black car with a driver and

a man in back. I assumed it was a high official or a wealthy landlord. As the driver honked at pedestrians to get out of the way, the man sat looking straight forward with the windows rolled up as if to keep the stench of Korea out.

When the Model T pulled to a stop in front of our house, Mother said, "Suk-bo, hide the daikons and get your father at once. Then go inside and clean up the house."

The administrator shut off his machine, and the engine went quiet. He got out of the car with a piece of paper in his hand and approached our house. He wore a wrinkled Western-style black suit that was too big for him, and thick, gold-framed glasses. I hid the basket of daikons and ran to where my father was working in his shack. It took a moment for my eyes to adjust to the dark. Father hunched over his bench, working on a bentwood yoke. His old saws and carving tools hung on hooks on the wall above him. Wood was scarce where we lived—the Japanese took nearly all the timber the woodsmen harvested—so my father's carpentry skills repairing plow handles and stools and carts were always in demand. He worked long hours, sometimes well into the night.

"*Appa,*" I said, "the administrator has come!"

Father set down his hammer and looked out the shack door. My father was not tall but strong and lean with hard black eyes. He wore a white bandana, tied tight around his head. He slowly took it off. "Suk-bo," he said, still looking outside, "go to the house. Go now."

As Father went around the front of the house, I hurried inside. I quickly put things in their place—the tea bowls in the open cupboard, the shoes lined up neatly at the front door, blankets folded at the foot of the sleeping mat. I hurriedly swept the floor. The Japanese insisted that we keep our houses neat and clean, and they often conducted surprise inspections. I heard once that the thatched roof of a farmer's house nearby was rotting and had maggots. To teach him a lesson, the official forced the farmer to eat the maggots.

After I'd cleaned up, I went to the latticed windows of the main room and pressed my ear against the *hanji* paper between the latticework. I strained to hear what the administrator was saying, but I could only catch a few words.

"Read this," I heard the administrator say in Japanese. And ". . . a new rule . . ." and ". . . your daughter is the right age . . ."

They were talking about me. I didn't know what the administrator was saying they wanted me to do, but I knew I would not want to do it. And who was I to have the administrator drive all the way to my village in his car? I was no one—a sixteen-year-old girl that nobody paid attention to. I held my breath and continued to listen.

"You will be notified," the administrator said. "It is your duty . . ."

"Yes, sir," I heard Mother say. I did not hear Father say anything.

The car engine coughed and rumbled to life. I cracked open the window and looked out. The car's gears engaged with a grind, and the wheels turned and spun in the mud. The automobile lurched along the road, trailing black exhaust as it went back from where it came.

My parents turned to come to the house, so I quickly closed the window and sat on a floor mat, pretending that I had been there all along. When the door swung open, they both glanced at me. Mother went to the basin and washed her hands. Father held a flimsy pink paper as if he didn't know what to do with it. Neither one said a word, and though I wanted to ask what the administrator had said, I knew I should stay quiet.

When Mother finished washing her hands, she sat on the mat across from me, and Father sat next to her. He set the pink paper on the floor. Mother looked straight at me. She was petite but strong and had a well-defined chin. "Suk-bo," she said, "you are sixteen years old now. You are a woman." Normally my father, a man and the head of the household, would be the one to speak first. Instead, he stared at the paper and let my mother talk.

"I married your father when I was your age. It is time for you to marry, too."

"I do not want to marry anyone," I said. "Kwan-so is two years older and he has not married."

"Your brother is a man," Mother said, "and men can wait to get married until they are older. And he is away at school and must finish his studies. Since you are no longer in school, you should think about getting married."

"I will not," I said under my breath.

"Suk-bo!" Father said. "It is important that you understand what your mother is saying."

Father was right, I was not always as respectful as I should be. Most times when I was disrespectful, my father would turn away or pretend he didn't hear what I had said. Mother, however, always scolded me. Sometimes she would swat me, although never very hard. Now it was Father scolding me. "I am sorry, Appa," I said, although I was not sorry at all.

Mother continued. "The Japanese have a new rule. They want Korean women to marry Japanese men. The rule applies to all unmarried women sixteen years and older. The administrator is informing all families with daughters that age. That is what it says on the paper."

"But we are Koreans!" I protested to my father, hoping he would agree with me. I knew Father didn't like the Japanese. He often said he thought they should leave Korea, though he said it only when Mother wasn't near.

My father didn't say anything. Mother went on. "Yes, we are Koreans. However, they want us to be Japanese."

"Why?" I asked. "Why must we always do as they say?"

"Because that is how it is with them," Mother replied.

"Well, I do not know any Japanese boys," I said.

I looked at my father. I hoped he would take pity on me as he often did and tell Mother we didn't have to follow their rules. But his shoulders were hunched and his eyes were unfocused. He looked like many of the men in my village, broken and resentful. Without looking up he said, "We could move to the north, Jo-soo. I know a man in Manchuria who can help me get work there."

Mother shook her head. "You want to go to Manchuria to join the rebels, Seong-ki," she said. "Anyway, our family is here."

"The police come to our village more often now," Father replied, his voice strained. "They came twice last week with their inspections and questions and new rules. Always their rules." He shook his head. "They arrested Mr. Pak last week. Mrs. Pak told me they bound his hands behind his back and kicked him before they pushed him into the car. Someday they will arrest me, too."

"They threaten you because you do not hide your disgust," Mother said. "If you were more careful and cooperated with them . . ."

"When does it stop?" Father bellowed, his jaw tightening. "Every month there are new rules, and you say we should cooperate. Now they want our daughter to marry a Japanese. They are destroying us."

There was a long pause, and the tension inside the house was thick like fog. Finally, Mother said, "Suk-bo, go pull the rest of the daikons."

I wrung my hands in front of my chest. "Please, *Ummah*," I pleaded, "don't make me marry a Japanese. We should do as Father says and go to Manchuria."

"Daughter!" Mother scolded. "Go now!"

I went outside and retrieved the basket, then went to the garden and kneeled at the daikons. Their leaves were bright green from the previous day's rain. As I pulled the radishes from the ground and brushed the mud off, I heard Father and Mother talking inside the house, quietly at first, then louder. They were arguing again. It wasn't proper for a woman to argue with her husband, but these days it happened every time the officials came to our village. I hated when they fought. I never really paid much attention to what they were fighting about. I would let them carry on and would go for a walk in the forest behind our village or visit a friend. Now, however, they were arguing about me.

I couldn't bear listening to them. I tried to shut my ears and turn my attention to the daikons. I grabbed one of the leafy tops and pulled. The top snapped off, so I dug around the root to free it. I pulled on the root's top, but it broke too, leaving half in the ground and half in my hand. I looked at the half daikon in my hand. I didn't even like daikons. We grew them because the official in charge of our village didn't take them from us. He said our poor soil made them bitter and sharp. As my father and mother fought inside the house, I threw the half daikon into the grass at the edge of the garden.

I thought of a boy I liked named Jung-soo who lived up the road. The son of Farmer Dho, he was lanky and shy and about my age. I couldn't say he was handsome, although he wasn't unpleasant to look at. Whenever the villages got together for a celebration, I'd catch him staring at me. We hadn't talked to each other yet, but now that I might be forced to marry a Japanese man, I planned to talk to Jung-soo at the next opportunity.

The back door flew open and Father stomped out. He marched into his shack and slammed the door. Soon I could hear him hammering on something.

Mother came to the garden and pulled daikons alongside me. After a while, she said, "Suk-bo, the Japanese are our rulers and we must obey them. Your father thinks we should fight them. But I fear that if we fight . . . well, you cannot lose a fight you do not take." She tried to smile, but it was as if she had forgotten how to. Over the past several years, her face had lost its once gentle beauty. Now it was thin, with lines around her eyes and mouth. Her chin had grown hard, and there was no life in her face.

After a few seconds, she said, "If they find someone for you to marry, that is what you will do."

"Why can't we go to Manchuria like Appa said?" I asked.

Mother stopped pulling the daikons. "Listen to me, Suk-bo. It would be very hard in Manchuria. We would have nothing and always be in danger. We would be hungry. This . . . this is a chance for you to have a better life."

"I do not care," I said. "I will not marry a Japanese."

"Yes, you will, Daughter," Mother said. She started pulling daikons again. "We will not talk about it any longer."

From Mother's tone I knew it would do no good to argue with her. So as Father pounded away in his shed, I pulled daikons next to my mother and worried about a Japanese man that someday I might have to marry.

FOUR

The next morning, I woke to the sound of Father working in his shed. He was hammering again, and his hammering was loud. I looked out to the main room of our house. It was earlier than I usually woke up, and the morning light bathed the room in muted colors. Mother was at the stove stirring something in the iron pot.

I rolled over on my mat to go back to sleep, but Father's pounding kept me awake. I remembered the new rule that Korean girls like me must be available to marry a Japanese man and knew I would not be able to sleep anymore.

I crawled off my mat and went into the main room. It was cool, but because my mother was cooking, the floor was warm from the *ondol* heating underneath the house. Mother glanced over her shoulder at me. "You are awake early, Suk-bo," she said.

"Why is Appa making so much noise?" I asked, rubbing my eyes.

"Yes," Mother said, "he is loud this morning, isn't he?"

"Why is he so loud?"

Mother pointed for me to sit at the low table. She brought a tea-kettle and two small tea bowls to the table. She poured the tea into the bowls. I took a sip, and the hot, bitter bori cha tea began to wake me up.

"Your father is angry," Mother said. "More so today than usual."

"Is he angry at the Japanese again?"

"Yes," Mother said, nodding.

"Is he angry about the new rule?" I asked.

Mother set her tea bowl on the table. "Suk-bo, there is something you should know about your father. We did not feel you needed to know this before, but now that you are older . . ." Mother gave me a smile, not like the forced smile she'd had lately, but like the gentle one I remembered from years earlier. My heart softened. I so wanted to go back to those days when Mother was tender and Father wasn't angry all the time.

As we sat at the table and sipped our tea, Mother told me about the time before I was born. She said the Japanese were strict then. The police beat and killed Koreans who did not obey them. Sometimes they killed for no reason at all. "It was a horrible time," Mother said. "We were always afraid."

Then Mother told me that in March of 1919, our people began to fight back. Students in Seoul issued a declaration of independence that sparked protests and riots all over the country. The provincial government called in the military to put down the riots, and the soldiers killed thousands of demonstrators. They arrested tens of thousands more, some of whom they shot in the streets.

"Your father wanted to join the resistance," Mother said. "But we had a young child—your brother—and I had just become pregnant with you, so I begged him to stay home, and he did. However, his younger brother, your uncle Chul-han, did not have children and joined the resistance. He went to Seoul and . . ." Mother looked into her tea bowl. "I am sorry to tell you, Suk-bo, your uncle was one who the police shot in the street."

I took a moment to think about this. I knew my father had had a younger brother, and I knew that he had died before I was born. I'd never thought to ask how he had died, and my parents had never told me. And now that I knew about my uncle, I saw Father in a different

19

way. Of course he hated the Japanese. Of course he was angry all the time. I would be angry, too, if the Japanese had executed my brother. In fact, though I didn't know my uncle, anger swelled inside me for what they had done to him.

"Why don't we fight them?" I asked. "I am not afraid."

"Huh," Mother said with a nod. "You have always been more spirited like your father. But after the demonstrations, we did not need to fight. Though we did not gain our independence, they were not so cruel as they were before. They encouraged us to help them build a new Korea. They gave us more independence. They were not as strict."

"Then why is Father so angry now?" I asked.

Mother sighed. "Times are changing," she said. "The Japanese are going back to the way they were before."

"Then we should fight them!" I declared. "Like Uncle did, like Father wants to."

"He and I have talked," Mother said. "We will stay here and do as the Japanese say."

Mother smiled at me again, but this time it was her forced smile. After a few seconds, she gathered our tea bowls and the teakettle and took them to the basin. She went to the stove and started stirring the pot. "I'm cooking rice. When it cools, you and I will make *dduk* for the festival tomorrow."

I wanted to ask again why we couldn't fight the Japanese, but I knew Mother would not answer me. So I went to the sleeping room and pulled on my day clothes. When I went back, Mother had prepared a small bowl of millet for my breakfast. When I finished eating, I had to do my chores. I went to the garden and pulled weeds from around the napa cabbage. I gathered sticks and dried grass, took them to the house, and put them in the wood box next to the stove. I swept the floor. Finally, I had finished my chores and it was time for me to study. I was studying Japanese writing, math, literature, and philosophy. Since

I was no longer in school—country girls like me rarely went to school after age twelve—Mother thought I should learn how to sew and cook. But Father insisted I continue to learn what they taught in the schools, and Mother did not mind that I did. I was glad she let me. I enjoyed my studies, and I was a good student.

But I didn't study that day. Instead, I decided to go to the forest behind our house to pick strawberries. That's what I said I wanted to do, but honestly, I just wanted to get away for a while. I was worried about having to marry a Japanese man someday, especially after the story Mother told me about my uncle. I needed time to think about what I should do.

I snuck out the back door, but before I went to the forest, I peeked into Father's work shed. He had stopped pounding, and he sat in front of his bench staring at nothing. I thought he was crying, and I would have been terribly embarrassed if he was. But when he turned to me, I saw that his jaw was hard and his eyes were like embers.

"Suk-bo," he said, "what do you want?" It was unusual for me to interrupt Father while he was working, and I thought he was angry at me.

"I . . . I," I stammered, "I want to tell you I am going to the forest to look for strawberries."

He nodded. "Yes," he said, his face softening a little. "Do not go too far."

"Yes, Appa," I said.

"Suk-bo," he said before I left, "you do not have to marry a Japanese man."

I loved my father, and now I was beginning to understand him. Though he could be strict, I knew it was because he cared about me. And like a strong, loving father, I believed he would protect me from the Japanese.

"Thank you, Appa," I said.

Father turned to his bench. I left and headed for the forest.

It was a lovely late spring day. Puffy white clouds slid lazily across the blue sky. The grass was cool from the spring rain, and the sun was warm on my shoulders. I looked for strawberries in open places where, when I was young, my mother had shown me they grew. I loved strawberries and was good at finding them hidden among the grass and low bushes. It wasn't long before I found a patch. There were only a few red berries hanging close to the ground. I picked them and dropped them in the bamboo basket I'd brought with me. Their sweet smell told me that they were ripe and ready to eat. I went farther into the forest to where I could no longer see the village. I found another patch, and farther on, another and another. In no time, my basket was full of red, ripe strawberries.

I went to an opening where the sun fell full on the ground. I set my basket down and sat in the grass. Here and there, birds flitted among the trees and chirped at each other. Squirrels chattered and bees buzzed. I heard something in the trees. I looked for it but didn't see anything. A small water deer perhaps, or a fox hunting a rabbit. I lay on my back. Soon, the heady smell of the pine forest and the cool grass beneath me cleared my head. Here, finally, I could relax and think about what I should do.

I had known some of the things that Mother told me about the Japanese. The people in the village were complaining more and more about how they were treating us. The men complained that the taxes were too high, leaving us with little money. There were rumors that the police were making arrests for petty reasons like refusing to speak Japanese or wearing white—which they said was a form of protest. Some families had moved to China. I never worried that trouble would come to me or my family. It is true that my father complained just like others. But he never committed a crime or did anything that the police would arrest him for. I thought we were safe and didn't need to be concerned about the Japanese. All that changed when the administrator came with the new rule.

I thought about what I would do if they said I had to marry a Japanese man. I did not like the Japanese. They were boorish and arrogant. Maybe Mother would agree to move to Manchuria. Maybe I could get the farmer's son, Jung-soo, to marry me instead. Or maybe, when they introduced me to the man they wanted me to marry, I could be ill-mannered and rude.

I thought about what I should do to be rude. I could refuse to bow and not answer questions. I could tell him that I thought he was ugly. I could spit out my tea and say it was cold. Maybe I could break something. Of course, it might get me in trouble with the police, and with Mother, too. But if it worked, Father would understand and tell me I was clever for thinking of a way out of having to marry a Japanese. Mother would have to agree.

Yes, that's what I would do. I would be rude—a monkey girl that no one would ever want to marry.

Pleased with myself, I put my hands under my head and looked at the sky. It was so blue and the air smelled so fresh. The sounds of the forest sang like a chorus.

I closed my eyes and let my mind drift. It went to our village and the people there I loved: my mother and father; Mr. Kwan, the blacksmith whose face was always covered with soot; the farmers—the Paks and the Kims, who hid food from their Japanese landlords and smuggled it to us. I pictured my brother, Kwan-so, studying at the Japanese school in Pyongyang. I hadn't seen him in over a year, and I missed him terribly. He was always kind to me, even though he liked to tease me about being petite. "You are a delicate flower," he would say to me when I complained about something. "But a flower with thorns!" I prayed I would see him again, soon. I thought about what Mother had told me about my uncle, and my mind drifted to Seoul, years earlier when the mob demanded independence. The people carried signs and shouted angrily at the police. I saw my uncle in the mob. He looked like my father, only younger. I saw soldiers pull him from the throng and tie his hands behind his back. They dragged him to the street. I saw a soldier raise his rifle and point it at my uncle's head.

I heard something in the forest again. It did not sound like the dainty water deer or a sneaky fox. It was something bigger. I snapped out of my reverie and sat up. I peered into the forest but saw nothing. Perhaps I imagined it. Then I saw something move behind a tree. My heart began to pound. Father had told me not to go too far into the forest, and I had gone farther than I should have. There were tigers in this part of the forest, and wild pigs, too.

I stood. "Who's there?" I shouted. I picked up my basket and held it close. "Is anyone there?" I heard no answer.

I started toward the village, walking at first, then running. Strawberries tumbled from my basket. Over my shoulder, I saw something coming toward me through the grass. I made for the trees, but whatever was chasing me was getting closer. I dropped my basket and ran as fast as I could. I made it to the trees but tripped on a root and fell. I rolled over on my back. The sun was in my eyes as a shadow appeared above me. I put my hand up to block the glare.

It was a man. He wore a white Western-style shirt and black trousers. He was young, only a year or two older than me. He was lean but not tall. He was handsome. He held out my basket to me. All the strawberries had fallen out.

I took the basket. "Who are you?" I demanded, my heart still racing.

He crouched next to me, resting his elbows on his knees. Out of the sun, I saw him better. His face was pleasantly lean but not long. His sparkling, liquid eyes were perfectly spaced and topped by almost feminine eyebrows. His hair was shiny black and trimmed above his ears, the way Japanese men wore it. He wasn't tall like Korean men, and his skin was dark, like the Japanese.

"Are you okay?" he asked, speaking Korean.

"Yes, I think so."

"I did not mean to scare you," he said. He looked both embarrassed and amused.

I was angry now. This man had indeed given me quite a scare. I stood up. "Who are you?" I asked again. "Tell me your name."

"I am Hisashi," he answered, still in his crouch.

"You are Japanese?" I asked.

"I am. What is your name?"

"I am Suk-bo," I replied, brushing myself off. "I have never heard of someone named Hisashi. You are not from around here."

"I'm from Sinuiju, not so far away."

"Sinuiju is a three-hour walk," I said. "That is far away to me. Why did you come here?"

"I am hunting for a treasure. I heard there are great treasures in this part of the forest." He picked a blade of grass and twirled it between his fingers.

"What sort of treasure are you looking for?" I asked.

"One that is beautiful to see." Hisashi examined the blade of grass.

"I have lived here all of my life," I said with a huff. "I know this forest well. There is no such treasure here."

"It is not only what you think it is," he said. "The value of a treasure is in the judgment of the one who wants it. For example, some might say that you are a treasure."

"You speak nonsense," I said. "How can a person be a treasure?"

"She can be beautiful," he said. "She can have a strong spirit. She can be unlike any other girl in the forest. That would make her a treasure indeed!"

His words made me uncomfortable, but a little excited. I said, "I do not believe you are looking for a treasure. I think you are a spy. You should not spy on people. You scared me and made me drop my strawberries."

Hisashi tossed the blade of grass aside. He extended his hand. "Come. I'll help you pick some more."

I didn't take his hand. He was Japanese, and I had learned not to trust them. They treated Koreans like me with contempt, and they were often cruel. The Japanese boys I knew—the sons of landlords and officials—liked to punch Korean girls and call us names. Once, a boy pulled my hair and pinched my breast when I got too close to him. He said I smelled like kimchi.

But this boy, this young man who held his hand out to me, was different. He didn't look at me the way other Japanese did. There was tenderness in his face. He was handsome, too, with his delicate features and lively eyes. And he spoke to me in Korean not Japanese. Still, he was Japanese, and I knew they could be slippery and two-faced. And just hours earlier, I had learned what they had done to my uncle. I couldn't possibly be attracted to this man.

"I have decided I do not want strawberries today," I declared. "They are not ripe. They are hard and will taste sour. I think I will go back home." I picked up my basket and said, "Goodbye."

"I will go with you," Hisashi said eagerly. "It is not safe for a girl to be alone in the forest."

"I am not afraid," I replied. "I can take care of myself."

"I will go with you anyway," he said and fell in step alongside me.

We went for a while without talking. Then Hisashi said, "Have you heard about the new rule where a Korean woman must marry a Japanese man if she is selected?"

"It is a silly rule," I said. "Japanese and Koreans should not marry. It is not right. I will not do it."

"Why does it matter if he is Japanese?" Hisashi asked. "It is only the naming that is your enemy. Is a man less handsome because he is Japanese? Is he less interesting? Does nationality defeat love?"

"Love? If it is love, there is no need for a rule."

"That is true," Hisashi said with a nod. "So tell me, do you think *I* am interesting and handsome?"

"Ha!" I scoffed. "You are not as handsome and interesting as you think you are."

"Don't you think I am just a little handsome and interesting?" he asked, still grinning.

I looked away so he wouldn't see me smile. I didn't answer, and we continued walking. Soon, we were at the field near my house. "I live over there," I said, pointing.

He faced me and gave a polite bow, which surprised me. A Japanese had never bowed to me before. Then he said, "I think I will come to this forest again. And when I return, I will no longer be Hisashi. Instead, I will have a Korean name. Then, perhaps, you will like me better."

I felt my cheeks go warm and didn't know what to say. Finally, I said, "You should not spy on girls in the forest." Then I ran through the field the rest of the way to my house.

And all that day, I couldn't stop thinking about the handsome, interesting man named Hisashi who was looking for a treasure in the forest.

FIVE

The next morning, Mother, Father, and I packed our haversack with herbed rice cakes Mother and I had made for the Dano, or spring, celebration with my mother's family. We'd cut back on rice for two months to have enough to make the cakes. Mother and I put on blue blouses, and Father wore a red shirt for the celebration. Around his waist, Father wore a twist of iris roots to ward off evil spirits.

When I'd returned from the forest the day before, I didn't tell my parents about the handsome young man named Hisashi. I didn't want to create a fuss. Mother would have scolded me for going too far away from the house. Father would have asked me about the man, and I would've had to tell him he was Japanese. That would have made Father angry, and he would have wanted to know more. Mother would have told Father to not be so angry, which would have made him stomp off to his shed. So I'd decided to keep the encounter to myself.

It was two miles to my uncle's house, where the festival would take place. We set out on the road with others from our village. There was the blacksmith, Mr. Kwan, and his wife and two girls—Soo-sung Kwan was a year older than me and Mi-sung two years younger. There was the farmer Mr. Kim, and his wife and their two young boys. I did not see the farmer Mr. Pak or his family. I remembered then that Father said the police had arrested him.

The spring rains had turned the forest and fields a deep green. The sun was out and the air was fresh and clean. I was excited. I loved visiting my uncle and aunt, my cousins, and our friends and neighbors. I loved the Dano holiday with the dances, games, and foods we only had at festivals.

My uncle's house was the largest house around. It had a tile roof, a big wooden door, and a veranda along the front. A persimmon tree stood in a large front yard, and fields lined the back. My mother's brother—his name was Hwan-gi—was younger than Mother. He had married into a wealthy family and moved in with his wife, Bo-sun, and her parents to help them take care of their farm. My uncle and aunt had a nine-year-old daughter named Soo-hee and a seven-year-old daughter named Jae-hee. Bo-sun's father and mother were too old to work on the farm, and I heard Father say that Uncle was struggling to meet the harvest quota the officials demanded of him.

By the time we got to the farm, there must have been forty people there. A man tuned the strings on his *gayageum*, as another set up his *buk* drum. Young children ran around in the yard as young children do. The Kim boys tried to climb the persimmon tree. Like me and Mother, the women wore blue, and like Father, the men wore red. The women were preparing a table of food—*dduk* sweet rice cakes, *jeon* pancakes with onions, kimchi, and bowls of *sujeonggwa* cinnamon punch. It had been a long time since I'd had food like this, and I couldn't wait until the ceremonies were over and it was time to eat.

Father went to talk to some men, and Mother and I went to the food table to give them our rice cakes. My aunt Bo-sun stood there holding Jae-hee's hand. My aunt was tall with square shoulders, and always wore a half smile, as if both amused and serious. She did not wear a blue blouse like the other women. Instead, she wore a long white dress. Mother frowned when she saw. "You should not wear white, Bo-sun," Mother said. "The Japanese forbid it."

"I wear white during the festival to say that I am Korean," my aunt replied. "We cannot lose our traditions, Jo-soo."

Mother set the herb cakes on the table and bowed her head, which surprised me because Mother was older than my aunt. I assumed it was because my aunt's family had been wealthy once. As we walked away from the table, Mother said, "Someday, I fear, your aunt will get my brother killed."

Mother and I stood with the rest of the people in front of the house waiting for the festivities to begin. I looked around for the farmer's son, Jung-soo, but I didn't see him. It was strange that he wasn't there, staring at me from inside the crowd. Maybe he was sick, or perhaps he'd gone to the school in Sinuiju or Pyongyang.

The blacksmith's daughter, Soo-sung, came to me and pulled me away from my mother.

"Did you hear about the new rule?" she whispered.

"Yes," I said. "The administrator came two days ago. He gave us a paper with the rule on it."

Soo-sung was taller than me, and she had an angular, disagreeable face. She lifted her chin and said, "I will not marry a Japanese man. We are going to run away to Manchuria, away from the Japanese and their rules."

"You are going to go to Manchuria? When?"

"Soon," Soo-sung replied, looking past me. "Before they match me with a Japanese man."

"Father wants to leave, too," I said. "But Mother says we should stay."

"If you stay, you will be forced to marry a Japanese. You will become a *chinilpa*."

"I will not help the Japanese. I will marry farmer Dho's son, Jung-soo. He likes me."

"Jung-soo? Haven't you heard? The police took his father's farm. They just took it without giving them anything for it. Mr. Dho took his family to Seoul to look for work."

I was shocked. It seemed that the Japanese were destroying families like the Paks and Dhos for no reason at all.

"I have a plan so that they will not want to marry me," I said.

Soo-sung looked down her nose at me. "What is your plan?"

"I will be rude to them. I will insult them and act up."

"That will not work," Soo-sung said, shaking her head. "They will beat you and make you get married anyway."

"Well, what will you do in Manchuria?" I countered. "I heard that the Chinese men there are ugly and rough. You will not want to marry them."

"I would rather marry a Chinese man than a Japanese," Soo-sung huffed. She walked away and disappeared into the crowd.

I went back to Mother, and it was time for the festivities to begin. My uncle stood on his veranda and quieted the crowd. He introduced his father-in-law, an old man with a white beard. My uncle bowed to his father-in-law and helped him to the veranda. Then, in a voice strained with age, the elderly man thanked the spirits of our ancestors for all they had given us. He acknowledged the other elders who were there, and we bowed to each one. He said it was good that we celebrated together so that we would remember our heritage.

And then the entertainment began. First, a group of players acted out the story of Dor-yeong Namu, the son of the spirit tree, and the great flood. A man holding tree branches above his head played Dor-yeong Namu. Women with blue ribbons danced around him, pretending to be the great flood. A narrator explained that during the flood, Dor-yeong saved a colony of ants from the water. Then he saved a swarm of mosquitos, a crane, a deer, a cow, and a tiger until he had saved all the animals of the world. Finally, he saved a young boy. A boy several years younger than me came onto the stage and held Dor-yeong's hand. The women with the blue ribbons left, signifying the flood was over. Then, two young women dressed in peasant clothes entered the stage. While the actor playing Dor-yeong, the boy, and the two girls danced, the narrator explained that Dor-yeong and the boy married two sisters and started the next race of humans. The actors left the stage, and the audience applauded politely.

Next came music and dancing. First, the men in their red shirts danced the *nongak*. They performed the farmer's dance, pounding drums that hung around their waist and clanging cymbals. Father and several other men marched and leaped in a circle around the drummers while spinning white ribbons on a stick. As he danced, Father looked like he was in a trance.

When the men finished, five women danced the *taepyeongmu*, the peace dance. The women glided and turned gracefully as a drummer played a slow rhythm. In the center was my aunt in her white dress. Her moves were skillful, and although she was the youngest, I could see she was leading the other dancers.

When the dancing was done, it was time for comedy and satire. This was my favorite part of the festival. I loved the banter between the satirists and the audience. I pushed to the front to get a better view. A man stepped into the center wearing a white mask to disguise himself. The mask had a long thick nose, bushy eyebrows, and huge ears. By the way he carried himself, I could see the masked man was young. I tried to see who he was, but with his mask on, I could not.

The crowd threw insults at him, pointed and laughed. I covered my mouth and laughed with them.

"You have a face like a donkey!" one person said.

"Are you as dumb as a donkey, too?" another shouted.

The man held up his hand. "Quiet!" he ordered. "I am a Japanese donkey, and you may not insult me!"

"A Japanese donkey?" a man said. "All Japanese are donkeys!" The crowd laughed again.

"You say Japanese are donkeys," the masked man said, "but if we are donkeys, you are pigs. And donkeys do work while pigs wallow in mud. We build roads and dams and bring electricity to you. We have brought order and efficiency, too." The man raised his palm to the sky. "Of course, you pigs have had to give us everything you own and change your wallowing way of life. But that is not too high a price to pay for all we have given you, is it?"

At this, the crowd hissed and whistled. I hissed with them.

"You ungrateful pigs!" the masked man shouted, pointing at the crowd. "Yes, we have stolen everything from you. But us donkeys have given you something even more valuable than these things I have said. We have given you someone to despise. Think of that!"

The crowd cheered. "That is true!" one person said.

"Yes!" said another. "We despise the Japanese donkeys!"

"Without us to hate," the masked man continued, "you would fight among yourselves, clan versus clan, as you did for hundreds of years. Without us donkeys, you would be poor pigs, trapped in your miserable past. Instead of despising us, you should thank us for uniting you!"

The crowd hissed again. Someone yelled, "We would rather be trapped in our miserable past than to have to live with donkeys!"

"Go home, donkey," another man said.

"You want us donkeys to go home?" the masked man asked. "Why should we go home? Korea has everything donkeys need—forests and fields, mountains and minerals. Korea is much too nice for pigs. It is much more suited for donkeys."

The crowd hissed and whistled. Again, I hissed with them.

"And you have beautiful women, too!" the man said. "More beautiful and charming than the homely donkeys on our island. For example . . ." The masked man scanned the crowd. He stopped when he saw me. "This girl here," he said, pointing at me. "This one would make a lovely donkey's wife, don't you agree?"

I think I blushed. I lowered my head and looked behind me for a way to escape attention. The crowd hissed and whistled louder. "We will never marry Japanese!" someone shouted.

"But of course, why would she marry a donkey when she can have a Korean pig who is content to be poor and wallow in the past?"

Someone said again, "Go home, donkey!" The crowd joined in. "Donkey, go home! Donkey, go home!"

I looked at the masked man, who was still facing me. Through his mask, I saw his eyes. They were focused on me as if he didn't hear the crowd's chants. This time, I'm sure I blushed.

Then the man looked beyond the crowd at something. The crowd turned to see what he was looking at. There, on the road, was a truck heading toward us.

"Who is that?" one person asked.

"The police!" another replied.

A murmur rippled through the crowd. I turned to the masked man and saw that he was running away. He ran behind the house, into the field. I wondered why he didn't just take off his mask and stay with the crowd, one among many.

The truck stopped at the yard and the crowd huddled close. Four policemen got out dressed in dark-blue uniforms, high boots, and squat hats with the police emblem on the front. Two carried batons. One held a rifle and another gripped a *shinai*.

"What is going on here?" the policeman with the shinai said. He tapped the bamboo sword in his hand as he talked.

My uncle stepped forward and gave the policeman a small bow. "We are celebrating spring," Uncle said.

"Spring?" the policeman said, mockingly. "You mean, you are celebrating Emperor Hirohito's birthday, don't you?"

My uncle did not respond. The crowd was dead silent.

The policeman strolled in front of the crowd as if he was doing an inspection. With each step, he tapped his leg with the shinai. "But I do not understand," he said. "If you are celebrating the emperor's birthday, you should not be wearing blue and red. And you should wave Japanese flags and sing songs of praise to the emperor. I do not see any flags. I didn't hear any songs for the emperor." He stopped at my uncle. "Were you singing songs of praise to your emperor?" he asked. "Perhaps you were singing 'Kimigayo,' our national anthem?"

My uncle lowered his eyes. "No, sir," he said.

"I didn't think so," the policeman said. He scanned the crowd. He stopped when he saw my aunt. She stood with her hands on Soo-hee and Jae-hee. He pointed at her with his shinai. "You there, the one wearing white. Come here."

My aunt told her daughters to stay where they were, and she went to the policeman. She did not lower her head to him.

"Why are you wearing white, woman?" the policeman asked, lifting the hem of her dress with his shinai. "Don't you know wearing white is forbidden? You aren't protesting, are you?"

"I am wearing white to preserve our heritage, sir," my aunt replied.

"Ha!" the policeman said. "There is no Korean heritage anymore. You are Japanese now, and you must respect our laws. Remove that dress at once."

My aunt hesitated, then she gave the policeman a nod. "Yes, sir," she said. She started for the house.

"Stop!" the policeman ordered. "Do it now. Right here."

My aunt turned back. She looked from side to side. "Here?"

"Right here, right now."

"No," my aunt said, shaking her head.

"No?" the policeman said, surprised. "You defy my order? I should arrest you and throw you in jail for a month. But then, Mother," he sneered, "who will take care of your daughters?"

The policeman glared at my aunt. "Take off your dress," he snarled, "or you will regret it and your daughters will be without a mother."

My uncle stepped forward. "Stop," he shouted. "This is not right." He approached my aunt.

The two policemen with batons intercepted him before he reached his wife. One swung his baton and struck my uncle hard on his thigh. The blow made a sickening thud and made him fall to the ground. The other policeman stood over my uncle with his baton raised.

My father took an angry step forward and the policemen braced for him. Before Father went two paces, Mother grabbed his arm. "Seong-ki, no!" she pleaded. Father didn't take his eyes from the policemen, but he stopped.

The policeman with the shinai glared at my father for a second, then addressed my aunt. "Remove your dress now or I will arrest you." My aunt stood still for several seconds, staring horrified at my uncle. Then she untied the sash around her waist. She pulled her dress from her shoulders and let it slip to the ground. She stood in front of the policemen, her husband, and the entire crowd in her undergarments.

The policeman nodded to the one holding the rifle and pointed at the white dress. The policeman with the rifle picked up the dress and threw it in the truck.

My aunt moved to go to the house. "Stay where you are, woman," the policeman said. My aunt stayed where she was, staring at the ground.

The policeman began to pace again. "So, you are celebrating spring instead of the emperor's birthday. Well, we need to correct that." He faced the crowd. "You should sing 'Kimigayo' for the emperor on his birthday. All good citizens of Japan should know our national anthem. Come now, sing it!"

The people in the crowd looked from side to side at each other and didn't sing. "What? You do not know it?" the policeman said. "Here, let me help you." He straightened his back, cleared his throat, and began singing in a baritone voice. *"Thousands of years of happy reign be thine . . ."* No one joined him, and he stopped.

He glared at the crowd as my aunt still stood to the side in her undergarments. "You know the anthem," the policeman barked. "If you do not sing it, I will start arresting people for being disloyal to the emperor. I will arrest this man first," he said, pointing his shinai at my uncle. "Now start singing with me."

He began again, and a few voices tentatively sang with him. *"Thousands of years of happy reign be thine . . ."* A few more joined in. *"Rule on, my lord till what are pebbles now . . ."*

"Good!" the policeman said condescendingly. "Everyone sing!"

Everyone sang, looking at their feet as they did. *"By age united to mighty rocks shall grow, whose venerable sides the moss doth line."*

"Excellent!" the policeman said. "You are all on your way to becoming outstanding citizens of the Japanese empire! And now that you've sung to the emperor, it is time for you to go home."

People stared nervously at the ground and did not move. "Now!" the policeman bellowed, slapping his shinai against his leg. "And if you gather like this again without permission, you will be arrested. Go!"

The crowd quickly broke up, people scrambling in all directions. My aunt ran to my uncle and helped him up. Women swept food off the table. The musicians hurriedly packed their instruments. Somewhere, a baby cried. I went to Mother and Father, and together we hurried down the road. Father took long, angry strides as we headed home. The entire way, none of us said a word.

SIX

Two days later, the administrator came to our village again in his Model T Ford. I spotted the car when I was helping in Mr. Pak's potato field. I didn't think much of seeing the administrator because he came often. I turned my attention to weeding the potatoes with the blacksmith's daughters, Soo-sung and Mi-sung. It was always the girls who helped on the farm. Like my brother, the young men were away at the Japanese schools in Sinuiju and Pyongyang, learning how to be good Japanese.

The police had still not released Mr. Pak for whatever he had done, and his fields were thick with weeds. We were on our second day of hacking away the weeds with our hoes. The previous day we'd worked until dark. I'd been exhausted and went to sleep without supper. In the morning, my hands were blistered and my back was sore, but I crawled off my mat and trudged down the road to Mr. Pak's field. I tied rags around my blisters and had been hoeing all morning when the car came puttering up the road.

"What does he want now?" Mi-sung asked, staring at the car.

"He probably wants to make sure we understand the new rule," Soo-sung grumbled.

"Will they make us marry a Japanese man?" Mi-sung asked.

"No," Soo-sung replied. "We will defy them as all Koreans should." She gave me a stiff look.

The car drove out of sight and we went back to our hoeing. Fifteen minutes later, the car came again, going back down the road.

"He stopped at your house, I think," Soo-sung said.

I didn't reply, and we continued to hoe for the rest of the day.

That night when I got home, Mother and Father were waiting for me. They told me that the administrator had indeed come to our house. "There is a Japanese family with a son who needs a wife," Mother said. "You are to go to Sinuiju tomorrow to meet the family. If the father approves of you, you will marry his son."

I looked at Father, hoping he would say we would go to Manchuria instead of going to Sinuiju. He just stared at his hands and said nothing.

"What is the boy's name?" I asked.

"The administrator did not say," Mother answered. "The family is Saito. The administrator said Mr. Saito is a high official in the provincial government."

"How old is the boy?" I asked.

"They said he is only a few years older than you," Mother said, trying to put on a brave face. "If they like you, you will not have to marry an older man. Since this boy is still young, you will live with his family in a nice house."

I tried to picture the house of Mr. Saito, the important official of the provincial government. The house would certainly have a *giwa* tile roof, a formal courtyard, and many rooms. They probably had gardens and servants, too. Mr. Saito most likely had a car and a driver.

I tried to imagine what his son was like. Was he handsome? Was he kind? Perhaps he had lips like a fish and was skinny and weak. Maybe he was stupid and dull and that's why his father was forcing him to marry a Korean girl. Perhaps he liked to hurt girls like me as the Japanese boys liked to do. I remembered my plan to be rude so that no one would want to marry me. I was sure that it would work, so I didn't ask any more questions.

Mother went to the stove. "I made *rousong* pork and rice for you," she said. "Come, eat your supper and then go to bed. We have a long day tomorrow."

The next morning, I arose before it was light outside. The administrator had told Mother and Father to bring me to the police station in Sinuiju, where someone would take me to Mr. Saito's house. It was a three-hour walk from our village to Sinuiju. Only Mother and I would make the trek. Father said he had to stay to work on a project. I wasn't sure if the administrator had told him he didn't have to go, or if he refused to. Either way, I was glad he wasn't going. I planned to be rude to Mr. Saito, and I didn't want Father to get into trouble for my behavior.

After I crawled off my mat, Mother filled the metal washtub behind our house with hot water. In the growing morning light, I sat in the tub and washed myself with soap the officials gave out, then washed my hair with calamus water to make it shiny. Mother poured a pail of water over my head to rinse off the soap. The water was cold and made me shiver. The night before, Mother had washed my gray dress. I didn't like that dress. It was coarse and dull and made me look plain. I had seen photographs of women in hanboks from before the occupation, and I always thought I would look pretty in one. But the officials didn't allow Korean women to wear hanboks, so I had never even tried one on.

I brushed my hair in front of the stove to dry it. Then, Mother twisted it into a long braid and tied it with a red silk ribbon with Japanese characters. I complained that I didn't want to wear the Japanese ribbon, but Mother said that I had to. "You must look like a proper young woman," she said. *A proper young woman.* I thought of how I was going to be rude once I got to the Saito house, and my stomach hurt a little. It certainly wasn't the way a proper young woman would act. But I pushed my stomach pain aside. I wasn't going to marry a Japanese man, no matter how important his father was.

When Mother had finished with my hair, I put on leather shoes that Father had patched and Mother had polished. They were too small for me and pinched my feet. I tied them loosely so they wouldn't pinch so much.

The administrator had instructed my parents to have me at the police station by early afternoon. It was still midmorning when Mother packed a bottle of water, the leftover rousong pork, and daikons in our haversack. Then, as Father hammered away in his shed, we set off down the road past the thatched-roof houses. Just outside the village, I saw Mrs. Pak, Soo-sung, and Mi-sung weeding the potato field. They looked at me when I walked by. I waved but they didn't wave back.

Clouds had moved in and a north wind promised rain, but Mother and I made good time. After an hour, we had walked to where we could see the Yalu River. Rice paddies in geometric patterns scaled the hills all the way to the riverbank. Farmers wearing pointed straw hats and hauling tube-shaped baskets on their backs bent over ankle-deep water, pushing seedlings into the ground. In another field, two men worked a pump wheel with their legs to flood a paddy. Every so often, a truck rumbled by, kicking up mud as it went. We had to scramble into the ditch so the mud wouldn't splash us. Poles with electric wires ran along the road. I remembered the masked man at the Dano celebration had said the Japanese had brought electricity to Korea. The wires were still several miles from our village, and I often wondered why we would need electricity.

As we were walking, my mind drifted to Sinuiju and the Saito family. Mother hadn't told me what to expect when we got there, or what they would ask me to do. Perhaps she didn't know. I wondered how an important Japanese family in Sinuiju knew about me, a poor carpenter's daughter miles away. I decided to ask. "Ummah," I said, "how did they find out about me?"

We took several steps before Mother answered. "I learned about the new policy months ago," she said. "And so, the last time I went to Sinuiju, I told the authorities about you. I want you to be matched with a good family, so I told them you were pretty and well-mannered." She looked at me out of the corner of her eye. "I did not tell your father what I did."

I wanted to stop right there, turn around, and march back to our village. Mother had offered me to be married to a Japanese man. She was giving me up! Days earlier, she had said marrying a Japanese man would be a better life for me. But I didn't want a better life. I was perfectly happy where I was.

I was hurt and angry at Mother, but I didn't say anything. I had a plan, and now I was more determined than ever to make Mr. Saito and his son reject me.

The rain held off and soon we were in Sinuiju. There were more trucks here, and cars, too. The electric poles carried dozens of wires, and I wondered why there had to be so many. The houses were close together, and they had tile roofs instead of thatch. Many people on the streets hurried here and there. I couldn't imagine where they were all going and why they had to hurry so much.

By the time we got to the police station—a drab one-story building with a shingle roof—I had blisters on my feet. My legs were tired and I was hungry. Mother gave me some pork, but it wasn't enough to make my hunger go away. I was thirsty, too, but our water was gone.

We went inside the police station. Electric lights hung from the ceiling, and telephones sat on wooden desks. I had never used a telephone, and I tried to imagine how it would sound to talk to someone far away. We went to a clerk at a desk. Though he wore his hair short like a Japanese, he was tall and light skinned like a Korean. Mother bowed. "My daughter, Suk-bo Yi, has come to see Mr. Saito," Mother said in Japanese.

The clerk looked at Mother, then at me. "Stay here," he ordered. I could tell from his accent he was Korean. He went into an office, and a few minutes later, a fat uniformed policeman came out, followed by the clerk.

"I am Sergeant Yamamoto," the policeman said. "Is this Suk-bo Yi?" he asked, nodding at me.

"Yes, sir," Mother said.

"I will take her to Mr. Saito," the sergeant said to Mother. "You are to stay here."

Mother bowed again, and instinctively I bowed to the sergeant. "This way," he said, and I followed him outside to the street.

Sergeant Yamamoto's pace was quick for a heavyset man, and I had to practically run to keep up with him. The blisters on my feet stung, and I cursed myself for not tying my shoes tight. I gritted my teeth against the pain and forced myself to keep pace. We turned a corner and were in an area of larger homes. A few even had gardens. Cars sat parked out front, like the ones I had seen on other visits to Sinuiju.

We stopped at a large house surrounded by a chest-high wall. It looked like a government building or a temple instead of one man's house. It was the largest house I'd ever seen, larger and grander than the others around it. A veranda several steps above the ground surrounded it. Its walls were white plaster. Slender beams supported wide eaves, and unlike the other houses, the slanted blue roof did not curve up at the corners. Beyond the house, a gardener in a straw hat pruned roses. Another raked the pebbles in a garden containing closely trimmed juniper trees and large rocks that looked like little mountains. One building looked like a garage and another could have been a gardener's shed.

Everything was square, neat, and clean. There was order and stature here. I remembered my plan to be rude and I swallowed hard. Perhaps Mother was right when she said this was a chance for a better life for me. But I didn't know these people. I didn't know how they would treat me, if they would be kind or cruel. And I didn't know anything about their son, the man who would be my husband. But it didn't matter. I didn't want to live here no matter how kind they were or if their son was smart and good-looking. I wanted to stay in my village with Mother and Father, away from the Japanese and their strange houses and demanding ways.

Before we stepped through the gate, Sergeant Yamamoto turned his fat frame to me. "Listen to me," he said, poking my chest. "Mr. Saito is the director-general of this province. He is a very important man. People say he will become governor-general someday. You must be on your best behavior. Do you understand?"

I backed away from his finger. "I will do what I must do," I answered. I didn't bow to him as I should have.

He gave me a hard look and I thought he was going to lecture me some more. Instead, he led me through the gate, up the veranda steps, and to the front of the house.

A middle-aged man in a white buttonless shirt and loose pants met us at the front door. The man was bald, had bushy eyebrows, and wore leather slippers. I didn't know if the man was Mr. Saito, but I assumed he was a servant because instead of bowing, Sergeant Yamamoto only nodded. "This is the girl," the sergeant said.

"Come with me," the man said, and I followed him to the house as Sergeant Yamamoto headed back to the police station. The man opened the door and we stepped inside a narrow, tiled entryway. He took off his shoes.

He pointed at my feet. "Take your shoes off here," he said. I thought I could start being rude by marching into the house with my shoes on. But removing shoes in a house was something I had always done. So I untied them and slipped them off. My socks were bloody from blisters. The man noticed my feet and said, "Wait here." He stepped into the house and spoke to someone inside. In a few minutes, he came back to the entryway and handed me a damp washrag and clean socks. I took off my socks and wiped the blood from my feet with the rag. I pulled on the clean socks.

"My name is Haru," the man said. "Follow me."

As he entered a large, open room, the man named Haru bowed low. I couldn't see anyone inside, so it puzzled me why he was bowing. When I stepped into the room, he said, "This is a Shinto house. You must bow when you enter." I didn't know why I should bow to no one, and for a second, I thought about not doing it. But I bowed nevertheless.

When I stood and looked around, I saw that I was in the most beautiful room I had ever seen. It had shoji paper sliding walls, and straw tatami mats covered the floor. A paper globe lamp hung from the ceiling. Inside a raised alcove hung a long scroll with Japanese characters and a lovely watercolor painting of a bamboo plant and a crane. On the floor of the alcove was a gold incense pot and an ivory carving of men in a long rowboat. Inside the alcove sat a porcelain bowl filled with water. A low ebony table surrounded by beige cushions was the only furniture. The room's size, proportions, and simplicity gave it both peace and power.

Haru said something to me, but I didn't hear him. He pinched my arm. I realized my mouth was open and quickly closed it. "Sit at the table on that side," he said, pointing. I sat, and he said, "Wait here." He slid open a door and disappeared on the other side.

After a few minutes, a woman in a white kimono came in with a tray holding a kettle, four small bowls, and a larger clay bowl with ground green tea leaves inside. The woman took no notice of me as she bent at the knees and placed the tray on the table. She knelt and laid out a beautiful silk napkin embroidered with an elaborate "S." She mixed the tea and water into the bowls, then left.

A wall opened and a middle-aged man and woman came in. The man was not tall, but square, and he looked powerful. He wore a dark waist-length robe over a light-gray kimono. The woman wore a simple white-and-black kimono. From the way they carried themselves, I knew they were Mr. and Mrs. Saito. They were the masters of the household and I should stand and bow to them. But it was time to carry out my plan. I lifted my chin and readied myself to be rude.

A few steps behind them, a young man walked in. He wore a white Western-style shirt and black trousers. His eyes sparkled. He carried a bowl of strawberries. It was Hisashi, the man I had met in the forest.

I gasped. Impulsively, I rose from my cushion and bowed. Mr. and Mrs. Saito returned my bow with a nod. Hisashi smiled at me knowingly. All three went to the alcove and washed their face and hands in the porcelain bowl. Then, we sat on our cushions around the table, Mr. Saito at the head, and Mrs. Saito and Hisashi across from me. Hisashi set the bowl of strawberries on the table.

Mr. Saito bowed at the table, then picked up his tea bowl. His short hair was beginning to gray at the temples. His face was square like his torso, and behind intelligent eyes, he did not betray his emotions. Mrs. Saito was a beauty with shiny hair pulled to the top of her head, and smooth light skin. Her face was delicate. She watched me closely and she, too, did not betray her feelings. I could see that with his almost feminine features, Hisashi was more like his mother. Unlike his parents, he wore a grin on his face.

Mr. Saito took a sip of tea and said, "I am Mr. Saito, and this is my wife, Koku, and my son, Hisashi. Have you been given a Japanese name?" His voice was full, loud, and deep.

I kept my eyes low. "No, sir. My name is Suk-bo," I replied in Japanese.

"I know your Korean name," Mr. Saito said, "but you are a Japanese subject now. You should have a Japanese name. I will see that you get one."

Here would have been a good place to be rude. I could complain that my Korean name was perfectly fine and I did not need a Japanese one. I could push my tea bowl aside and say I preferred Korean tea instead of the Japanese tea. I could cross my arms and refuse to answer their questions. But I looked at Hisashi and held my tongue.

Mr. Saito said, "Hisashi went camping a few days ago and picked these strawberries. He thought you might like them. He says they are perfectly ripe and sweet. Have some."

I bowed to Hisashi. He smiled at me, and in his smile, I saw the kindness I'd seen in the forest. "Thank you," I said. I took a strawberry and bit into it. It was indeed ripe and sweet.

"Hisashi is my second son," Mr. Saito said. "My eldest has a Japanese wife. He lives in Tokyo and is an officer in the army. However, to fulfill the Imperial Government's law to assimilate your people, we have offered to have Hisashi marry a Korean woman. You are a candidate."

I swallowed and said, "Thank you, sir."

"Tell me," Mr. Saito said, "how do you feel about the Japanese?"

With the sweet taste of wild strawberries in my mouth and Hisashi grinning at me from across the table, I changed my mind about acting rude. Perhaps Mother was right and I would find a better life here. It would be a lovely house to live in, and I would have a new and exciting life in Sinuiju. I might even go to Japan someday. And, I must say, Hisashi was very handsome.

But now, I had a problem. Mr. Saito was asking me how I felt about the Japanese. I knew my father hated our Japanese masters, and I had come to feel the same way. I had learned that they executed my uncle. And just a few days earlier, I had seen what the police did to my aunt at the Dano festival. But even though Mr. Saito was the perfect picture of a robust Japanese man, he didn't seem to be that way. Mrs. Saito hadn't said anything, but she looked to be gracious and pleasant. And then there was Hisashi. He had picked strawberries for me. I decided it wouldn't be so dreadful to marry him.

I remembered what the masked satirist had said at the festival. "Sir," I said finally, "you have built roads and dams and have brought electricity to Korea. Your people have brought order and productivity, too. Without you, we would still be a backward nation, fighting among ourselves, clan versus clan, as we did for hundreds of years."

"Ha!" Hisashi said. "That is a good answer!"

Mr. Saito raised an eyebrow. "Is that how you really feel, or is that what you were told to say?"

"No one told me what to say, sir."

"I see," Mr. Saito said. "Well, you are right. Korea's only salvation is to become Japanese."

Mrs. Saito lifted her chin. "Have you learned to sew and cook?" she asked. Her voice was cool and even. "We would expect you to be a proper wife to our son."

I thought for a second that I should lie and tell her that I was a fine cook and could sew anything. But I shook my head. "I am sorry, ma'am," I answered. "I do not know how to cook and sew. I study literature, mathematics, and philosophy instead. But"—I lifted my eyes to Mrs. Saito—"if I am chosen, I would be keen to learn what you think I need to know to be a proper wife to your son."

Mr. Saito grunted. "Literature and mathematics and philosophy. It is unusual for girls to learn these things. Would you continue your studies if you married my son?"

"I would want to, sir," I answered. "Under your direction, of course."

Mr. Saito stared at me for a while. Then he turned to Hisashi. "Son, do you have any questions for this girl?"

"Yes, *Tōchan*," Hisashi said. "I do." He put a serious look on his face and said, "Tell me, Suk-bo, do you like the strawberries, or do you think they are hard and sour?"

I smiled a little and said, "I like them very much, thank you. They are ripe and sweet."

"Yes, I thought so, too," Hisashi said. His eyes twinkled.

After a few seconds, Mr. Saito stood, signaling that the meeting was over. Mrs. Saito and Hisashi stood with him, and I did, too. "That is all

I have time for," Mr. Saito said. "You may go. We will let your parents know our decision."

"Tōchan," Hisashi said, "it has started to rain. Suk-bo has a long walk back to her village. You could send her in your car."

"Yes, yes, yes," Mr. Saito said with a wave. "I will have Haru arrange it."

I bowed to Mr. and Mrs. Saito as they left, and now, I was alone with Hisashi. He led me to the entryway and I put on my shoes. We stepped outside to the veranda under the eaves to stay out of the rain. I touched the red silk ribbon in my hair as we waited for the car.

Hisashi grinned at me again. "I saw you the other day," he said.

"You did?" I said. "Where?"

His grin grew to a full smile. "At your festival. I was the man in the mask."

"You were?"

"Yes," Hisashi replied. "I borrowed the mask from one of the entertainers. It was a good performance, don't you agree?"

"It was," I said, grinning at him.

"You used what I said to answer my father."

"It was a good answer, I think," I replied. "Tell me, why did you come to the festival?"

"I wanted to see you again. It was fun until the police came."

"They humiliated my aunt," I said with an accusatory tone.

"I'm sorry they did. It is not right what the police do sometimes."

The car pulled up and the chauffeur opened the door for me. Before I left, Hisashi touched my arm. "Here," he said. "These are for you."

He handed me an embroidered table napkin with something inside. I opened it and saw the strawberries he had picked. I lowered my eyes to him. "Thank you," I said.

"Have a good trip," Hisashi said and gave me his kind smile again. I felt my cheeks get warm.

Mr. Saito's automobile was big and black like the one I had seen in Sinuiju years earlier. The driver was a Korean man about twenty years old with the Japanese name Isamu. When he saw me, he regarded me with what I thought was disdain. I brushed aside his look and said nothing to him as we went to the police station to pick up Mother. On the road home, Mother and I sat in the back, me with the strawberries in my lap, and Mother looking embarrassed to be riding in such a grand car. The road was rutty and the car lurched from side to side, but I didn't mind. I didn't get to ride in a car often, and I thought it was great fun.

As I looked out the window at the rain falling on the rice paddies, I felt happy. I was beginning to like the idea of marrying Hisashi. I believed he would be a good husband for me, and I believed I could learn to be a good wife. When Mother asked how the meeting went, I told her I thought it went well. At this, she nodded and tried to look pleased. But in the softness of her eyes and in the lines around her mouth, I could see that she was sad.

SEVEN

Mr. Saito said he'd inform my parents of his decision about me, but he hadn't said when. So for the next several days, I went about doing my chores, studying my lessons, helping in the fields, and continually looking at the road for the administrator's car to come. As the days went by without hearing from Sinuiju, I thought Mr. and Mrs. Saito had rejected me. I was upset that they thought I was unworthy of marrying their son. I wanted to know what they thought was so terribly wrong with me. I had behaved properly instead of rudely. I'd answered their questions as best as I could. It seemed that Hisashi liked me. I wanted them to accept me, and I wanted Hisashi to accept me, too. At night on my mat, I fantasized about strolling the grounds of the beautiful house, driving around in the big black car, and living in Sinuiju. I fantasized what it would be like to lie with Hisashi, stroke his chest, kiss him, make love to him.

But, after many days, I'd settled into my routine, and my mind began to change. I grew uneasy about marrying a Japanese and living in a house and city I knew nothing about. It would be a strange world for me. I thought about how I would miss my parents and my brother when he came home. I would miss my village and my strolls in the forest. I began to think that I had made a mistake by not sticking with my plan to be rude so that Mr. Saito would reject me.

In the end, I wasn't sure how I felt. Though I wasn't sure about his parents, I liked Hisashi with his sparkling eyes and almost pretty face, and I wanted to see him again. Mother and Father said nothing about it, although in the heavy silence of our house, I could tell they disagreed about what to do should Mr. Saito select me.

One night when we sat down for our evening meal of millet and beans—our monthly allotment of rice had run out days earlier—Father informed me that my uncle needed me on his farm. "Since he hosted the Dano celebration, the administrator sent his laborers to work in the factories in Pyongyang," Father said. "His girls are young and not much help. He will need you for several days."

"Does she have to be gone that long?" Mother asked.

"She will go for as long as Hwan-gi needs her," Father replied.

"Perhaps I should go, too," Mother said.

"No, I need you here." There was a pause. Then Father said, "You are worried about your sister-in-law."

Mother nodded. "Suk-bo, we should tell you about your aunt Bo-sun. She is . . . eccentric in many ways. She has dangerous ideas and strange behaviors. She says the spirits talk to her and that she can see the future. You must be careful what you believe."

"I would not say her ideas are wrong," Father said with a glance at Mother, "although it is true that sometimes she says strange things. Listen to your mother, Suk-bo. You must be careful with your aunt."

We said nothing more, and when we had finished eating, I packed a rucksack of clothes for my stay.

It was another rainy day when I walked to my uncle's house. By the time I got there, I was wet, and mud caked my shoes. My head hurt. When she saw me coming, my aunt came out of the house with a blanket and threw it over my shoulders. "You should have waited to come until the rain stopped," she said.

She led me inside the house. Soo-hee and Jae-hee were waiting at the door. "Look, Soo-hee," Jae-hee squealed, "it is Cousin!" The girls grinned at me.

"Leave Suk-bo be," my aunt said. "She needs to get dry. Go to the other room. You can see your cousin later." Disappointment crossed the girls' faces, but they did as they were told and left. My aunt went to the stove and lit a fire. I huddled in front of the flames. Though it was warm, I was shivering. My aunt put a kettle of water on and tossed in some herbs. She looked at me with a worried expression. She opened my rucksack and took out a change of clothes. "Take off those wet things," she said. "Put these on."

I put the dry clothes on, and she hung my wet ones on a hook next to the stove. She served me the brew of herbs, which warmed me. I no longer shivered. But now, my headache was worse. After a few minutes, my eyes grew heavy. My aunt went to a room and came back with a mat and another blanket. She placed the mat in front of the stove and I lay on it. She covered me with the blanket. Soon, I was asleep.

I couldn't say how long I slept. When I awoke, Jae-hee was standing above me, staring. "Ummah, Cousin is awake!" she squealed.

"How do you feel?" my aunt asked.

"Better, I think," I said.

Jae-hee slid up to me and showed me her doll. It had on a blue-and-white silk hanbok. An elaborate gold *binyeo* held the doll's hair in place. "This is Cor-ee," she said. "She is the empress of Korea. Someday I will be an empress, too."

"Let Suk-bo wake up, Daughter," my aunt said from the stove. "You can show her Empress Cor-ee later. Go and do your studies with Soo-hee."

Jae-hee pouted but took her doll and disappeared into the other room.

I sat up and looked around. My uncle's house was much larger than my parents' house. It had a *maru*—a large open main room with a kitchen, eating area, and family sitting area. The floor was polished wood plank, much smoother than ours. A chest with brass hinges stood against a wall. The kitchen had an iron cookstove, a sink under a window, and a Chinese hutch. Sliding latticed doors led to other areas of the house.

"Where is Uncle?" I asked.

"He is helping a neighbor butcher a shoat," my aunt replied, stirring a pot. "We will have pork for the next few days." She stood straight with her shoulders back. She wore her usual half smile. I thought she might be embarrassed to see me since I'd seen the police humiliate her. But she showed no sign of embarrassment, as if she was above being embarrassed.

"You took a chill on your walk here," Aunt said. "Rest today and you will be well tomorrow."

"Thank you, *Sookmo*," I said, calling her by the respectful name for my mother's brother's wife. "I feel better having slept."

She studied me from across the room. "You talked in your sleep," she said. "You said things."

"I did?" I was surprised. I'd never talked in my sleep before. Or at least no one ever told me I did.

"Tell me," my aunt said, looking into the pot she was stirring, "who is Hisashi?"

I tensed. I wasn't sure if I should tell my aunt that the officials might make me marry a Japanese man. My parents had told me to be careful what I said to her. "He's someone . . . I met," I said, hoping she wouldn't ask any more.

"I see," my aunt said. "Hisashi is a Japanese name. He is Japanese?"

"Yes."

"Is he your age?"

"Two years older, I think."

"Is he handsome?"

"Please do not tease me, Sookmo," I said.

My aunt took the pot from the stove and sat next to me. "I hear there is a new rule that some Korean women will have to marry Japanese men. This man who you met, is he married?"

"No."

"I see," she said with a slight nod. "You don't want to talk about this Japanese man who is two years older than you and is not married."

I didn't know if this was a question or a statement. It was as if she was scolding me for something terrible I'd done. I thought I should apologize, but I didn't know what I would be apologizing for.

My aunt went to the stove. "Hwan-gi will be home soon and he will be hungry. I was able to get a chicken. Hwan-gi hasn't had meat in many days. He works so hard. You should play with the girls. They would enjoy that. It is important that families stay close."

An hour later when my uncle came trudging through the back door, muddy and wet, I was feeling normal again. His daughters and I greeted him with a bow. My aunt helped him change out of his muddy clothes, and we all sat at the low table and ate chicken with a handful of rice. My uncle had my mother's well-defined chin, only he looked younger, and he was thinner. He looked like he needed a long rest. He said, "The rain will clear tonight and the sun will be out tomorrow. We have a lot to do, Suk-bo. The cabbage and beans need weeding, and we must finish harvesting the winter daikons. I will need help with the roof. Some of the tiles slipped during the winter."

"Yes, *Sookbu*," I said. He nodded to me, and I could tell he was grateful that I was there to help. It sounded like he would need me for several days, and I worried how many more questions my aunt would ask about Hisashi.

When we'd finished the meal, my aunt put both children to bed. Shortly after, I curled up on a mat in a room off the back of the house and fell fast asleep.

I woke in the middle of the night and didn't know where I was. I'd been dreaming. I sat up in a fog. I shook my head. Eventually, my mind cleared and I saw the dark outline of the room. I remembered I was in my uncle's house and I breathed again. I tried to recall if I'd been having a nightmare. Perhaps I had been dreaming about living in the Saito house, a married woman. Maybe I was dreaming about fighting the Japanese with my father in Manchuria. Though I couldn't remember it, my dream left me with a sense of foreboding.

I was going to have a long, hard day, and I had to get more sleep. I took a few breaths to calm myself, lay down and pulled the blanket over me, and closed my eyes.

I heard something move—shuffling feet and muttering. It was my aunt's voice. The muttering was angry and tense, and I thought she was arguing with someone. I pushed off the blanket and put my ear to the door. I heard her say, "Why is it so?" and "Leave me be!" I slid the door open a crack and peeked into the main room. There in the shadows, my aunt paced back and forth like a ghost in nightclothes. She was alone. She waved her arms and shook her head. She looked at something in her hand and said, "I do not want this thing."

I stepped from behind the door. "Sookmo," I said, "what is wrong?"

She snapped her head around and her eyes flashed. She rushed to me. She grabbed my shoulders and brought her face inches from mine.

"You cannot marry him, this Japanese man!" she whispered. Still holding my shoulders, she turned her head to the side. "But you have to marry him, don't you?"

She took a step back and seemed to be thinking something through. Her breathing returned to normal, and her eyes no longer flashed. Finally, she said, "I am sorry for scaring you, Suk-bo," as if she'd suddenly realized what she had done. "Come. We must not wake Hwan-gi."

I wanted to go back to my mat, to crawl under the covers as if nothing had happened. But the vision of my aunt angry and confused wasn't going to let me sleep. So I followed her outside to the front of the house. We sat on the veranda. It was warm for the middle of the night. The clouds had moved away, and the stars twinkled in the night sky.

"This man," she said after a while. "Tell me about him."

I was reluctant to tell her about Hisashi. She had said I couldn't marry him, and then for some reason, she said I had to. I wanted to know why. So I told my aunt how I had met Hisashi and how his father, the director-general who lived in Sinuiju, might make me marry his son. I told her that I believed Hisashi was kind, that he had given me strawberries and spoke to me in Korean. I said we had not yet heard if they had chosen me.

"What does he look like?" my aunt asked.

"He is not tall like a Korean, but he is not short, either. His hair is shiny. He has a pleasant face."

"He sounds nice," my aunt said. "But he is Japanese. Most families are refusing to give up their daughters. I think most Japanese men don't want to marry Koreans, either."

"Mother thinks I should marry him. Father thinks that we should flee to Manchuria. Who is right, Sookmo?"

In her white nightclothes and with her hair down, my aunt looked like a *mudang*, a shaman who talks to spirits. I sensed spirits all around her. They must have been who she was talking to earlier. "Oh, my niece," she said softly, "it is more complicated than you can know. The spirits of our ancestors speak to me. They cry for Korea. They beg us to fight for our country. But the spirits give me vision, too. I see what will happen if we fight."

"What will happen?"

She shook her head. "Many will suffer and many will die. So this is the question you must answer: Is it better to fight for Korea and die quickly? Or is it better to surrender and die slowly?"

With her strange aura and even stranger words, I now understood what my parents had said about my aunt. It seemed like she was speaking in riddles. Surely my decision to accept marriage to Hisashi—if and when it would come—or to resist and flee to Manchuria, was not as grave as she indicated. How could I, a sixteen-year-old girl, help save Korea by resisting? And why would I die if I surrendered?

Finally, I said, "With respect, Sookmo, I do not think the decision I make will matter much."

"I see," my aunt said. "Let me show you something." She held out her hand and, though it was dark, I saw she held a comb with an ivory inlay of a two-headed dragon. It was the most beautiful thing I'd ever seen.

"What is it?" I whispered.

"It was given to me by my grandmother," my aunt replied. "The dragon's spirit speaks to me. It also gives me vision."

I looked at the comb in my aunt's hand. In the dark, the two-headed dragon seemed alive. It stared at me. I thought I heard it speak.

My aunt said, "When this comb with the two-headed dragon came to me, it was a sign that I was chosen to speak for the spirit of Korea. The spirit tells me to fight for our country. But the vision it gives tells me what the cost of fighting will be. It prevents me and Hwan-gi from joining the rebels with our girls. But you, you have a different choice. Your father's way is dangerous. You could be killed. But your mother's way will be no less perilous. If we yield to Japan, our country will die. And then we will all be cursed by the two-headed dragon."

My aunt sighed. "I do not know. Maybe your mother is right. Maybe it is lost already."

"You cannot lose a fight you do not take," I said. "Mother told me that a few days ago."

"Huh, yes," my aunt said, nodding. "She would say something like that. But consider this. Maybe you lose something more important if you do not." She faced me. "Know this, Suk-bo. If you marry this man, you invite the curse of the two-headed dragon. It will not be easy to bear the curse. It might kill you just as surely as the Japanese would kill you for being a rebel."

She closed her hand around the comb. "You are the only one I have told about this comb, Suk-bo. I do not know why I did. Please keep it a secret. I have sworn to protect it."

She looked at me, and her half smile grew sad. "Come," she said. "You must sleep. You have hard days ahead."

I went to my room and lay on the mat. But the image of the two-headed dragon floated in my mind, and I did not sleep well that night.

EIGHT

The decision from Sinuiju came while I was working for my uncle. After six days of hard work, I was so tired I didn't even think to ask about it when I got home. But after I'd rested for a day, I noticed there was tension in the house like after Mother and Father had a bad argument. In the morning, Father left through the front door instead of going to his shed. Mother hunched over the low table and looked at nothing. I asked where Father was going.

"He's going to buy a mule," she said.

"A mule? What for?"

"He is taking us to Manchuria," Mother replied without looking up.

"We are going to Manchuria?"

Mother looked at me and I could see that she had been crying. She said, "While you were gone, the administrator came. He said Mr. Saito wants you to marry his son."

I was stunned. So many days had gone by since I had met Mr. and Mrs. Saito that I was certain they had not chosen me. But now that I knew they had, I didn't know how I felt. Of course, I was thrilled that they thought enough of me to have me join their family. But I remembered what my aunt had said about the decision I had to make—to be killed for fighting the Japanese or to be cursed by the spirit of the two-headed dragon. The more I thought about what she had said, the more I hoped that they wouldn't choose me so that I wouldn't have to decide. Now I had to. Then again, it appeared that Father had already made the decision for me.

"What will we do in Manchuria?" I asked.

"Your father says he knows someone there who will give him work, but I do not believe him. I think he wants us to join the rebels." Mother shook her head.

So, we were going to be rebels in Manchuria. I'd heard that the rebels there were hardscrabble men and women with guns who fought for Korean independence. Their stories were full of bravery and heroism and gave us all hope, although in hushed conversations, most people believed that independence was just a fantasy.

My aunt had said that fighting the Japanese could cost me my life but that it would save Korea. I remembered the story of my father's brother and how the police had shot him in a street in Seoul. I remembered that they had arrested Mr. Pak, and he still hadn't come back. I remembered how the police had treated my aunt at the Dano festival. I saw how hard all the people of my village worked and how little the Japanese gave back. I remembered the two-headed dragon on my aunt's comb and how it seemed to speak to me. And though I liked the thought of being with Hisashi, and living in the big house in Sinuiju would be exciting and glamorous, it felt like fighting was the right thing to do.

"When will we leave?" I asked.

"Tonight," Mother answered. "We must travel in the dark."

"Ummah," I said, "I do not know for certain, but I think maybe, Father is right."

Mother gave me a look. "You have been talking to your aunt," she said. "Go. Pack your rucksack with clothes. Do not take too much. It is a long way to Manchuria."

I went to the sleeping room and gathered clothes, a hairbrush, and several of my books. When I thought about how far we had to travel, I put half of the books back. Then, I put them all back. I couldn't think of why a rebel would need books. I wondered what the rebels would have me do when we got to Manchuria, how I would help with their fight. Perhaps they would make me cook or sew or learn how to be a nurse. Maybe they would ask me to fight with a gun. I had never shot a gun before. In fact, I had never even butchered a chicken.

I heard Father come through the front door. Mother didn't greet him. "I bought a mule," he said. "I will get the beast tonight so we do not raise suspicion. We will leave when it gets dark. We have to make many miles before the sun comes up."

I went to finish packing my rucksack. When I finished, I left the house. Father was in his shed, putting some of his tools into a canvas bag. I snuck around the side so he wouldn't see me and went into the garden.

The morning promised a hot afternoon. The heavy air didn't move, and the earth started to slow its pace. As I strolled through the napa cabbage and carrots, I thought about what we were going to do. I remembered my brother told me he had read that Manchuria had fields of grass as far as the eye could see. It was so cold there in the winter that horses froze solid and they could do nothing with the carcass until it thawed in the spring. In the summer it was so hot that no one worked during midday. Manchuria had rivers much wider than the widest part of the Yalu River and mountains taller than any in Korea. But the strangest thing of all was there were no Japanese.

It sounded like a strange place indeed, nothing at all like my forest and village. I would miss this place dreadfully—the gossipy blacksmith's daughters, Soo-sung and Mi-sung; old Mrs. Choi; the farmers, Mr. Kim and Mr. Pak, and their families. I'd miss my aunt and uncle and my cousins. And I'd miss the forest—picking strawberries, watching the water deer step so lightly on the forest floor it was like they were stepping on eggs, listening to the birds sing their songs. I realized how much I loved this place and I didn't want to leave. I thought about Hisashi and how exciting it would be to live in Sinuiju. It made me sad that I wouldn't see him again. But a young woman like me wasn't supposed to argue with her father. We had to go to Manchuria.

I heard something on the road. I saw Mr. Saito's car making its way to our house. Behind it was the administrator's Model T. I ran to Father's shed. "Appa," I said, "Mr. Saito's car is coming! The administrator, too."

"Go to the house," he said, shoving the canvas bag with his tools in a corner. "Make sure it is clean."

I ran into the house where Mother was frantically cleaning. I grabbed the straw broom and swept the floor. Mother dusted the open cupboard and straightened the cookware. She checked to make sure the table was square with the room.

"Maybe they heard we were running away," I said.

"No," Mother said, placing the cushions neatly around the table. "If they did, they would have sent the police."

Father came through the back door, wiping his forehead. He joined us at the window. "We must be careful," he said. "They cannot know about our plans."

The administrator got out of his car and hurried to the front of our house. Mr. Saito's driver opened the black car's back door and Mr. Saito stepped out, followed by Hisashi. My heart skipped a beat when I saw him wearing the same white shirt and black pants as the other times I'd seen him. Mr. Saito looked official, dressed in a Western-style suit with a high white collar and a black tie. As he got out of the car, he donned a hat with a brim, looking ever so much like a stalwart Japanese dignitary. As Mr. Saito and Hisashi approached our front door, Mr. Saito's driver went to the trunk and took out a heavy wooden box with rope handles.

"*Konnichiwa!*" the administrator said excitedly from the other side of the door. "The director-general calls on this house!"

Father shot a look at Mother. "You will have to help me with my Japanese," he said. Mother nodded. Father opened the door and bowed. "Please, come in," he said in his broken Japanese.

Mr. Saito came in first and took off his hat and then his shoes. The administrator and Hisashi followed him and took off their shoes. When our eyes met, Hisashi gave me a quick smile. I lowered my eyes. The driver came in with the wooden box, and Mr. Saito pointed to the middle of the room. "Put it there," he said. The driver set the box on the floor and then went back to the car.

Mr. Saito looked around. My father motioned to the table with his head slightly bowed. "Sit?" he said.

The administrator stepped forward. "The director and his son have come to talk to you about your daughter. You should make tea."

"Yes, sir," Mother said with a bow. She hurried to the stove and started a fire. She poured water in a kettle and set it on the stove. She tossed in some tea.

Father gave Mr. Saito a cushion, and the director-general sat at the low table. He placed his hat next to him. The administrator and Hisashi sat on the floor behind him. I stood off to the side.

The administrator smoothed his wrinkled suit. "It is a great honor for you to have the director-general visit your house," he began in a high-pitched voice. "He is a great man and . . ."

Mr. Saito raised his hand and the administrator went silent. Mr. Saito cleared his throat. Then, in his full voice he said, "As the administrator has told you, I have come to talk to you about the decision to have your daughter marry my son."

I glanced at Hisashi, who sat straight and looked at his father.

"As you know," Mr. Saito continued, "Korea is now Japan. It is divinely ordained that all of Asia come together under one roof. Emperor Hirohito is the pillar that supports the roof."

Mother came to the table with a tray. On it were a teapot and several tea bowls. Her hands trembled as she poured tea into the bowls and handed them to Mr. Saito, the administrator, Hisashi, and my father. She bowed away and sat behind Father.

Mr. Saito took a sip of tea. Then he continued. "Our great emperor wants all his people to share the empire's good fortune. But to share, we must make sacrifices."

Mr. Saito looked at me. I was still standing off to the side. Then he looked at my father, who kept his eyes low. Mr. Saito said, "The decision has been made for your daughter to marry my son so that our people will become one. This is what you must do. But our emperor is abundantly benevolent and so, I have come here today from my post in Sinuiju to show the emperor's appreciation for your obedience."

Mr. Saito raised his hand, and the administrator went to the wooden box. It was heavy for him and he struggled to set it in front of my father.

"I was told you are a carpenter," Mr. Saito said to Father. "This is for you."

Father looked uncomfortable and didn't move to open the box. Instead, he stared at it, and I thought he was going to tell Mr. Saito that he didn't believe the Japanese were ordained to rule Asia and that his daughter couldn't be bought. Finally, he leaned forward and lifted the lid. Inside was a stunning set of saws, knives, carving tools, files, and a hand plane. A stiff leather strap held each tool in place. The tools themselves were magnificent. The polished steel blades looked hard and sharp, and the blond wooden handles looked smooth and stout. My father stared at them for quite some time. Finally, he said, "Thank you, sir."

Mr. Saito looked pleased that Father seemed to like the gift. The director-general took another sip of tea. Then, he said to me, "Come, sit, Suk-bo." I sat at the table next to Father. "I have two things for you," Mr. Saito said. "First is a new name. We will call you Miyoko Saito after you marry my son. Miyoko means 'good child,' which I am sure you will be. I have had the papers readied to change your name.

"The other gift is this." Mr. Saito reached inside his jacket and pulled out a small, leather-bound book. "You said you would like to continue your studies, and you shall. Here is a book for you to study. It is the basis of the Japanese authority. It is in Japanese, of course, and might be difficult for you. Hisashi will help you with it."

He gave me the book. It was *Kodō taii, The True Meaning of the Ancient Way,* by Hirata Atsutane. I nodded and said, "Thank you, sir."

Mr. Saito looked pleased. Then he said, "The wedding will take place in ten days at my house in Sinuiju. As is the Shinto tradition, it will be a small ceremony. We've invited only immediate family. I will send a car for Suk-bo . . . Miyoko, the day before the wedding so we can prepare her. I will send a car for you the morning of the wedding," he said to Father and Mother. "After the wedding, your daughter will live with Hisashi in my house. I assure you, she will be treated well."

Mr. Saito put his hands on his knees. "And now," he said, "I must get back to my post." He stood, and everyone stood with him.

"Father," Hisashi said, "I would like to spend a few minutes with Suk-bo before we leave."

"Yes, yes, yes," Mr. Saito said. "I suppose that is appropriate. The administrator and I can talk business in the meantime. Do not be too long."

"Thank you, Father," Hisashi said. He put on his shoes. "Come for a walk with me."

I nodded and went out the back door with Hisashi.

It was starting to get hot when we went to the field behind the house. White, billowy clouds were growing in the hills beyond the forest, promising an evening storm. In the grass, crickets jumped out of the way as Hisashi and I walked side by side. My heart was beating a little fast, and I was afraid I might say something silly. We walked a while without saying anything.

"It is quite something that Father would make the trip here to talk to your father," Hisashi finally said. "I encouraged him to do it, though I did not think he would. But here we are. My father is an honorable man."

"Does he truly believe that Japan is destined to rule Asia?" I asked.

"Oh, yes," Hisashi replied. "He works very hard for the emperor. Someday Father might be prime minister."

"My father doesn't think Japan should be here," I said, afraid that I was being too bold.

"Most Koreans agree with your father. I'm not sure what to believe."

We went a little farther, and then Hisashi said, "How do you feel about marrying me?"

I didn't know how I should answer his question. I'd only seen him twice before—in the forest and at his home. I suppose I saw him at the Dano festival, too, but I didn't know he was the man behind the mask. Truthfully, I really didn't know him at all, but he had been kind to me and I sensed a tenderness in him. I decided to trust him and tell him how I really felt.

"I am nervous about it. I do not know anything about you."

"Yes, that is true. But you think I am handsome and interesting, don't you?" he said with a grin. "You did not say so in the forest that day."

I blushed and grinned, too. "Yes, I do," I said.

Hisashi grew serious. "To be honest, I am nervous about it, too. Father says I must marry a Korean woman because that is what the government has ordered. I was not sure I wanted to until I saw you in the forest. That is why I came that day. To see you."

"You *were* spying on me," I said.

Hisashi chuckled. "I suppose I was."

"It seems like it was just yesterday," I said. "I never said thank you for the strawberries."

"Yes, well, it was my pleasure to pick them for you."

He touched my arm and we stopped walking. He faced me. "I have something else for you."

He reached inside his pocket and took out a small rectangular box. He held it out to me. "I thought this would look good on you. I hope you like it."

I took the box and opened it. Inside was a two-pronged silver *kanzashi* hairpin. At the end was a circle of silver finely etched with trees and a crane on a pond.

"It is from Tokyo," Hisashi said nervously. "I would have bought a binyeo for you, but Father would not approve. Japanese women wear these for special occasions," he said, running his words together as if he'd forgotten how to breathe. "Maybe you could wear it for the wedding. If you like it, that is. Do you like it? Is it okay? What do you think of it?" He looked at me pleadingly.

"I like it very much," I said. It was, in fact, the most beautiful thing I'd ever held in my hand.

He breathed a sigh of relief and smiled. "Try it on."

I hesitated. Here was a man I didn't know who had given me a most intimate gift. But in ten days, if we did not run away to Manchuria, he would be my husband. So as Hisashi watched, I reached around and loosened my braid, letting my hair fall over my shoulders. I folded my hair over and fastened it to the top of my head with the silver pin. I lifted my eyes to Hisashi.

"You are beautiful," he said simply. "A true treasure." He touched my cheek. Now it was I who could not breathe. And then I knew I could not go to Manchuria with Father and Mother.

Hisashi nodded toward the house. "We must get back. Father is waiting."

I took the hairpin out and braided my hair again. I put the pin in the box, tucked it inside my dress, and we walked to the house. When we got there, Mr. Saito and the administrator were waiting in their cars for Hisashi. At the front of the house, Hisashi nodded respectfully to Father and Mother and then to me, too. I bowed to him. I pressed the place inside my dress where I had put the hairpin. He waved at me as he climbed into the big black car. My parents and I watched as the two cars headed toward Sinuiju.

NINE

"We are not going to Manchuria now, are we?" I asked Mother and Father after Mr. Saito's car disappeared down the road. The three of us sat at the low table. The box of new tools was still where the administrator had placed it on the floor in front of Father. Father laid a dull pink paper on top of the box.

"What is that?" Mother asked.

"The administrator gave it to me when he left," Father said. "I don't know what it says. I do not read Japanese."

It wasn't true that Father didn't read Japanese. Most everyone in Korea could read Japanese. He wasn't good at it—certainly not as good as I was—but he could read enough to get by. Most of the time, he simply refused to read anything except Korean.

He pushed the paper at Mother. She picked it up and read it to herself. When she finished, there was a worried expression on her face.

"What does it say?" Father asked.

Mother handed the paper to me. "Here," she said. "You read Japanese better than I do. Make sure we know what it says."

I did my best to interpret what the paper said. It was addressed to Father and said that Mr. Pak was not going to return to his farm and that Father was to take it over. The administrator would hold Father responsible for producing the same amount of vegetables as Mr. Pak had. A shortfall would result in punishment. Father was to start his new responsibilities immediately, before the farm fell into too much disarray.

Father stared at the box of new tools. "Well, this does not seem like much of a gift now, does it?" he said. "And so, to answer your question, Suk-bo, yes, we are going to Manchuria."

"Seong-ki," Mother pleaded, "if we go now, we will disobey a direct order. Mr. Saito came all the way from Sinuiju to give you his gift. It would be an insult to an important man like him. It would be dangerous for us to leave now."

Father continued to stare at the box. "I am not a farmer, Jo-soo. And Suk-bo is not Japanese."

"We could send word to Pyongyang for Kwan-so to come home," Mother said. "Our son could help on the farm. We could make it work."

Father raised his fist and brought it down hard on the box of tools, putting a crack in the lid. "When will we stop letting them oppress us?" he growled. "When will we stand up for ourselves? They are taking everything away. They are killing us. I won't let them. We must fight! We leave for Manchuria tonight."

Father pushed away from the table. Before he left, I cried out, "Appa, I will willingly marry Hisashi. I believe Mr. Saito when he says they will treat me well. And Hisashi is nice." I reached inside my dress for the box Hisashi had given me. I opened it and showed Father the hairpin inside. "He gave me this," I said.

"It is kanzashi," Father said, as if the word tasted bad. "It is Japanese."

"I do not want to go to Manchuria," I said.

Father looked at me. There was anger in his eyes, and his chin was firm. "We leave for Manchuria tonight," he said again, "and you are going." He marched out of the house through the back door.

I'd never disobeyed my father before. I'd always done exactly what I was told. I did so, because that's what I was expected to do. Sure, there were times I wanted to do something else, like when Father said I had to help Mother in the garden and I wanted to go for a walk, or when he said I needed to run an errand when I wanted to read one of my books. And sometimes, I would interpret his request to my advantage, like when I would take a long way around to do his errand and visit the Kwan girls. But I never directly disobeyed him. And I would never have dreamed of doing so for something this important. Until now.

I had decided the second Hisashi gave me the hairpin that I was going to marry him. I was prepared to argue with my father and even disobey him if I had to. Now, Father said we were going to Manchuria.

But what could I do? I couldn't run to Hisashi and tell him Father was fleeing to Manchuria. They would arrest him and throw him in prison like they'd done to Mr. Pak. I couldn't run to my aunt, either. She would agree with Father and send me right back home. My brother in Pyongyang was too far away. I could hide in the forest, but I certainly couldn't hide there for ten days.

My mother was the answer. She had argued with Father about the Japanese for as long as I could remember, and like me, she wanted to stay. But how far would she go? She was Father's wife, and wives were supposed to obey their husbands.

"Ummah," I said, "I will not go. I am staying here to marry Hisashi as you said I should." Saying this, defying my father, was terrifying. It was as if I was defying not just Father but tradition itself. I was rejecting our way—that a daughter never disobeys her father. And I was agreeing to marry a Japanese man.

Mother gave me a satisfied look. She said, "I will stay here with you. If both of us stay, your father will stay, too. I will tell him." She tried to put on a brave face, but her once-square shoulders sagged, and I saw that her fights with Father were taking away her beauty and grace. I felt a pang of guilt for taking sides. And I was afraid that Father would hate me for siding with Mother. I wanted it to be like it was before, when he wasn't angry all the time and Mother's shoulders didn't sag. But those days had disappeared years earlier, and I knew that after this day, they would never come back. So I sat quietly at the table as Mother went to the shed to talk to Father.

Mother returned after just a few minutes. I hadn't heard any arguing or shouting or pounding from the work shed. Mother didn't say a word about what she and Father had said, and I didn't ask. All day, I heard nothing from the shed, and I didn't see Father at all. I didn't know if he was working or if he had gone to Mr. Pak's farm. Perhaps he'd left for Manchuria without us. That evening, I emptied my rucksack as Mother put away what she had packed. She dragged the box with tools to the shed. After the sun set and I lay on my mat for sleep, all I knew was that I was not going to Manchuria that night and that in ten days I would marry Hisashi.

I didn't see Father the next morning, either. When I awoke, I asked Mother where he was. "I do not know," she said. "He never came into the house last night. I went to the Pak farm this morning to see if he was there. Mrs. Pak said he never came."

"He must have gone to Manchuria," I said.

Mother did not reply. We sat in silence as I ate a quick breakfast of millet and beans. Then, I set about doing my chores. I listened for noises from Father from inside his shed, but I heard nothing. I looked out to the forest but didn't see him there. The new box of tools with the cracked lid had not moved from where Mother put it the night before.

I finished sweeping the floors while Mother sat at the table and did nothing. I wanted to ask what we would do now that Father was gone. I knew what would happen to me. I would live in a beautiful house with servants and good food. Mother, however, needed Father. Without him, she would be like poor Mrs. Choi, dependent on the generosity of the village. And now the village did not have Mr. Pak or Father, and it would surely suffer.

I sat in the sleeping room trying to do my studies. I picked up the book Mr. Saito had given me—*The True Meaning of the Ancient Way*, by Hirata Atsutane. I opened it and began to read. It detailed what it called the "pure ancient Japanese culture and traditions," and laid out a case for rejecting Chinese, Confucian, and Buddhist thinking. The author called it "Kokugaku"—Japanese national learning.

As I read about the history of Japan, the image of my aunt's comb with the two-headed dragon came to me. I saw the dragon's eyes and claws, and a sense of foreboding washed over me. I thought of what my aunt had said—that the spirits of the dragon would haunt me if I married a Japanese man. I quickly closed the book, and the image of the two-headed dragon went away.

Father still hadn't come home by the time we had our evening meal of chicken broth and vegetables. I was beginning to believe that he'd indeed fled to Manchuria without us and I would never see him again. I couldn't imagine life without my father. He had always been good to me, even when he was angry. He worked hard to support our family, and I always felt safe with him near. Now that he was gone, it was as if our family had lost a leg and would fall over in the slightest breeze. I was racked with guilt because I'd defied him.

Mother and I cleaned up from our meal and went to our mats for sleep. But I didn't sleep right away. I lay awake, thinking of Father, hoping that he was okay. I wondered if he was thinking about Mother and me. I wondered how far he had gone in one day. I tried to envision where he might be on his journey. Was he still in Korea, heading north through the mountains? Or had he crossed the Yalu River into China and then turned north? I tried to picture a map from my studies to see what the best route for him would be. I began to think that Mother and I should have gone with him.

I was getting drowsy when the front door opened. Mother rushed to the main room, and I followed close behind her. My father stood in the door. There were dark circles around his eyes as if he hadn't slept in two days. His hair was a mess.

"Seong-ki!" Mother cried. She ran to him and embraced him. He did not return her embrace. Mother pulled away and lowered her eyes.

"I'm hungry," Father said, and went to the table and sat. Mother hurried to the stove and started a fire. As I stood in the doorway, Mother put on a kettle of tea and a pot with water and rice she had hidden in a small sack under the pots. She chopped some vegetables and tossed it in with the rice.

Father sat at the table hunched over. "Suk-bo," he said.

I took a step into the room. "Yes, Appa?"

"Since you refuse to go to Manchuria, you and I will start working on the Pak farm tomorrow. You still have eight days to be a Korean, and I expect you to work like one. We will go before it is light."

"Yes, Appa," I said.

"Go to sleep now," he said. "You will need the rest."

I went to my mat, but I stayed awake a long time. I listened to hear Mother and Father talk, but I heard nothing.

The next morning Father woke me when it was still dark. We ate a quick breakfast and went to Mr. Pak's farm. All that day, I worked alongside my father, cleaning the farmyard, pulling carrots and daikons in the root field, and weeding the soybeans. Mrs. Pak did what she could, and at every turn, she bowed and thanked Father for his help. She brought us tea and made lunch and dinner. When dusk came, she said that we should go home, but Father refused to quit. We worked until it was too dark to see, then we worked another hour. All the time, Father only talked when he said what we were going to do next. I wanted to talk with him as I had done all my life. I wanted to tell him that we had tomorrow to do more work and that we should go home and rest. But I didn't dare say anything. I knew Father was punishing me for defying him, and I quietly accepted the punishment.

By the time we headed home, my hands were bleeding and my back and legs ached so much I could barely walk. As I collapsed into bed, Father said, "We start early again tomorrow."

"Yes, Appa," I said as I fell asleep.

We kept to the same schedule for the next two days. By then, my hands were even worse than they'd been before. Every day I wrapped them in rags, but all the same, yellow calluses grew thick on my fingers and palms. Mother made a solution of vinegar, onion, and salt to soak my hands in at night so the calluses would not build up. I could soak them for only a few minutes before I fell asleep. The sun was baking my skin and it was turning dark. Each night, Mother rubbed oil into me. My back and legs no longer ached, but I was so bone-tired that I didn't eat well. I was losing weight and turning hard. I worried that I would look like a poor farm girl on my wedding day. The way Mother ministered to me, I knew she was worried, too, but she never said anything to Father.

The hard work didn't seem to affect Father. He did twice as much as I did, and though he wasn't a farmer, he knew just what to do. Mrs. Pak was always thanking him, but he didn't reply. He said almost nothing both at work and at home. He never smiled. His expression was a combination of resolve and resignation—resolve that he would make the Pak farm an example of what he could do; resignation that he had to do it for the Japanese.

On the fourth day, the Kwan girls came to help us weed the soybeans. As she scratched around the plant stalks with her hoe, Soo-sung said, "I hear you are marrying a Japanese man. So you will be a chinilpa." She twisted the word "chinilpa," as if it was a curse word.

"I am not a chinilpa," I countered. "I am not collaborating with the Japanese. It is what the authorities say I must do. If I refuse, they will throw Father in prison, and then the village will not have enough to eat."

"We still have Mr. Kim's farm," Soo-sung said. "We will have plenty to eat. You should go to Manchuria instead of marrying a Japanese. It is too bad you didn't marry the farmer's son Jung-soo before he left for Seoul. I heard he liked you. Who are you marrying?"

"He is the son of the director-general. He lives in Sinuiju."

Soo-sung looked at me askance. "Hmm, the son of the director-general. You *are* a chinilpa."

I didn't respond. I took my hoe and worked two rows over where I didn't have to talk to Soo-sung.

By the sixth day, Father had the farm in good order. The fields were clean of weeds and the farmyard was neat. We had harvested the first crops of carrots, daikons, and cabbage. When the administrator came in a truck to take our harvest, he looked at the farm and didn't say anything to Father about falling short of his quota. Father loaded the truck, and the administrator said he would be back in two weeks.

All those days, Father and I worked side by side as if we were strangers. I wanted to say I was sorry for defying him, and truly I was. But even with the hard labor Father was putting me through, I did not regret staying instead of going to Manchuria.

That night, we went home before it was dark. Mother prepared a meal of rice and beans. I ate well. I was less tired than the previous days. I think I was getting used to the hard work.

Mother said, "In three days, Suk-bo will have her wedding. She should rest tomorrow."

To this, Father said nothing. He finished his rice and went to his mat to sleep.

TEN

When the wedding was only two days away, I had many questions. I didn't know what I should take with me. I didn't know what I should do to prepare for the wedding. I didn't know what I should wear or how I should wear my hair. And I didn't know how to make love to a man. I wanted to ask Mother for advice, but I sensed she wasn't in a mood to talk. She was concerned that our defiance had broken Father. She watched his every move and attended to his every need. She rarely said anything to him unless he spoke first.

When I woke up, it was light outside and Father was already gone. I had slept late. I wasn't tired and my body didn't ache like it had each of the previous six days.

Mother was at the stove when I went into the main room. When she saw me, she said, "I have made rice and egg for you."

I was surprised she had an egg. We only had eggs when the Paks or Kims smuggled them to us instead of giving them to the Japanese. "Where did you get an egg?" I asked.

"Your father gave it to me last night and said it was for you. I saved the rice from our allotment. Here, take it."

Mother held out a bowl. It was nearly full with rice, onions, and a cooked egg. It was twice as much as I usually ate. I took it and sat at the table.

"Eat it all," Mother said as she brought me a bowl of tea and sat across from me.

I had no trouble eating everything. When I finished, Mother gathered the bowl and took it to the rinse bucket. I sat at the table, imagining what my life soon would be like. I thought of Hisashi. I thought of our wedding night.

Finally, the question spilled from me. "Ummah, how do you make love to a man?" I supposed Mother wouldn't answer my question or would say that I shouldn't worry about it. So I was surprised when she put the bowls aside and sat at the table. She smiled gently, the way she smiled years earlier. Her loose braid fell gently down her back.

"I was only a year older than you when I married your father," she said. "I did not know what to do, either. I was afraid to ask my mother. She did not like Seong-ki. I think it was because he was a Yi. Or perhaps it was because she thought he was a rebel." She grinned. "She was right about that."

Mother closed her eyes as if she was dreaming. "I was so in love with your father then. He was handsome and strong and full of life. My heart raced every time I saw him. I could not wait to be with him. And though I worried about what to do when we were finally together, when it happened, it was . . . well . . . We loved each other and it made our lovemaking beautiful."

Mother took a sip of tea and regarded me over the top of her tea bowl. "So, tell me," she said, "how do you feel about this man?"

I shrugged. "I do not know. I have seen him so little."

"How do you feel when you see him?"

"Well," I said, blushing, "like you with Father, I suppose. My heart races a little."

Mother nodded. "I think then, making love to him will be beautiful, as it was for me."

My mother's words made me feel less afraid, and I was grateful she had talked to me. Then I asked, "Do you still love Father?"

Mother's smile faded. She nodded weakly and looked inside her tea bowl. "Yes, I do," she replied. "Very much. But his spirit is broken. Men are not strong like women. When a man's spirit is broken, it never heals. Still, I love him. True love, Suk-bo, is not conditional. It is much deeper. It comes when the passion ends. Then it becomes a commitment you make every day for the rest of your life." She looked at me and smiled, but it was once again her sad, forced smile.

A lifetime commitment. Was that what I was agreeing to? Could I commit myself to a Japanese man for the rest of my life?

She stood from the table. "You should rest today. Pack your books and some clothes. Mr. and Mrs. Saito will give you what you need when you go there tomorrow."

"Is Father going to the wedding?"

"I do not know," Mother said simply. I wanted to probe, but I knew it wouldn't be wise.

Mr. Saito's car came for me the next day as the sun climbed over the hills in the east. It was a bright, warm day with not a single cloud in the sky. The birds sang and flitted about as birds do on a sunny day. You could almost hear the grass grow in the field behind our house. I stood at the front door and watched as the car rolled up the road trailing a cloud of dust. I half hoped that I would see Hisashi driving the car, but as it drew near, I saw that there was only Mr. Saito's driver, Isamu. The car pulled to a stop in front of our house, and its trail of dust drifted away in the breeze. Behind the wheel, Isamu spotted me, and for a second, I thought I saw him scowl.

Isamu got out of the car and gave me a stiff nod. "I have been ordered to take you to Mr. Saito's house," he said. "Are you ready?"

Mother had woken me early that day. As usual, Father had left for the Pak farm before it was light outside so it was just Mother and me. I took a bath in the metal washtub behind the house. Mother put salts in the water and lilac petals, too. As I soaked in the soft, fragrant water, Mother filed the calluses on my hands and scrubbed the dirt from under my fingernails with a stiff brush. After my bath, Mother combed my hair, braided it, and tied it with the red silk ribbon. She had pressed my gray dress and helped me put it on. From somewhere, she had found white maquillage that she rubbed on my face, neck, and hands to lighten my sun-darkened skin. When she finished, she stepped back, looked at me, and said, "Suk-bo, you are beautiful."

Mother had never doted on me like this before, and she had never told me I was beautiful. Right then, I wanted to throw my arms around her, hold her, and never let her go. But I knew those days were gone for me. So I nodded and said, "Thank you, Ummah."

Now from the doorway, I stared at Isamu and couldn't say if I was ready. I was unable to move or utter a single word. Mother came behind me with my rucksack. She put a hand on my shoulder. "You must have courage, Suk-bo. This is what is best for you."

Until then, I'd never had to have courage. I had lived under the protection of a loving mother and father, and an older brother who looked out for me. Now I was going to live in a strange house with people I didn't know. My family would be miles away. Mother was right; I had to have courage.

I turned to Mother, and this time I threw my arms around her. I squeezed her tight as a tear rolled down my cheek. She hugged me for a few seconds and then pushed me away. She looked into my face and wiped the tear from my cheek. "Go now," she said softly. "Your father said he is coming to your wedding. We will be with you tomorrow."

Right then I thought I should run into the forest to hide. But inside my rucksack, I had packed the hairpin that Hisashi had given me. I remembered how nervous he was when he gave it to me. I remembered how he smiled when I said I liked it. So I took in a deep breath and went to the car. Isamu didn't come around to open the car door for me as he should have. So I opened the door myself and climbed into the back seat of Mr. Saito's big black car, and we drove away from my house.

Isamu and I didn't talk as we drove to Sinuiju. I had hundreds of questions I wanted to ask, but I could tell he didn't want to talk to me. So I looked out the car window and tried to think of the answers to my questions. Eventually, I realized I couldn't know the answers and would just have to see what happened.

When Isamu pulled the car up to the house, the bald butler named Haru and the woman who had served the tea when I visited weeks earlier stood side by side at the front door. Haru wore the same buttonless white shirt, loose pants, and leather slippers as when I saw him before. His face showed no emotion. The woman looked elegant in her white kimono and hair arranged so that it framed her face. This time, Isamu jumped out of the car and opened my door. But with his back to Haru, he gave me a hard stare as he offered his hand to me. I looked away from him and climbed out of the car with my rucksack. I bowed to Haru and the woman.

"Welcome, Miyoko, to this household," Haru said with a professional nod. He gestured to the woman next to him. "This is Yoshiko. She is the head housekeeper here. Come. You have much to do today."

Haru and Yoshiko led me into the house. I was careful to remove my shoes and bow when I entered the main room as Haru had instructed me to do weeks earlier. They took me to a room in the back with a low bed on a frame. I saw a simple blond-wood chair, the likes of which I had never seen before, and a shoji screen. A chest with brass hinges sat next to the bed. Two young women, one petite and pretty, one tall and gangly, stood by and bowed when Haru and Yoshiko came in. They wore plain purple kimonos and had light skin, so I assumed they were Korean.

"Yoshiko will take care of you," Haru said evenly. "First, you must be fitted for your wedding dress. Later, we will go over what you will do in the wedding. I expect you to do exactly what we tell you. Do you understand?"

"Yes, sir," I said.

Haru left and Yoshiko stood in front of me. "Put your rucksack next to the bed," she said. Her voice was gentle and comforting. She nodded at the chest. One of the young women opened it. Inside was a white kimono and a large headpiece that looked like a round kite with a long tail.

"Try on the *tsunokakushi* first," Yoshiko said. "Sit."

I sat on the chair as the gangly assistant took the headpiece out of the chest, and with the help of the pretty assistant, they put it on me. It was heavy and cumbersome. It covered my head and shielded my eyes from the sides.

"Ma'am," I said, "I have a hairpin that Hisashi gave me. I would like to wear it for the wedding if I may."

Yoshiko shook her head. "No, this is a Shinto wedding. The tsu-nokakushi headpiece symbolizes your resolve to become a gentle and obedient wife. It hides the horns of jealousy and selfishness. A hairpin would be inappropriate."

Yoshiko pushed the headpiece lower on my head so that it nearly covered my face. She stepped back and examined me. "It will do as is," she said evenly. "Now, take it off and put on the kimono."

The assistants lifted the headpiece from me and set it aside. As I took off my gray dress, they took the kimono from the chest. It was the most beautiful piece of clothing I'd ever seen. It was white silk covered with subtle raised designs of peacocks. A thick white bow and tassels hung from the front. In the back was a much larger bow with a strap that hung the length of the kimono.

The young women raised the kimono over my head, and I ducked into it. It was heavy and made me feel small. Yoshiko stood in front of me and pulled and tugged on it. "It is the right length but it is too big in the middle," she declared. "You were larger when I first saw you."

She was right, I was larger then. Over the previous several weeks, I had lost weight from working for my uncle and on the Pak farm. I hoped she wouldn't also notice my dark skin and rough hands.

"We will have to take in the chest and waist," Yoshiko said. "The shoulders should be smaller, too. But we do not have time for it. Kiyo, Fumiko," she said to the assistants. "An inch in the chest and two in the waist. Go now."

The women helped me out of the kimono and left with it. Yoshiko examined me as I stood in front of her wearing just my undergarments. "You have been in the sun," she said, shaking her head. "You are dark like a plum and I'm afraid that the makeup you have on does not hide it. Also, the sun has bleached your hair and your hands are rough. Tomorrow we will use oshiroi powder on your face and camellia oil for your hair. Tonight, as you sleep, you will wear gloves soaked in coconut oil for your hands. We will give you the appropriate undergarments, too. You will look fine for your wedding."

The door slid open and Mrs. Saito stepped in. Yoshiko nodded to her, but I was too shocked and didn't think to bow.

"Leave us, Yoshiko," Mrs. Saito said. Yoshiko nodded again and I was surprised she didn't bow to the lady of the house. Then I was alone with Mrs. Saito.

She wore the same black-and-white kimono she had on when I first saw her weeks earlier. She had her hair pinned up the same way Yoshiko did so that it framed her face. She was expressionless as she glided over to the chair and sat. Still in my undergarments, I reached down and picked up my gray dress.

"Leave it on the floor," Mrs. Saito said. "It is appropriate for you to be in your undergarments given what I am about to say."

I dropped the dress and stood in front of Mrs. Saito like a child. She examined me from my head to my toes. She did not reveal if she approved of what she saw or if she was disgusted with me. "Tomorrow you will marry my son," she finally said, her voice cool and controlled. "You should know that I do not approve of this union. Hisashi is . . . sensitive, and he needs a strong Japanese wife, not a weak Korean girl like you. But my husband is a patriot, and he believes we should do what the emperor says, no matter how foolish it is. So he has given our son to the empire to support the idea that Koreans should be Japanese. I do not think it is wise for us to mix. It will dilute Japanese blood."

She lifted her chin. "But as the wife of an important man, I am expected to follow my husband without question. And that is what I will do. However, you should know this." She leveled her eyes on me, sending a shiver through my body. "You will be Hisashi's *Korean* wife," she said, as if the word "Korean" was dirty. "When the time is right, he will have a proper Japanese wife. Of this, I am sure. It does not matter what my husband believes. And when that time comes, you will go your separate way along with any bastard children you have."

She kept her eyes on me and let her words sink in. It seemed like time had stopped. I wasn't sure if I'd heard her correctly. The words "Korean wife" kept ringing in my head. I think I started to shake. I'd thought Mr. and Mrs. Saito would treat me well. That's what Mr. Saito had promised. But according to her, I would be nothing more than a mistress for Hisashi. I wouldn't be a respectable wife at all. And I wouldn't be able to love him as I had dreamed I would. Right then I thought I'd made a mistake.

Mrs. Saito stood from the chair and went to the door. She slid it open. Before she left, she said, "I expect our time together, however short, will be . . . cordial. As long as we understand each other, there is no need for hostility. Goodbye, Miyoko."

She went out the door, and I quickly put on my gray dress.

I stayed in the room with the low bed all day. Haru and Yoshiko came in shortly after Mrs. Saito left and drilled me on what I was to say and do in the wedding ceremony. Haru was strict and scolded me when I got something wrong. He often flicked his finger on my head to emphasize a point. Yoshiko encouraged me to try again and praised me when I got it right. They told me that the wedding would take place midafternoon the next day and that only the immediate family would attend.

The pretty servant girl named Kiyo brought me a supper of miso soup, rice, vegetables, and strips of grilled beef in a bento box. It was the first time I'd had beef in many years and it was delicious. When Kiyo came to take away the bento box, I thought I saw a look of disapproval on her face the same as Isamu had given me earlier in the car.

The next day as Yoshiko looked on and instructed them what to do, Kiyo and Fumiko bathed me, put camellia oil in my hair, and applied oshiroi powder on my face and hands. They put me in the wedding kimono, which now fit perfectly, and then put on the tsunokakushi headpiece. Yoshiko tugged and pulled on the kimono and headpiece until they were just right. Finally, she declared that I was ready.

We went to the entrance of the large main room where I had first met Mr. and Mrs. Saito. Under the large headpiece, I had to turn completely to look around and see anything. I saw a man wearing a black cylindrical hat and a blue priest's garment. Mr. and Mrs. Saito were there. He wore a smart Western-style black suit with a white shirt and gray tie. Mrs. Saito looked stylish in an elaborate red kimono. She held herself straight and without expression.

It was only after I looked closely that I recognized my parents, who wore kimonos. I had never seen them in kimonos before. I was sure they didn't own them so I assumed the Saitos had provided them. Mother looked lovely in her blue kimono. She held her shoulders back and smiled at me when our eyes met. Father, on the other hand, looked as if he was a prisoner and his kimono was prison garb. He stared at his feet and never looked up.

Then Hisashi came in. He was strikingly handsome in a black kimono with a black-and-white striped pleated skirt. He smiled at me and my heart skipped a beat. He came to me, took my hand, and led me to the priest who stood in front of the *kami dana*, the miniature Shinto altar.

The priest washed our hands. He said a prayer to Shinto gods as he asked for a blessing on our marriage from the *kami*—the emperor and the spirits of nature. We said our vows and sipped sake three times, representing heaven, earth, and man. Mr. and Mrs. Saito and Mother and Father sipped sake, too, and everyone toasted us saying "*Kampai!* Drink up!" Everyone, that is, except Father, who continued to stare at his feet.

And when it was done, I looked at Hisashi, my new husband, who seemed genuinely pleased to have me as his wife. I looked at Mother and Father, and sweet sorrow filled me that my life with them was over. I saw Mr. Saito in his suit and tie. He looked the very picture of a proud Japanese patriot. I looked at Mrs. Saito, who held her chin and eyes level.

I took my husband's hand. At that moment, I could have been happy. But now that I was the wife of a Japanese man, I saw the two-headed dragon from my aunt's comb. Its eyes were afire and its claws raked the air. It was talking to me. "Korea!" I thought I heard it say. "Dare not forsake your people!"

ELEVEN

Mother had said that if I loved Hisashi and he loved me, our wedding night would be beautiful. I didn't know if I loved him. I didn't even know what love between a man and a woman was. All I knew was that my heart beat fast when he was near. He had been kind to me and called me by my Korean name. My hand tingled when he took it to lead me to the priest. I willingly gave my vows to him.

I didn't know if he loved me either. He always seemed excited to see me. He'd said his vows, too. But his mother had said I would only be his mistress, and I worried that he felt the same way.

After the wedding reception—a brief gathering with tea and a variety of vinegared rice and raw fish served with silver chopsticks and on gold-rimmed porcelain plates—I said goodbye to my parents, and Isamu took them home in Mr. Saito's car. I felt scared and alone as I watched the car drive down the road with Mother and Father looking awkward in the back seat. I wondered when I would see them again.

When the servants cleared away the food from the reception, Hisashi and I went to his room on the other side of the house from where I had spent the previous night. He told me we were on the men's side of the house, but since we were now married, I would live with him there. The room was much larger than the one I had stayed in. There was a low table and chairs without legs, the seats resting on the floor like cushions. Off to one side was a low bed on a frame like the one I'd had in my room, only this bed was much larger. Against a wall was a desk and a shelf with books. A scroll with a watercolor painting of the sea and a snowcapped conical mountain hung next to the desk. A *tansu* clothing chest sat against another wall. Someone had lit incense in a bowl on the table, and the room smelled spicy and sweet.

I still wore my wedding dress. After the reception, Yoshiko had said I could take off the cumbersome headpiece, and Kiyo and Fumiko had taken it away. Hisashi still wore his black kimono with a white-and-black striped skirt.

He faced me. His eyes were nervous and his breathing was a little fast. "We are husband and wife now," he said. He grinned shyly.

From inside my kimono, I took the silver kanzashi hairpin that I had hidden there before the wedding. I showed it to him. "I wanted to wear this for our wedding, but Yoshiko said it would be inappropriate. I do not think it would be inappropriate for me to wear it now, do you?"

Hisashi smiled at me, and this time, his smile was not so shy. "I would be honored if you would wear it," he said with a nod.

I gave him the hairpin and turned my back to him. I lifted my hair off my neck and twisted it on top of my head. He didn't do anything. After a few seconds, he said, "I . . . I don't know how it should go."

With my back to my husband and holding my hair up, I smiled to myself. I said, "Just push it in so my hair will not fall."

He put a hand on my hair and I felt the metal tines gently slide against my scalp. I faced him. "It looks nice," he said.

He took my hand and led me to the bed. My hand tingled where he held it. It was like I'd forgotten how to breathe. I dropped his hand and stepped back. I untied the obi of my kimono. I slipped the kimono from my shoulders and let it fall to the floor around my feet. I unbuttoned my silk undergarment and opened it. Hisashi's mouth was open as I stood in front of him. He came to me. He put his hand on the side of my face and I leaned into it. He slipped his other hand underneath my undergarment and around to my bare back. He pulled me into him.

As he came close to kiss me, I heard the words his mother had said the day before. *You will be Hisashi's* Korean *wife. When the time is right, he will have a proper Japanese wife.* Suddenly, I felt unclean and Hisashi's touch was cold. I pulled away.

Hisashi looked hurt and confused. "What is it?" he asked. "Did I do something wrong?"

I shook my head. "No, I'm sorry."

He stood in front of me for a moment. Then he closed my undergarment around me. He sat on the bed and invited me to sit with him. As I sat next to him, I was embarrassed and didn't know what to say.

Finally, he said, "I think I understand. But please know this, Miyoko . . . Suk-bo. I will never hurt you."

I believed him. Though I had only seen him a few times and didn't really know him well, in my heart, I knew he was true. I was ashamed for rejecting him. "It is not you," I said.

"Please tell me, what is it?"

I hesitated. Then I blurted out, "Will you take a Japanese wife someday?"

He looked shocked at my question and I saw I had hurt him again. "Whatever makes you think that?" he asked, as if I had just accused him of cheating on me.

I wanted to tell him what his mother had said, but I knew I shouldn't. He might get angry with her and confront her about it. Then there would be no peace for me in the Saito household. So I said, "I am just a poor Korean girl. Everything here is so different, so grand. I cannot imagine that you would have me and not a Japanese wife."

Hisashi took my hand. He peered into my face with his liquid eyes. "Listen to me, Suk-bo," he said softly. "I think you are beautiful. I have thought so since I saw you in the forest that day. You made me laugh when you got angry at me for making you spill your strawberries. I saw in you the kind of woman I could love, and I knew that I wanted to marry you. It does not matter that you are Korean. I know in my heart that you will be a fine wife."

Relief washed over me and I wanted to cry. In that moment, I no longer cared what his mother had said. This man—this handsome, kind, and gentle man—was saying in his way that he loved me. And now, I knew what love was and I knew that I loved him, too.

I leaned into him and we kissed. His lips were warm and tender. My heart raced. He put his arms around me and pulled me in close. He opened my undergarment and pressed his hands against my back. His touch was soft and gentle. And there, on the low bed in Hisashi's room, surrounded by the sweet, spicy smell of incense, we made love.

And it was, as Mother had said, a most beautiful thing.

Before the wedding, I didn't know what I would do when I lived at the Saito household. I had worried that I wouldn't be able to continue my studies and that I would be bored with nothing to do. But as it turned out, I didn't need to worry. Mr. Saito allowed me to continue my education, although with a strong emphasis on Kokugaku—Japanese learning. Kokugaku loyalists believed the Japanese were naturally pure and destined to rule all of Asia. They believed in strict adherence to "the way"—discipline, order, and purification—and that Emperor Hirohito was divine. In the afternoon, I received instruction from Yoshiko on how to be a Shinto wife. She taught me the proper way to conduct a tea ceremony, how to greet people—a level chin and a firm eye to those in positions below me; a bow of the head and diverted eyes to those in positions above. She taught me how a Shinto household ran—everything on a strict schedule and perfectly organized. Haru taught me that they did everything with the utmost respect for the emperor and Japan. I studied the *Kodō taii, The True Meaning of the Ancient Way* that Mr. Saito had given me. Every morning we washed ourselves in front of the kami dana altar and said prayers. Every night we bowed to the emperor and prayed for his health. Instead of the strict routine boring me, over time I grew to appreciate the serenity of it.

Even so, I knew my place. I wasn't invited to receptions with Japanese officials or to Shinto services outside the house, even though Hisashi always went. I stood behind Hisashi when we were with others. I wasn't allowed out of my room during my monthly bleed.

I didn't mind. Although Haru could be harsh, it was comforting to have him and Yoshiko tell me what to say and how to act. I never had to do any chores like I'd done when I lived with my parents. The servants did everything. Kiyo and Fumiko were always only a step or two away, ready to provide anything anyone might need. An old Korean cook named Ai never left the kitchen. Her young assistant served the meals. One gardener took care of the grounds and Zen garden, while another looked after the vegetable garden and orchard. A handyman was always working on the house, although it seemed to me that the house was perfect and didn't need any work. Except for Haru and Yoshiko, all the servants were Korean with Japanese names. It was strange to have them bow to me. Some of them were much older than I was, and Haru scolded me to stop bowing to them. It made me a little sad to stay upright when I should have bowed to my elders. It was as if I was no longer one of them. And I saw, by the way they looked at me, that they felt the same about me.

Once I got used to life in the Saito house, I was happy. Even so, I missed my parents terribly. I hadn't seen or heard from them in many months. I wanted to know how they were. I wanted to visit them, but I thought asking for permission would imply I didn't like being with Hisashi. So I never asked.

Hisashi told me he wanted to be a medical doctor, so he spent hours every day with private tutors. He always had his nose in a book about medicine. Sometimes he went away for days at a time with his father on official government business. I missed him when he was away and was never comfortable while he was gone. But he always returned, and his joy in seeing me told me he missed me, too. When he could, he spent time with me. He was always tender and kind. We made love often. He smiled whenever he looked at me. I loved him so much it hurt.

One day a year and a half after we were married, Hisashi announced that he was tired of his studies and asked if I wanted to go with him for a bicycle ride in Sinuiju. I'd gone out on my own only a few times since our wedding day, but never far from the house. I eagerly accepted.

It was midafternoon on a warm day in early fall when Isamu got the bicycles from the garage and had them ready for us at the road. My brother had taught me how to ride a bicycle—he had an old rusty one that he had found on the side of the road and fixed up—but I hadn't ridden one in a long time and I was afraid that I'd forgotten how. I wore a plain kimono, and Hisashi wore his usual white shirt and black trousers. The bicycles were nothing at all like my brother's. They were shiny and new and had chrome wheels and handlebars. Hisashi held my hand as I hiked my kimono over the bicycle frame and found the pedals with my feet. I pushed on the pedals, and soon I was gliding along as if it was only yesterday that I had ridden my brother's rusty bicycle. I felt light and free with the wind in my face. Hisashi mounted his bicycle and quickly caught up to me. His strides were long and I had to practically push myself to keep up. As he pedaled, his shirt billowed out. He held his chin high and he looked pleased. It made me happy that my husband was so contented. It didn't seem that I needed to worry that someday he would take a Japanese wife, although truthfully, I still did.

As we rode past blocks of houses into the city center, Hisashi told me about Sinuiju. "It is an important port," he said. "They bring logs down the Yalu River to mill and ship to Japan. Dandong, China, is just across the river, and a bridge connects the two cities."

We entered the heart of the city and came to a park bordered by a street on one side and a railroad line on the other. I saw the open area of the Yalu River beyond the end of the park. Street vendors sold fish and rice cakes to people strolling along the tree-lined path. We got off our bicycles and steered them as we walked. An elderly woman held out a red scarf embroidered with a crane with a red head. I stopped for a moment and admired it. Hisashi came alongside me.

"Do you like it?" he asked.

"It is pretty," I replied.

"Then you shall have it," he said. He turned to the woman. "How much?"

"Four yen."

Hisashi reached into his pocket and produced a five-yen coin. He gave it to the woman and she handed him the scarf. She reached inside her pocket for change. Hisashi raised his hand. "There is no need," he said. The woman bowed a thank-you to him.

Hisashi held out the scarf to me and I took it. "It is too expensive," I said, admiring the embroidery.

"I do not agree," he said. "The red-crowned crane is a symbol of longevity and fidelity. I give it to you as I have given you my promise to be a faithful husband. Anyway," he said with a grin, "it will look nice on you."

"Thank you." I wrapped the scarf around my neck and showed it to him.

"I was right," he said. "It does look nice on you." If we hadn't been in the city, I would have kissed him right then.

We walked our bicycles to the end of the park. Hisashi pointed to the river. "Look over there. It's the bridge I told you about."

I had only seen the bridge across the Yalu River from far away, on the road to my parents' house. At that distance, it was a thin line across the river. But up close, it was an amazing sight. On top of huge stone piers, twelve steel spans reached all the way across like a giant snake coming in and out of the river. They had swung the center span perpendicular to the rest of the bridge, cutting the snake in half.

"Why is that part open?" I asked.

"It's a swing bridge," Hisashi answered. "That section swings open to the side to let ships go through."

"But there are no ships going through now," I said. "Why is it open?"

"To prevent people from crossing."

"Why do they have the bridge if they don't let anyone cross?"

"Because our relationship with China is not good," Hisashi replied. "There is talk that we will go to war with them."

I wanted to ask why Japan and China would want to go to war with each other, but I was asking too many questions and I didn't want to ruin the pleasantness of our outing. We walked along the Yalu River for a while. The river was muddy and flowing as if it was alive and slithering to the sea. On the docks, men unloaded heavy wooden boxes from ships with ropes attached to masts. The rigging creaked and groaned under the weight of the cargo. Fishermen shouting at each other in Japanese heaved ashore baskets filled with their catch. The acrid fish smell filled the air. We walked our bicycles a little farther and came to two soldiers guarding the dock. They had rifles, and on their arms they wore a broad white band with red kanji characters. When they saw us, they brought their rifles to their chests.

Hisashi reached out his hand to stop me. "Kempei tai," he uttered, staring at the soldiers with the white armbands. "We should go no farther."

I had never seen the military police before. I had heard of them, of course. Everyone knew about the Kempei tai. Soo-sung, the black-smith's daughter, once told me that they tortured people for informa-tion about the resistance by pouring water in their mouths to make them think they were drowning. She had said they had spies throughout Korea looking for rebels, and when they found them, they shot them. I didn't believe her then. But now, seeing them clutching rifles and eyeing us, I was not so sure.

"What are they doing here?" I asked.

"That building over there," Hisashi said, nodding to a two-story brick building away from the dock. "It's a brothel."

"A brothel?" In front of the building door were soldiers in a line. They laughed and shuffled their feet as they waited. The door opened and the soldier in the front of the line went inside. I had heard of brothels before. Soo-sung once showed me pictures of women with heavy makeup and fancy outfits and said that men paid money to have sex with them. But I thought brothels were only in the big cities of Seoul and Pyongyang, not in Sinuiju.

"We should leave," Hisashi said.

I stared at the line of soldiers waiting to get inside the brothel. I saw a young woman in a window on the second floor. I couldn't see if she was wearing makeup or dressed in fancy clothes.

"Quickly!" Hisashi said.

We mounted our bicycles and pedaled to the park. There, Hisashi bought rice cakes and we ate them as we walked our bicycles again. I wanted to ask Hisashi more about the brothel, where the women came from, if they were Japanese or Korean. But since I had moved into the Saito house, I had learned that some questions were best unasked.

When we finished our rice cakes, Hisashi said, "Suk-bo, I have something to tell you." He kept his eyes on the path as if he would rather walk than talk. "It is good for me, but I am afraid you might not like it."

For a second, I panicked, thinking he was going to tell me that he had found a Japanese wife and that I would now only be his mistress. But though I worried about it constantly, it didn't make sense. I knew he loved me. I saw love in how he looked at me, in the way he encouraged me to keep up my studies, in how he called me by my Korean name when we were alone. And I was sure that it was his love I felt when I lay with him at night. Even so, I was not sure.

"What is it that you think I will not like?" I asked, looking at the path with him.

"I am going away for a while," he said. "To Tokyo to study medicine. Father has arranged an apprenticeship with an important man there. He is Surgeon Major Shiro Ishii of the Imperial Army. Doctor Ishii is doing new work on bacteria and chemicals and how they can harm people. The apprenticeship will give me an advantage when I go to medical school."

"How long will you be gone?" I asked.

"Six months," Hisashi responded. "Maybe longer, but less than a year. I should be able to come home for visits."

"I am your wife. I should go with you."

He faced me. "I will live on a military base. It will be long hours, but"—he put a hand on my arm—"I promise I will write often." He offered a tender smile.

"I will write every day," I said, choking back tears.

Hisashi nodded. "I believe you will, my wife. I believe you will." He put a hand on my arm and looked into my eyes.

"There is one more thing you need to know," he said. "I know how my mother feels about you. She says things sometimes, and I've heard her arguing with Father."

I looked at my feet.

"Well, she is wrong, Suk-bo. Do you understand what I am saying? She is wrong. Now that we have been together, I know you are the finest woman I could have married."

Though we were in the park with people around, and though it wasn't proper to show affection in public, I threw my arms around him. "Don't leave me, Hisashi," I breathed. "Please don't leave me."

He put his arms around me and said, "It will only be a short while and then we will be together again."

We held the embrace for a precious moment. Then, we walked our bicycles all the way back home and didn't say anything more. As we walked, I wondered and worried how I would manage living in the Saito house without my beloved Hisashi.

TWELVE

Hisashi left for Tokyo two weeks later. Isamu drove him to the train station in Sinuiju where he was to catch the train to Seoul and then a ferry to Japan. He took a black leather suitcase and books in a satchel. He waved goodbye to me as I stood on the veranda fighting back tears. Six months, he had said. Maybe longer. He would try to write every week, he had said.

From the time he'd told me he was going to Tokyo, I'd clung to him like a frightened child clings to her mother. I never let him out of my sight. When he studied, I'd sit beside him with my books pretending to read. When he said he had to stretch his legs, I'd say I needed to stretch my legs, too. We ate every meal together. We made love every night. When we were alone, I put my hair up and pinned it with the silver hairpin he had given me.

I think he understood why I clung to him the way I did. He continually said, "It will be for only a few months," or "It will give us a prosperous future," or "Imagine how happy we will be when I return." I gave him the red scarf he'd bought me in Sinuiju so that he'd remember me. He thanked me and said, "I promise I will always keep it with me as I keep you in my heart." His tenderness made me even sadder. I counted the minutes until he was to leave. I'd count the seconds until he returned.

The day he went away, I never left our room. I lay on the low bed with my face close to where he slept, drinking in the scent of him. I leafed through the books he'd left behind, running my fingers over the pages that he had touched just days earlier. I went to the tansu chest and took out the clothes he didn't take with him. I draped them over the chair and laid them on the bed like he did, pretending he was still there. I skipped the midday meal and then the evening meal, too. I wore the silver hairpin all day.

That night, Yoshiko came and asked if I was well. I told her I was, but I wanted to be alone.

"You cannot stay in your room all day," she said, picking up Hisashi's clothes and folding them into the chest. "You must attend prayers tomorrow morning and take your meals with the family at the usual time. Do you understand?"

I sat on the end of the bed looking at the floor and didn't answer. She came to me and held out her hands. "Look at me," she said.

I put my hands in hers. As it always was with Yoshiko, she revealed no emotion. Her face was neither sympathetic nor stern. Like the hair that she always had perfectly folded on the top of her head, she was a portrait of fortitude. "You must be strong," she stated. "Hisashi loves you and he will return someday. Until then, you must hold your chin up and be with the family." She held her eyes on me and gave me a nod. She dropped my hands and left the room.

Yoshiko's reassurance helped me sleep that night. Or perhaps I was exhausted with grief. The next morning, I attended prayers with Mr. and Mrs. Saito, Yoshiko, and Haru at the kami dana altar. At the morning meal, it was just me and Mr. and Mrs. Saito. I was terribly uncomfortable sitting alone with my in-laws. After we bowed to the table, Kiyo and Fumiko brought the breakfast and tea, I kept my eyes low and poked at my food with my chopsticks. I think Mr. Saito knew that I was uncomfortable. In his husky voice he said, "The doctor who Hisashi is studying with, Major Ishii, is doing important work for the empire. It is fortunate that I was able to get Hisashi an internship with him."

"Yes, sir," I replied.

Mrs. Saito kept her eyes forward and her chin level as she ate. She said nothing. It was as it always was with Mrs. Saito. She said very little to me. We were cordial, as she had said we should be when she declared I would only be Hisashi's Korean wife. But in the cool way she looked at me, in how she ignored me, in how she said "Miyoko" with a slight lift on the final *o* as if my very existence was in question, I knew that her opinion of me hadn't changed. So I kept my distance. I prayed that the love I had with Hisashi would prove she was wrong.

Mr. Saito picked up a slice of pear with his chopsticks. "Hisashi will learn much working with Doctor Ishii," he said, examining the pear slice. "It will help him when he goes to medical school."

"Yes, sir," I replied. Mrs. Saito continued to sit straight with her eyes forward. She took small bites of food as if she was only tasting it.

"It is good for the empire," Mr. Saito said, finally putting the pear slice into his mouth. "For the emperor."

"Yes, sir," I said. I continued to poke at my food.

Mr. Saito looked at me sideways and swallowed the pear. After a moment, he sighed as if he was frustrated with me. He picked up his napkin and wiped his mouth. He set the napkin on the table. "I must go to Pyongyang this evening," he announced. "I am not sure how long I will be away. I will ring Haru and tell him when I am to return."

Then I said, "I want to visit my parents. I have not seen them since the wedding. May I, sir? Please?"

"Yes, yes, yes," Mr. Saito said with a wave of his hand. "Of course. Isamu will drive you."

Mrs. Saito turned her head toward him, and her eyes narrowed ever so slightly. Then, she faced the table again. Mr. Saito bowed to the table and got to his feet. Mrs. Saito and I stood with him and bowed. As they left through the sliding door, Mrs. Saito gave me one of her cool looks.

I sat at the table again. Kiyo and Fumiko came in to clear away the tea and food. As Kiyo took the teapot from the table, I caught a look of hostility in her eyes. I'd seen the look before. It was the look the servants gave me when they thought I wasn't looking.

"Why do you look at me like that?" I demanded. I was angry that Hisashi had left me alone here in this house. I was furious that the servants looked at me like I was a traitor.

Kiyo didn't seem at all surprised by my outburst. "I am sorry, ma'am," she said prettily, although she didn't sound sorry at all. "Did I look at you the wrong way?" She gave a most condescending half smile. Fumiko awkwardly clutched tea bowls and gawked from behind Kiyo.

"You think I'm a chinilpa for marrying Hisashi, don't you? Well, I am not a traitor. I married him because they made me do it. But now, I love him. And he loves me too, I know it. What difference does it make that he is Japanese and I am Korean? Should I hate my husband just because you hate the Japanese?"

Kiyo held her condescending half smile. "Of course not, ma'am."

Before she could leave, I asked, "What is your Korean name?"

"I am sorry, ma'am," Kiyo said. "I am only known as Kiyo."

"Jin-ee," Fumiko interjected from behind Kiyo. She glanced at Kiyo, then looked at me. "My name is Jin-ee."

"Mine is Suk-bo," I said to Fumiko, who was still clutching the tea bowls. "We can call each other by our real names when we are alone."

Fumiko nodded at me. Kiyo's half smile remained on her face as if she had painted it on. With the teapot in her hand, she went out through the door. Fumiko gave me a quick smile and followed Kiyo.

I wasn't able to see my parents right away. Mr. Saito was touring villages in his province and Isamu drove him. I wouldn't have minded the delay if I'd still been with Hisashi. But now that he was gone, I didn't have anything to do and I was lonely. I tried to keep up with my studies, but I couldn't concentrate for more than a few minutes. Haru and Yoshiko had taught me what I needed to know about being a Japanese wife and living in a Shinto house, so I received no more lessons from them. I only saw Mr. and Mrs. Saito at meals when Mr. Saito was home. The Korean laborers didn't want anything to do with me. Yoshiko was always pleasant, but she was older and busy running the household. The days were growing short and a cold wind blew from the north. I seldom went out.

I missed Hisashi terribly. I would sit for hours trying to picture where he lived in Tokyo, what he was doing for Doctor Ishii. I wrote a letter to him every day on fine rice paper and in my very best handwriting. I gave each one to Haru to mail. Hisashi had told me he would try to write every week. It had been almost two months since he'd gone away and I still hadn't gotten a letter from him. At first, I thought it was because the mail must take a long time to travel across the sea from Tokyo. When after a month I still hadn't gotten a letter, I convinced myself it was because he was busy at his new job and that I would get a long letter from him any day. But now that two months had passed, I worried that he didn't care about me anymore. Tokyo was certainly full of beautiful women who would lust after a handsome man with a bright future like Hisashi. Images of glamorous women flirting with my husband, pawing at him, whispering in his ear that he should have a proper Japanese wife plagued my mind. I practically went crazy with jealousy. Most days I cried and didn't want to get out of bed. Yoshiko would come to me and, in her steadfast way, convince me to attend morning prayers.

I slept poorly. One cold night, a strong wind shook the fallen leaves outside my window and made the tree branches groan. I lay alone in my bed with the blanket wrapped tight around me, trying not to think about Hisashi. It was dark—the oppressive dark that only comes in winter. I squeezed my eyes closed and tried to shut my ears to the wind.

I wanted to cry, but I'd already cried that night and had nothing left inside me. Fatigue seized my entire body. I started to drift off.

When I was nearly asleep, I sensed there was something next to me. With my eyes closed, I whispered, "Hisashi." There was no reply. I wanted to open my eyes, but I couldn't. "Hisashi," I said again.

Then I saw the two-headed dragon from my aunt's comb. It was there, next to me. Its eyes were red with fire and it was clawing at me. Its tongues flitted angrily. Its tail thrashed the air. Behind the dragon were people, hundreds of them, perhaps thousands. They were Koreans and they were shouting at me. "Chinilpa!" they said. "Chinilpa!"

"Leave me alone!" I screamed. I threw off the blanket and sat up. My heart was racing and my breaths were short. For some reason, I felt nauseous. I looked at the bed next to me. The dragon and the people were gone. I looked around, but only saw darkness.

On the other side of the latticed door a person came holding a candle. The door slid open and Yoshiko stepped in. She came to my bedside. Her hair was down and the candle illuminated her face, making her look like a ghost.

"Miyoko," she scolded, "you have awakened the entire house with your shouting."

Then I said, "May I visit my parents tomorrow? Mr. Saito said I could."

Yoshiko sighed. "I will check with Mr. Saito," she said. "Now, go to sleep and do not shout any more. Mr. Saito is traveling again tomorrow and needs his rest."

She took the candle and left. I lay down and wrapped the blanket around me again. I felt so alone. I wanted to shut my eyes and go to sleep, but I was afraid that the two-headed dragon would haunt me again. And I was still nauseous. So I lay on my side facing the place Hisashi had slept and prayed that the two-headed dragon would not return.

The next day, Yoshiko informed me that the chauffeur could take me to see my parents whenever I was ready. I was excited and I wanted to go at once, so I pulled on my leather shoes and my *haori* outer coat and went outside to the garage. I found Isamu sitting on the floor in the back of the garage smoking a cigarette. He wore a dark, loose-fitting shirt and a small black cap. Underneath his hat he had pulled his wavy hair into a short tail. He didn't get up when he saw me.

"Yoshiko said you will take me to see my parents," I said. "I would like to go now."

Isamu took a puff from his cigarette and blew the smoke into the air. "And you, the Korean wife of the Japanese son, want me to jump up and take you at once."

"Yes," I said, surprised at his tone. "Yoshiko said you would."

Isamu took another long pull on his cigarette and snuffed it out on a post. He tossed the butt in a tin can on the ground next to him. He sighed as if I was a great inconvenience. He pushed himself up and went to the front of the garage and stood next to Mr. Saito's car. "Okay, let's go."

He did not open the car door for me, so I opened it myself and climbed in the back. Isamu backed the car out of the garage, and we drove through the outskirts of the city and up the road toward my parents' house.

Isamu didn't say anything while he drove. I thought about what he'd said when I asked him to take me. *Korean wife of the Japanese son . . .* I wanted to ask him why he'd said that, but I knew why. He despised me for marrying Hisashi. He thought I was a chinilpa. I wanted him to know that I truly loved Hisashi and that I was just as Korean as he was. I wanted to be friends with him.

"Thank you for taking me, Isamu," I said, trying to break the ice between us.

"Byong-woo," he replied.

"Excuse me?" I said.

"My name is Byong-woo," he said, keeping his eyes on the road. "They call me Isamu, but my real name is Byong-woo."

"Ah," I said. "Then I shall call you Byong-woo. My name is Suk-bo." He didn't reply and kept driving.

"Where did you learn how to drive a car, Byong-woo?" I asked.

"Look," he said, "I was told I had to drive you to your village. I was not told I had to talk to you."

"That is a rude thing to say," I said. "What if I told Yoshiko about your attitude?"

"Then I would know for sure you are a chinilpa," he replied.

I decided not to say anything more. If he wanted to be rude, if he thought I was a traitor, there was nothing I could do or say to change his mind. So I sat in the back and looked out the window.

I wondered what I would find when I saw my parents. I hoped that with me gone, they had rekindled the love they once had. I was sure that on the Pak farm Father had filled the biweekly quota of food for the administrator. In the few days I'd worked alongside him, it was obvious he had a knack for farming and relished the hard work. Mother only wanted me to be happy, and I wanted to tell her that I was. Of course, with Hisashi away, I was miserable and insecure, but Mother didn't need to know that.

We pulled into my village at midday. It was warm for winter, but even so, patches of ice dotted the road and snow clung to the hilltops. We drove past the farmers' fields that lay fallow for the winter. Mr. Pak's farm looked weedy and unkempt and I wondered why Father had left it that way. We drove to my parents' house and Byong-woo turned off the car. He rolled down his window and took out a cigarette. He lit it and started smoking, all the while looking out the front window as if I wasn't there.

I got out of the car and looked at my parents' house. Like the Pak farm, it was unkempt. I had never seen it like that before. Mother and Father had always insisted on keeping the house and garden orderly and clean so the administrator would not punish them. I went to the door and pushed it open. A cobweb grabbed at my face. There were no cooking pots at the basin and no wood next to the stove. The floor mats were gone. So was the table. I took a step in and called out, "Ummah? Appa?" There was no reply.

I went to Father's work shed. The box of tools Mr. Saito had given him was still sitting on the floor where Mother put it a year earlier. Father was not there and his old tools were gone. I went to the root garden. They hadn't planted that year and the garden was full of weeds. I looked down the road to the Kwan house. Smoke drifted from the chimney—they were there. I took a step toward the house to ask them where my parents were. Then I remembered that Mr. Kwan's daughter, Soo-sung, had called me a chinilpa. I went to the car and climbed into the back seat.

"I want to go to my uncle's house," I said.

Byong-woo gave me a look over his shoulder. "I was only told to take you here," he replied.

"Please, Byong-woo," I said. "It is only a mile or two farther on."

"No, I will not," he said.

I was livid. There he sat in the driver's seat of Mr. Saito's car, pretending that he was better than me. "You!" I said. "You and the other servants, you all live under Mr. Saito's roof and eat his food, no different than me. If you are so noble, why aren't you fighting in Manchuria? Why do you accuse me of being a traitor when you are no better?"

"I did not marry a Japanese," he replied.

"No, but you drive a Japanese man's car because if you did not, they would punish you the same as they would have punished me if I hadn't married Hisashi."

He paused for a moment to think about what I'd said. Then he tossed his cigarette butt out the window. "Your uncle's house is on this road?" he asked.

"Yes," I answered.

Without a word, he started the car and we drove to my uncle's house.

THIRTEEN

My young cousins, Soo-hee and Jae-hee, dressed in coarse wool winter coats, played in the front yard of my uncle's house as we approached. When she saw us coming, Jae-hee ran into the house, and soon my aunt was at the front door. Bo-sun gathered the girls to her and held them against her *chima* skirt. She stared at the car. Byong-woo pulled it alongside a persimmon tree just outside their front yard and turned it off. I got out of the back and started for my aunt. I walked halfway, and then I ran the rest of the way and threw my arms around her.

"Sookmo!" I cried. "Aunt! I am so happy to see you."

"Ummah, it is Cousin!" Jae-hee squealed. She hugged me as I hugged my aunt.

My aunt put a hand on my shoulder. "Suk-bo," she said, "you have returned after all this time."

I pushed back from her. "I went to see my parents. They are not at their house."

My aunt looked away. "Jae-hee," she said, "show Suk-bo your new doll."

My young cousin pulled me into the house. She threw off her coat and then ran and got her dolls. One was the doll named Cor-ee she'd shown me on my visit before I married Hisashi. The new doll was a male dressed in a man's hanbok. As my aunt brewed tea at the stove, Jae-hee told me about the dolls as Soo-hee looked on. "The boy is named Jung-soo," Jae-hee said. "He and Cor-ee are married." I glanced at my aunt, who stayed facing the stove. I suspected she encouraged the girls to name their new doll Jung-soo, the name of the farmer's son who I liked before I met Hisashi.

My aunt came to the table with the tea and told Soo-hee to take Jae-hee so she and I could talk. Soo-hee took her sister by the hand, and they took their dolls to the other room. My aunt poured tea into bowls and handed me one.

It felt good to be with someone I'd known before I was married. It felt good to speak Korean again. I asked, "Where are my parents, Sookmo? Please tell me."

My aunt regarded me for a minute. "You have not visited in a long time," she said. "Now you come and you have a nice haori coat and fine leather shoes. The last time you came, you walked instead of being driven in a car. You had Korean clothes and shoes with holes in them."

"Sookmo, please," I said.

My aunt sighed. Then she said, "A few months after your wedding, your parents went to Manchuria. They have been gone well over a year. Your mother had made a deal with your father. She said she would go with him to Manchuria once you were safe. We have not heard from them since they left."

"Manchuria," I said.

"What did you expect?" my aunt said. "Your father could no longer work for the Japanese. It was killing him. And your mother had nowhere to go if your father left without her. It was a reasonable decision. I am sorry to have to say this to you, Suk-bo, but it is not likely you will see them again."

My aunt's words struck me like a slap. I couldn't imagine never seeing my parents again or feeling their loving touch. Now that they were gone, I realized I'd taken them for granted—the joy of the talks I'd had with Mother when we worked side by side in our vegetable garden, watching Father in his shed turn a piece of raw wood into a chair. I would miss them terribly. And I felt guilty. I had fallen in love with a Japanese man and I was taking comfort in a Japanese house. I'd been so involved with Hisashi that I hadn't visited my parents. And now, they were gone. No wonder Kiyo and Byong-woo and all the Koreans hated me. I *was* a chinilpa. "It is my fault," I cried. "My parents ran away because I married Hisashi."

"No," my aunt said. "Honestly, they did the right thing by going to Manchuria. It is time we fight the Japanese. I would have gone with them if not for the girls. But"—her face softened—"do not blame yourself. I know that your mother pushed you into the marriage. I would not have done the same."

"Hisashi is in Tokyo studying to be a medical doctor," I sobbed. "I write to him every day, but he does not write to me. I love him and cannot bear to be without him. His mother said that he will take a Japanese wife someday, and then I fear they will kick me to the street."

"I warned you your way would be difficult," she said.

"I do not care," I said. "I love him and he loves me."

"But he does not live with you and you are afraid he will take a Japanese wife."

I didn't want to argue with my aunt about my decision to marry Hisashi. It would be impossible to tell her how much I loved him and how happy we'd been together.

"What about my brother?" I asked, changing the subject. "Did Kwan-so go with them?"

My aunt's eyes went cold. "No," she said. "He is still in Pyongyang studying the Japanese way. He is smart, your brother, but he forgets who he is. He thinks he will prosper by being Japanese. I do not expect him to ever come back to us."

I remembered how my brother had taught me to ride his bicycle in the road in front of our house. I remembered how he teased me for being skinny. I remembered how he made me feel safe when Father was away. "If he does not come back, then my family is gone," I whispered.

"I told you that you would pay a price for taking the path you chose," my aunt said. "I am sorry the price has been so steep."

After a while, I said, "I have been haunted by the dragon from your comb."

"Yes," my aunt said with a faraway look, "it haunts me, too. The spirits of our ancestors are angry. They are afraid that we are forgetting them. I'm sorry, Suk-bo, that I showed you the comb with the two-headed dragon. But it is important that you know about the curse."

We sat together for a long time without saying anything. My aunt stared at her tea as if her mind was far away. After a while her eyes focused and she finished drinking, then told me I should do the same. "It is bori cha," she said. "Korean tea." She gave me a sly smile.

My uncle came home a short while later. The three of us sat at the low table with the girls, and we talked about how well the crops did that year and how winter had come early. They asked me about life in Sinuiju, and I told them about Mr. and Mrs. Saito, how Haru was strict and Yoshiko was kind. I told them about the strange ways of a Shinto household. While we talked, Jae-hee pestered me to play with her and Soo-hee, and finally, I did. I'd forgotten how it felt to be with family. I'd forgotten what it was like to be home.

From outside the door, Byong-woo said, "Miyoko, we must go back."

My aunt went to the door and invited Byong-woo to come in and have tea with us. He declined and repeated that he and I had to get back. "We have been gone too long," he said from the door.

I hugged Soo-hee and Jae-hee. I bowed to my aunt and uncle. "Stay strong," my aunt said. I went to the car, and Byong-woo and I headed back to Sinuiju.

The weak winter sun was already dropping when we drove down the icy road. It was turning cold again, and the mud on the road was freezing, making the car bump along uncomfortably. Byong-woo looked at me in the rearview mirror. He wasn't wearing his chauffeur's hat, and his black wavy hair fell around his shoulders. He'd rolled down the window a crack to blow out his smoke. Even so, the car smelled like cigarettes. "What did you learn about your parents?" he asked. "Where did they go?"

I wasn't sure what I should tell him. I didn't know him well. He might be a spy for the Japanese or, more likely, for the rebels. Or maybe he was just a chauffeur. But when I thought about it, it didn't matter if I told him. My parents were in Manchuria far away. If Byong-woo was a Japanese spy, there would be nothing he could do to my parents. If he was a rebel, he'd be pleased that they had joined his cause and perhaps he'd regard me more favorably.

"They went to Manchuria," I said. "My father did not want to work for the Japanese anymore."

Byong-woo looked away from the mirror. Then he looked back. "Manchuria?" he said.

"Yes, that is what my aunt told me."

"Are you sure?"

"Yes," I said, starting to feel a little uneasy. "Why do you ask that way?"

Byong-woo turned his eyes to the road. "Miyoko . . . Suk-bo," he began, "what you said earlier was right. I do have a comfortable life driving Mr. Saito's car. But like you, that does not mean that I have abandoned our people. So I will tell you something that could put me in trouble with Mr. Saito. The Japanese have made great advances against the Chinese army. They now control all of northern China."

I took a minute to absorb what Byong-woo had said. I thought he was mistaken, or perhaps he was playing a cruel joke on me. "It's not true," I said. "My aunt did not say anything about that. How do you know?"

Byong-woo pulled the car to the side of the road and let it idle. He put his elbow on the seat and faced me. "I know because I am the chauffeur for the director-general of this province. I know things that others, like your aunt, are not supposed to know. I'm telling you the truth. The Japanese occupy all of Manchuria, and they are at war with China for control of the rest of the country."

In my mind I saw my parents fleeing the Japanese. I saw soldiers with rifles surrounding them. I remembered what my mother had said about how the Japanese had shot my father's brother. I shook my head. "They will be okay," I said, trying to shake away the images. "It will be no different for them than if they had stayed here."

Byong-woo looked away. "I do not think so," he said. "They are arresting any Koreans they find in China. They say they are all rebels."

This struck me like a shot. My parents *were* rebels; that's why Father wanted to go to Manchuria. I tried not to think of what the Japanese would do to my father and mother if they captured them.

Byong-woo pulled the car onto the road and we bumped toward Sinuiju again. Byong-woo said, "Tell me, Suk-bo, how do you feel now about marrying a Japanese man?"

I didn't answer him. The soldiers who were arresting Koreans in Manchuria were different from Hisashi. My husband was kind and gentle. Sensitive, his mother had said. Surely my husband wouldn't take part in murdering.

We drove for a while longer in silence. Then Byong-woo decided to press his questions. "Suk-bo, do you love Hisashi?" he asked.

"Of course I do," I replied, surprised at his question. "He is a good man, not like what you think."

"Oh, I agree he is. He is not like most Japanese. Neither is his father. Mr. Saito does not always agree with the government, although he is careful to hide his feelings. Japan wants to rule all of Asia and the

Pacific, too. They are building a great army, navy, and air force. There is no stopping them now that they have defeated the Chinese. But Mr. Saito is a patriot. He would never disagree with the emperor. He does his job and says nothing."

"Why do you ask if I love my husband?" I asked.

"Because you never write to him," Byong-woo replied. "He sends you letters every week, but you do not send any to him. That is rather strange, I think."

"It's not true!" I exclaimed, pushing myself to the edge of my seat. "I write a letter every day!"

"You do? Well, that *is* strange indeed. I am the one who takes the mail to the post office. I have never seen a letter from you."

"I give them to Haru."

"Haru gives the mail to me. And he would not take your letters if he was not instructed to do so by either Mr. or Mrs. Saito."

"Hisashi has written to me?" I asked, grabbing the back of Byong-woo's seat. "Where are the letters? Who did you give them to?"

"I give them to Haru," he replied. "Again, he would deliver them to you unless he was instructed not to."

I clutched Byong-woo's seat. "I have to get them! Please, Byong-woo, you must help me."

Byong-woo shook his head. "I am sure if they don't want you to have them, the letters have been burned. Although I would not trust Haru, I think I would blame Mrs. Saito."

"Why?" I cried. "Why would she do such a thing?" But I didn't need Byong-woo to answer my question. I pushed myself into my seat. Hisashi, my dear Hisashi, had written to me after all. I desperately wanted to know what he'd written in those letters. Did he say he still loved me? Did he miss me? Did he ask why I didn't write to him? I ached that he thought I didn't write. I had promised to write every day, and he must wonder why he wasn't getting letters from me.

As the lights of Sinuiju came into view, I tried to think what to do about the letters. I said, "Byong-woo, I need your help. I can give my letters directly to you and you can give me Hisashi's letters. No one needs to know."

The chauffeur shook his head. "I will not take that risk. Anyway, they will be suspicious when you no longer give Haru your letters."

"I will write two letters! I will give one to Haru and the other to you."

"What about the letters from Hisashi?" Byong-woo replied. "They will become suspicious when they see no more letters from him."

"No, they will not," I countered. "Since he has not gotten any letters from me, they will think he has stopped writing. Please, Byong-woo. It will work. They will not catch you."

Byong-woo again shook his head. "No," he said simply. "Haru is far too shrewd for that."

I was angry at him, frustrated, and desperate. It was as if the news about my parents, the invasion of Manchuria, and Hisashi's letters had turned my entire world upside down. I needed Byong-woo's help, but he was refusing. Finally, I burst out, "You refuse to help another Korean so that you can keep your easy job. I am not a chinilpa, *you* are, Byong-woo. Or should I call you 'Isamu'?"

"Say what you will about me," Byong-woo replied. "But listen to me carefully, Suk-bo. You must not tell anyone you know about the letters or what I have told you about Japan and China. It will be dangerous for me and for you, too."

As we drove into Sinuiju, I started sobbing, heaving full-bodied sobs like I'd never sobbed before. "Please, Byong-woo," I sobbed. "Please deliver the letters."

Byong-woo did not answer. He snuffed out his cigarette, put on his chauffeur's hat, and drove the car to the Saito house.

FOURTEEN

The morning sickness came two days after I visited my aunt. When I awoke, my stomach churned. I thought I had caught an illness, but I didn't feel feverish. When I sat up and swung my legs over the side of the low bed, foul-tasting bile rose from my stomach into my throat. I thought I was going to vomit. I lay down and closed my eyes. My chest burned and my stomach roiled as if something inside was squeezing it. And then I was sure I was going to vomit. I quickly rolled onto the floor and vomited a watery, stringy mass onto the mat.

I stayed on my hands and knees for some time, and eventually the nausea went away. I got up and slid open the door. "Kiyo!" I called. "Fumiko!" I went back to the bed and sat. I clutched my blankets tight around me.

A few seconds later, both women came to the door. "What is it, Miyoko?" Kiyo asked.

"I am sick," I said. "I vomited on the floor."

Kiyo spotted the mess. "I will get Yoshiko while Fumiko cleans up."

A few minutes later, Fumiko was back with a pail and rag cleaning up my mess when Yoshiko came in with Kiyo behind her. Yoshiko's hair was up as usual. "You are sick?" she asked, sitting on the bed alongside me.

"I feel fine now," I said. "It lasted for only a few minutes."

"I see," Yoshiko said. Her face was emotionless. "Do you have a fever?"

"No," I answered.

"Are you dizzy?"

"No," I answered again.

"Kiyo," Yoshiko said, "make some ginseng tea, strong and hot, and bring it at once."

"Yes, ma'am," Kiyo said.

"Fumiko," Yoshiko said, "finish cleaning and leave us."

"Yes, ma'am," Fumiko said with a bow. She took one more swipe on the mat with her rag and followed Kiyo out of the room.

Yoshiko addressed me squarely. "Tell me, Miyoko," she said, "when was the last time you had your monthly bleed?"

I paused a minute to think. Then, I said, "It has been over two months."

"Two months," Yoshiko said. "You stay here in bed. Haru will call the doctor on the telephone. I think you are pregnant."

I sipped the ginseng tea Kiyo had brought me and waited for the doctor to arrive. At first, I thought Yoshiko must be wrong. I hadn't thought anything was unusual about missing my monthly bleeds. It sometimes happened when I had to work long hours in the fields or when Father, Mother, and I went a week or more with not enough to eat. But here I had plenty to eat and I didn't have to work at all. I knew that women sometimes got sick in the morning when they were pregnant. Mother had told me about it and hinted that morning sickness had afflicted her when she was pregnant with my brother and me. I concluded that Yoshiko's diagnosis was probably right.

My head spun with a million questions and worries. I wouldn't have Hisashi's support during my pregnancy. My husband was hundreds of miles away, and it would be months before he'd return. And Mother and Father were in Manchuria trying to escape from the Japanese army, or perhaps they were prisoners . . . or dead. I felt so alone without the ones I loved to help me. I only had Yoshiko, Kiyo, and Fumiko. I didn't know how any of them would feel about me having Hisashi's baby. Yoshiko would probably be all business as usual. She would see to it that the household staff took good care of me and my baby. Haru would be all business, too, although I remembered Byong-woo said I shouldn't trust him. Kiyo would probably disapprove of the baby as much as she disapproved of me. I wasn't sure how Fumiko would feel.

And then there was Mr. and Mrs. Saito. I presumed that Mr. Saito would be pleased that a Korean woman was having his son's baby and that he was fulfilling his duty to the emperor. Mrs. Saito, on the other hand, would not be pleased at all. Having a child—Hisashi's child—would make it more difficult for her to drive me out of her family. She would hate me for it and hate my baby, too.

Even so, I was delighted that I was pregnant. Hisashi would love our child, I was sure of it, and he would love me for giving him one. He would be a good father and we would grow closer through our child. I so wanted to tell him about the baby growing inside me. But how? They weren't delivering my letters. So though I was thrilled, I was also terribly frustrated and alone, and all I wanted to do was cry.

The doctor came midmorning wearing a black suit and carrying a black leather bag. As Yoshiko stood by, he took my pulse, listened to my heart with his stethoscope, and felt around my neck. He pressed his hands on my belly. He asked about the timing of my monthly bleeds. He asked if my breasts were tender, and I told him that I'd noticed they were.

He stood from the bed and addressed Yoshiko. "As you suspected, she is pregnant," he declared. "It has been two months, or thereabouts. The baby will come in the summer."

As the doctor packed the stethoscope in his leather bag, he gave Yoshiko instructions on what I should and should not eat, and how much rest I should get. He said he'd return in two weeks to check on me. Yoshiko said she understood. She thanked the doctor with a slight bow, and he took his bag and left.

"I will have Kiyo bring more ginseng tea and plain rice," Yoshiko said. "Rest now, as the doctor said."

"But I feel fine," I protested. "The sickness is gone."

"Do as I say," Yoshiko said.

"Yes, ma'am," I replied and lay down on the bed.

Before Yoshiko left, I said, "How will we tell Hisashi?"

"After you have rested, you can write a letter to him."

"But the letter . . . ," I said. I hesitated. I remembered that Byong-woo said I shouldn't reveal what I'd learned about the letters.

"Yes?" Yoshiko said. "What about the letter?"

"It will take so long to get to him," I said.

Yoshiko nodded. "Perhaps Haru can send a telegram. Now rest. I will be back in an hour to see how you are feeling."

"I do not believe Haru will send a telegram," I said.

"He will if Mr. Saito asks him to. I will make a suggestion."

"Thank you, Yoshiko," I said. I was truly grateful. As she left, I knew that Yoshiko, in her firm, demanding way, was going to take care of me.

That morning I wrote a long letter to Hisashi about the baby. Tears fell onto the paper as I wrote because I knew my letter wouldn't reach him.

The next day, I asked Yoshiko if Haru had sent Hisashi a telegram about the baby. "No, he did not," she said. "I told him about your pregnancy and suggested he send Hisashi a telegram. He said he would only send a telegram if Mr. Saito instructed him to, and Mr. Saito is traveling again. Anyway, he said it was not necessary because you had given him a letter that presumably told your husband about the baby."

"What if the letter gets lost?" I asked, trying to hide my anguish.

"You write to him every day," Yoshiko replied evenly. "I do not think they will all get lost. Now, stop worrying. You need to relax or your sickness will get worse."

I was not able to relax as Yoshiko said I should, and over the next several days and weeks, the morning sickness got worse. It came every day. Yoshiko had Fumiko place a clean bowl next to my bed every night, and every morning I filled it with my sickness. One day when the vomiting was so bad that I thought I might turn inside out, a vision came to me. It was the two-headed dragon from my aunt's comb, and it was in my belly where the baby was supposed to be. It thrashed its head and whipped its tail inside me. When I finished vomiting and the nausea went away, I lay on the bed, but the dragon was still with me, calmer now, but there waiting for another chance to torment me. It felt like when the time came, I would give birth to the two-headed dragon. I wondered what it was trying to tell me. I worried that it would cause the baby to be grotesque or born with two heads. I worried that the dragon was trying to kill my baby.

As time went by, I didn't gain weight like I was supposed to, and Yoshiko called for the doctor. When he came, he had me step on a spring scale and wrote down my weight. He pressed his hands on my stomach. When he had finished, he prescribed a combination of traditional herbs and modern medicines to combat the morning sickness and calm my nerves. Every morning, I took the medicines, and they helped a little with the morning sickness, although I always felt the two-headed dragon inside me.

The herbs and medicines eventually worked well enough that I could attend the morning prayer and meal. Mr. Saito had returned, and when he, Mrs. Saito, and I entered the main room, we washed our hands and bowed all the way to the floor at the kami dana altar. Mr. Saito said a prayer and thanked the emperor for his blessings. Then, we went to the table, and Kiyo and Fumiko brought our morning meal.

I had not talked to Mr. and Mrs. Saito about my pregnancy. For the past several weeks while I had been sick, I had stayed in my room. And they hadn't come to visit me, either. I assumed Mr. Saito hadn't visited because he just returned from Seoul and Pyongyang and was very busy. I assumed Mrs. Saito didn't visit me because she disapproved of me having Hisashi's baby.

The meal went as it had before my morning sickness had come. Mr. and Mrs. Saito talked about the household and Mr. Saito's busy schedule. Eventually, Mr. Saito said, "How are you feeling, Miyoko? I hear you have had the morning sickness."

"I feel better, sir, with the medicine the doctor prescribed."

"Are you getting enough to eat?"

"Yes, sir," I replied.

Mr. Saito nodded. "You are in most capable hands with Yoshiko."

Then I said, "Does Hisashi know about my pregnancy?"

Mr. Saito raised his eyebrows. "I would hope he does. You wrote to him, did you not?"

I looked at Mrs. Saito, who was staring at me with narrow eyes and a firm chin. I remembered that I could not tell anyone I knew they weren't delivering the letters. But I was desperate. I looked away from Mrs. Saito and said, "Yes, sir. I write to him every day. But I have not heard from him. I have not received a single letter from him since he left."

Mr. Saito cocked his head and looked surprised. "Is that true? Well, that is indeed strange. I have received several letters from him. Yours must have gotten lost. I will have Haru investigate."

I shot a quick glance at Mrs. Saito, who was facing the table. We finished our meal in silence and then, Mr. Saito announced he was going to Seoul again and would be gone for several weeks. We all stood together, bowed to the table, and Mr. and Mrs. Saito left through the sliding door.

Even with Mr. Saito's help, I still did not get any letters from my husband. I asked Haru if he had learned anything about letters to me from Hisashi. He replied that he was investigating as Mr. Saito had directed him to. I wanted to tell him that I knew he was not delivering them, but I bit my tongue.

On one of those late winter days when the sky is clear but the air is not cold, I went to the Zen garden. The gardener had raked the expanse of white pebbles into neat concentric circles around three islands of boulders, meticulously sculpted plants, and closely trimmed moss. A short stucco wall topped with gray-green tile ran along the back of the garden. Hisashi had told me once that the pebbles represented the sea, the boulders the land, and that they had sculpted the plants to look like clouds. The garden was sublimely beautiful. Mr. Saito spent hours here, and I often came here to sit and think.

My stomach had settled for the day and I was starting to gain weight. I missed Hisashi terribly. I wondered what he was doing at that moment, if he was thinking about me as I was thinking about him. I looked at one of the Zen garden boulders and pretended it was the island of Honshu. I picked a place on the boulder where Tokyo would be. I set my eyes on that place and sent my husband my love.

I heard steps behind me. It was Byong-woo wearing a coat and his chauffeur's hat. He rarely came to the garden, so I was surprised to see him. As he approached, he snuck a look over his shoulder at the house. When he was next to me, he gave me an envelope. "Hide this in your coat," he said. "Do not let anyone see it." Then, he walked on as if he hadn't even noticed me.

I slipped the envelope inside my coat. I looked around the grounds and then at the house. Through an opening in one of the sliding walls, I saw Haru staring at me. I quickly turned back to the Zen garden. I pressed my arm against the envelope inside my coat. Could it be a letter from Hisashi? My heart raced. I sat for a few more minutes before going in to my room.

FIFTEEN

My heart sank when I tore open the envelope only to see that the letter inside was not in Hisashi's handwriting. The first page was a note from Byong-woo that he had written in Hangul. I sat on my mat and read it.

> *Suk-bo,*
> *Enclosed is a copy of Hisashi's latest letter to you. I cannot give you the actual letter because I had to give it to Haru. You must destroy this note and letter immediately after you read it. If someone finds it, they will arrest me.*
> *I had to copy it quickly but I did my best. Remember to destroy this letter and note. Do not let anyone know about it. Beware of Haru.*
> *Byong-woo*

I flipped to the next pages. It was, in fact, hastily done. He'd left off a hash mark here or a curl there on the characters and I couldn't decipher some of it. But there was enough to see that it was a letter from Hisashi. I started to cry. I had a letter from my husband, from Hisashi! And though it was not the actual letter he had written, though it wasn't in his handwriting and he hadn't touched the paper, the words were his.

I pushed through my tears and read the letter. Hisashi said that he'd heard I was pregnant, but he didn't say how he'd found out. He said he was thrilled and that he couldn't wait to be at my side to support me. He hoped the baby would be strong and healthy and he was excited to be a father. He said he'd do everything he could to return before the baby came.

The letter went on to talk about his work, but this part was cryptic and didn't sound at all like Hisashi. Usually, when he was excited about something, he went on and on about it. But there was no excitement in his words. There were only a few short sentences and that was all. I decided that Byong-woo must have left some parts out.

Hisashi's letter went on to say that he still had not received a letter from me and that he didn't understand why. He wondered if his letters were reaching me. The letter ended by saying that he missed me and hoped that he would hear from me soon. He said he'd continue to write. He signed off, *With deepest love, your husband, Hisashi.*

I clutched the letter to my chest and started to cry again. They were tears of relief to know that my husband still loved me. I hadn't needed to worry all this time. He wasn't looking for a Japanese wife in Tokyo. He loved me, he said—*with deepest love!*—and his words set me free from my fears.

But my tears were from frustration, too. I was frustrated and angry that my husband wasn't getting my letters. I was terrified that he would think I didn't care. I wanted to march up to Mrs. Saito and tell her I knew she was destroying my letters and insist that she stop. But I thought better of it. If I said anything, they would arrest Byong-woo and I would be in trouble with Mrs. Saito.

I read Hisashi's letter again and again. I tried to decipher the characters that Byong-woo had copied incorrectly. I wanted to meet with Byong-woo in secret to ask him more about the original letter, but I knew I shouldn't. Finally, after I'd memorized each character and each sentence, I took the letter and Byong-woo's note to Hisashi's desk and burned them in an incense bowl.

My morning sickness never went away, but with the medicines, it was at least bearable. I continued to gain weight, and soon my belly grew large.

I still wrote a letter to Hisashi every day and gave it to Haru. I never got one from Hisashi, and I received no more copies from Byong-woo. I wanted to ask Byong-woo if he would make a copy of Hisashi's letter again, but I knew that Haru was watching me, so I never did.

Gradually, winter lost its grip on Sinuiju and gave itself over to spring. And as spring grew into summer, my belly grew heavy, making it difficult to walk. I had constant heartburn, sometimes so bad that I had to lie down until it went away. The baby kicked my ribs. I had expected that it would have come by now, but it seemed content to stay put and kick me. I remembered sitting with my parents in our house after dinner when my mother told me that I was late coming out of her when she was pregnant with me. She said I kicked constantly and then I came a month late. "You did not cry for the first month and we thought something was wrong with you," she'd said.

My father grinned. "We still wonder sometimes," he teased. Remembering this made me cry a little.

One night, there was a terrible summer storm. It started with wind and lightning and thunder that shook the house as if the spirits were angry. When I was young, I always enjoyed a good summer storm. But now, without Hisashi by my side and my belly heavy with child, the storm's tumult felt like a bad omen.

When the rain came, the pains came, too. Lying in my bed, I wasn't sure what they were at first. It wasn't at all like heartburn or the baby's kicks. I didn't feel nauseous. It was cramping, like when I had my monthly bleeds, only much worse. The pain lasted a short while and went away. After a few minutes, the pain came back harder. And this time, the two-headed dragon came roaring with it, clawing at my insides, angry, fighting to be free.

I limped to the door and called for Yoshiko, who came dressed in her nightclothes.

"I think the baby is coming."

She nodded. "I will have Haru get the doctor. Go to your bed. I will be back with Kiyo and Fumiko."

A few minutes later, Yoshiko, now wearing her head housekeeper kimono and with her hair up, was at my bedside again, along with Kiyo and Fumiko. The servants laid a birthing mat on the floor and helped me onto it. They brought in towels and rags and a pitcher of water. They gave me a special tea that Yoshiko said would help with the pain.

Yoshiko kneeled alongside me and held my hand. "Squeeze my hand when the pain comes," she said, as if someone giving birth in her household was a common occurrence. "Do not fight the pain. Soon, you will feel water inside you let loose. Do not worry. It is normal."

Yoshiko knew just what to do, and her courtly demeanor made me less afraid. As I waited for the next pain to come, I realized I didn't know much about the head housekeeper. I didn't know if she'd had children herself, or if she was married or not. I didn't know how she felt about politics, religion, or if she believed that Koreans like me were inferior. She was the head housekeeper and supremely skilled at her job. And now, her job was to help me deliver my baby.

As the storm raged outside, the pains came again. Soon, as Yoshiko had predicted, there was a watery gush, as if something burst inside me. Kiyo and Fumiko cleaned the mess with towels. I thought perhaps the baby had come, and I raised myself up on my elbows and asked Yoshiko what it was. "Your water broke as I said it would," she said. "It is what should happen. The baby will come soon. Lie down now."

I lay on the mat and closed my eyes. Though the room was cool, I was sweating.

I had so wished that Hisashi would be with me when the baby came. I wanted to cry, but before I could, there was another flash of lightning and crash of thunder and with it came another pain, harder than any before it. I cried out. Yoshiko helped me onto my elbows and I pushed at the pain to make it go away. The pain eased and I lay down and tried to catch my breath. My head and heart pounded. Yoshiko wiped the sweat from my forehead with a rag.

The door slid open and the doctor came in. The rain had soaked his coat and black leather bag. "How long between the contractions?" he asked, throwing off his coat.

"About three minutes," Yoshiko replied. "They are coming faster."

The doctor rolled up his sleeves, hurriedly washed his hands, and then squatted at my feet. He spread open my legs. "I see the head," he said. "It is close."

The pain came again. It was almost unbearable, as if the baby was trying to kill me. "Push," the doctor ordered. "Push hard."

As Yoshiko held my shoulders and the doctor watched between my legs, I pushed. The doctor reached inside me and grabbed something.

"I must turn the baby," he said.

Something inside me moved. Then, in a gush, I felt something slippery slide out between my legs. The doctor caught it and held it in his hands.

"What is it?" I cried, seeing a red, watery lump in the doctor's hands. It was a baby.

The doctor forced the baby's mouth open with his fingers. He snapped his finger on its buttocks, but nothing happened. I started to panic, thinking the baby was dead. I began to sob.

"Hush, Miyoko," Yoshiko said, holding my shoulders. "Be patient."

The doctor snapped his finger on the baby's bottom again, harder this time. The baby flinched and opened its mouth. It squeaked and let out a high-pitched cry.

"Blanket," the doctor said. Kiyo handed him a blanket, and the doctor wrapped the baby in it. He handed the bundle to me. "It is a boy," he said. "I will have to look him over, but from what I can see, he is healthy."

I looked at the squirming bundle in my arms. It no longer cried. My baby's little chest rose and dropped with each quick breath it took. He rolled his head back and forth as if he was trying to work out a kink in his neck. He blinked his eyes open and looked beseechingly at me. I ran my hands over his bald head, and he whimpered and closed his eyes.

I immediately loved him. My son! I wanted to both cry and laugh with joy. I looked at the doctor and said, "Thank you."

The doctor grunted. "You may hold him while I clean up. Then I must examine him."

I looked at Yoshiko, and for the first time since I'd known her, I saw the corners of her mouth curl up ever so slightly. There was a glint in her eye. "It is a beautiful child," she said. "Congratulations."

And then I looked beyond Yoshiko. There, standing just outside a half-open sliding door, a figure looked in. I focused on the face and locked eyes with it. It was Mrs. Saito, and her eyes were as fierce as the storm outside. I pressed my baby close to my chest and looked away.

Haru named my baby Masaru. Customarily, Mrs. Saito should have named him. But she wasn't interested in my baby. I secretly gave him the name Young-chul. I called him Masaru when we were with others, but when I nursed him, I whispered, "Young-chul, my *nae eolin wangja*, my little prince." I loved him more than I ever thought it was possible to love anything. When I held him, my heart ached. He could make me cry just by gripping my finger with his little hand or resting his head against my chest, or simply looking up at me with his dark, questioning eyes. I thought he looked like Hisashi and I yearned to share him with my husband.

Fumiko loved Young-chul, too. Kiyo refused to have anything to do with him, so the duty of helping me take care of my baby fell to Fumiko. She would coo at Young-chul and tell him he was handsome. She was quick to take him when I asked for help. She held him for hours at a time. I think Yoshiko liked my baby, too. Of course, she was businesslike, always concerned with making sure Young-chul had everything he needed. But once, when she thought I wasn't looking, I saw her run her hand over Young-chul's face and smile down at him.

When Young-chul was four months old, I was sitting in one of the low chairs in my room nursing him when Mrs. Saito came in followed by Haru and a man I'd never seen before. I was surprised to see them. I'd rarely seen Mrs. Saito since Young-chul's birth. She was avoiding me. I only saw Haru when I gave him my letters to Hisashi, which I still wrote every day.

"What is it?" I said as they filed in.

"We have come to examine the baby," Haru said coolly.

"Why?" I said, pulling Young-chul from my breast and covering myself.

Mrs. Saito stood next to the door with her arms folded as Haru and the other man came to me. I pressed Young-chul close to my chest. "Tell me what you want with my baby," I demanded.

"As I said," Haru replied, "we need to examine him. Do not be difficult and give him to this man."

I held Young-chul closer, making him squirm. "Who is he? Why does he need to examine Young-chul . . . I mean, Masaru?"

Haru leaned over me and pulled my arm away from my baby. The other man took Young-chul and went to the bed with him. He opened his case and took out some instruments and a pad of paper. Young-chul started to kick and cry.

I lunged for my baby. "No!" I cried. "What are you doing?"

Haru placed himself between me and the man. He raised his hand. "He will not hurt Masaru, but you must not interfere with the examination."

"Who is he? What is he looking for?"

Haru dropped his hand. "His name is Doctor Suzuki and he is an expert from the government. Mrs. Saito brought him here all the way from Seoul."

"All the way from Seoul? Why? What is his expertise?" I kept a careful eye on the fat doctor as he unwrapped Young-chul from his blanket. Young-chul cried louder when the blanket came off, and it was all I could do not to push past Haru and go to him.

"He is an expert in genetics," Haru replied simply. "Now, let him do his work."

"Genetics?" I exclaimed. "But why? Do you think something is wrong with my baby?" The doctor pulled out a tape and measured Young-chul's height, the length of his arms and legs, and the circumference of his head. With a protractor, he measured the width of Young-chul's head, the length of his nose, and the distance between his eyes. He looked into Young-chul's eyes with a magnifying glass. After each measurement, he wrote something on his pad. Young-chul was wailing now, the full-throated baby's wail that only a mother can quiet. I took a step toward the bed, but Haru stopped me with his hand. I desperately tried to think of what the doctor was looking for. I looked at Mrs. Saito, who still had her arms crossed and looked on with a cold stare.

Finally, the doctor turned to Haru and Mrs. Saito and said, "I have what I need." Haru stepped aside and I ran to Young-chul, who was red from crying. I wrapped him in his blanket and held him close to my chest. I kissed him on the top of his head and whispered, "Shee, my little prince. Sheeee." Soon, my baby stopped crying and fell asleep.

Holding my baby, I faced Doctor Suzuki and Haru, who conferred with Mrs. Saito. Mrs. Saito nodded to the doctor and said, "That will do." Haru escorted the doctor from the room and left me alone with Mrs. Saito.

"What was the doctor looking for?" I said. I kept my voice low so I wouldn't wake Young-chul. "What are you doing?"

Mrs. Saito raised her chin to me. "Nothing you need to know now." She started to leave.

I was furious with her. This I could not let stand.

"I do not believe you," I exclaimed before she could leave. "I think you are up to something and I will not let you get away with it. You think I am a whore for your son, but you are wrong. You are wrong! I love Hisashi and he loves me, too. I know you are trying to force us apart. But it will not work. Do you understand? We love each other and when he comes home, we will still love each other despite your deceitful plans."

Mrs. Saito kept her back to me as if my rebuke was just an afternoon breeze rustling the leaves. "Oh yes, Hisashi," she said coolly. "I forgot to tell you. He is not coming home anytime soon. He will be away for many more months. That must be a great disappointment for you." Then she left, sliding the door closed behind her.

SIXTEEN

As Mrs. Saito said, Hisashi didn't come home until months later. One morning, Yoshiko told me he was coming that afternoon. He'd been gone for a year and a half, and I was so excited to see him, I skipped the morning meal. I spent all morning bathing myself, brushing my hair, and putting it up just so with the silver hairpin. I applied just the right amount of oshiroi powder on my face. I put on my best kimono. I bathed Young-chul, who was nine months old now. I scented him with lilac water and dressed him in his finest silk clothes.

On a glorious April day, he arrived in the back of Mr. Saito's car, sitting alongside his father. As the car pulled up to the house, I stood on the veranda holding Young-chul, who watched the commotion with great interest. Mrs. Saito, Haru, and Yoshiko stood alongside me.

When Hisashi climbed out of the car, I almost didn't recognize him. He wore a tan army uniform that was a size too large. His jacket had buttons on the front, pockets on both sides of the chest, and yellow epaulets on each shoulder. Underneath his black-billed army hat, his face was thin. He had a slight bend in his back. When he saw me, he took off his hat and smiled weakly. I wanted to run to him, throw my arms around him, kiss him, and show him our beautiful son. But it would make a scene, and making a scene was not the way of a Shinto household.

Mr. Saito came to the veranda, and all of us bowed to him. "Look who is here!" Mr. Saito said joyously. "Our son, Lieutenant Saito of the Imperial Army." He stepped aside, and when Hisashi stepped forward, Haru and Yoshiko bowed to him. He didn't acknowledge their bows because he was staring at me.

Mrs. Saito smiled at Hisashi. "Welcome home, Son," she said, reaching a hand to him. Hisashi only glanced at her before turning to me. Mrs. Saito dropped her hand, and the smile fell from her face. She flashed a look at me.

With his hat under his arm, Hisashi came to me. He looked at Young-chul, who buried his head into my chest. "He's beautiful," Hisashi said.

"He looks like you," I said, fighting tears.

Hisashi raised his eyes to me, and I saw that the sparkle in them—the sparkle that had melted my heart—was gone. His beautiful hair had lost its shine. He looked like a different man.

"Come!" Mr. Saito insisted with a wave. "Hisashi is tired and hungry. He has been working much too hard and needs to put on some fat to fill out his new uniform. Haru, Yoshiko, have the household prepare a proper meal for my son. Tomorrow after he has rested, we will have a feast to celebrate his return. We will invite all of Sinuiju. We will spare no expense. Come, come!"

We all went inside the house and bowed toward the kami dana altar. Mr. Saito told Hisashi that he should get some rest. "Then later," he said with a hand on Hisashi's back, "I want to hear about your work with Doctor Ishii." He patted Hisashi's back, and Mr. and Mrs. Saito went to their part of the house while Haru and Yoshiko went to give orders to the staff to prepare a meal and organize the feast. I gave Young-chul to Fumiko and led my husband to our room.

I went to him. I put my arms around him and hugged him hard. I put my head against his chest. It felt so good to have him in my arms. It was as if I was holding the very thing that gave me life. "Oh, my husband," I said. "You cannot know my joy that you are here again."

He didn't return my embrace. He stood in a slight slump with his arms at his side as if I wasn't there. I pushed away. I started to panic that he didn't love me anymore. "Why don't you hug me?" I pleaded. "Aren't you happy to see me? Don't you love me anymore?"

He looked at the bed. "I have loved you since the day I met you," he said feebly. "But I am tired."

My anxiety turned to guilt for worrying about myself and not about his well-being. He was exhausted and ill. It looked like he didn't have enough strength to take another step. I took his hand and led him to the bed. I unbuttoned his jacket and helped him remove it. I pulled off his boots. He lay on the bed facing away and brought his knees to his chest. I slipped out of my kimono and lay next to him. I stared at his back and wanted to touch him, kiss him, make love to him. But he didn't move. And that is how we stayed for the rest of the afternoon.

When it was time for the evening meal, I put a hand on Hisashi's shoulder and said we had to get ready. He didn't respond, so I gently jostled him. "Hisashi," I said, "we must go." With effort, he pushed himself out of bed and dressed in his usual white shirt and black pants. His pants were too big for him, and I had to cinch the belt so they wouldn't fall.

I tried to talk to him as we got ready. "You will feel better when you have time to rest," and "You can play with your son later," and "After dinner perhaps we can take a walk and you can tell me about your work." His response was always one word. "Yes," "Okay," and "Perhaps." I wanted to tell him that I wrote letters to him every day. I wanted to know how he came to be in the army and what lay ahead for us. I wanted to tell him all about Young-chul. But it was obvious that he did not want to talk.

The meal the staff prepared was fit for a prince. Kiyo, Fumiko, and the cook's assistant spread it out, and it covered the big table edge to edge. There was vinegared rice with raw fish, vegetables in dashi broth, boiled quail eggs, grilled fish, two kinds of soups, and, to wash it down, tea and sake. I gave Young-chul to Fumiko, and, after washing our hands and faces and bowing to the kami dana altar, we sat at the table, me next to Hisashi, and Mr. and Mrs. Saito across from us. Yoshiko stood back from the table and gave quiet orders to Kiyo and the cook's assistant.

Mr. Saito was in a particularly good mood. "My son has returned," he said, "and he is an Imperial Army lieutenant! I'm told he is one of the army's youngest officers."

Mrs. Saito looked content. She was more animated than usual, nodding as she said, "Yes, it is good to have him back," and "I am sure he is the most handsome officer in the army, too."

Hisashi picked at his food and tried to respond to his parents' flattery. "Yes," he replied, "it is good to be home," and "They are making many young men officers these days," and "I do not know about being the most handsome." I saw that he was putting on a show for his parents. But I had seen him earlier, curled up in bed and unresponsive to me. Something was haunting him and he didn't want his parents to know. For the most part, he was succeeding. Mr. Saito went on and on about how proud he was of his son and how he had a great future. He talked about how quickly Hisashi would climb the ranks in the army and how he would be an important medical doctor someday.

"Son," Mr. Saito said after a while, "you have not eaten much. And here your mother had the staff prepare all of your favorite foods."

"I am sorry, Father," Hisashi replied. "I am not hungry right now."

"Yes, yes, yes," Mr. Saito said. "You are tired from working so hard and traveling. Rest for the day and tomorrow, too. In the evening, we will have a grand party to celebrate your return."

Hisashi lowered his head. "That will not be possible, Father."

"What? Why?" Mr. Saito asked.

Hisashi folded his hands in his lap. "I have to leave tomorrow," he declared.

"Tomorrow?" I cried out.

"So soon?" Mrs. Saito asked.

"Yes," Hisashi answered. "Doctor Ishii is building a medical camp in Manchuria outside of Harbin. I have orders to join him there as soon as possible. Coming home was only a stopover on my way."

I almost burst into tears. I wanted to throw my arms around him and cling to him to keep him from leaving again. He needed more than one day to regain his strength. I needed more than one day with him to be sure he still loved me.

Hisashi looked sideways at me. "I am sorry," he said.

"Well," Mr. Saito said, clearly surprised, "I can place a call to try to give you more time here."

"No, Father," Hisashi said quickly, "it will do no good. Doctor Ishii—*Colonel* Ishii now—has influence with the generals in Tokyo. He has taken a liking to me and wants me with him. Please do not make any calls."

"As you wish," Mr. Saito said with a shrug. "As you wish."

Mrs. Saito stared at her son, her face creased with concern. "When will we see you again?" she asked.

"I do not know," Hisashi answered, looking away.

"We can visit in the morning," Mr. Saito said, trying to sound upbeat. He pushed away from the table and stood, and we all stood with him. Mr. and Mrs. Saito left, and Fumiko and the cook's assistant started to clear away the food. Fumiko brought in a fussy Young-chul. "Masaru is hungry," she said as she gave me the baby.

I followed Hisashi to our room, carrying Young-chul on my hip. As I nursed him, Hisashi watched me, expressionless. I wanted to ask him if I could go with him to Manchuria, what he would do there. I wanted to ask him how long it would be before he returned. But he looked so tired I didn't have the heart to press him for answers. He curled up on the bed. While I nursed Young-chul, I gazed at my husband and worried how I could possibly rekindle our love in just a few hours.

Hisashi slept all night and into the morning. We missed prayers and the morning meal. I thought he'd wake up when Young-chul fussed for me to feed him, but he never moved. I was so concerned about my husband, I didn't sleep. I wanted to know what was bothering him. I worried that he didn't love me anymore because he'd found a Japanese wife. I thought he might be angry that he didn't get letters from me. But the only meaningful words he'd said were that he'd always loved me. I clung to those words like a drowning woman clings to a wood plank. I prayed that he'd feel better after a long night's sleep so we could talk before he had to leave.

Midmorning, Hisashi sighed and uncoiled his legs from his chest. I'd given Young-chul to Fumiko and sat on the mat watching my husband sleep. When he roused, I hurried to his side. "Hisashi," I said, "you are awake. Do you feel better?"

"A little, I think," he replied. "What time is it?"

"You slept all night and it is midmorning. Are you hungry?"

"I suppose I am," he said. "I must get dressed. I have to be at the train station by noon."

He swung his legs over the side of the low bed. I kneeled in front of him. "I'm so worried about you," I said. "You are troubled."

"That is true," he said with a nod.

I took his hands. "Oh, my dear husband, tell me what is wrong. I want to help you."

Hisashi put a hand on my shoulder and gently pushed me away. In his face, I saw incredible sadness like I'd never seen in him before, like I'd never thought was possible in the man I'd first seen that day in the forest. I began to sob. "Why are you so sad? Please tell me! Is it because you didn't get letters from me? I wrote to you every day as I promised I would. But they did not send them. Your mother and Haru, they did not send them and they never gave me your letters, either. I love you, Hisashi. Please know that I never stopped loving you." I began to sob uncontrollably.

"I know you do," Hisashi said. "And as I said, I've always loved you, too."

He sat on his bed and looked at his feet. "But now, I fear the way for me to prove my love will be the hardest thing for me to do. I must ask you to stop loving me."

I squeezed my eyes closed. I shook my head. "What did you say?"

He sighed a choking sigh as if he was trying not to cry. "I said, we have to stop loving each other."

My heart stopped and my mind went numb. I couldn't think. "That does not make sense. Why?" I asked.

"I cannot tell you," he replied, shaking his head woefully. "It has to do with my work with Doctor Ishii. I can tell you nothing more."

He stood and began to pace. "You have to forget me," he said, turning angry. "I will forget you, too. That is what we must do. That is why I came home—to tell you that we cannot be married anymore."

"You have a Japanese wife!" I cried. "You married a woman in Tokyo and now you are throwing me aside just as your mother said you would."

"I would never do that," he said.

"You are lying! You don't have the red scarf I gave you. You said you would keep it to remember me by, and now you don't have it anymore!"

"I am not lying," Hisashi countered. "As I said, it has to do with my work."

"How? Why?" I asked, wiping my tears on my sleeve. "We have a son—our son, *your* son—and he needs a father. Surely you do not mean to abandon your son!"

"I will talk to Father and he will take care of you and our son," Hisashi replied. "I will do it before I go. You will not be abandoned."

"Why can't we be married any longer? Please tell me. What happened in Tokyo?"

Hisashi stopped pacing and stared at the wall. "They made me an officer in the medical corps. The *youngest* officer in the medical corps," he said with a wry smile. "I will be a doctor someday and make Father proud. But what I must do—what they have made me do and what I will do while I wear the uniform of the Imperial Army—means that we can no longer be in love." He faced me. "Although it will destroy me, it is the right thing for you. It is as simple as that," he said with a shrug. "And now I must go."

I was dumbfounded, looking at my husband as I would look upon a stranger. The world fell away as if it was dissolving into a void. I couldn't move. I couldn't speak. I didn't dare let myself cry or I would have spilled myself out and died right there.

Hisashi put on his uniform. He gave me a look that was both sad and resolute. Then, he slid open the door and left.

SEVENTEEN

He left the same way he came—in the back of the big black car. Under the same perfect blue April sky as when he came, Mr. and Mrs. Saito, Haru, Yoshiko, Young-chul, and I watched from the veranda. I wore my best kimono and had put my hair up and pinned it with the silver hairpin. He gave me one last sad look before he climbed into the back seat. After that, he didn't acknowledge me, as if he was determined to forget me and was telling me again that I had to forget him, too.

As the car passed through the gate, I was too numb to cry. It was as if my heart was leaving with him. After the car disappeared, I dragged myself to my room. For some time, I sat on the mat with Young-chul, trying to make sense of what Hisashi had said to me, but I couldn't. How could I ever stop loving him? How could he stop loving me? I imagined all manner of reasons why he said we couldn't love each other anymore. But I always came back to the one reason that made the most sense—my husband had taken a Japanese wife. But he'd said he hadn't. He'd said it was about his work. He'd said he loved me. And he was not the type of man to lie about something like that.

Young-chul must have sensed my distress because he started to fuss. Kiyo knocked on the door and offered to take him. I was surprised at this because Fumiko usually took Young-chul. I told her I was fine, but she came to me and took Young-chul anyway. She leaned in and whispered, "Do not worry. I will take care of your son." As she left, I wondered why she felt she needed to reassure me about Young-chul.

I was too exhausted to remove my kimono when I curled up on the bed. I hadn't slept well in days and I needed to clear my mind. I pushed away the images of Hisashi, frail and sad, saying we couldn't be married anymore. I tried to stop imagining what he was doing for Doctor Ishii that made him say those terrible things.

And then I realized what I had to do. Mother had said that love was a commitment you made every day for the rest of your life. Well, I would stay committed to Hisashi for the rest of my life, no matter what he'd told me to do. It didn't matter what he was doing for Doctor Ishii. It didn't matter that Hisashi was trying to stop loving me. Just as I'd chosen to marry him, I'd choose to keep loving him.

There was a knock on the door and Haru came in. He held his hand out. "Come," he said. "Mr. and Mrs. Saito want to talk with you in the Zen garden."

"Now?" I asked. "Is it about Hisashi?"

Haru lifted me up by my arm. "They are waiting," he said. "Do not make them wait any longer."

Haru's grip was firm as he dragged me through the house to the side door off the kitchen. I tried to break free from him, but I could not. "What is this about?" I asked. "You are hurting me." I had to lift my kimono so I didn't trip on the hem.

"Do not fight, Miyoko," Haru said. "It will be best for you if you do not fight." As we passed through the kitchen, the cook and her assistant kept their eyes on their work.

Mr. and Mrs. Saito sat on the bench facing the Zen garden. Haru pushed me to stand next to Mr. Saito. He kept his hold on my arm.

As usual, the gardener had raked the pebbles into neat concentric waves around the boulder islands and dwarf juniper trees. This was normally a place of serenity for me, where I came to clear my mind.

Now, tension filled the air as if the pebble waves were the waves of a tsunami. Mr. Saito stared at the garden but he was not in his meditating pose. His eyes were unfocused and his face was sad. He drew in a long breath. "Miyoko, you have brought shame to our family," he said. "I promised that you would be treated well here, and that is what we have done. In return, you betray my son and mock my generosity. It brings me great sorrow."

"Sir," I said, "I would never do that. Why do you say I did?"

Some papers sat on the bench next to Mr. Saito. Still looking at the garden, he picked them up and raised them over his shoulder. He said, "This is a report from Doctor Suzuki. He examined your baby some time ago. The report says it is not Hisashi's baby." He set the report back on the bench.

I was stunned. I couldn't believe what Mr. Saito was saying. I couldn't believe any of this was happening to me. "It is not true!" I cried. "He *is* Hisashi's baby! The doctor is wrong."

Mrs. Saito faced me. There was a spark in her eyes and a slight lift of her mouth at the sides. "Doctor Suzuki is an expert in the differences between the races," she said. "I thought there was something peculiar about your baby, so I brought the doctor here. After he examined the boy, he gave me the report. According to his analysis, your baby is purely Korean. He has no Japanese traits whatsoever."

"It is not possible," I protested. "I only love Hisashi!"

"I recall," Mrs. Saito said coolly, "that you and the chauffeur were alone the day you went to visit your parents. Haru learned that your parents were not there. They had fled to Manchuria to join the rebels. Yet for some reason, you and Isamu were gone the entire day. The timing of your pregnancy is right for it."

Everything was upside down. The sky was the earth and the earth was the sky, and I was trapped somewhere in between. My head spun. "It isn't true!" I cried out. "I would never betray Hisashi. Ask him! He will tell you that my love is true."

"We told him about the report," Mrs. Saito said. "That is why he was so sad. He said he is willing to leave you if his son is cared for and you aren't harmed. We will take care of the boy. As for you . . ."

I shook my head to try to make everything right side up. "He said it was because of his work! He is sad because of something about his work with Doctor Ishii."

Mr. Saito turned to me. "It has nothing to do with that," he said. "Doctor Ishii is doing important medical work for the empire. He chose Hisashi because my son is gifted and he works hard. My son honors me. You, however, do not, and you must face the consequences."

Mr. Saito stood, and Mrs. Saito rose with him. "Come," he said. Mr. Saito walked toward the front of the house followed by Mrs. Saito, me, and Haru, who still held my arm. We walked around the corner and there, waiting for us, were two police officers. One had a pistol on his belt. The other held a length of rope. When I saw them, I froze. Haru gripped my arm harder and pushed me toward the officers.

Mr. Saito said, "I am sorry, Miyoko, but you brought this on yourself." Mrs. Saito lifted her chin and gave me a most satisfied look.

"My son!" I said. "What about Young-chul?"

"Young-chul?" Mrs. Saito mocked. "Who is Young-chul? Oh, you are asking about Masaru, but I see you have given him a Korean name. That proves you know he is Korean."

"No!" I said. "I just . . . He is Hisashi's son! I only wanted him to have both a Japanese and Korean name. You are making a mistake! I did not betray Hisashi. I wouldn't!"

"Enough of these lies," Mr. Saito bellowed. "It makes me sad." He motioned to the police officers, and the one holding the rope stepped forward. Haru held on to my arm. I tried to jerk free, but he just held on tighter.

"No!" I screamed. "I have done nothing wrong!"

The policeman approached. "If you fight, I will have to hurt you," he said.

It was useless to resist two strong men, so I stopped fighting. A strange calm came over me. Standing there under the bright blue sky, I saw everything was right side up again. I looked at Mr. Saito. "You are wrong, sir," I said directly. "I love your son. I always will." He looked away.

As Haru turned me so the policeman could bind my hands, there was the sound of a car starting. Then, slowly, Mr. Saito's car came from the garage and approached us. Byong-woo sat behind the wheel, focused on the policeman with the pistol on his belt. He pulled up to us and stopped. He left the car running and opened the door. The policeman put his hand on his holster.

Byong-woo got out of the car as if it was just another day for him to drive someone somewhere. Except now, he wasn't wearing his chauffeur's hat. As he came around the front, I saw he had a pistol in his hand. He raised it and pointed it at the policeman. "I have been wanting to kill a Japanese policeman for years," he sneered. "Do not give me an excuse or I *will* shoot you." The policeman dropped his hand from his holster.

"What are you doing, Isamu?" Mr. Saito roared. "Put that gun down."

"My name is Byong-woo," the chauffeur replied, "and I am a member of the resistance. I am sorry, Mr. Saito. You are an honorable man. It is your country's occupation of my country that I resist, not you. Anyway, I think your wife has convinced you that I am the boy's father and the police will arrest me, too. I assure you that I am not the father. Mrs. Saito's lies are only a plot against her daughter-in-law."

Byong-woo pointed his pistol at the policeman next to me. "Let her go," he demanded. The policeman stepped aside, but Haru still clung to my arm. I tried to twist free, but he would not let go.

"Let go of her, Haru," Mr. Saito ordered.

Mrs. Saito stepped forward. "No, Haru!" she said, her eyes flashing. "Keep hold of her. She is a whore."

"What are you doing, Wife?" Mr. Saito said.

She stared at Byong-woo. "Isamu will not shoot. He is a chauffeur, not a warrior."

As Haru held on to me, Byong-woo pointed his pistol at Mrs. Saito. His face was hard and resolute. He focused on her. "No, Isamu!" Mr. Saito said.

Mrs. Saito didn't move and returned Byong-woo's stare. She sneered at him. Byong-woo lifted the pistol a little and pulled the trigger, sending a shot just above her head. The shot was loud and made everyone recoil. Mrs. Saito went slack-jawed and took a full step back, her eyes wide with fear.

Byong-woo leveled his pistol at Haru again. "*You* I will not miss," he said. "Now let her go."

Haru hesitated and then released his grip on me. Byong-woo reached behind him and from his belt, he took his chauffeur's hat. He tossed it on the ground in front of him. "We are not Japan's slaves," he said. All the while, he held the pistol on Haru.

"Get in," he said to me.

I ran to the car and climbed into the back seat. With his pistol still leveled on Haru, Byong-woo went to the driver's side. He jumped in, put the car in gear, and stepped on the accelerator. The car lurched forward. There was a shot from behind us, and the back window shattered. I screamed and put my hands over my head.

"Get down!" Byong-woo shouted as the car roared onto the road. I dropped between the seats as we raced along. There was another shot and I heard a metallic ping on the back of the car. We turned a corner and then another, each turn pitching me to the side. My head hit the door. I climbed onto the seat. Byong-woo was expertly steering the speeding car through the streets of Sinuiju.

"Where are we going?" I said, my heart racing.

"To the river. There is a boat for us there."

"Young-chul!" I cried. "I cannot leave Young-chul! We must go back."

"If you do, they will arrest you and you will never see your son again."

"What will they do to him? What will they do to my son?"

"He will be fine," Byong-woo said as the river came into view. "Kiyo will take care of him."

"Kiyo?" I said.

There were sirens in the distance, several of them. Byong-woo pointed the car toward the river. The bridge to China was just ahead of us. The car sped along the dock. Then Byong-woo slammed on the brakes, sending me tumbling against the front seat. The car screeched to a stop. Byong-woo got out and opened my door.

"This way," Byong-woo said. "Quickly!"

I climbed out. The sirens were louder now, only a few blocks away. A trawler was moored to the dock. A man in fisherman's clothing reached for me from the gunwale. Another man hopped off the boat, climbed into the car, and sped off.

"Get in the boat," Byong-woo said. I grabbed the man's hand and he pulled me aboard. Byong-woo jumped in after me. "In the hold," he said pointing to an open hatch. Byong-woo followed me and closed the hatch behind us. The hold was cramped, dark, and slimy. It reeked of fish. Byong-woo huddled close to me. I could smell cigarette smoke on him. After a few seconds, I heard the two police cars with their sirens blaring coming along the dock. The sirens grew louder and louder and soon they were alongside us. Then they roared past.

After the sirens faded, the boat engine sputtered to life, and in a few seconds, I could feel we were on the open water. Exhaust fumes combined with the stench of the hold made me nauseous.

"Where are we going?" I said to Byong-woo, only inches from my face.

"To China," he replied.

"Will Young-chul be there?"

"No," Byong-woo said.

"When will I see him again?"

"I do not know. It might be a long time. But do not worry."

"Kiyo will not take care of him!" I cried. "She doesn't like him."

"There is Fumiko and Yoshiko, too. As I said, he will be all right."

Sitting inside the close, dark hold, my heart swelled with anger and grief. I punched Byong-woo's chest. I punched him again and again. "You took me from my son!" I cried. "Take me back to my son!"

Byong-woo let me punch him and didn't say anything. And when I could punch no more, I brought my hands to my face and cried.

EIGHTEEN

Present Day, Los Angeles

"Doctor Ishii," I say to Ms. Yi, "of Unit 731?"

On the table inside the interrogation room, the recorder's light continues to glow red. Ms. Yi stares at it with watery eyes. Her head nods ever so slightly, and I can't tell if she's answering yes or if her head shakes because of her age.

Finally, she says, "Yes, Anna. That Doctor Ishii."

"Who's he?" Detective Jackson asks from behind me. I'd almost forgotten he was there with us. "What's Unit 731?"

Ms. Yi continues to stare at the recorder and doesn't answer, so I do. "I think we should let Ms. Yi tell her story."

Jackson just shakes his head. I turn to Ms. Yi and put a hand on her arm. "Ma'am, would you like more tea?"

She nods and says, "Yes, please."

"Detective?" I say. "More tea for Ms. Yi."

Jackson doesn't get out of his chair as he opens the door and hands the teapot to someone on the other side. "What's this Unit 731 you're talking about?" he asks, shutting the door. "I've never heard of it."

I nod. "You're not alone. Most Americans don't know about Unit 731."

"So, what is it?" Jackson insists. "What does it have to do with the murder?"

"We don't know if it's a murder, Detective," I say quickly.

He ignores me and leans into Ms. Yi. "Does this Unit 731 have something to do with your parents?"

"I do not know," Ms. Yi replies. "I never saw them again after my wedding day." She looks at her hands. "However, they went to Manchuria and that is where Unit 731 was."

"So," Jackson says, "the deceased was your husband and you murdered him because something happened at this Unit 731. Am I right?"

"You are impatient, Detective," Ms. Yi says. "As Anna says, you will have to listen to the rest of my story for answers to your questions."

The door opens and a man in a white shirt and tie gives Jackson the teapot. He whispers something to the detective.

"I gotta leave for a minute," Jackson says. "I'll be right back."

Jackson leaves and I'm alone with Ms. Yi. I study her. She doesn't look tired from telling her story and I marvel at her strength. I can tell she wants to continue. I reach over and shut off the recorder.

"Unit 731," I say. "My god . . ."

Ms. Yi just stares.

"Ms. Yi," I say, "is there anything you want to tell me while the detective is gone? About Hisashi or your parents or what happened at Unit 731?"

"No," she answers. "It is all in my story."

We sit quietly while we wait for Jackson to return. I should probably press Ms. Yi for what happened in the nursing home. I should know who the dead man is and her relationship to him. But I think I need to listen to her story, too. I try to hear what they're saying on the other side of the door, but I can't. I think I'm supposed to find out what's going on, but I don't know the protocol. I decide to stay with my client.

Finally, Jackson returns. He shoots a look at me and sits in his chair. "There's a ruckus out there," he declares. "Media's all over this story and the DA wants to know what I got so they can press charges. My lieutenant is pressuring me to wrap this up. How much longer will it be?"

"It will take as long as it takes," Ms. Yi answers. "Now, where were we?"

"You'd just escaped from the police and were going to China," I say, pouring tea for her.

"Ah, yes," Ms. Yi sighs. "Without my little prince." The pain in her face has returned.

"We can take a break for a while, Ms. Yi," I say. "Don't worry about what they want outside. Take your time."

"No," she says with a shake of her head. "It is important that you hear my entire story. Then, Detective Jackson here will have what he wants."

Ms. Yi takes a sip of tea and stares at the recorder. "Your machine is off," she says.

Jackson leans over and punches the recorder on. The light glows red again.

"China," she says with a sad smile. "The rebels."

NINETEEN

Manchuria, China. 1939

My breasts were swollen and painful, and all I could think about was how Young-chul was missing his feedings. The discomfort was a persistent reminder of how Hisashi had abandoned me and how I had abandoned my son.

The boat rocked, making me seasick. The closeness made me sweat. Inside the hold, Byong-woo leaned on me heavily and snored. I couldn't believe he could sleep. I guessed we'd been on the water for an hour, maybe more. They'd closed the hatch and I couldn't tell if it was dark outside.

Finally, the engine slowed. The hull made a crunch sound against sand, and the boat stopped. Byong-woo woke with a start. He rubbed his eyes and pushed open the hatch. Cool air poured into the hold.

"You can come out now," a voice said in Korean.

Byong-woo climbed out of the hold and reached a hand to me. I grabbed him and he pulled me up into the dark night. In the half-moon light, I saw that we'd stopped on the riverbank.

"This is where you get off," the fisherman said. He held something out to me. "Take off your kimono and put this on," he said.

I pulled off my kimono and took the clothes, the loose pants and shirt of a peasant man. I put them on and cinched them tight with the waistband. He handed me a pair of leather shoes. I took off my zori and put them on.

"Your hair," Byong-woo said, pointing.

I tied my hair into a man's braid that hung down my back. Byong-woo jumped off the bow and helped me down. He splashed out of the river and started up the bank. At first I didn't want to go, but then I sloshed after him. We were on a path of sorts leading through the trees and bushes. Branches grabbed at my arms and legs and swatted my face. With some effort, I scrambled to the top of the bank. Byong-woo pulled me up the last few feet into an opening. By then, my eyes had adjusted to the dark and I saw that we were standing on the bund of a rice paddy.

Byong-woo sat on the bund and emptied the water from his boots. I did the same. Then he said, "This way."

"I don't want to go," I said. "I want to go back."

"Huh," Byong-woo replied. "Do what you will."

I stayed put while Byong-woo set off. Before he disappeared into the darkness, I followed him. We walked along the embankment away from the river. The bund was narrow and I had to be careful where I stepped so I didn't fall into the paddy. The moon reflected silver off the paddy water, the air was cool and still.

Eventually, we came to a narrow road heading away from the rice paddy.

After a while, I said, "Where are we going?"

"There is a house some ways from here. They are Chinese rebels who are our allies. They will help us."

"We are in China?"

"Yes," Byong-woo replied.

"Are we going to stay at that house?"

"Only for a day."

"Then where will we go?"

"To Manchuria. To a rebel stronghold."

"Are my parents there?"

"I do not know," Byong-woo said.

"Can you take me to my brother? He is in Pyongyang."

"No," Byong-woo answered. "Anyway, I hear he is a chinilpa. He might turn you in."

I decided not to ask more questions. Byong-woo kept a steady pace and I fell behind. I was terribly confused about everything that had happened over the last several days. Hisashi had said we couldn't stay married even though I knew he still loved me. Mr. and Mrs. Saito had accused me of infidelity though I never would've betrayed my husband. And now I was separated from my son. I tried to imagine what he was doing, where he was sleeping in the big house. I wondered how they would feed him. Perhaps they'd hire a wet nurse, although Mrs. Saito probably would refuse to pay for it. Then, Young-chul would have to have goat's milk and watery rice. Kiyo said she would take care of him and I had to believe she would. But Mrs. Saito had said before my wedding that she would cast out any children that I would have with Hisashi.

I wanted to stop and demand that Byong-woo take me back to Young-chul. But I knew he wouldn't. Anyway, Byong-woo had said we were in China, across the Yalu River. I had no way to get to my son.

Byong-woo noticed I was lagging. "We must hurry," he said. "It will be daylight soon. We are not safe. Come quickly!"

I tried to push aside the worry about Young-chul and caught up to Byong-woo. The road ran along the base of a forested hill, and in the distance I saw the shadow of a house. The sky was growing light. It was deathly still, the soft, quiet pause that comes before the vigor of a spring day. Byong-woo went to a tree and crouched behind it. He cupped his hands over his mouth and gave three soft whistles. In the stillness, the whistles carried over the road and into the forest. Soon, two whistles came from the house.

Byong-woo took my arm and said, "It is safe."

We hurried to the back of the house, where the door opened for us. We stepped into a dark room, and I sensed the presence of people there. Someone closed the door behind us, while someone else lit a lamp. The light illuminated the faces of three men. One was elderly with a gray beard and round wire glasses. The others were younger. They had the dark features of Chinese and stared at us warily.

Byong-woo bowed. *"Ni hao,"* he said, using the formal Chinese greeting.

The elderly man nodded. "You are Byong-woo?" he asked in Chinese.

"I am," Byong-woo replied.

"We were told you would be alone," the old man said.

"This woman is Korean. The police were about to arrest her. She did not commit the crime they accused her of, so I brought her here with me."

"That was a perilous decision," the man said. "We have heard that they are hunting for this woman. Not just the police . . . but the Kempei tai, too. There is a reward."

"I will take responsibility," Byong-woo replied.

"You have put us all in danger. Why do they want this woman so badly?"

"They made her marry the son of the director-general in Sinuiju. She had his son, but they accused her of being unfaithful."

"If she married a Japanese, why is she worth saving?" the man said, eyeing me. The thick lenses of his glasses enlarged his eyes.

Anger swelled inside me. Why did this man have the right to judge me? I stepped forward. "They forced me to marry him, but I admit that I love him," I said, careful to use the right Chinese words. "Yes, he is Japanese, but that does not mean I am a traitor. My husband is an honorable man and he loves me. Do you understand? And now, they have taken everything from me. My parents, the man I love." The words caught in my throat. "They took my son. I will not rest until I have them back."

There was a glint in the man's eyes, magnified by his glasses. "And what if you do not get them back?" he asked.

"Then I will die."

"As we all must do," the old man said with a nod. Then he faced Byong-woo. "You must hide here today," he said. "Rest well. You have a long journey ahead."

He motioned to one of the younger men. "Take them to the hiding cave."

The young man swung a rifle over his shoulder and led us to a cave not far from the house.

The cave was damp and cold and only big enough for two people. After we'd crawled in, the young man stuck his head in. "I will bring water and rice."

"Cigarettes, too, if you have them," Byong-woo said without raising his head. The man nodded and went away.

I folded my legs beneath me and sat on a mat across from Byong-woo. My mind was dull, my eyes heavy. I closed my eyes and saw the faces of Hisashi and Young-chul. I wanted to reach for them, embrace them, but before I could, an uneasy darkness overwhelmed me, and I fell asleep.

I didn't wake until night. When I opened my eyes, everything around me was in shadows and I didn't know where I was. I couldn't understand why it was cold and damp or why I was lying on the ground.

I rubbed my eyes and looked around. I saw the faint light of the cave opening and I remembered. The ache for Hisashi and Young-chul came rushing back. I wanted to go back to sleep to make the ache go away. I pulled my knees to my chest and closed my eyes. My entire world was gone. Maybe it would have been better if they had arrested me and put me in prison. Then, Hisashi could come back and rescue me and we could take Young-chul away from Mrs. Saito.

I heard voices outside the cave. It was Byong-woo, talking to someone in Chinese, but I couldn't understand them.

Someone came into the cave. I opened my eyes but it was too dark to see who it was. "Suk-bo, wake up." It was Byong-woo.

"I am awake," I said.

"We must leave at once," he said, offering a hand to me.

"I don't want to go," I said. "I want to go back to Young-chul."

"If you go back, you will be shot," Byong-woo said. "I don't want to hear any more of this. You must come now. The Kempei tai is in this area looking for you. Come, quickly!"

My heart felt like stone as I followed Byong-woo out of the cave. It was early night. A line of light lit the western sky, and the moon had not risen yet. I saw the outline of the trees.

The young man who had brought us to the cave motioned for me to follow him. "This way," he said. He had a pack slung over one shoulder and a rifle over the other.

"Where are we going?" I asked.

"North," he replied. "We will walk all night."

Byong-woo and I followed the man along a path. He walked quickly and even Byong-woo struggled to keep pace with him. When I fell behind, Byong-woo came and helped me. The young man never looked back and never slowed his pace.

After several hours my legs ached from walking and I was hungry and thirsty. We stopped at the edge of a clearing on the top of a hill. Our guide squatted behind a bush and scanned the clearing. "You rest while I check the path ahead. This is a dangerous place. Japanese soldiers are all around. Be quiet and do not move from here." He handed Byong-woo his pack. "There is water and food inside," the man said. "A few cigarettes, too. Take care not to eat too much. We have a long way to go." He disappeared into the dark.

Byong-woo and I sat behind the bush. He opened the pack, took out a water poke, and gave it to me. "Drink," Byong-woo demanded. Though I was thirsty, I only took a small drink.

He took out a round wheat *bing* and gave me half. The brown bread was hard. I tore off a small piece and put it in my mouth. I chewed but did not swallow.

"We will not have much to eat for many days," Byong-woo said. "If you ever want to see your son again, you must eat and drink."

I swallowed the wheat bread and then took a few more bites.

"Eat slowly," Byong-woo said. "Let it satisfy you."

He handed me the water poke again, and I took a bigger drink this time. The bing and water gave me some strength. I began to focus on surviving so that someday I could see Hisashi and Young-chul. "How long will we have to run?" I asked.

"It will take many days to get to where we're going. But I think after today, we will be safe from the Kempei tai. They do not want to confront the rebels."

"What will we do when we get there?"

"We will join a rebel group led by a man the Japanese call 'The Tiger.' I must warn you that you must be careful what you say and do there. They are stern people who will not tolerate insubordination."

"What if I do not want to join the rebels?"

"Then you can go back to face Mrs. Saito and the Kempei tai," Byong-woo said with a look. He crossed his legs and took a cigarette from the pack. He lit it, careful to hide the flame. As he smoked, he studied me.

I inspected the remaining bing in my hand. I wanted to eat the rest of it, but I thought about the journey ahead. I slipped it into my pocket.

I asked, "What will happen to Young-chul?"

"As I told you," Byong-woo replied, blowing smoke in the air, "he will be fine."

I looked at him. "How do you know? Mrs. Saito told me before my wedding that she would banish me and any of my children to the street when she could."

"Mrs. Saito," Byong-woo said bitterly. "Mr. Saito is an honorable man. He is misguided, but honest and ethical. On the other hand, Mrs. Saito, she is the devil."

He looked at me directly. "Your son will be fine. I know because Kiyo will see that he is."

"But Fumiko is the one who takes care of Young-chul, not Kiyo."

"Fumiko is weak," Byong-woo said. "I do believe she is fond of your son, but she is in love with Haru, though he only uses her for his own pleasure. You see, Haru is a spy for the Kempei tai. They do not trust Mr. Saito. They question his loyalty to the emperor."

"But Mr. Saito has always spoken as if he is loyal."

"Yes. He is the director-general and an educated man. But he and Hisashi are much alike. They are sensitive and that is not something that fits well in the new Japan."

"What about Yoshiko? Is she a spy, too?"

Byong-woo shook his head. "She is a mystery to me. I was never able to find out much about her."

"So, Kiyo will take care of Young-chul," I said. "I never thought she liked me."

"She didn't. She thought you were a chinilpa for marrying Hisashi. I must admit, I thought so, too."

"Do you still?" I asked.

"I am not sure," he replied, snuffing his cigarette out. "We will have to see."

After a while, our guide came back and said it was safe to go on. We walked all night and hid and rested in the forest the next day. The guide squatted behind a bush with his rifle as we rested. I don't think he ever slept. When darkness came, we hiked all night and rested during the day. We drank water from streams and dug roots to eat. After four days of hiking, the forest gave way to rolling hills covered with wheat fields, and I remembered what my brother had told me about Manchuria. It seemed like you could see until the end of the earth. It was cold at night and warm during the day.

I kept pace with our guide and Byong-woo. My legs were no longer sore and my breasts were no longer full. I was growing strong, like I had when I'd worked the fields. I tried not to think about Young-chul, but he was always with me. I tried to imagine how Kiyo would treat him. I thought about Hisashi. I wondered how close I was to him. Perhaps his camp was just over a hill or in the next valley. I sent my love to him and resolved to survive this ordeal so that someday I would see him again. I thought about my parents who were here, too. They, like Hisashi, might be close by. Perhaps they were where I was going. Perhaps I would see them soon.

On the seventh day, the hills had turned to low mountains, broader and farther apart than those in Korea. A group of men with rifles met us in a valley. The men talked with our guide and then all but one quickly marched off. Our Chinese guide gave us a quick bow and headed back from where we came with his rifle and backpack over his shoulder. The other man bade us to follow him. We crested the hill and made our way into another valley. In the high places, men with rifles stared at us from behind boulders. The valley twisted and narrowed into a glen with a dry riverbed. Beyond a few weather-beaten trees stood tents and huts made from sticks. Six horses stood in a pen. Dozens of men in tattered clothes milled about, many who carried rifles. Others had pistols in their belts.

We stopped in an open area, and the man who we'd been following said, "Wait here." We stood as the rebels examined us from a distance. There must have been sixty or seventy in all. I saw women in the group and was surprised to see that some carried pistols in their waistbands.

The women looked tattered and hard. Some wore their hair down and untied, which was inappropriate given that they were among men.

A man came out of a tent followed by several other men. Tall, and with a purposeful walk, he wore a dark plain tunic jacket and high leather boots. He had his hair cut short. He walked up to Byong-woo and me.

"Welcome, Byong-woo," he said without bowing or extending his hand. "I am pleased you made it here without incident. Thank you for your service to the resistance. We will talk later."

Byong-woo bowed to the man and said, "Thank you, Commissar."

The man faced me. "So, you are Suk-bo," he said. "The one who the Kempei tai wants so badly. I am honored to meet you. My name is Kim Il-sung."

TWENTY

I bowed to him and asked, "Are my parents here?"

"Come to my tent," Il-sung said. "We can talk there. Byong-woo, I will send for you later."

As Byong-woo walked away, I followed Il-sung to the compound's largest tent, furnished with a low table and mats. Oil lamps cast flickering shadows against the tent walls. What looked like rolled-up maps were scattered on the floor and leaning against the walls. Il-sung motioned for me to sit at the table and sat across from me.

Under thick brows, Kim Il-sung's eyes were both intelligent and penetrating, as if he saw and understood everything around him. His short hair accentuated the squareness of his face. He held his shoulders straight, yet he looked relaxed. He was young—I guessed that he was in his late twenties. But from the way the other men submitted to him, he was clearly the leader.

"Tell me about your parents," he said.

"They are from a village outside Sinuiju, sir," I replied, avoiding his eyes. "They came to Manchuria over two years ago."

"And you are a Yi, if I heard correctly," Il-sung said.

"Yes, sir. My father is Seong-ki Yi. He is a carpenter."

Il-sung nodded. "Yes, I remember hearing about a carpenter named Yi and his wife who joined the resistance about that time."

I looked up. "Please, sir, tell me where they are. I have not seen them in years."

"Ah, yes. You have not seen them since you married Hisashi Saito, the son of the director-general," Il-sung said flatly. "I learned about you from Byong-woo's reports."

My shoulders sagged. I had grown weary of telling everyone that they forced me to marry Hisashi, but that I loved him nonetheless. It didn't seem to matter to anyone, and it wouldn't do any good to argue with this man.

"Do you have any other relatives?" Il-sung asked. "A brother or a sister?"

"I have an older brother," I answered. "His name is Kwan-so. He is studying at the school in Pyongyang."

"The Japanese school. A Korean attending that school is a chinilpa. Does your brother support the Japanese occupation of our country?"

"I do not know, sir," I answered.

"Well, Suk-bo," Il-sung said, "I have my doubts about you, who would marry a Japanese man instead of fighting them with your parents. We will give you an opportunity to prove you are not a chinilpa like your brother. We are a unit of the Anti-Japanese United Army. Along with the Chinese, we conduct raids on Imperial Army outposts. Someday, we will drive the Japanese dogs from our homeland. I expect you to help. For now, fetch water and do what Ki-soo tells you. Eventually, you will learn how to fight.

"As for your parents . . ." His voice softened. "There was a carpenter Yi with a unit not far from here. The Japanese overran them six months ago. Most were killed. Some were captured. No one escaped. I cannot say what happened to your parents—if they were killed or if they were captured."

Il-sung regarded me for a while. I looked at my hands and hoped my parents were with those who'd been captured and not killed.

Il-sung waited for me to say something. Finally, he motioned to the guard at the door. "Take Suk-bo to the women's quarters," he said. "She can rest for today, but tomorrow, she must put in a full day's work."

He turned to me. "That is all."

A stick hut with a green canvas tarp covering the roof served as the women's quarters. Cast-iron kettles, pots, and straw baskets sat alongside a firepit, and I watched a woman not much older than me start a fire with sticks and grass. She eyed me warily as the soldier led me to the hut.

"This is where you will live," the soldier said, pointing at the hut door with his rifle. "You have everything you need here." He nodded at the woman at the firepit. "This is Ki-soo. She will teach you what you need to know."

The soldier turned on his heel and marched away. I stuck my head inside the hut. The musky smell of unwashed people invaded my nose. As my eyes adjusted to the dark, I saw a woman lying on a mat. She opened her eyes to look at me and then rolled over. I couldn't tell if she was sick or just resting.

I pulled out of the hut and looked around. The morning sun made everything bright. Inside the compound, people brushed the horses and others worked on the trucks. A group of men sat in a circle, cleaning rifles. Women lugged *toks*, balancing the tall clay pots on their shoulders as they walked. I saw Byong-woo heading to Il-sung's tent accompanied by a soldier. He saw me and our eyes met for a split second. His look reminded me that I needed to be careful about what I said and did here.

The woman named Ki-soo had the fire going. The grass crackled and curled in the flames. She poured water in a kettle and hung it on a spit over the fire.

"How can I help?" I asked. I was determined to survive my time here with the rebels. I was determined to get back to Young-chul someday.

"We heard that a woman was coming," she replied without looking up. "What is your name?"

"I am Suk-bo," I answered.

"You are the one who was married to a Japanese man?"

"Yes, I was," I replied with a little too much force. "But I am here now and I would like to help. Now tell me please, what can I do?"

Ki-soo smiled to herself. As she lifted the lid of a basket and measured out some rice, she said, "I was told you will rest today. Take a mat inside the hut. When you are rested, there will be more than enough for you to do."

I went inside the hut and lay on a mat away from the other woman who, this time, didn't open her eyes. I stuffed a blanket under my head, but it was stiff and coarse and scratched my face. It also stunk, so I pushed it aside. I closed my eyes and tried to picture my parents' faces. It seemed like a lifetime ago that I had last seen them at my wedding. The images of them were fading from me. I remembered my father's strong hands, but I couldn't remember the details of his face. I remembered that my mother was small but strong, but I couldn't picture her eyes. I missed them so much. I prayed they were still alive.

I thought of my brother. My aunt and Byong-woo had said he was a chinilpa, but I didn't see how the young man I'd looked up to all my life could have changed so much. I hadn't seen him for years and I missed him. I wanted to see for sure if it was true what they said about him. I would try to find him someday.

I thought about Hisashi and Young-chul, but I had to quickly push those thoughts away. If I was to see them again—if I was to hug my son and lie with my husband and feel his breath against my neck—I would have to endure being here with Kim Il-sung and the rebels. I could see that it was going to take all my strength. I would need to be careful, as Byong-woo had said. But I was going to do it for Young-chul and Hisashi. So I cleared my mind and let sleep take me away.

I awoke while it was still light outside. The woman who'd been in the hut with me was gone and I was alone. I rubbed my eyes and pushed myself off the mat. I was still tired and needed more sleep, but I was determined to survive. I went outside. The sun was at its early afternoon angle, turning everything a harsh yellow and forcing me to squint. A lazy lethargy had replaced the bustle of the morning. People lay in the shade of tents and trees while horses munched grain and swished their tails.

I went to a group of women that included Ki-soo. "Are you rested already?" she asked as the others inspected me. I could see contempt in their eyes.

"Yes," I said. "I am ready to help."

"Good," she said. "You have been assigned to water detail with Young-ee. Later, you will help fetch water."

"Yes," I replied. "Is that all I will do?"

Several of the women laughed without covering their mouths. Ki-soo grinned. "Yes," she said, "that is all you will do today."

I sat in the shade with the other women. Young-ee introduced herself. "I am from Pyongyang," she said. "My father was a Christian minister there. We had to run away when the Japanese started to persecute Christians."

I guessed that Young-ee was about my age. She was my height, but thick boned. And where I was light skinned and soft from living with the Saitos, she was dark from years in the sun. Her hair that she had braided in a tail was stiff and dull. Her eyes flitted from side to side as she talked.

"How long have you been here?" I asked.

"Four years."

"Are your parents here?"

She shook her head and looked around as if someone was watching her. "No. They were killed."

"I'm sorry," I said.

"It is okay," she said with an out-of-place smile. "I have everything I need here. You do, too. You will see."

Her odd smile stayed in place, but her eyes moved about. She leaned in to whisper to me. "I shouldn't be friends with you because you married a Japanese man. But we can be friends when we are alone."

"Yes," I said. "We can be friends." Young-ee nodded and then stopped talking to me.

None of the other women introduced themselves. They talked very little as if they knew they shouldn't expend energy. Then, when the sun dropped, the women began to stir. One by one, they headed off in different directions.

Ki-soo came to me. "Go with Young-ee to fetch water. She will show you what to do."

We collected four toks from a storage tent and put one on each shoulder. I followed Young-ee out of the compound and along a dry riverbed. As we carried the clay pots, Young-ee shared gossip about the others.

"You have to watch out for Ki-soo," she said. "She is young, but Commissar Kim favors her. They say she is a good shot with a rifle. They say she has killed a Japanese. She will hit you if you do not do your job. You will see."

"Okay," I said.

"The other women are not so bad. Jeon-suk is lazy. She always says she is sick, but I think she is just pretending to get out of work."

"What about the men?"

"You must be wary of them," Young-ee said, walking fast. "My advice for you is to join up with one. That one you came with looks nice. Stay away from Jin-mo. He and Ki-soo are sweet on each other."

"Which one is Jin-mo?"

"He is the handsome one."

"Thank you for your advice," I said, "but I cannot be with a man. I am married."

"Some of the other women are married, too. But that does not matter here. You need a man or all the men will be after you. You will see."

"Do you have a man?"

"No," Young-ee replied faintly.

I wanted to ask how far we had to go for the water, but I decided I would find out soon enough. I asked, "Why do you call Il-sung 'commissar'?"

"It is a communist title. Commissar Kim is a communist. He expects all of us to be communists, too. After you have been here a while, he will talk to you about it."

"I do not know anything about communism," I said. "Are you a communist?"

"I am what Commissar Kim wants me to be. You will be, too. You will see."

We came around a knoll and saw an area in the distance with tall trees and green grass. Young-ee set her toks on the ground and crouched behind a rock. I put my toks down, too, and crouched next to her.

"That is where we get the water. It is a spring. We must be sure no one is there before we go in."

We watched together until Young-ee was satisfied. We lifted the toks again and hurried to the spring. Green trees and bushes surrounded a small pond. Young-ee slowly approached the pond, looking to her left and right as I followed. "You have to watch out for mamushi," she said. "I hate snakes. And mamushi are poisonous."

When we got to the pond's edge, Young-ee slapped her hand on the water, making a loud splash. "I do this to scare the mamushi away," she explained. When Young-ee was sure no poisonous snakes were in the pond, we filled our toks with water. Young-ee expertly lifted the heavy toks to her shoulders, but I struggled, almost dropping one. When I had them both on my shoulders and was supporting them with my hands, we headed back. The toks were very heavy and they pushed into my shoulders, making my back ache. We hadn't gone halfway to camp when my arms grew tired and I was afraid I would drop the pots.

"I need to rest," I said.

Young-ee didn't stop walking. "We cannot," she said. "It is unsafe out here."

"Why don't they use the horses or one of the trucks to fetch the water?"

"They make too much noise," Young-ee answered. "Anyway, they need to rest the horses and save fuel for the trucks."

We were within sight of the camp when I could no longer feel my arms, and the pain in my shoulders was so sharp, I could not go on. I took the toks from my shoulders and dropped one, spilling the water. Young-ee looked at me in horror, still balancing the toks on her shoulders.

"We do not have time to rest!" she cried. "And you spilled the water. Now we will have to make five trips instead of four. Come, quickly!"

"Five trips?" I said, rubbing my shoulders.

"Yes," Young-ee replied. "Come now, quickly. We have to finish before it is dark."

Young-ee watched as I struggled to get the toks onto my shoulders again. "Do not worry," she said as we started walking again. "You will get used to it. You will see."

Young-ee was wrong—I never did get used to it. Every day we fetched water from the spring—four morning trips and four at night. Each trip took an hour. On hot summer days when the men and horses needed more water, Ki-soo made us go for more. Between the morning and evening trips, we relaxed in the shade or napped in the hut. I could never get enough to eat, and I lost weight. My shoulders and back ached constantly. My skin turned dark, and my hair became stiff and wiry like Young-ee's. I knew life with the rebels would be hard, but I never dreamed it would be like this. Perhaps I could run away and find my brother in Pyongyang. But I was in territory controlled by the Imperial

Army, a long way from Pyongyang. If they caught me, they might kill me or send me to prison. And I didn't even know which direction to go.

I did little else than fetch water every day, rest during the breaks, and sleep at night. Though it looked bad for her to be my friend, Young-ee never left my side because no one else would listen to her chatter. She talked constantly about this or that. She gossiped about which man was trying to be with which woman. She told me about her parents and about Christianity. She said she believed that Jesus had been a great prophet. She said she had memorized many passages from the Bible and she often recited them aloud. She told me that Commissar Kim had been a Christian once, but he had rejected Christianity when he became a communist. I didn't mind her talking. Listening to her kept my mind off Young-chul and Hisashi.

When winter came, one wool blanket was not enough to keep us warm inside our stick hut, so the women pushed our mats together and combined our blankets to make one big one. We slept close so our bodies warmed each other. Ki-soo and several other women didn't sleep in the women's hut, instead going off at night to be with their men. Jeon-suk cried herself to sleep nearly every night. The other women never tried to comfort her.

Time moved slowly in the rebel camp. Every month or so, the men went on a raid, taking them out of camp for days or weeks at a time, while the women stayed back, gathering food and doing their daily chores. I stuck to the routine of fetching water with Young-ee in the morning and evening. Every day, I thought of Hisashi and Young-chul.

One summer morning after I'd been in camp over a year, the man named Jin-mo came on a horse, galloping into the compound. He stopped at Commissar Kim's tent and said something to the guard at the door. The guard ducked inside the tent as Jin-mo galloped away. The guard came out and ran to talk to the men. Then, everyone started scrambling about.

Ki-soo ran over to one of the men to find out what was going on. "We have to move," she said when she returned. "The Japanese are near. The men are planning a raid and it is not safe here."

The women sprang into action. Young-ee took my hand and led me to the horses. "We need to get a lot of water. We can use the horses."

"But I thought it was too dangerous to use the horses," I said, running with her.

"The danger of staying here is greater," she said. "Quickly, quickly!"

We took two horses, and Young-ee got slings. We cinched the slings on the horses, hung six empty toks on each one, then led them to the spring. When we got to the knoll, Young-ee went ahead as I held the horses. She came back after a few minutes and declared it was safe, so we led the horses to the pond.

Young-ee had just dipped a tok into the water when from within the grass, a mamushi snake uncoiled and struck her arm, sinking its fangs deep into her flesh. Then it quickly slithered away. Young-ee dropped the tok and screamed. She gripped her arm. The horses started, so I grabbed the leads. They reared and snorted, but I held firm. Young-ee looked at me wide-eyed. "I have been bitten! I have to get back!"

She started to run. "Wait!" I said. "We have to get the water." Young-ee kept running toward camp. I looked at the horses, still carrying the empty toks. I untied the toks and took them to the pond. I slapped the pond to scare away the mamushi, then kneeled at the pond's edge. As quickly as I could, I filled each tok and tied it onto the horses. I grabbed the horses' leads and hurried to camp.

I caught up to Young-ee halfway to camp. She was stumbling about and looked confused. "Which way do I go?" she cried.

Her arm was swelling and her eyes swam. A streak of blood dripped from the bite in her arm. I dropped the leads and went to her. "I'll take you," I said. "Get on my back." I crouched and lifted Young-ee onto me. On my back, she was not much heavier than the toks that I carried every day. But the load was awkward and Young-ee couldn't hang on.

She moaned and rolled her head. "I am going to die," she sobbed. "I do not want to die."

"You will not die," I said, hiking her body higher. "Hang on as best as you can." I grabbed the horses' leads and ran as quickly as I could all the way to camp, carrying Young-ee on my back.

Byong-woo saw me first. He was with other men loading a truck with tents and supplies when he spotted me struggling with Young-ee, who had stopped moaning and was limp on my back. He ran to us. "What happened?" he asked, taking Young-ee.

"She was bitten by a mamushi!"

"Take the horses to Ki-soo and tell her what happened," he said. "Have her bring Chun-ja with her medicines."

I led the horses to Ki-soo, who was helping other women load cookware into a wooden cart. "Young-ee has been bitten by a mamushi!" I shouted as I approached. "She needs Chun-ja with her medicines!"

Ki-soo told one of the other women to get the medicine woman and told another to take the horses. "Where is she?" Ki-soo asked.

"Byong-woo has her over by the trucks."

I followed Ki-soo as she ran to Byong-woo. He had Young-ee on the ground on her back. Young-ee's arm was swollen to twice its normal size and as purple as a plum. Byong-woo sliced into the wound with his knife.

"How long ago was she bitten?" he asked me.

"I do not know, exactly," I answered. "Maybe a half hour. I had to get the water first. I came as quickly as I could." I put my hands to my chest. I was worried that I'd made a mistake for getting the water instead of helping Young-ee.

Byong-woo stopped cutting the wound and stuck his knife into the ground. He leaned on his knees. "It is too late to suck out the venom," he said. "Chun-ja is her only hope."

Then, from across the compound, Commissar Kim strolled toward us. As he walked, he examined the scene in front of him. When he saw the commissar, Byong-woo grabbed his knife and stood. We all stared as Il-sung approached. When he got to us, he looked down at Young-ee. "What happened?" he asked.

"She was bitten by a mamushi," Byong-woo answered.

"Were you able to suck out the venom?" Il-sung asked, still staring at Young-ee.

"No. It is too late," Byong-woo said. "She was bitten a half hour ago. Suk-bo stayed to get the water. Chun-ja might have potions and we can—"

"Suk-bo did the right thing to get the water," Il-sung said. He looked at Byong-woo. "Leave her. We do not have time."

"Yes, Commissar," Byong-woo said with a nod. He sheathed his knife and walked away, leaving Young-ee lying on the ground. Ki-soo walked away, too. Il-sung started back to where he'd come from.

"Wait!" I shouted. "We cannot just let her die!"

As I stared at their backs, they continued to walk away. I ran to Il-sung. "Commissar Kim," I cried, grabbing his sleeve, "we must try to save her! Please!"

Il-sung did not stop. "Go and help with the water," he said.

"But sir," I pleaded, still holding his sleeve, "Chun-ja has medicines!"

He continued walking and looked at me as he did. His face was expressionless. "Young-ee is dead. If we take the time to try to save her, we might all die." He stopped and pulled my hand from his arm. "Now go to the water. We need it for our escape."

I stood in the compound, looking at Il-sung's back as he walked away. He went to a group of men, one of whom held a map. Il-sung leaned over the map, pointing at it and talking to the men.

I looked at Young-ee, unconscious on the ground. I couldn't believe they were letting her die. I looked around the compound. The men and women of the rebel camp went on with their tasks and didn't seem to notice my friend Young-ee dying in front of them.

TWENTY-ONE

It took us an hour to break camp. Ki-soo assigned Jeon-suk to help with the water horses. Each of us took a lead and we went northeast with the rest of the rebels. There were sixty of us in all. Commissar Kim rode a horse along with Jin-mo and two other men. Byong-woo drove one of the trucks—a run-down army truck loaded to the springs with diesel fuel, tents, and supplies. The other truck was a three-wheeler with handlebars like on a motorcycle, the engine behind the driver, and a cargo area behind that. It carried rifles and ammunition. Four men walked in front of the truck, clearing away boulders and branches. The rest of us walked on foot behind.

The company moved quickly over a hill, down a valley, and across a grassy plain. It was cloudy, but it didn't look like it would rain. The clouds kept the heat away, and soon we were far from our camp. As I led my horse alongside Jeon-suk, all I thought about was Young-ee dying in the dust behind us. We didn't even take her with us so we could bury her.

By midafternoon, the grassy plain fell away into a valley and we stopped. Jeon-suk and I brought water to the men and horses and watched as Commissar Kim gathered his lieutenants to study a map.

Commissar Kim nodded when Jin-mo pointed to a line of trees down the valley.

"We are not far from where we will make camp," Jin-mo said when he came to us. "It is in that valley. We will need the truck, so you will have to haul the supplies by hand. The men will be away for several days. We will leave a few men to guard the camp." Jin-mo went to the group of lieutenants who were studying yet another map. Byong-woo and two other men unloaded his truck, putting the tents and supplies in a pile. Those of us staying behind began to assemble the supplies into packs.

Byong-woo came to me. "We need the water horses and the remaining water. Put the toks in the truck."

"What will we do for water?" I asked.

"You will be near a river," he said. He hesitated as if he wanted to say something. Then he finally said, "Take care, Suk-bo. I will return soon."

Jeon-suk and I hauled the toks to Byong-woo's truck. Two men took the water horses and put saddles on them. About a dozen men climbed into the truck. Four others climbed into the back of the three-wheeler. Then, they took off.

Darkness had fallen by the time the rest of us had hauled the tents, supplies, and water to the new camp in a low woodland with aspen and tamarack trees. We were mostly women—fifteen in all. But some men were with us—one who had lost an arm, three who were too old to fight, and two able-bodied men who had stayed behind to guard the camp. We set up two tents, and after a quick meal of millet porridge and tea, the women crawled under blankets and went to sleep.

The next morning, our water supply was low, so I roused Jeon-suk from under the blanket and we gathered the toks. I wasn't sure where we could get water, so I asked one of the elderly men named Won-ho.

"We are close to the Mudan River," he said. He pointed the direction I should go. "Be careful that no one is there."

I turned to leave. "Wait," he said. He reached inside his shirt and pulled out a pistol. "Can I trust you with this?" he asked.

"Yes, sir," I answered, looking at the pistol.

He handed it to me. "Put it in your waistband. Fire two shots if there is trouble."

I'd never held a pistol before. It was heavier than I'd expected. I looked at it, then at Won-ho. He pointed at a small lever on the side. "That is the safety latch. Put it in the down position and pull the trigger to fire it. It is not hard."

I nodded and put the pistol in my waistband. Jeon-suk and I shouldered our toks and started walking.

It was less than a half mile to the river. The Mudan was not nearly as wide as the Yalu, but it ran much faster over boulders and across sandbars. It was lined with aspen trees whose leaves quaked nervously. Jeon-suk and I hid behind bushes and scanned the river to see if we were alone. I kept a hand on the pistol. We didn't see anyone, so we hurried to the river and filled our toks. I was afraid Jeon-suk would have trouble carrying the heavy toks to camp. She was younger than I was and she was frail. Yet she shouldered the toks as well as Young-ee had.

The others had not set up any more tents by the time we got back. "We do not know if we will stay here," Ki-soo said. "There is no sense in making a full camp until the men return."

Jeon-suk and I made one more trip for water, and then we had nothing more to store it in. I gave the pistol to Won-ho. "When the men come back," he said, "you should learn how to use it."

In the afternoon, one of the men came into camp with a deer he'd shot. Two women butchered it while others started a fire to smoke the meat. Won-ho and another man took nets to the river and caught fish that they cleaned and hung over the fire. That night, we each had a taste of venison and fish, though we saved most of it for when the men returned. I hadn't had meat in many months, and though the venison was tough and the fish had bones, they were delicious. As it started to get dark, I led some women to the river where, after making sure we were alone, we stripped down, bathed ourselves, and washed our clothes. The river was cold and I could only bear it long enough to scrub the grime from my skin, dunk my head in, and run my fingers through my hair. I shivered as I dried myself, and yet I felt better than I had in weeks. I'd forgotten how good it felt to be clean.

The men did not return the next day or the next day after that. The hunter shot another deer and two rabbits. The fishermen caught more fish. The women gathered roots and plants from the forest. They found ginseng and leaves for tea. Soon, the food baskets were full.

On the fourth day at the new camp, the men returned. Jin-mo came into camp before the others, riding his horse. The horse's tongue hung out, and its mouth foamed. We gathered around Jin-mo as he dismounted, and he handed the reins to one of the men. "It needs water, feed, and a rubdown," Jin-mo said. He pointed to two other men. "You two come with me. We need help to get the truck through the forest." Then he addressed the group. "The others will be here in two hours. They are tired and hungry. Get ready for them." He hurried back from where he came, the two men following close behind.

Jeon-suk and I resupplied the water as the rest of the women prepared food and laid mats for the men. The fishermen caught more fish and put them on the cook fire so the fighting men could have fresh meat when they arrived.

Eventually, we heard the truck coming. The rumble grew louder, and soon, the truck, followed by the three-wheeler, appeared through the woods. In front of the truck, the two men from camp cleared away forest debris to make a path. Behind were the fighting men with Commissar Kim high on his horse. He held a rope tied to the neck of a man whose hands were bound together. The man slouched forward and stumbled as he walked. He wore a Japanese uniform.

We all rose to meet them. I stepped to the front of the group staring at the soldier. My heart beat fast as I thought it might be Hisashi. But as they came close, I saw that the soldier was shorter than Hisashi and had a round face. One of his eyes was swollen shut.

The trucks stopped at the edge of camp. Byong-woo got out from behind the wheel and looked around. When he saw me, he nodded and gave a slight smile. Il-sung dismounted and led the prisoner to the group. Up close, I saw the soldier's good eye was wide with fear. He was barefoot and his feet were bloody.

We gathered in front of Commissar Kim. "We have had a great victory in our raid against the invaders," he said without emotion. "Though two of our men were killed and another three were injured. But we killed many Japanese and we captured this dog." He jerked the rope, making the soldier stumble. "We brought him here to interrogate him."

He pointed at Chun-ja. "Chun-ja, get your medicines and do what you can for the injured men. They are in the truck. The rest of you, take care of the men and horses. Set up the rest of the camp. We will stay here for the winter."

As Chun-ja and two other women hurried to the truck to tend to the injured men, Commissar Kim and Jin-mo took the soldier to a tree. They tied him to the trunk with a rope around his neck, forcing him to stand so that he wouldn't choke. I helped the women feed the men and tried not to look at the soldier struggling to stay upright on his bloody feet.

As the men ate, the women set up the rest of the camp. They raised the tents and gathered branches to make huts. They spread blankets and mats. After the men had eaten, they crawled into tents to sleep. All except for Commissar Kim, Jin-mo, and Byong-woo, who went to the soldier, now slumped against the tree and pulling the rope tight around his neck. I thought the soldier was dead, but when they untied him, he gasped and moaned. They dragged him into the woods.

Seeing the soldier stagger, cry, and plead for his life, I thought of Hisashi. He too was a Japanese soldier, an officer in a camp somewhere here in Manchuria. He might be close to where we were. Perhaps he was with the company that we'd just raided. Maybe he was one they'd killed.

As I watched them disappear into the forest with the prisoner, I wanted to stop them from what they were going to do. I wanted to explain to them that some Japanese were good people and that no one deserved to be tortured and killed. I wanted to tell them that I loved a Japanese man. But I knew it would do no good to plead for the man's life. The raid had killed two of our own, and by the look on his face, Commissar Kim wanted revenge.

Now that the men were back, we would need a lot more water. I got Jeon-suk and we gathered the toks. I went to Won-ho, got his pistol, and tucked it into my waistband. Then, Jeon-suk and I headed to the river. Unlike Young-ee, Jeon-suk didn't talk much. She'd always kept to herself, sitting to the side when the women chatted before going to bed. So I was surprised when she came alongside me and started talking.

"Why are they torturing him?" she asked as we walked.

"They want information about the Japanese, I suppose," I replied.

"But he is a private. He won't know anything."

She was right. The soldier wore a private's uniform and he wouldn't have any valuable information. We didn't say anything more. When we got to the river, a shot rang out from where they'd taken the soldier. As Jeon-suk filled her tok, she started to cry. I thought of Hisashi, and I wanted to cry, too, but I pushed my cries down inside where I was becoming hard like stone.

We spent the fall and then winter at the camp by the Mudan River. It was colder than any winter I'd known. The nights were long and the days short and dreary. Snow piled against the tents and huts. We made hard, icy paths in the snow from tent to tent and to the river. I was never warm and I was always hungry. They put me last in line to get food, so I never had enough to eat. At night under the blankets, the women made me sleep on the end where one side of me was always cold. I knew why they treated me the way they did. I'd married a Japanese.

During the day, we did our chores but little else. On especially cold days, we stayed inside the tents, huddling close to stay warm. Every day, Jeon-suk and I made trips to the river for water. Though the river ran fast, we often had to break through ice with rocks. I wrapped my hands in rags to keep them from freezing. Midwinter, the leaders decided to shoot one of the horses. They said it was to save feed for the other horses, but I think it was to provide food for us. They shot the animal on a bitterly cold day, and the women quickly butchered it, steam rising from the carcass as they cut into it. They smoked the meat before it froze. They dragged the carcass to the river where, over the next two weeks, the crows and eagles picked it clean.

I hadn't talked to Byong-woo much since our escape from Sinuiju. Now that we had idle time, he often sought me out. When Jeon-suk pretended to be sick, Byong-woo volunteered to help me fetch water. I think he did it to be with me, but I didn't mind. His interest in me kept the other men away. Besides, Byong-woo was a strong porter and, unlike the always-sullen Jeon-suk, he liked to talk. Now that he didn't have to wear the chauffeur's cap, he wore his long wavy hair down. The sun and Manchurian wind gave him a rugged look that sat well on him.

One day when winter was beginning to lose its grip, Jeon-suk refused to come out of the tent, so Byong-woo and I went to the river with the toks. He smoked a short brown cigarette as we walked. "Our raids have Commissar Kim in good standing with the rebel leaders," he said. "There is talk that they will put more men under his command. We are lucky to have him as our leader."

"Yes," I said. I wanted to say that I thought Il-sung had been wrong to leave Young-ee to die and that I didn't approve of them torturing and killing the soldier the way they did. But I decided it was best to hold my tongue.

We walked a little farther. Then I asked, "Why did you save me in Sinuiju? Why didn't you just escape on your own and let the police take me?"

"It was a big risk," Byong-woo said. "If they had caught us, they would have tortured me and then shot me."

"Then why did you do it?"

"I guess I felt sorry for you," he replied.

"But I was happy with Hisashi," I protested. "And I had Young-chul. You took me from my son."

"You did not have Hisashi anymore. And Mrs. Saito was taking you away from Young-chul, not me. I arranged for Kiyo to take care of him. This is better for you."

"This?" I asked as we came to the riverbank. "Living here in Manchuria like this?"

"Yes, this," he answered bluntly. "Here, fighting the Japanese as your parents did. I hated it in Sinuiju. I was a slave in a chauffeur's hat. I would much rather be here in the cold. Anyway," he said with a quick look, "I saved you because I wanted you to come with me." He tossed his cigarette butt to the side and dropped to his knees. He began filling the toks.

We filled the water toks and headed to camp without talking. After we'd dropped them off, Byong-woo said, "Suk-bo, tell me. How do you feel about me?"

"You saved my life," I replied. "I am grateful."

"Just grateful? That is all you can say?"

I smiled at him and walked away.

Eventually, the daylight grew longer and it wasn't as cold at night. The women did not sleep as close together and the ice paths turned to mud. One day, Jin-mo went off on his horse. Three days later he returned with fifty more rebels, who set up camp next to us. They were hardscrabble men and women dressed in rags. I thought they looked pathetic. Then I looked at my own ragged clothes and noticed how calloused and cracked my hands had become. I hadn't brushed my hair in months. I could feel my ribs sticking out and that my face was thin. I'd become just like them.

When the snow finally melted, a feeling of relief filled the camp. We'd survived the winter. People spent more time outside the tents. Jeon-suk didn't pretend to be sick as often. Byong-woo and several other men worked on the truck and three-wheeler. Still others practiced hand-to-hand combat with the new people, each group showing the other new moves. Women went to the woods in search of plants and roots to restock the food stores. Hunting parties shot more game. Men constantly cleaned their rifles.

Not much happened in camp for several months until one day, after a storm, Jin-mo came to me. Il-sung's handsome deputy rarely took notice of me, so I was surprised when he called my name. "Suk-bo," he said, "come with me. Commissar Kim wants to talk to you."

I hesitated, not sure if I'd heard him correctly. "Come, come!" Jin-mo said, waving his hand. "Do not make him wait."

I followed him to Il-sung's tent. Jin-mo opened the tent flap and motioned me inside. I stepped in as Jin-mo, staying outside, closed the flap. The commissar sat at his table, which was set with two tea bowls and a teapot. Il-sung saw me and bade me to sit with him. Whenever I saw him, I was surprised how a man not much older than me could be so charismatic. Now, inside his tent, his aura was strong.

I kept my eyes low as Il-sung poured tea into the tea bowls and set one in front of me. "The new people brought tea from China," he said, "so we do not have to drink that swill. Drink."

Il-sung had never offered to drink tea with me before. In fact, he hadn't spoken three words to me since Young-ee died. I knew why. It was because he didn't trust me. But I'd worked hard for the rebels for nearly two years, and now, he was offering me tea. Perhaps, I thought, I had earned his trust.

I took a sip and it was, in fact, the best tea I'd had since I'd lived in the Saito house. Sipping his tea, Il-sung kept his eyes on me. "You are the water girl," he said from over his tea bowl. "I have been told that you are strong and you never miss a day of work. That is admirable, exactly the traits our rebellion needs."

"Thank you, sir," I said.

He set his tea bowl down. "I should tell you that several of our new comrades have information about the raid on the unit your parents were with. They said that your father was a brave soldier, but he and your mother were captured. It is not likely you will see them again. I am sorry."

I looked into my tea bowl. I'd hoped that my parents were not killed. But the thought of them as prisoners was worse. I wanted to cry for them, but I choked back my tears so I wouldn't cry in front of Commissar Kim.

Il-sung took another sip of tea and said, "I have been thinking about you, Suk-bo. I was concerned that you are sympathetic to Japan because of feelings you have for your husband. How do you feel about what we are doing here, fighting the Japanese?"

"I do not know," I said, shaking my head. "My father hated them. My mother was afraid of them. They turned my brother into a chinilpa. If it is true what you say about my parents, they have destroyed my family. I think they are destroying Korea, too."

"They are," Il-sung said. "And China, too."

I looked at Commissar Kim. "But Hisashi is not like that. He is a kind man. He does not support what Japan is doing in Asia. When we were alone, he used my real name."

"Are you sure about him?" Il-sung asked.

"Yes, sir. I know it in my heart."

"Well," Il-sung said, "we have learned something different about your husband."

"What do you know?" I said quickly. "Tell me, please."

Il-sung lifted his chin at me. "Byong-woo said that your husband was going to work for Doctor Ishii here in Manchuria. We have learned that Doctor Ishii has set up a camp in Harbin, less than two hundred miles north of here, near where they captured your parents. They say it is a sawmill, but we know it is not. No timber goes in and no lumber comes out. Only prisoners go in, but they do not come out. The Japanese conduct experiments there—cruel experiments on prisoners."

"Experiments?" I shook my head. "Hisashi would not be involved in something like that."

"Oh?" Il-sung said. "Was Byong-woo wrong about what your husband was going to do?"

I looked down. "Hisashi only said he was going to work for Doctor Ishii."

"Yes," Il-sung said, picking up his tea bowl. "Your husband is helping Doctor Ishii conduct experiments on prisoners—prisoners like your parents." He took a sip of tea and stared at me.

"No," I said. "It cannot be true. You're saying that so that I will disown him."

"It is true and you know it," Il-sung said.

I thought about it for a minute. Perhaps Il-sung was right. Maybe it was why Hisashi was so distraught the day when we were last together. Maybe it was why he'd said we couldn't be married anymore. It made sense, but I couldn't make myself believe it.

I wanted to reach out to my husband. I wanted to tell him I knew he was a kind and gentle man and that he would never hurt anyone. He was less than two hundred miles away, Il-sung had said. Over the hills and valleys of those miles, I sent my love to him. I prayed that he would receive it.

And then I became angry. Why had fate done this to Hisashi and me? Why couldn't we have a love like we'd had that precious year before he went to Tokyo? Why did I have to suffer?

"It is the curse of the two-headed dragon," I said to myself.

"What did you say?" Il-sung asked. "A two-headed dragon?"

"Yes," I said, nodding. "My aunt told me that if I married Hisashi, I would be cursed by the two-headed dragon. I saw it once. It is in a comb she has."

"A comb?" Il-sung said with raised eyebrows. "Tell me about it."

"It had a gold spine. The dragon was made from ivory inlays. It was beautiful. My aunt said her mother gave it to her."

"I see," Il-sung replied. "Where does your aunt live?"

I remembered that my aunt told me I shouldn't tell anyone about the comb. Il-sung seemed to be very interested in it, and I realized I'd made a mistake telling him about it.

"It is nothing," I said, shaking my head. "The gold was fake, and the dragon wasn't ivory at all. My aunt said she was going to throw it away."

Il-sung smiled wryly. "But you said it was beautiful. And you think the dragon has cursed you."

"No," I replied. "It is just something I say."

"Where does your aunt live?" Il-sung asked again.

"She . . . she lived outside of Sinuiju," I replied, "but she and my uncle moved to Seoul. I have not seen them in years."

"I see," Commissar Kim said. "Well, as I said before, I have been thinking about you. I want you to prove that you are with us. I am promoting Byong-woo to third in command behind Jin-mo. Byong-woo has many skills and is passionate about our cause. He knows how to make bombs. I want you to work with him. It is dangerous but important work."

"I would rather fetch water, sir," I replied.

"Yes, well," Il-sung said, leaning back. "Your son—what is his name? Young-chul, is it?"

I snapped my head up. "What about my son?" I asked. "Where is he? What can you tell me about him?"

A dry smile spread across Il-sung's face. "Byong-woo arranged for one of our people—Kiyo, I think he said her name was—to take care of him. I hear your son is doing well in her care. But I cannot say how the boy would do if we told Kiyo to put him on the street. He is half Japanese, so no Korean would take him in. He is half Korean, so the Japanese would not want him either. The poor boy would starve. I think our comrade Kiyo is his only hope to survive."

I pictured Young-chul alone on the streets of Sinuiju, where no one would take him in. My prince was only a toddler, and without Kiyo, he would surely die. They wanted me to help make bombs. It was a dangerous job, Il-sung said. But they had Young-chul.

I bowed my head to Commissar Kim. "I would be happy to help Byong-woo," I said.

"Good," Il-sung said. "Your service will be valuable to us. And as long as you are working with Byong-woo, you should be his woman. It will prove to us that you no longer love a Japanese soldier."

Although Byong-woo seemed to be a good man, and I knew he wanted me, I couldn't picture myself being with him. I was still in love with Hisashi and I always would be. I wanted to tell Commissar Kim how I felt about my husband. I desperately wanted to try to make him understand. But I knew it wouldn't do any good, so I said nothing.

"Think about it, Suk-bo," Il-sung said. "And now, you may go."

TWENTY-TWO

As Commissar Kim said, Byong-woo was an expert with explosives. The new people had brought chemicals and black powder that they stored in a small tent fifty yards from the main camp. The black powder was in sacks and the chemicals in toks. The chemicals gave off a suffocating odor that gave me a headache. When I told Byong-woo the smell bothered me, he said the chemicals had to stay inside the tent out of the weather. "It is the acid you smell," he said. "You never get used to it."

A little way from the tent a tok sat buried inside a pit with only the top exposed. It was covered with a heavy lid. "That is where we keep the mercury fulminate," Byong-woo said, pointing.

"Mercury fulminate?"

"It's the catalyst. The main explosive is black powder, but the tricky part is the catalyst. We use mercury fulminate. It is unstable and dangerous."

"Why do you need a catalyst?" I asked.

"Black powder can make a good bomb," he said. "But using a catalyst makes a much more powerful explosion. We do not have much fulminate, so we must make more. The new people brought what we need. I'll teach you how. Then, I will show you how to make a bomb."

Over the summer, I worked with Byong-woo making fulminate of mercury. I didn't like the thought of making bombs to kill people, but I was trapped. All I was doing now was making fulminate. When the time came to make a bomb and use it to kill someone, I would have to decide what I would do.

During that time, I didn't learn much about Byong-woo. I sensed he didn't want to talk about his past. He was focused on killing Japanese. He never once asked me to go to his tent at night. I think he hoped that our time together would make me want to go to him on my own. But I never did.

As we worked, Byong-woo told me news of the war. "The Chinese report that the Japanese are in southern China now," he said. "They are killing innocent civilians wherever they go. We have learned that a few years ago when they took Nanking, the soldiers raped women and killed babies with their bayonets. They cut off the arms of young boys so they could never get revenge." He shook his head. "I hate the Japanese. I want to kill as many of them as I can."

What he was saying couldn't possibly be true. I had lived with Japanese all my life. Sure, they could be cruel like when they made the farmer eat the maggots from his rotting roof, or what they'd done to my aunt during the Dano celebration. And if the rumors were true, they tortured the rebels they caught for information. But raping women and killing babies? Surely it was an exaggeration. And I knew for certain that Hisashi would never be involved in such atrocities.

"Not all Japanese are like that," I said.

"You are talking about Hisashi," Byong-woo said. "You are right. I cannot imagine your husband doing such terrible things. But he is complicit. He is an officer in the army that is raping women and killing babies." He looked at me sideways.

If what Byong-woo said was true, an Imperial Army officer like Hisashi was, indeed, complicit. But though I saw him wearing a uniform when he'd come home from Tokyo, I could not picture my husband as a soldier. I only saw him as a carefree young man with short, shiny hair and an infectious smile, spying on me in the forest behind my house. I refused to believe he knew what the Japanese were doing. I refused to believe he was helping Doctor Ishii conduct human experiments. I refused to stop loving him.

When we finished for the day, I went to camp, leaving Byong-woo at the bomb-making tent. I went to the eating area and took some dried fish and millet. I sat away from the others and tried to eat, but I didn't have an appetite. I set my food next to me and drew my knees to my chin. I tried not to think of Japanese soldiers killing babies with their bayonets.

By the end of the summer, Byong-woo and I had run out of mercury and had made enough fulminate "for several good bombs," as Byong-woo said. "Now it is time for you to learn how to make a bomb."

Byong-woo got a paper cylinder about the size of a carrot from inside the tent. He got a sack of black powder and put some inside the cylinder. "The tighter you pack it, the bigger the explosion," he explained. "This is just a small one for practice, so we won't pack it tightly." With a stick, he poked a small opening in the powder. He took a large pinch of fulminate and gingerly pressed it into the opening. "Treat the fulminate as you would a baby bird," he said. "Be gentle with it. Do not press it too hard." He closed the cylinder with beeswax. Then he folded a crease in a sheet of rice paper and poured in black powder. "This is how you make a fuse," he said. "A little powder makes the fuse burn slowly. A lot of powder will burn more quickly. You must decide how fast the fuse should burn depending on the situation you are in. For this one, we will use just a little." He rolled the rice paper into a long, thin snake and pinched the ends closed.

We'd made a small bomb. "Big enough to show you what it can do," Byong-woo said. "But not so big to use too much material." We took our bomb to the forest far away from camp and placed it in the tall grass in an open area. It was a lovely fall day with blue skies and a gentle breeze that made the aspen leaves quake. Byong-woo showed me how to set the fuse into the bomb by making a small hole in the beeswax with a stick and pushing the fuse into the fulminate. He gave me a sulfur match. "Light it," he said. "Then run with me to behind that tree over there. It is a small bomb, but it can kill you." I struck the match and held it to the fuse. The fuse caught fire and started to fizz and spark. I ran with Byong-woo to behind the tree and covered my ears. In a few seconds, the bomb went off. The shuddering explosion was bigger than I'd expected. Crows took wing and cawed noisily. A covey of quail flushed from the woods. I looked around the tree at the crater the bomb had created. Where there was once grass, there was now only dirt. I was thrilled that our bomb had worked so well, but I was horrified by its power.

Byong-woo took out a cigarette and lit it. "Well done," he said, staring at the smoke from the explosion.

We stood for a while. The smell of burnt gunpowder hung all around us as smoke drifted high in the air. Finally, Byong-woo said, "My father and his father before him made fireworks. My father taught me how to make them, too. That's where I learned how to make fulminate and work with black powder. When I was a boy, I worked alongside my father to make shows for the New Year celebration in Sinuiju. It took us months to make the fireworks for the show. On New Year's night it was a thrill to see what we made shoot off over the Yalu River. We made red and blue and green bursts high above the river. They were like flowers on fire that lived for only a few seconds. Afterward, people would bow to my father and thank him for the show. They would give him money."

He took a puff from his cigarette. "Then one day when I was thirteen years old, the police came to our house and arrested my father. They took the black powder and chemicals and the paper we used to make fireworks. They accused my father of making bombs for the rebels. My father was a peaceful man. He never made a bomb in his life. He only made fireworks. But after that day, I never saw my father again. After they arrested him, I decided to use what he had taught me to fight the Japanese. I joined the rebel underground in Sinuiju and taught them how to make bombs. They got me a job as Mr. Saito's chauffeur so I could spy on him. I've been waiting ever since to get back to making bombs."

Byong-woo faced me. "As you know," he said, "we set off fireworks to ward off evil spirits. When I was young, I truly believed the fireworks my father and I made kept evil away. Now when I make an explosion like this one, I think of it destroying the evil spirit of the Japanese."

"It doesn't just kill spirits," I said. "It also kills people."

He sneered. "Just like spirits, if the people are evil, they deserve to die." He tossed his cigarette butt into the weeds.

We walked back to camp side by side. As we neared camp, Byong-woo said, "You have done well, Suk-bo. But Il-sung and Jin-mo do not trust you. If you are to survive here, you need to be with a man. I am in good standing with Commissar Kim. He has put me third in command behind Jin-mo. It is an important position. Being with me will help you. I would be kind to you."

Byong-woo took my arm and made me face him. "Some night I will send for you," he said. "Think about what it means for you to be with me. Think about what message it sends if you refuse."

I pulled away from him and met his eyes. Then I ran to the women's tent.

He sent for me a week later. The messenger was Ki-soo. She came to where I was resting near the cooking area and sat next to me. She brought her knees to her chin. "You should go to Byong-woo tonight," she said while looking out over the camp. "It would be the right thing for you to do."

I had come to respect Ki-soo. She was Jin-mo's woman and he was second in command. And though she was young, she was in charge of the women. She was level-headed, but she was strict, too. Once, when Jeon-suk refused to fetch water, Ki-soo kicked her out of the women's tent and had everyone in camp ignore her. She didn't give Jeon-suk anything to eat. Jeon-suk stayed outside of camp for three days, shivering in the cold and snow. On the morning of the fourth day she came back, bowed to Ki-soo, and said she would be glad to fetch water. Ki-soo made Jeon-suk fetch water alone that morning, and then she accepted Jeon-suk as if nothing had happened. After that, Jeon-suk never again refused to do her chores.

Now, Ki-soo was telling me I had to forget that I was married to Hisashi and be with Byong-woo. If I refused, they'd discipline me as they did Jeon-suk. They would also label me a traitor and kick me out of camp. They might hurt my son.

"Yes, ma'am," I said.

"Good," Ki-soo said. "Go after the sun sets." Then she left me sitting alone.

Just before sunset, I went to the river, stripped off my clothes, and cleaned myself in the cold, clear water. I twisted my hair into a braid. I washed my clothes and wrung them out. I had to put them on while they were still wet. I went to camp and headed to Byong-woo's tent. I stepped inside and bowed. A lamp threw shadows against the tent walls. Byong-woo sat on a mat. Next to him was a bottle and two cups.

"You came," he said.

Though he wasn't as handsome as Hisashi, Byong-woo was pleasant to look at. He'd washed and put on clean clothes. And although he'd lost weight, with his long wavy hair and rugged good looks he didn't look like the rough, unkempt rebel I'd come to know.

"Come," he said, putting a hand on the mat next to him. "Have some *makgeolli* with me."

I kept my eyes low as I sat next to him. My heart beat fast and every muscle in my body tensed. He took the bottle and poured the milky-white rice wine into the cups. He handed one to me. I took a sip. It was strong and harsh, not like the sweet makgeolli Hisashi bought in Sinuiju.

"Commissar Kim grants his senior officers a few privileges," he said, lifting his cup high and examining it. "I get cigarettes and mak-geolli. Neither are good, but they're better than nothing. Makgeolli is very hard to get, here. I saved my ration for you." He grinned at me. "Drink!" he said.

I took another sip and the wine started to warm me. Byong-woo emptied his cup and poured himself another.

"I am glad you decided to come here," he said. "Now that I am third in command, I have this tent to myself. I want to share it with you. You must not like the wine. You aren't drinking much."

"As you said, it isn't good."

"Hah!" Byong-woo chuckled. "It is not, but it does the job." He lifted his cup to his mouth and emptied it.

He looked at me. "You asked me once why I saved you in Sinuiju. I told you it was because I felt sorry for you. But it was more than that. It was because I was attracted to you." He lifted my chin with his finger. "You are a beautiful woman, Suk-bo. I want you to be my woman."

I shook my head. "I love Hisashi," I said.

He jerked his finger away. In the shadows of the tent, Byong-woo's eyes turned cold. "Hisashi!" he said as if it was a curse. "He works for Doctor Ishii and you have heard what they do in their camp. Is that the man you are in love with?"

"I have only heard what you say," I said, "but I don't believe it. You are making it up to make me hate him. I will always love him, no matter what you and Commissar Kim say."

Byong-woo snorted. "What is love if you can love a man like that?"

"Love is a commitment you make every day for the rest of your life," I said.

"Then why did you come here to my tent?" Byong-woo asked.

"I do not know," I answered. "Perhaps it was a mistake."

Byong-woo grabbed my arm. "I am not Hisashi," he said, "but I am Korean. You are Korean, too." He pulled me into him and kissed me. I put my hands on his chest and tried to push him away, but he was too strong. He grabbed my hair and pressed his mouth into mine. The makgeolli bottle fell over, spilling its contents onto the mat.

"No!" I cried.

"I am doing this for you," he said. "If you don't have me, they will kill you. Don't make me force you."

I knew that I couldn't fight him. If I resisted him, they would think I was a chinilpa and they would, indeed, kill me. And they'd put Young-chul on the street where he would die. I stopped struggling and forced myself to breathe. I relaxed my shoulders. I lay back on the mat. I opened my dress. Byong-woo clumsily unbuttoned his trousers and climbed on top of me. As he thrust himself inside me, I tried to pretend he was Hisashi and that we were making love. But there was no love in what we were doing, and all I felt was pain. And there I broke my promise to my beloved Hisashi.

I stayed with Byong-woo from then on. I had become his woman. But every time we had sex, every time he touched me or when Il-sung, Jin-mo, or Ki-soo regarded me as if I was now one of them, I felt guilty. Guilt clung to me like an odor I could not wash away. At night after sex, when Byong-woo fell asleep, I cried into my hands. I prayed to the spirits of my mother and father to help me. I prayed to Hisashi to forgive me. I wanted to run away, back to Sinuiju, back to when I was with Hisashi and we were happy. But I was two hundred miles away, and Hisashi had said we couldn't be married anymore. I could never return. So I did my duties, stayed with Byong-woo, and tried to cope with the guilt.

I wasn't sure if Byong-woo loved me. Although I could tell he was attracted to me, our being together seemed mostly utilitarian for him. Having a woman gave him the stature he needed to command respect from his troops. I tended to his needs. We had sex most nights—a clumsy, perfunctory act that only helped him fall asleep. We ate together to show Byong-woo's men that he had a woman. We worked together. He was kind to me as he had promised. But emotionally, my relationship with him was the same as it had been when he was the Saito chauffeur.

Truly, I didn't care if he loved me or not.

Byong-woo's position as third in command kept him busy. Every day he drilled the men on how to conduct raids. He led target practice. He inspected weapons and the status of the ammunition, vehicles, and horses. As Il-sung and Jin-mo plotted their next raid, Byong-woo made sure the men were ready for it.

Il-sung was away often during that time. The rumor around camp was that he was meeting with Joseph Stalin of Russia or Mao Zedong, the head of the Chinese communist party. I didn't think it was possible that Il-sung would meet with such important men. But the rebel raids under Il-sung had been successful and apparently, he was quickly moving up in the rebel organization.

One day before the snow came, Jin-mo informed us we were moving south, "closer to our homeland," he said. After he'd issued his orders, the entire camp went into action. The women took down tents and packed cookware, dried fish, venison, and the roots and plants they'd gathered. The men took up their weapons. I helped Byong-woo put the black powder, fulminate, and bomb-making materials in the truck.

The Spirit of the Dragon

Byong-woo turned his attention to his other duties, and I went to help Jeon-suk fetch water. We put the water toks on the horses and led them to the river.

"How is it being the woman of an important man?" Jeon-suk asked.

"It is not as easy as you think," I replied, feeling guilty again.

"You have your own tent," Jeon-suk said. "You are served food with the men before the women are served. The women respect you now."

"I suppose," I said.

We'd come to the river and Jeon-suk untethered a tok from the horse and dropped to her knees to start filling it. "I know why they chose you to be with him and not me," Jeon-suk said with a look of satisfaction.

"Oh, why?"

"Because you married a Japanese man."

"But I am with Byong-woo now."

"Yes, and he is teaching you how to make bombs, isn't he?" Jeon-suk said, strapping a tok onto a horse. "There were two before you who made bombs. They were both orphans. They sent them on missions where they were killed. They used them just like they are using you."

As I strapped a tok onto a horse, I wondered if Jeon-suk was right. Though I'd tried to show that I was not a chinilpa by taking up with Byong-woo, they would never forget that I'd married Hisashi. My love for him would brand me for the rest of my life. For the time being, I was useful to them, helping Byong-woo make bombs and being his woman. But I knew that Byong-woo didn't love me, not the way Hisashi did, not the way my mother said true love should be. And I would never love him either. So when the time came, they would send me on a mission as they'd done to the orphans. And then they would be done with me, the cursed woman who'd married a Japanese man.

TWENTY-THREE

The winter sky was as gray as slate when we left. All together there were one hundred of us. Il-sung and two of his lieutenants rode on horseback, leading the procession. Jin-mo was far out front, scouting, watching for the Japanese. Byong-woo drove the big truck as he always did. Four men walked in front of it, clearing the way. I followed behind, keeping a watch on the fulminate and black powder that we'd packed into the truck. We left the three-wheeler behind because Byong-woo said there was not enough fuel for both vehicles to make the trip.

We hiked for ten days over hills and through valleys. At night, I slept inside the truck with Byong-woo out of the cold. Every day we rose when it was still dark and made camp after the sun set.

By the twelfth day, the landscape looked like Korea, with granite peaks and pine forests. "Are we in Korea?" one of the women asked as we ate rice and dried venison.

"No," a lieutenant replied. "But we are not far." He pointed south. "Over those hills is the Yalu River."

The Yalu River. I thought of Young-chul. The Saito house where I'd last seen my son was less than a mile from the Yalu. I could see from the high hills around us that we were far upriver from Sinuiju, but still, it was the Yalu River, a place I knew. It was near where I'd grown up. It was where I last saw Hisashi.

I closed my eyes and let my mind travel over the hills and down the river to Sinuiju. My mind walked through the city park and past the houses. I came to the gate of the Saito house. There in front of me was the beautiful house with its white plaster walls and blue roof. I saw Young-chul on the veranda. He was a toddler now, playing with a ball. Kiyo stood behind him, watching. I reached for my son, but he didn't see me. I wanted to call to him, but I couldn't bring up the words.

"Suk-bo," someone said.

I snapped out of my daydream and opened my eyes. There above me was Byong-woo. "Yes?" I said, shaking away the image of my son.

"Come with me," he said.

It was getting dark and the wind was picking up as I followed Byong-woo to the shelter of some trees away from the rest of the rebels. Commissar Kim was there with Jin-mo and two of their lieutenants. We stopped and waited as the men examined maps and talked. They all nodded. The lieutenants bowed to Il-sung and headed to the rebel camp.

Jin-mo waved for us to come close. Byong-woo and I went to Il-sung. I kept my eyes low.

"Suk-bo," Commissar Kim said, "Byong-woo tells me you have learned how to work with bombs. That is good. We will need you for our next raid."

Jin-mo stood in the shadows behind the commissar and watched me closely. Il-sung continued. "We will strike the Japanese in our homeland tomorrow night. In the morning, you will cross the Yalu River with the fighting men, where we will strike an army compound. We need you to sneak around to the opposite side and set off a bomb to create a diversion. If you can do it so it kills Japanese, all the better. When the bomb goes off, we will attack. If all goes as planned, we will kill many Japanese."

I kept my head bowed but felt the eyes of the others on me. A gust of wind swept through the gathering.

"Of course," Commissar Kim continued, "if the bomb does not go off, we will not have an advantage. And then, many of our comrades will be killed."

Commissar Kim crossed his arms over his chest. "What we are asking you to do is dangerous. There is a chance you will be captured or killed. But you will do it, Suk-bo. I remind you that we still have your son. It would be tragic for the boy if you betrayed us."

Jin-mo came forward and nodded at Byong-woo. "Byong-woo will help you with the bomb, but we will need him with us," he said. "One of the men will guide you to where you need to go. You will have to manage the final stage on your own."

"The final stage?" I said.

"Getting back without getting killed or caught," Byong-woo said.

I didn't want to do what they were asking me to do. I didn't want to kill anyone, even Japanese soldiers. But I had no choice. They had Young-chul and they had me. "I understand," I said. "I will do my best."

That night inside the truck as the wind howled, I couldn't fall asleep. I could tell Byong-woo wasn't sleeping, either.

I said, "Will we make the bomb in the morning?"

"I have already made it," Byong-woo answered. "It is a big one."

"I'm afraid," I said.

"It is normal to be afraid before a battle."

"What should I do if they capture me?"

"There is nothing you can do. They will torture you for answers about us. You should resist, but you will not be able to for long. By the time you give in, we will be far away."

"Will they kill me?"

"If they capture you, yes. But"—Byong-woo moved himself so our faces were close—"they won't. Listen to me, Suk-bo, and listen well. After you light the fuse, run to the river as fast as you can. When you get there, go downstream. Do not rejoin the fighting men or go back to camp. If you do, they will kill you."

"Our own people will kill me? I don't understand. Why?"

"Just do as I say. You will be on the Korean side of the river. Only move at night. In three days, you will come to a town called Wiwon. Find a fisherman named Xu-han. Tell him you are my wife. He will help you."

"He will help me do what?"

"What you do then is up to you, Suk-bo. Just remember what I did for you."

"What is happening, Byong-woo? Why are you telling me this?"

He leaned in, and in the dark, I saw his face clearly. For the first time, I saw compassion in his eyes. "I am saving you again, Suk-bo," he said. "Now, stop asking questions and try to get some sleep." He rolled away from me and curled up behind the steering wheel.

I pulled my blanket to my chin and tried to understand why Byong-woo wanted me to escape from the rebels after I set off the bomb. I could not think of a reason. If I did my job creating a diversion, surely Il-sung and Jin-mo would be pleased with me. I would be a hero at camp. The women would accept me and the fighting men would treat me as if I was one of them. The stigma of being married to a Japanese man would be gone. But instead, Byong-woo wanted me to run.

I leaned against Byong-woo and he put an arm around me. He smelled like cigarettes, but I'd grown fond of the smell on him. I usually thought of Hisashi when I lay with him. But for some reason, this time I did not. As the wind howled outside the truck, I reached up and pressed Byong-woo's arm into me.

I didn't sleep that night. I expected that we'd rise before it was light, but the sun was already up when the men outside began to stir. Byong-woo woke with a start. He sniffed and shook himself awake. "We have to go," he said.

Outside, the wind had died, but low dark clouds filled the sky. Byong-woo took me by the shoulders and made me face him. "Remember what I told you last night," he said. "The town of Wiwon. A fisherman named Xu-han." I nodded that I remembered.

We went to where the women had prepared a meal of rice and vegetables. We ate in silence. When we'd finished eating, Jeon-suk brought water to the fighting men, who filled their waterskins. Ki-soo and another woman gave out dried meat and *geonppang* hardtack.

We sat for a while, waiting. Men checked their rifles and then checked them again. Others scratched at the dirt with sticks while still others stared off into the distance. Eventually, Jin-mo said, "It is time to go."

Byong-woo pointed to the back of the truck. "The bomb is in a sack in the truck. Get it and come with me."

I got the sack, heavy with the bomb inside, and we went to where the fighting men had gathered. I remembered the explosion of the small bomb Byong-woo and I had set off, and I wondered what kind of power this bomb would have. I assumed it would be huge and deadly.

Jin-mo addressed the men who had their rifles slung over their shoulders. He gave a briefing of the mission and divided them into two groups. He would lead the frontal assault, he said. Byong-woo would lead a second assault from the side once the Japanese started to advance. Commissar Kim would direct the raid from the rear, and he and a handful of men would guard the retreat.

Then, Il-sung stepped forward. He took several seconds to scan the group of men. Then he said, "We fight for our mothers and fathers and for all who came before us." His voice was powerful and filled with passion. "We fight for our children and our children's children and for all who will come after. We fight for our country." He looked at the gray sky. He nodded. "It looks like it will rain," he said. "That is fitting.

We will rain fury on the Japanese dogs." He looked at the men with fire in his eyes. "Fight today, men, with the courage of the righteous!" The men shook their rifles and nodded eagerly. I glanced at Byong-woo. He wasn't nodding with the others. Instead, he was staring at me.

And then we set off. The men moved quickly, and after several hours of hiking we'd crossed over the hills and looked out over the Yalu River. It was much smaller than it was in Sinuiju. We went to the riverbank and started to cross, the men holding their rifles and ammunition above their heads. The water was cold, and I was afraid that the bomb would get wet. Byong-woo helped me keep the sack above the water. The river came up to my chest, but I was able to wade across without having to swim.

After we'd crossed the river, we were in Korea. At the river's edge, I took a deep breath and filled my lungs. The sweetness of my home flowed through my veins. For the first time since I'd left Sinuiju, everything seemed familiar and safe. I was home.

I didn't have time to savor the feeling. The group quickly climbed the bank and gathered around Jin-mo. "The Japanese camp is less than a mile away," he said. "This is where we split up. My group to the right, Byong-woo's to the left. Commissar Kim and his men will stay here. Keep low. It will be dark soon."

Jin-mo looked at me. "Suk-bo," he said. "Go with this man."

A tall, lanky man named Dae-ho stepped forward. He held his rifle with both hands as if he couldn't wait to use it. He jerked his head, telling me to follow him. I picked up the sack with the bomb and we headed straight as the rest of the men split into two groups.

Dae-ho moved quickly, and I had to run to keep up. We crossed a field and then another. Just as Il-sung had predicted, a cold rain started to fall. The dirt turned to mud, making it hard to walk. We reached a line of trees and Dae-ho held out his hand for me to stop. By then, it was almost dark. The rain made a splattering sound on the mud. Through the rain I saw an open area on the other side of a field and the shape of tents inside. Light from lamps dotted the camp and men moved about.

Dae-ho pointed. "Take your bomb and set it off as close as you can to the camp. Stay low. If they see you, wait until they get close and then set off your bomb. Kill as many of them as you can."

I took the bomb out of the sack. It was a stiff cardboard box and was much bigger than the one I'd set off in the field with Byong-woo. I looked at the fuse. It was short, less than a foot long. I felt inside the sack to see if there was a longer fuse, but there was nothing.

"The fuse is too short," I said.

Dae-ho nodded. "It has to be short so it will burn quickly and the enemy won't see it."

"But I won't be able to get away."

"Most likely you will not," Dae-ho said. He held out a match. "I was ordered to shoot you if you don't light the fuse. I was also told to tell you to remember your son."

I did think of my son, and my shoulders sagged. I realized they'd been planning this all along. Though I'd become Byong-woo's woman and learned how to make bombs, they'd used me just as Jeon-suk said they would. I wasn't ready to die. I'd endured all this time with the rebels, hoping to see Hisashi and Young-chul again someday. I wanted to see my parents' house in the village, too. But it wasn't going to happen. If I didn't do what they said, if I didn't light the short fuse, they would kill me and my son.

I grabbed the match from Dae-ho and glared at him. "Tell Commissar Kim that if he does not keep his promise to take care of Young-chul, I will haunt him for the rest of his life."

"Just light the fuse," Dae-ho said.

I pushed the bomb back into the sack. I walked into the field, keeping my eyes on the tents and men in front of me. A strange calm came over me. As I crossed the field, I thought of Hisashi. It had all started with him. By marrying him, I had invited the curse of the two-headed dragon, and it had led me to this. As I walked through the rain toward the camp, I was at peace. I'd had a great love with Hisashi. We'd had only a short time together, but it was more than I'd had a right to expect. We would never have it again. I'd had to betray my husband with Byong-woo. Perhaps setting off the bomb was the best way for it to end.

Three-quarters of the way across the field, I could see the faces of the Japanese soldiers. I was close enough to hear their voices. I remembered that Il-sung said I should try to set off the bomb so it killed as many soldiers as possible, but I wasn't going to do it. I believed that, like Hisashi, some Japanese were good men. They didn't deserve to die and I wasn't going to kill them. I would set off my bomb away from the camp where it would kill no one except me.

I took the bomb from the sack and set it on the ground. I dropped to my knees. I found a rock to strike the match with. I lit the fuse. I lay in the mud next to the bomb. The rain fell harder, splashing all around me.

As the fuse sparked and hissed, I thought the two-headed dragon would come to laugh at me, but it didn't. There was only the cold, wet mud underneath me and the bright yellow sparks of the fuse. The sparks quickly reached the bomb and I closed my eyes and waited for the explosion. The fuse hissed for a second more, and then it stopped. I opened my eyes and saw it had gone out. I put my finger where the fuse met the bomb. The fuse had burned all the way inside. I remembered Dae-ho said he'd shoot me if he didn't see me light the fuse. Well, I had lit the fuse but the bomb didn't go off. I looked behind me and didn't see Dae-ho. I took the rock and broke open the box. There was no fulminate or black powder inside. There was only sand.

"Byong-woo," I said aloud.

I heard gunfire from the other side of the camp. Soldiers shouted and began to run around. They gathered in small groups with officers pointing the directions they should go. A truck started, then another. A machine gun fired from inside the camp at targets on the other side.

"A town called Wiwon," I said to myself. "A fisherman named Xu-han."

And then I ran. I ran across the muddy field to where I'd left Dae-ho. Rifle fire from the camp grew more intense. The machine gun thundered and there was a loud report from a mortar explosion. A shot rang out from somewhere in front of me. A circle of mud splattered at my feet. Through the rain, I saw a yellow flash. A bullet whistled past my head. It was Dae-ho and he was trying to kill me.

I dodged to my left and ran to the line of trees at the edge of the field, slipping and falling in the mud as I went. I crawled behind a bush and lay on the ground. I heard the sloshing of footsteps approaching, so I pulled my knees to my chest. The footsteps came closer and stopped inches away. I held my breath. The rifle fire from the battle in the camp was constant now. The machine gun never stopped firing. Another mortar lit up the sky. From the mortar's light I saw Dae-ho standing above me with his rifle at his shoulder. He scanned the field for me. As the light faded, he lowered his rifle and turned away, running toward the river.

I stayed where I was, not sure if Dae-ho was still looking for me or if he had gone back to join the rebels. Eventually, the battle was farther away, at the other side of the camp. The rain soaked through my clothes, and I began to shiver.

I lifted my head above the bush. I didn't see Dae-ho. I ran toward the river. Mud clung to my shoes, making it hard to run. I came to the riverbank, where I heard the battle raging upstream. The rebels had retreated. From the sound of the gunfire, the Japanese were not far behind them.

Three days, Byong-woo had said. Downriver. Wiwon. I moved as quickly as I could along the river. In the dark with a hard rain falling, I couldn't see where I was going. Bushes and branches grabbed at my legs. I wasn't making progress so I climbed up the bank. I was drenched and very cold. I found a hollow that gave cover from the rain. I curled up inside it.

I heard the battle far away now and I guessed the rebels were in full retreat. I had not set off the bomb to create a diversion for them and they probably assumed I'd betrayed them. And as I shivered inside the hollow, I prayed that they would not kill my son.

TWENTY-FOUR

Although Byong-woo had told me to travel at night, I couldn't see well in the dark and was constantly tripping and running into branches. I ripped a gash in my leg that looked bad. I hit my head on a branch, raising a lump. I was making little progress, so I decided I had to travel when I could see. I walked high above the riverbank away from the deadfall and trees that hung over the river. I drank rainwater from ditches and dug roots to eat. I watched for Japanese soldiers and the rebels. I thought it was ironic that I was wanted by both.

On the third day, I got dysentery and I had to stop. As cramps racked my stomach, I found a ravine and hid under an overhang. I vomited, but for three days I'd only eaten roots and leaves so all that came up was a stringy, green mass. After a day in the ravine, the dysentery had eased, but I was hungry, cold, and exhausted. The gash in my leg throbbed. Every breath was a chore; every move, painful. I wanted to stay in the ravine. But the rebels were going to put Young-chul on the street. I had to get to Sinuiju to save him. But first, I had to get to Wiwon.

I pulled myself out of the ravine and headed downriver. I crossed over fields and pushed through thickets. I waded across the tributaries.

I was making progress but grew weaker by the hour. I no longer had the energy to watch for the Japanese or the rebels.

Midmorning on the fifth day, I came to a road that ran alongside the river. The Yalu was wide here—twice as wide as where the rebels had crossed. I took the road and soon saw a village. I stood in the road in a daze. I looked at myself. My clothes were rags and my shoes were torn apart. Cuts covered my face and hands. The gash on my leg was hot and red. My hair had pulled out of its braid and hung in strings around my head. I reached up to twist it into a braid again. I did one turn, then two. The world began to spin. I couldn't feel my legs. I hit the ground with a dull thud. Everything went dark.

I awoke to the face of an old man looking at me. Above him was a thatched ceiling like the one in the house I'd grown up in. The man said something, but I couldn't hear him. I turned my head to the side and saw a window and sunshine outside. I heard a voice. I turned to the man. His lips moved and the voice I heard was his. "You," I heard him say. "Now!"

I closed my eyes and concentrated on what he was saying. "Wake up," the man said. "You, wake up now!"

I opened my eyes. "Yes," I said.

The old man grinned a crooked grin. "Good!" he said. He shuffled to an iron stove and poured something into a tea bowl. He brought it to me. "Medicine," he said. "Drink it."

I tried to push myself up, but everything hurt. I lay back down. The man lifted my head and brought the bowl to my lips. "Drink!" he said. I took a sip. The liquid was hot and bitter. I pushed it away. "Drink it all," the man insisted. He lifted the bowl to me again, and I drank everything inside.

He laid my head down. "More in a little while," he said. "Now, you rest." I turned to the side and watched as he took the tea bowl to the stove. His hair was pure white and untied so that it fell down his back. His clothes hung on him as if he'd shrunk since he'd put them on. Though it was winter, he wore sandals instead of shoes.

I was under a blanket, lying on a mat. I wasn't wearing my shoes, and someone had put clean clothes on me. I felt something cool on the gash in my leg. The bump on my head throbbed.

"Where am I?" I asked.

"What?" the old man said.

"Where am I?" I repeated, louder this time. The medicine was starting to wake me.

"I cannot hear you," the man said. He came and dropped to his hands and knees next to me. He pointed his right ear at me. "Shout into my ear," he said.

"WHERE AM I?" I said as loud as I could.

"Ah," the man nodded, "you are a guest of the house of Mr. Wu, in the village of Wiwon," he said proudly. "I am Mr. Wu!"

"How did I get here?"

"What?" The old man leaned his ear to me again, making his white hair fall over his face.

"HOW DID I GET HERE?"

Mr. Wu nodded. "My grandson brought you to my house. He found you lying in the road."

"HOW LONG HAVE I BEEN HERE?"

"Two days," Mr. Wu replied.

Two days. I tried to push myself up again. "Young-chul," I said. "I have to get to Sinuiju!" I got halfway up, then collapsed onto the mat.

"You will not go anywhere," Mr. Wu scolded. "In one hour, you will have more medicine. Then you will eat. I am making fish stew." He pushed himself from the floor and went to the stove.

I dozed for a while and then Mr. Wu gave me more medicine. Though I was still weak, I was able to sit up. I saw that someone had put leaves on the gash in my leg and covered it with a cloth. It still hurt, but it itched, too, and I could tell it was healing. Mr. Wu brought me a bowl and chopsticks. Inside the bowl was a hot milky stew. The aroma was heady. "Eat," he said.

With the chopsticks, I picked up a piece of fish and ate it. It tasted wonderful. I took another bite of fish and then carrots and onion. I lifted the bowl to my mouth and sucked in the broth. I hadn't had food this good since I'd left the Saito house.

"More?" Mr. Wu asked.

I nodded, and he took my bowl to the stove and filled it. I ate the second bowl and set it next to me. The hot stew warmed me and I felt better.

"Thank you," I said with a bow of my head.

"The medicine will heal you," he said, taking my bowl. "The stew will make you strong."

He put the bowl in the wash bucket and came and sat in front of me. "Who are you?" he asked. "Who is Young-chul?" He turned his ear toward me.

"I am Suk-bo," I said, remembering to talk loudly. "Young-chul is my son."

"Where do you come from?" He turned his ear to me again.

My mind was clearing and I remembered that I was wanted by the rebels as well as the Japanese. I didn't know who this man was. Wu was a Chinese name, so he might be a Chinese rebel or he might be a spy for the Japanese.

"I come from Sinuiju," I shouted into his ear. "I am looking for a fisherman named Xu-han."

Mr. Wu threw his head back and laughed. "Xu-han is my grandson! Why do you want Xu-han?"

"I am married to Byong-woo," I replied.

Mr. Wu stopped laughing. He pushed himself up and went to the iron stove. "Xu-han will be back tonight," he said sternly.

As he stirred the pot, he shot a look at me from over his shoulder. I could tell he didn't want me in his house. It had to be something about Byong-woo. I knew I didn't have the strength to go to Sinuiju on my own, so I lay down and pulled the blanket over me. I closed my eyes and waited for Xu-han to come home.

Xu-han came as it started to grow dark. I'd slept a little more but was awake and lying on the mat when he arrived. Mr. Wu sat in the room cross-legged, repairing my shoes with a thick needle and thread.

Xu-han was tall and had the lean features of someone who worked hard. He had his hair pulled into a topknot. He wore a dark coat and pants that stopped just over his knees. He took off his boots and walked through the house barefoot. He carried a straw basket that he dropped next to the stove.

"She is awake, *Zuzu*," he shouted to the old man. I was surprised he used the Chinese word for grandfather.

Mr. Wu pushed his needle into the sole of one of my shoes. "She is looking for you," he said. "She is Byong-woo's wife."

"You are Byong-woo's wife?" Xu-han asked.

I sat up and faced him. "We were together," I answered, "but we are not married. How do you know Byong-woo?"

"Byong-woo is my cousin, my *sachon* on my mother's side."

"Byong-woo is Korean," I said, "but your name is both Korean and Chinese. Your grandfather is Chinese."

"Yes. My grandfather married a Korean woman. I am one-quarter Chinese. So is Byong-woo."

"He is?" I said, thinking it was ironic that he'd criticized me for marrying a Japanese man.

"Are you a rebel?" Xu-han asked.

"I lived with the rebels," I said. "Byong-woo took me to them."

Mr. Wu looked up from his work. "I do not want trouble with the Japanese," he said. "Or the rebels."

"You hate the Japanese," Xu-han shouted at the old man, "and now you hate the rebels, too."

"All of this fighting," Mr. Wu said. "It is foolish. People killing each other for no reason. When will it stop? When will there be peace? Yes, I hate people who make war in my country." The old man started working on my shoe again.

"I brought home fish, Zuzu," Xu-han shouted. "You should clean them before they spoil."

Mr. Wu grunted and set down my shoe. He went to the stove and picked up the basket Xu-han had brought in. He got a knife from next to the stove and went to the back of the house.

Xu-han came and sat in front of me. He nodded to where his grandfather had gone. "He cannot hear with his ears," he said with a head shake, "but he hears just fine with his eyes. He worries about me. I am all he has left."

Xu-han stared at me. "Tell me, were you with the rebels that attacked the Japanese camp north of here?"

I nodded. "Yes."

"Was Byong-woo with them?"

"Yes, he was."

"That is not good," Xu-han said. "We have heard reports. The Japanese built up their army for a push to wipe out the rebels in Manchuria. Your group underestimated the size of the encampment they attacked. They were routed. Only a few managed to escape."

I looked at my hands. I thought of all those who I'd known over the past two and a half years. Jeon-suk, Ki-soo, Jin-mo, Byong-woo. If only a few escaped, they killed or captured the rest. I felt guilty for having deserted them. Then again, I never really was one of them. They'd used me and threatened to hurt Young-chul.

"Byong-woo said you would help me," I said. "I must go to Sinuiju as soon as possible."

Xu-han shook his head. "That is risky. It is a difficult time. The Japanese have become more aggressive. They have taken nearly all of China and they think they are invincible. There is talk they will attack America soon. If they defeat the Americans, no one will stop them and they will do whatever they want to us."

Xu-han let what he said sink in. Then, he asked, "Why do you want to go to Sinuiju?"

"My son is there."

"Your son? I did not know that Byong-woo had a son."

"He is not Byong-woo's son."

"You had a son with someone else?"

I didn't know what I should say about marrying a Japanese man. I thought Xu-han would throw me out of his house. But he was both Korean and Chinese. Surely, he would understand. "I was forced to marry a Japanese man. We had a son together. I had to leave him in Sinuiju."

"I see," Xu-han said. "I will take you. We will have to go at night. Rest tomorrow. We will leave after dark. Your leg should be better by then."

"Thank you," I said.

"Do not leave the house until we leave. No one should see you. We can trust no one."

"Yes, sir," I said with a bow of my head.

That night, I slept in the main room while Xu-han and his grandfather slept in the sleeping room. I awoke from a vision of Hisashi, troubled as he was when I last saw him. I was shaken and couldn't go to sleep again. The snoring in the other room was impressive as

I got up, wrapped myself in a blanket, and went to the door. My leg felt better as I stepped into the front garden and looked at the stars. They were like a sea of twinkling lights. I thought of a song Mother sang to me about stars when I was a little girl. I tried to remember the words. I hummed the melody and the story came back. It was about Cheonjiwang, the Celestial King, who came to earth and married a human woman, Bujiwang. They had twin sons named Sobyeolwang and Daebyeolwang, who were the Big Star King and the Small Star King. The brothers had a riddle contest to decide who would rule the human world. Sobyeolwang won, and an angry Daebyeolwang became the ruler of the underworld. Together, the brothers represented good and evil. I tried to find the stars Mother had said were Sobyeolwang and Daebyeolwang, but I didn't remember which ones they were.

I thought about the war against the Japanese. Were they evil like Daebyeolwang? It certainly seemed they were. But Hisashi wasn't evil. Yet even he had followed the Japanese leaders. He was an officer in their army. He was complicit in their evil. For the first time since I met him, I was angry at him. He'd abandoned me and our son to fight for the Japanese. Perhaps it was true that all Japanese were evil.

I went back to bed and awoke the next morning to Mr. Wu and Xu-han arguing. I lay on my mat, pretending to sleep, and listened.

"It is unsafe," Mr. Wu said.

"You worry about me too much, Zuzu," Xu-han countered.

"They killed your mother and father."

"The Japanese didn't kill them. They drowned."

"They drowned because they were trying to escape to China."

"I don't want to argue about them again," Xu-han said. "We need to decide what to do."

"I have mended her shoes," Mr. Wu said. "We will get her some clothes. We can give her dried fish and a waterskin. She made it here on her own. She can make it to Sinuiju on her own, too."

"She would have to go by land. They are building the dam at Sup'ung so she can't follow the river. If she goes by road, they will stop her and ask questions. I can take her where we will not get stopped."

"You are reckless, Xu-han. You cannot know they will not stop you. And if they catch you smuggling a rebel, they will arrest you."

There was silence for a while. Finally, Mr. Wu spoke up. "She can go through China to Dandong. I can take her. It is less risky in China and I have family and friends there. They are not as likely to stop an old man and a woman."

"Yes, that might work, Zuzu. I can take you across the river in my boat. Yes, that is what we will do."

"And if they catch me and shoot me," Mr. Wu said, "well, I am an old man."

That night, the three of us left after dark. It was cold and perfectly still. I followed Xu-han and Mr. Wu to the river where we climbed into Xu-han's fishing boat, a narrow Japanese *amibune* with a long square bow. Nets and buoys that smelled like fish lay in the bow. I sat on the nets, and Mr. Wu sat cross-legged in the middle as Xu-han worked a pole attached to the rudder. With a few expert strokes by Xu-han, we were in the current and soon reached the opposite shore in China. I jumped out of the boat onto the shore. Xu-han carried his grandfather on his back and set him down on shore. He handed us both rucksacks.

"Four days to Dandong and four days back," Mr. Wu said. "Although, I will want to stop and visit friends on the way back. Then, who knows how long it will be?"

"Do not take too long, Zuzu, or I will become a worrier like you," Xu-han replied. "And the worst of winter is yet to come. You won't be able to travel when the rivers freeze."

Xu-han faced me. "My grandfather can take you to Dandong. To get to Sinuiju, you will have to cross the bridge. I am sorry. That is all we can do. Please, if they catch you, do not tell them about us. Good luck, Suk-bo."

"I promise I will say nothing about you," I replied. "Thank you."

Xu-han climbed into his boat, pushed off, and disappeared into the blackness of the river.

"This way," Mr. Wu said. We shouldered our rucksacks and climbed up the bank and onto a path. As we started walking, I felt almost normal again. My head no longer hurt where I'd bumped it, and the gash on my leg was healing. Xu-han had found clothes for me—a chima skirt and loose *jeogori* blouse both made from coarse wool. Mr. Wu had done a good job fixing my shoes. Before we'd left, I'd bathed in the washbasin behind Mr. Wu's house and tied my hair into a braid.

We walked on the path for an hour in the dark, and then Mr. Wu led me over a hill to a shack. He went inside and stuck his head out. "We will rest here for the night and start again in the morning. Come."

I went inside where it was dark and musty. The floor was dirt. I'd expected that we would travel all night, but Mr. Wu curled up in the corner and soon, he was snoring loudly. I lay down too, but I didn't sleep.

Mr. Wu slept until well after the sun was up. I thought about waking him but decided against it. He awoke with a lazy yawn and sat up. His long white hair fell over his shoulders. "We need tea," he said.

"Shouldn't we be going?" I shouted into his good ear.

"Yes, we should. First, tea." He went outside and gathered some dried grass and sticks and brought them to the side of the shack. From his rucksack, he took a tin cup and a pinch of tea. He poured water into the cup from his waterskin, tossed in the tea, and set it on the sticks and grass, then started a fire with a match.

"Aren't you going to have tea, too?" he asked, warming his hands over the fire.

I sighed. I wanted to get going, but apparently we were going to have tea first. "Okay," I said with a shrug. I took my cup and made tea alongside Mr. Wu.

After the tea brewed, we sat against the shack and drank. Mr. Wu sipped his tea and looked like he might take all day to finish it. He looked out over the hill and nodded as if he was pleased to be in China again.

Finally, I asked, "Why did you agree to take me to Dandong? You said you didn't want trouble with the Japanese or the rebels."

"Xu-han tells me you want to get to Sinuiju because your son is there," he answered. "He said you married a Japanese man."

"I was forced to marry him," I said. "His mother did not like me and tried to have me arrested. That is why I escaped with Byong-woo. I had to leave my son there. I have to get back to him."

"Why didn't your mother-in-law like you?"

"Because I am Korean."

"Ah, yes," Mr. Wu said. "I married a Korean woman, too. Of course, it was not the same as marrying a Japanese. Still, I understand what it is like to wed someone outside of your people."

"Did you love your wife?"

"Oh, yes," Mr. Wu said, looking into his cup. "Very much. Her name was Jun-li. We were happy, although my mother did not like her very much."

"What about your wife's mother?" I asked. "Did she like you?"

"Ha!" Mr. Wu laughed. "Not at all. She thought I was smug, wanting to marry a Korean woman. It was only because my family had money that they agreed to the marriage. However, it would not have mattered if they had said no. Jun-li and I loved each other, and that is all that mattered. People are prejudiced because they do not know we are all small parts of the same spirit. The spirit is in everyone and in all things—the mountains, the sea, the birds, and the fish. It does not matter where someone was born or what they look like or what language they speak. They are us and we are them."

I sensed that what Mr. Wu was saying was true. It did not matter that Hisashi was Japanese and I was Korean. We had shared something. We had connected. Perhaps we'd touched through the spirit Mr. Wu was speaking of.

I looked at Mr. Wu and smiled to myself. Here was someone who understood my situation with Hisashi. And if there was one person like Mr. Wu, there must be others: married women and men from different races and clans like Mr. Wu and his wife, Korean women who fell in love with Japanese men. For the first time since I'd fallen in love with Hisashi and faced the scorn of both Koreans and Japanese, I didn't feel so alone.

Mr. Wu pointed his chin at me. "What about you? Do you love your husband, the man they forced you to marry?"

I nodded. "I do. His name is Hisashi. But I am angry at him for leaving me."

Mr. Wu nodded with me. "Yes, love is difficult. And that is why I agreed to take you to Dandong."

We'd finished our tea and Mr. Wu declared it was time to go. We shouldered our rucksacks and found the road again. And then we set off for Dandong.

TWENTY-FIVE

It took us four days to get to Dandong, just as Mr. Wu said it would. At the Hun River, a large tributary to the Yalu, we had to use a ferry. Mr. Wu did his best to talk the oarsman out of charging us his fee by making up a story about how I, his granddaughter, was taking him to the hospital in Dandong because he had only a few days to live without medicine. But the oarsman was unmoved and Mr. Wu grudgingly paid him. All the way across the river, Mr. Wu berated the poor oarsman for being unsympathetic to a dying old man.

We saw Japanese soldiers only once—a troop truck going north that forced us to jump into the ditch. I was afraid they were going to stop and ask questions. But they seemed to be in a hurry and just kept going.

We spent a night at the house of Mr. Wu's cousin. The man was as deaf as Mr. Wu, and his wife was petite and shy. Mr. Wu's cousin didn't seem pleased to see Mr. Wu, although he agreed to feed us and put us up for the night. We left in the morning without saying goodbye.

Despite his age and small size, Mr. Wu was a strong walker. I was still a little weak and had to push myself to keep pace. But I was determined to get to Dandong and find a way across the bridge to Sinuiju.

We came to Dandong in the afternoon of the fourth day. The city teemed with people all going somewhere. Mr. Wu bragged about how much more beautiful the Chinese city of Dandong was than the unpleasant Korean city of Sinuiju. He pointed out the Great Wall in the hills above the city. "It begins here and goes all the way across China," he said. "Imagine that! A wall two thousand miles long. The Chinese are extraordinary people indeed!"

I'd heard of the wall the Chinese built to keep out invaders from the north. But though I'd grown up less than thirty miles away, I'd never seen it. Now, looking at it as it snaked through the mountains, with its gray brick walls and pagoda towers, I had to admit that it was impressive. And it was true that Dandong, with its brick buildings and wide boulevards, was a beautiful city.

Mr. Wu said goodbye outside the city center. He gave me some Chinese yuan. "I do not have yen," he said. "These yuan are only good here, in China. They will do you no good in Korea. There is enough for a few days." He pointed to the river. "On the other side of the river is Sinuiju. They guard the bridge, so you must find a way to get across."

I bowed to him. "Thank you, Zuzu, for helping me," I said. "I am most grateful."

Mr. Wu nodded to me. "Take care, Suk-bo. I hope you find your husband. True love is a rare treasure. Goodbye."

Mr. Wu walked away and I was alone in Dandong. I had no idea how I would get to Sinuiju. I walked through the city center and to the Yalu River. There before me was the bridge Hisashi had shown me years earlier. It seemed like a lifetime ago. I looked across the river. I saw the train station and where Hisashi and I rode our bicycles. I saw the building where the brothel was.

Kempei tai soldiers in wool coats guarded the entry to the bridge, inspecting each person as they went by. I watched as they pulled a man from the procession. The man kept his head low as the soldiers stood over him, asking questions. Suddenly, one of the soldiers grabbed the man by the arm and marched him toward a building that flew a Japanese flag. The people crossing the bridge pretended not to notice as the man pleaded with the soldier to let him go.

I had an idea. I took the yuan Mr. Wu had given me and counted it. It wasn't much, but perhaps it was enough. I went to the city center and walked along the main street full of people going here and there. I looked at the shops and businesses. I spotted an apothecary and went inside. Behind the counter, a Chinese man with a long beard and round glasses inspected me.

"What do you want?" he asked.

"Excuse me, sir. Do you sell makeup here?"

"Why do you want makeup? It is not for women like you."

"Please, sir," I said. "I have money."

"If you want," he said, giving me a look through his glasses. He pointed to a shelf against a wall. "Over there."

Jars and bottles of makeup and perfume sat on the shelf. I tried to remember what the women in the brothel wore in the pictures that the blacksmith's daughter, Soo-sung, had shown me years earlier. White powdered face. Lips painted red. Highlighted eyes.

I took a jar of powder and red lip paint to the man. "I want to buy these," I said.

"Twelve yuan," he said.

Mr. Wu had only given me eight yuan. I asked, "How much for just the lip paint?"

"Five yuan," he answered.

"What can I buy for three more yuan?"

"An eye pencil," he said. "Prostitutes use it to highlight their eyes."

I picked up an eye pencil and took it to the counter. I gave him my money and left the store. I went to a side street away from the crowd. I looked at my reflection in a window. I hadn't seen myself in years, and I was shocked at how old I looked. I was no longer a girl. I was thin, and my clothes were dirty from four days of walking. My shoes were muddy. I ducked into an alley and took off my jeogori blouse. I brushed the dirt off as best as I could and shook it out. I put it back on and did the same with my chima skirt. I wiped the mud from my shoes. I went to the window. I applied the paint to my lips and used the pencil to highlight my eyes. I dipped my finger in the red and rubbed it into my cheeks. I stepped back and looked at myself. I wasn't nearly as made up as the women I'd seen in Soo-sung's picture. But hopefully, it was good enough.

I went to the main street. I turned toward the Yalu River. People stared at me as I walked past. I wondered if I'd put on too much lip paint. I kept my head low.

I got to the bridge, to the line of people waiting to cross. The woman in front of me glanced at me and shook her head. The line moved forward, so that I was seven people from the front, then four. I was close to the Kempei tai guards wearing their white armbands with the red Japanese character. They inspected each person as they came to the front of the line. They asked questions. Then it was my turn to face the guards.

"I have not seen you before," a guard said, examining me. "Who are you and why do you want to go to Sinuiju?"

"My name is Miyoko," I said, bowing and remembering to use my Japanese name. "I was told I could find work in Sinuiju."

"What kind of work are you looking for?" the guard asked.

"I want to work in the brothel," I said.

"Ha!" the guard laughed. "Is that why you painted your face? Well, I hope they will hire you. If they do, I will be sure to visit." He leered at me for a second, and then said with a nod, "You may cross."

The bridge's ironwork curved above my head, and the giant concrete piers rose from the river below as I walked across the bridge. Trucks rumbled along the roadway, making the bridge shake. The walkway was high above the brown water of the river. It hurt my stomach to look down, so I kept my eyes on the person in front of me. I prayed I wouldn't see anyone I knew.

Before I got to the other side, I wiped off the lip paint and eye pencil on my sleeve. I ran my hand over my lips to make sure I'd gotten it all off. I reached the end of the bridge and stepped onto the dock. I had made it to Sinuiju.

The town was much the same as when I'd been here before with Hisashi. There were fewer people here than in Dandong. Fishermen worked on their nets, and crews on boats unloaded cargo. Downriver the brothel was guarded by the Kempei tai soldiers.

I walked upriver to the park where Hisashi had bought the red scarf for me. I looked from side to side, afraid that someone I knew might see me. I quickly walked through the park and into the part of town with houses. I tried to remember which way it was to the Saito house. I turned a corner, then another. I saw a house I recognized. I walked a block farther, where I recognized more houses. I was in the right part of town.

I was out of breath as I came to the street where the Saito house was. I only thought of Young-chul. He would be three years old now. He wouldn't remember me, but I had to see that he was all right. I needed to be careful. If Mr. or Mrs. Saito spotted me, or Haru or Yoshiko or Kiyo, they would call the police and have me arrested.

Two houses down was the huge Saito house surrounded by the chest-high wall. The blue roof hung above the white plaster walls like blue sky over white sand. I snuck up to the wall and crouched low so only my head was exposed. I scanned the grounds. They had covered the vegetable garden with straw for the winter. They had raked the Zen garden. As always, everything was square, neat, and clean.

It was quiet in the compound. The gardeners were gone and Mr. Saito was not sitting in the Zen garden. There was no one on the veranda. It was almost as if they'd abandoned the house. I thought about climbing over the wall, going to the house, and looking in. But it would be too risky. If someone was there, they would catch me. So I sat on the ground below the wall and tried to think of what I should do. I hadn't known anyone in Sinuiju other than the friends of the Saitos. If I went home to my village, my parents wouldn't be there. Perhaps the blacksmith, Mr. Kwan, would take me in. I thought of my aunt and uncle who lived up the road from us. I could go there. But it would take hours and there was no guarantee they would still be there. Anyway, I just wanted to see my son.

I heard voices coming from the house and lifted my head above the wall. Yoshiko, her hair up and wearing her white kimono, stood on the veranda. At her side, holding her hand, was a young boy, three years old. He wore a blue kimono and his hair was in a topknot.

It was my little prince, my son, Young-chul. My heart broke when I saw him. Tears welled in my eyes. I stifled a cry. My son was so handsome in his kimono. He looked like a little man—a three-year-old copy of Hisashi. And he was alive! The rebels had not put him on the street as they'd threatened to do. He looked healthy and happy, just as I'd prayed he would be. I wanted to jump over the wall and sweep him into my arms. I wanted to tell him I was back and I'd never leave him again. I wanted to hug him, kiss him, and tell him how much I loved him.

Through my tears, I saw him hug Yoshiko's leg. She put her hand on his head and smiled down at him. He held on to her for a second, then held her hand again. They casually strolled along the veranda.

My son had bonded with Yoshiko. My joy at seeing Young-chul turned to anger at Yoshiko for taking my place. I should be the one my little prince hugged. I should be the one whose hand he held. She had stolen him from me, and I hated her for it.

I rose from behind the wall and glared at Yoshiko. I wanted to scream at her for what she'd done. Then, she looked out from the veranda, and our eyes met. She froze for a second, then said something to Young-chul. He ran inside the house.

She'd seen me, and soon the police would be after me. I ran down the street past the houses and into the park. People strolling on the pathways stared as I ran, and I realized I was making a scene. I stopped running and walked. I didn't hear sirens or see the police. I was exposed, so I had to go somewhere to hide. But where? There was the train station, but there would be too many people there. I came to the dock, but there was no place to hide. I saw two women wearing makeup and dressed in kimonos heading toward the brothel. I ran to them before they reached the guards.

"Please," I said. "I need help."

The taller one said, "Why do you need help?"

"I need a place to hide," I answered.

The shorter one stepped forward. "Hello, Miyoko," she said coolly.

It was Kiyo. I barely recognized her in her makeup and fancy kimono. In place of the delicate prettiness she'd had before, her face showed a hardness.

"Kiyo!" I exclaimed. "You are a Korean. Help me."

She sneered. "Help you? You who married a Japanese? A chinilpa?"

She grabbed my arm, and over her shoulder she said, "Guards! Here is someone you have been looking for."

"No, Kiyo," I begged, trying to pull away. "Please."

Kiyo held me firm, and the guards came before I could break free.

"Who is this?" one of the guards asked.

"She is Miyoko Saito," Kiyo said, still holding my arm. "She is the daughter-in-law of Director-General Saito. She escaped two years ago after she betrayed the director-general's son."

"Are you Miyoko Saito?" the guard asked. Anger welled inside me. I had endured life in the rebel camp for two years. I had escaped their treacherous plot to kill me. I had made it to Sinuiju and I had seen my son. And now, they'd caught me.

"I am Suk-bo Yi," I answered, staring at Kiyo.

"What is your Japanese name?" the guard demanded.

"I am Hisashi Saito's wife," I said defiantly. "I am not a rebel and I am not a chinilpa. I don't care about any of that. I just wanted to see my son."

"Come with me," the guard said, taking my arm from Kiyo. "You need to go to the police station so we can learn who you really are."

As the guard led me away, Kiyo said, "Goodbye, Miyoko." Then she turned and headed to the brothel.

It was the same police station Mother and I had walked to before I met Mr. and Mrs. Saito for the first time. The Kempei tai soldier never let go of my arm. When we got inside, he had me sit on the floor against a wall while he talked to a desk clerk. The clerk glared at me, then went into an office. A few seconds later, he came out with a fat police sergeant. It was Sergeant Yamamoto, the same man who had escorted me to the Saito house that first day.

"It *is* you!" the sergeant said when he saw me. "Guard," he said to the Kempei tai soldier, "take her to the interrogation room."

They took me to a windowless room with a three-legged stool and a chair against a wall. The Kempei tai guard told me to sit on the stool, which was so short that when I sat, my knees came to my chest. The guard brought the chair to the door and sat.

We stayed there for quite a long time—the guard leering at me every so often—until finally, the door opened and a short, slim man in a suit came in carrying a bowler hat. He nodded for the guard to leave, then sat down. He had a light mustache over thin lips that curled up ever so slightly at the corners. His eyes were close set over a pointed nose.

"I am Major Ito," he said, reaching into his jacket pocket. He took out a pack of American cigarettes and took one out. He brought it to his lips and lit it with a match. "I am Kempei tai. You are Miyoko Saito. Your Korean name was Suk-bo Yi. Correct?"

"Yes, sir," I said. I was terrified. I remembered what I'd heard about how the Kempei tai tortured people. I thought it was all an exaggeration, and that even if it were true, it would never affect me. But here I was, being interrogated by a Kempei tai major. My legs started shaking and it was difficult to breathe.

The major took a long draw on his cigarette and blew the smoke toward the ceiling. "You escaped two years ago with a known rebel, Byong-woo Chung, whose Japanese name was Isamu. Correct?"

"He forced me to go with him, sir. I did not want to leave my son."

"You mean, Byong-woo's son. He is the boy's father, correct?"

"No, sir. Hisashi Saito is the father."

Major Ito flicked ash from his cigarette onto the floor. "We have information that says otherwise. Have you ever had sex with Byong-woo?"

"No, sir," I said. "I mean, not before then."

"Oh, but you have since then? So, you had sex with him after you escaped and you expect us to believe that you were not romantically involved before? Then why is your child one hundred percent Korean? We have a report from a Doctor Suzuki . . ."

"It's not true!" I cried. "It was a plot by Mrs. Saito. Young-chul is Hisashi's son!"

"If he was Hisashi's son, why did you run off with the rebels?" The major took another puff from his cigarette.

"I told you. Byong-woo . . . Isamu forced me to go with him."

"I see," the major said. "What did you do for the rebels while you were with them?"

"I mostly fetched water, sir," I replied.

"Water? Hmm. Did you do anything else?"

I knew I couldn't tell him about making bombs with Byong-woo, even though I'd never made a bomb that hurt anyone. Yes, I had lived with the rebels, but I was never truly one of them. They had used me and I had escaped from them just as I'd escaped from the Japanese. But how could I make the major understand? It was best if I said nothing.

"I just fetched water, sir," I said.

Major Ito shook his head. "I do not believe you are entirely forthcoming in your answers, Miyoko Saito. And we have questions about where you were with the rebels, who their leader was, their planning, etcetera, etcetera. However, we will have to continue in another place. Somewhere more . . . quiet." He snuffed out his cigarette on the bottom of his shoe. He picked up his bowler hat from the floor. He stood and opened the door.

"Sergeant," he said, "have the prisoner transported to our interrogation post outside of town at once. I will meet her there."

He faced me. "I will see you in a little while, Miyoko Saito. Until then, you should think about how you will answer my questions."

I stood from the stool. "Please, sir," I cried. "I am telling the truth!"

"Well, before the sun rises, we will have the truth from you." His eyes narrowed, and the corners of his mouth turned up. He put on his hat.

Sergeant Yamamoto stepped into the doorway. "Sir," he said, "there is a problem."

"A problem?" the major asked. "What kind of problem?"

The sergeant glanced at me, then looked at the major. The major stepped out and closed the door behind him.

I heard talking on the other side of the door. It was low at first, then it grew louder. The major started shouting. "I do not care!" I heard him say. The sergeant said something in reply, but I couldn't hear.

"This will not stand!" the major said. I heard him stomp away.

A few minutes later, Sergeant Yamamoto came in. "Someone is here for you," he said.

I quickly followed him out of the room to the lobby. There, waiting at the desk, was Yoshiko, dressed in her white kimono. When she saw me, she held out her hand. "Come with me, Miyoko," she said.

I took her hand and followed her outside. Night had settled in and it was dark. There, in front of the police station was Mr. Saito's black car. "Get in the back," Yoshiko ordered. I did, and she climbed behind the steering wheel. She started the car and put it in gear. She pointed the car toward the Saito house.

"What is happening?" I asked.

"I am taking you to the house."

"But Mrs. Saito will have me arrested again!"

"She and Mr. Saito are in Tokyo," Yoshiko replied as we turned a corner. "They will not be coming back."

"But how did you get the police to let me go?"

"I made a call to Mr. Saito in Tokyo. He is still the director-general here in Sinuiju, although not for much longer, I'm afraid. I convinced him to set you free."

"How did you do that?"

"Well, you see, Miyoko," Yoshiko said, looking at me in the rear-view mirror, "Mr. Saito is my father."

TWENTY-SIX

Yoshiko pulled the car to the courtyard and led me through the front door. I expected to see Haru, but no one greeted us. We stepped through the entryway and into the main room. Yoshiko bowed and gave me a look that told me I should bow, too. "This is still a Shinto household," she said. I bowed to the room as I'd done when I lived there.

It felt strange to be back in the beautiful house with the shoji sliding walls, low ebony table, and tatami mats covering the floor. Though it was strange, it was comforting, too. It was a place I'd been happy.

"Fumiko!" Yoshiko said. "Come at once."

A second later, Fumiko, looking thinner and more gangly than the last time I saw her, came in and bowed. When she saw me, her mouth opened.

"Prepare Miyoko's room," Yoshiko said.

"Yes, ma'am," Fumiko replied. "Which one?"

"Her room. The one she had with her husband. And have Ai make tea."

"Yes, ma'am," Fumiko said with a bow. She gave me a quick smile as she left.

Yoshiko motioned to the ebony table. "Sit," she said. "We must talk."

"I would like to see my son first," I said. "Please?"

Yoshiko nodded. "Of course."

As she led me to the room, she said, "He is sleeping, and we must not wake him. He will be confused about who you are and won't go back to sleep. You can see him for only a minute."

She slid open the door to a room. There on the mat was a small lump covered with a blanket. I went to him. They had taken out his topknot, and his black hair was a tangle. His face was perfectly proportioned. Under the blanket, his body was lithe and athletic. He was perfect.

I had prayed for this moment, but I'd never dared believe it would come. And now that I was inches away from my little prince, tears of joy ran down my cheeks. All the suffering I'd endured with the rebels and the hardship of getting to Sinuiju faded from my memory. I'd have endured a thousand times as much for this one moment of joy. I wanted to wake him and tell him I'd returned. But Yoshiko was right: it would only confuse him, so I held back. Through my tears, I looked at Yoshiko. All the anger I'd had for her for taking my son was gone. "Thank you," I whispered. She returned a simple nod.

I wiped away my tears and we went to the main room. We sat at the ebony table. Fumiko had set out tea that Yoshiko poured into two bowls.

"I'm sure you have many questions," Yoshiko said, cupping her tea bowl. "In time, your questions will be answered."

As we sipped our tea, Yoshiko told me that her mother had died when she was young. Her father, Mr. Saito, was destined for high government office. "Governor-general of Korea," she said. "Maybe Japan's prime minister someday." But he needed a wife to fulfill his political ambitions, so he married the current Mrs. Saito when Yoshiko was just five years old. They had Hisashi two years later.

"Because I was a daughter from a previous marriage," Yoshiko explained, "once they had a son of their own, I was no longer an important part of the new family. My older brother was away in school then, so he was out of the house. Still, my father insisted that I move with them to Sinuiju when the emperor appointed him director-general. Even so, my stepmother insisted that no one knew that I was Mr. Saito's daughter from his first marriage. So I fell into the role of house supervisor and supported my father any way I could."

Yoshiko went on to explain that the government had assigned Haru to be Mr. Saito's assistant in Sinuiju. Haru hired Kiyo and Fumiko. Yoshiko never trusted Haru. "We discovered he was a government spy," Yoshiko said. "He was a snake. He gave reports about my father to the Kempei tai. The military does not like my father. They think he is sympathetic to Korea and China. In time, they moved against him with the help of Haru's reports. They denounced him, effectively ending his career. Haru left shortly after. He is now an officer in the Kempei tai."

"I saw Kiyo," I said. "She's the one who turned me over to the police."

"Yes, Kiyo," Yoshiko said, shaking her head. "She was part of the resistance. Byong-woo was, too, as you know. The fact that they were here in the house put a stain on my father's record. When Haru found out about Kiyo, he gave her the option to go to a prison camp or work in the brothel. She chose the brothel.

"Then, about four months ago, when it became clear that they would remove my father from office, my stepmother went to Tokyo, saying she would never return to Korea. My father stayed here for a month, then he went to be with her."

Yoshiko set her tea bowl on the ebony table and continued. "I stayed to take care of my father's house. We have a reduced staff now. Old Mr. Lee does the gardening work of two men. Ai, the cook, stayed, too. We hire out handiwork and anything else we need."

"What about Fumiko?" I asked. "Byong-woo told me she was in love with Haru."

"She was, but he did not love her. He treated her poorly. And, I should tell you, she cares for your son. She refused to leave after Haru left. She has been a great help."

I nodded. I was thankful that Young-chul had people who cared for him. I was glad I was back in this house.

And then I asked, "What about Hisashi?"

Yoshiko looked into her tea bowl. "He has not come home since you saw him last. As far as we know, he is still in Manchuria. He stopped writing about a year ago. I am sorry, I can tell you nothing more."

She looked at me again. "You should know that I love Hisashi as if he was a full-blooded brother. He and I were close growing up. He always comforted me when Mrs. Saito was cruel. He has a good heart."

"Yes, I know," I said. "I pray that his heart isn't broken."

We were quiet for a while. I thought of my own brother, Kwan-so. The rumor in the rebel camp was that the Japanese were making Korean men join the Imperial Army and putting them on the front lines. I wondered if that had happened to Kwan-so.

Then, Yoshiko said, "We need to talk about Masaru. Kiyo volunteered to take him after you left, but I took him instead. I am his aunt. It was my duty. I have raised him as if he was my own. I must tell you that I love him, and he loves me, too."

"But I am his mother," I complained.

"Yes. I knew there was a chance you would return, but truthfully, I did not think you would. I have thought a lot about what to do if you did."

I was afraid Yoshiko would say that she had to be Young-chul's mother and that I had given up that right when I escaped with Byong-woo. If she did, I wasn't in a position to fight her. She was in charge of the household and she said she loved Young-chul.

"What have you decided?" I asked apprehensively.

"He knows I am his aunt. I could not pretend to be his mother for when . . . if Hisashi came back. How would it be for a child to have his parents be brother and sister?

"But," Yoshiko sighed, "I was raised without a mother. I know how important it is to have one. You gave him life, but I gave him a home. So we will do this. We will both raise him."

I wanted to argue that I was Young-chul's only mother, but I knew Yoshiko was doing a great favor for me. She could have easily let the police take me and continued to raise Young-chul on her own. Now, she was offering to share Young-chul with me. For the first time, I saw Yoshiko clearly. Though she could sometimes be imperious, she had a good heart just like Hisashi and her father. I was certain that she'd been good to Young-chul while I was with the rebels and that she would continue to be. As much as I wanted to have Young-chul to myself, she was right. If Young-chul could not have his Japanese father, perhaps he should have his Japanese aunt.

I bowed my head. "I would be honored to share my son with you. But may I make a request?"

"You may," Yoshiko replied.

"I would like to call him Young-chul, his Korean name."

"That would not be wise with what is happening in Korea today," Yoshiko replied. "And it would confuse him. No, you should not use that name."

"Yes, ma'am," I said.

"Good," Yoshiko said with a nod. "Tomorrow I will introduce you to Masaru. He won't know you and will cling to me. You must accept this. For the time being, we will say you are a friend of his father's. When he has accepted you, we will tell him you are his mother. You should spend time with him, but you must be careful not to push yourself on him. He is sensitive like his father."

"What have you told him about Hisashi?"

"I have told him his father is a brave soldier and we do not know when he will return. I told him that his father loves him and thinks of him every day."

"Yes, that is the right thing to say," I said. "I believe it is true."

We'd finished our tea and I was exhausted from the day's ordeal. My head spun with all Yoshiko had told me. I couldn't wait until the morning when I would start to get to know my son again.

I went to the room where I'd been Hisashi's wife. It was exactly as it'd been before, with its low bed and desk to the side. Fumiko had laid out nightclothes on the sleeping mat for me. I put them on, crawled under the blankets, and was soon fast asleep.

I awoke not sure where I was. I thought I might be in prison or with the rebels or that perhaps the entire ordeal of the past few years had been a nightmare. I think I called out. Soon, a light appeared outside my room. The door slid open and Fumiko, holding a candle and looking awkward in her sleeping clothes, came in.

"Miyoko," she said, "are you all right?"

I shook my head to clear it and remembered where I was. Fumiko had a look of concern on her face. "Yes, Fumiko," I said. "I was not sure where I was. But now I remember."

"It is still early, Miyoko," Fumiko said. "You should sleep some more." She started to leave.

"Fumiko, come. Sit with me," I said, switching from Japanese to Korean.

Fumiko came to my mat. She set the candle on the floor and sat alongside me.

"Tell me about my son," I said. "Tell me about Young-chul."

"Masaru. Young-chul. I forgot that is what you named him," she said in Korean.

"When it is just us, we will call him Young-chul. I remember your name is Jin-ee. Mine is Suk-bo."

"Only when we are alone," Fumiko said. "The Japanese are very strict now."

"Okay. Only when we are alone. So tell me, Jin-ee, what is Young-chul like?"

Fumiko's face lit up. "He is a most wonderful child," she said. "He is full of life, curious about everything. He loves boats. His favorite toy is a boat Yoshiko bought for him. He takes it everywhere. He begs to go to the pond in the city park to play with it. He loves to go to the river and watch the boats."

"Do the Japanese know he is half Korean?"

"Yoshiko is careful not to let people know," Fumiko replied. "She thinks they would treat him poorly if they knew."

"What about the Koreans? Do they know?"

"Since Hisashi is his father," Fumiko replied, "after you left, the cook's assistant and the young gardener treated him as they did all Japanese. I think that is why Yoshiko dismissed them."

"What about you?" I asked.

She looked at me pleadingly. "I love him. I truly do," she said. "It does not matter to me if he is Japanese or Korean. He is a kind and gentle boy."

"Thank you," I said.

We were quiet for a while. Then Fumiko asked, "You will not take Young-chul away, will you?"

"No. I will stay here with him until Hisashi returns."

"Hisashi," she said, looking down again.

"What is it? What can you tell me about my husband?"

Fumiko looked at her hands. "There are rumors that Doctor Ishii is doing evil things in Manchuria."

"Yes," I said. "I have heard the same rumors, but I do not believe them. Hisashi would never do something like that."

"I do not believe he would, either," she said.

She looked up at me. "There are rumors that Japan is going to lose the war. If they do, Korea will be free again."

"Then we can use our real names all the time," I said.

Fumiko smiled, and I saw she was glad to have me back. I was someone she could talk to, and I could talk to her, too. "You need your sleep," she said.

"Yes," I replied. "I am tired. Good night, Jin-ee."

She took the candle and went to the door. "Good night, Suk-bo," she replied.

The next morning, I arose early. Fumiko must have been waiting for me because she came into my room right away with a bath towel and one of my kimonos from when I'd lived there before. "It is a big day for you, Suk-bo," she said. "You will meet your son this morning. I am here to help you prepare. I have poured a bath for you."

I went to the bathing room and washed in the wooden tub. It was glorious to bathe in hot water again, and I would have loved to stay and soak. But I was anxious to meet my little prince, so I scrubbed myself, washed my hair, and put on the kimono. Fumiko was waiting for me when I returned. I sat on my mat with my back to her as she combed out my tangles.

When she finished braiding my hair, she stepped back and examined me. She reached inside her kimono. "I have something for you." She pulled out the silver hairpin that Hisashi had given me. I bit my lower lip.

"When you left, Kiyo took it. But when Haru sent her to the brothel, I took it from her. She was angry, but she did not dare fight me. And now, I am returning it to you."

"Thank you, Jin-ee," I said. "I would like to wear it when I meet my son."

Fumiko nodded. She took the hairpin and put it in my hair. I asked for a hand mirror and she gave me one. It made me sad to see my reflection. While the hairpin was beautiful, I looked completely different than the last time Young-chul had seen me. My hair was coarse, and my skin was dark and rough. I looked much older.

Fumiko must have seen the despair in my face. "You look fine, Suk-bo," she said. "I will ask Yoshiko about getting camellia oil for your hair and aloe for your skin. The household does not have much money for luxuries, but she will agree."

I gave the mirror to her and said, "I want to meet my son now."

She smiled at me and said, "Come with me."

I met Young-chul in the great room. Yoshiko and I were waiting for him at the kami dana altar when Fumiko brought him in. He wore his blue kimono and they'd put his hair into a topknot. Now that I saw him close, the resemblance to Hisashi was amazing. He had his father's sparkling eyes and feminine eyebrows. His skin was light. It was all I could do to not run to him and hug him. As we all washed ourselves, then bowed at the altar, Young-chul eyed me suspiciously.

When we were done, Yoshiko said, "Masaru, you must bow to our guest. Her name is Miyoko. She is a friend of your father."

Young-chul gave me a quick bow and then sidled next to Yoshiko at the ebony table. Fumiko left to fetch our breakfast.

I gathered my composure and said, "I like your topknot, Masaru."

Young-chul pressed his face into Yoshiko's arm. Yoshiko gently pushed him away. "When someone gives you a compliment, you must say thank you."

"I don't want to," Young-chul said.

"Masaru, you must learn to do what is right. Say thank you to Miyoko."

"Thank you," Young-chul said softly.

Fumiko and Ai brought in tea and a breakfast of rice cakes, grilled fish, and vegetables, and set them on the low table. Yoshiko bowed a thank-you to the meal, and I remembered the Shinto tradition of giving thanks. Yoshiko said, "Masaru, you must bow to say thank you to the emperor for our food. Miyoko will bow, too."

I bowed and Young-chul gave a quick bow with me. Yoshiko poured tea and motioned that we should eat. Young-chul watched me carefully as I took some food. Yoshiko gave him a plate of food, which he did not touch.

"Eat your breakfast, Masaru," Yoshiko said.

He didn't eat. He kept glancing at me and turning away when I looked at him. I wondered if somewhere deep inside, he recognized me. He and I had bonded, mother and child, in the short time we'd had together. I had suckled him, played with him, and held him when he cried. Did he remember? I wondered.

"Masaru," I said, picking up a sweet rice cake, "do you like dduk? I like them very much, although I have not had them for a long time."

He studied me for a moment. Then he said, "What is dduk?"

"Oh," I said, realizing that I'd used the Korean word for sweet rice cakes. "I mean mochi. Do you like mochi?"

"I like the ones with honey." He grabbed a rice cake with honey and took a bite.

My heart was filled with happiness. I'd started to reconnect with my son. Yoshiko was right when she said it would take a long time. But it had started, and it felt like the first time I'd seen him, it felt like the day he was born. We would be mother and child again someday, and I could barely contain my joy.

While we ate our breakfast, Young-chul behaved like toddlers do. Yoshiko had to remind him to use his chopsticks. The slightest thing distracted him. He wanted to go to the kami dana altar and play with the ivory carving there. Yoshiko gently instructed him on the proper behavior for a young boy, and he did his best to obey. I saw by her gentle way that Yoshiko was a good mother. And I saw by Young-chul's response that he was sensitive like his father and playful and mischievous like him, too.

As difficult as it was, I heeded Yoshiko's advice and didn't push Young-chul to talk to me. Though I hadn't had a proper meal in years, I didn't care about the rich food or the good tea. I let my heart and soul fill with the joy of being with my son, my little prince, Young-chul.

TWENTY-SEVEN

Over the next several weeks and months, I focused on rebuilding my relationship with Young-chul. Fumiko was right about him. He was bright and curious and full of life. All day he skipped around the house getting into this and that. He asked questions about everything and listened carefully to the answers. He was sensitive, too. When Yoshiko or Fumiko told him he shouldn't do something, he would go quiet as if he was thinking over what he'd done. After a few minutes, he would bound away on another adventure.

Though I desperately wanted Young-chul to love me, I didn't push myself on him. We ate meals together and I'd ask him about what he'd done that day. We talked about insects he saw in the garden. He asked how the clouds stayed in the sky.

And we talked about boats. Fumiko gave me a book on naval history from Mr. Saito's study. I showed the book to Young-chul and read it to him on the veranda. He studied the drawings and memorized the boats' names. He said he wanted to go to England someday to see the tall ships there. I didn't tell him that they made today's warships out of steel and that they had cannons that killed at great distances.

After several months, Young-chul and I had become friends. Yoshiko was still the one he went to when he scraped a knee or when he didn't feel well. She was still the one who put him to bed at night. Yoshiko let me have my time with my son, but it was clear that she was in charge of his upbringing. Though I wanted it to be different, I was thankful for what I had.

During this time, my body began to recover from the difficult years with the rebels. I filled out and my hair regained its luster. The scars on my leg and head receded until I could barely see them. I had fewer nightmares. But as I grew stronger, I worried more about Hisashi. It had been so long since I'd seen him. Everything in the Saito house reminded me of him: the Zen garden where we talked for hours, the big room where we ate our meals, our bed where we made love. Every time I looked at Young-chul I thought of my husband. I missed him terribly and desperately wanted to be with him again. And Young-chul needed a father.

I asked Yoshiko if I could write to him.

"It would not be wise," she answered. "The Kempei tai screen all letters. If they see one from you, it will keep you in their minds. When my father is no longer director-general, it will be difficult for me to keep them from arresting you.

"Anyway," she continued, "it will do no good to write to Hisashi. My father wrote him often, but he did not believe his letters got through. My father was a powerful man so he made inquiries. When I asked him what he had learned about Hisashi, he told me he'd learned nothing."

When Hisashi first left for Tokyo, I'd promised to write him every day. I wanted to keep my promise. I wanted him to know that I still loved him, even though I was angry with him for abandoning me. But I had to heed Yoshiko's warning and I never wrote a single letter.

For months, I didn't leave the compound. When I first came to the household, Yoshiko said it would be unsafe for me to go to Sinuiju. "The police will look for the slightest reason to arrest you," she'd said. "And I imagine the Koreans will not be kind to you, either."

So, I stayed at home. Yoshiko often took Young-chul to the city park or to the river to watch boats, leaving me with nothing to do. I looked for ways to help around the house. But despite having a skeleton staff, the household ran smoothly under Yoshiko's leadership. One day, I went to Mr. Saito's study. When I'd lived there before, I wouldn't have dared to set foot inside his study. But Yoshiko had gone out with Young-chul and the house was quiet, so I went in. The room was simple and neat like the rest of the house. The floor was covered with tatami mats, and latticed shoji doors lined the walls. There was a low mahogany desk, and in a corner on a stand was the red-and-white Japanese flag. Off to the side was a full bookcase.

I went to it. Dozens of books lined the shelves—books on philosophy history, science, politics, and literature. Several were on Asian history, religion, and Shintoism. On the bottom shelf were books I'd never seen before—books on ethics and human rights and democracy. They were written in Japanese, Chinese, French, and English. I remembered when I was growing up, Father and Mother had wanted me to learn math, philosophy, and literature even though I was a girl, and how I'd hurry through my chores so I could read my books. I remembered how I'd read alongside Hisashi when he studied his medical books. It had been years since I'd read anything. The sight of all those books rekindled my passion for reading.

I didn't take any of them. Yoshiko was the head of the house, and this was her father's study. I left the study and at dinner that night I asked Yoshiko if there was something I could read.

"My father has books in his study. Take what you want, but be sure to return them. He might want them shipped to Japan someday."

Later, I went into Mr. Saito's study and looked more closely at the books. I selected one on world history. I took it to my room and started reading. I read all day and well into the night when I should have been sleeping. I finished it in two weeks, making notes on rice paper like Hisashi had done when he studied. Then, I went to the study and selected a book on philosophy. I finished that one in a week. In just a few months, I'd read twenty of Mr. Saito's books.

One day after I'd finished yet another book, I went to Mr. Saito's study to get a different one. I'd read half of the books on the top shelves. I scanned the dog-eared, worn books on the bottom shelf. Most had notes sticking out of the pages. At the end of the shelf was a book in French titled *Les Misérables*. I picked it up and examined it. It was filled with notes in Mr. Saito's handwriting—more so than any other book. I flipped through the pages. I couldn't read French, but the letters and words were fascinating. Mr. Saito's notes were passionate. *YES!* he wrote next to a sentence underlined twice. *Japan needs to learn from this* he'd written on another page. I put the book back and took one from an upper shelf.

That night at dinner, I asked Yoshiko about the strange book in French. "*Les Misérables*," she said with a nod. "It was Father's favorite book. It is a story about evil, lies, and injustice."

"You have read it?" I said. "I didn't know you could read French."

"French?" Young-chul said, poking at his food with his chopsticks. "What is French?"

"It is the language of diplomacy," Yoshiko answered.

"What's diplomacy?" Young-chul asked.

"It is how nations get along with each other," Yoshiko replied. "Now stop poking at your food and eat."

Yoshiko and I shared a grin at Young-chul's boyishness. She said, "Father insisted I learn French. I had a tutor for years. He also insisted I read *Les Misérables*."

"I would like to read it someday," I said.

"Someday you should. Unfortunately, there are no translations in Japanese or Chinese that I know of. In the meantime, there is something else you should read in my father's study. It is a play by William Shakespeare translated into Japanese. Have you heard of him?"

"Yes, I have," I answered. "He was English, as I remember. I've never read anything he wrote."

"You are correct, Shakespeare was English. He wrote poetry and plays. You should read his play *Romeo and Juliet*. I believe you will find it most interesting."

"Thank you," I said. "I will."

That night, I replaced the book I'd selected earlier and took two books from the bottom shelf. I took *Les Misérables*, though I didn't read French. And I took *Romeo and Juliet*. The book was in Japanese and was thin, but Mr. Saito had written almost as many notes in this book as he'd written in *Les Misérables*. I took the books to my room and started reading the story of Romeo and Juliet.

Two households, both alike in dignity,

In fair Verona, where we lay our scene,

From ancient grudge break to new mutiny,

Where civil blood makes civil hands unclean.

From forth the fatal loins of these two foes

A pair of star-crossed lovers take their life;

Whole misadventured piteous overthrows

Do with their death bury their parents' strife.

I read the entire play in one night.

When I lived with the rebels, the two-headed dragon never haunted me. But now that I was back in Sinuiju, living in a Japanese house, it visited me often. It would wake me at night like a chilling draft or an eerie sound. I'd lie on my mat and remember the warning my aunt had given me when she showed me her comb. I felt the dragon strongest when I sat in the Zen garden by myself. I used to love being in the garden with Hisashi. We'd talk there about his passion for medicine, what our children would be like, our future together.

I hadn't believed in the curse when I was with Hisashi. But everything I'd gone through over the past years made me wonder if the curse was real. I worried how it would affect my future. I wondered what it was trying to tell me. I wanted it to go away, but it never did.

One fall day after I'd been back at the Saito house nearly a year, I sat at the Zen garden wrapped in my coat when Yoshiko came and sat next to me. She looked over the garden with its raked white pebbles and green islands. She didn't say anything at first, and I got the sense that there was something important on her mind. I drew my coat tight around me.

"I have heard from my father," she finally said. "He says the war has turned against Japan. The Americans are winning battles in the Pacific. Months ago, bombs actually fell on Tokyo. The Chinese army continues to fight in the south of China. Russia threatens in the west."

"Why are you telling me this?" I asked.

"Because," Yoshiko replied, "my father wants me to sell the house. He needs the money. If I can find a buyer, I will go back to Tokyo."

"And will you take Masaru with you?" I asked.

"I don't know."

"If you take him, I will go, too."

"Japan is not a place for Koreans," Yoshiko replied. "Especially if we lose the war."

"There are thousands of Koreans living in Japan. I can be just another one. I will not leave my son again." I looked over the Zen garden. I saw the two-headed dragon staring at me among the branches of the sculpted juniper trees. I heard it whisper to me on the winter breeze.

"Well, it might be some time before we find a buyer," Yoshiko said. "We will see what we can do at that time. I wanted you to know."

And then I said, "I think we should tell Young-chul . . . Masaru that I am his mother. It's time he knows."

"I will think about it."

Yoshiko started to leave, but before she did, I said, "I want to ask for a favor."

"Yes?"

"I want to visit my aunt and uncle. They live up the road from my village. Will you take me there?"

"They are likely not there anymore. The war displaced many of your people. But I will see what I can do. Perhaps I can get gasoline for the car and drive you there. It would be safer for you if we drove."

"Thank you," I said.

Yoshiko left the garden and went into the house. I stayed and tried to understand what the two-headed dragon was telling me.

It was many months before Yoshiko could get enough gasoline to take me to see my aunt and uncle.

"When can we go?" I asked.

"Tomorrow," she replied.

It was a bright and cold winter day when we left. After the morning meal, we gave Young-chul to Fumiko and set off in Mr. Saito's big black car. Yoshiko drove, and I sat in the front next to her. She was the only woman I'd ever seen drive a car. She gripped the steering wheel hard and sat on the edge of her seat as if she was determined to make the car do what she wanted. The car lurched and bucked when she let out the clutch.

"When did you learn to drive?" I asked.

"I taught myself," she said, keeping her eyes fixed on the road. "I had to. When you and Isamu left, there was no one to drive the car. I'd seen what the chauffeur did when he drove, so I copied him. It was not as easy as I thought it would be. There were times I was afraid I was breaking the car. But I kept trying it, and eventually I got it to work." She grinned. "It's actually kind of fun."

"Thank you for taking me," I said.

"You're welcome," she replied. "We won't be able to stay long. The sun sets early this time of year and I do not want to drive in the dark."

As we drove into the hills outside of Sinuiju, I was thankful for Yoshiko. We'd bonded through our shared love for Young-chul and, I think, because we were women on our own. Still, she was older than me and in charge of the household. And she was Japanese. Though she didn't treat me like Japanese treated Koreans, I knew my place with her.

Sunlight on the dormant fields made the air shimmer as we drove. Yoshiko gripped the wheel hard and tried to avoid ruts as the car rumbled along the dirt road. Sometimes I was afraid she was going to drive into the ditch. We crested a hill and then another. I remembered walking this road with Mother when I first visited the Saito house. I was nervous about seeing my village. I wondered if I'd see the Kwan girls. I wondered if I'd see my aunt and uncle when we got to their house.

We crested yet another hill and then, before us, was my village and my parents' house. The house was deserted. The thatched roof had caved in. The garden was thick with frozen weeds.

As we drew close, I pointed. "There, that is my house."

Yoshiko slowed the car. "Do you want to stop?" she asked.

My heart ached at the sight of my house in such a condition. But I had to stop. "Yes, please," I answered softly.

Yoshiko pulled the car to the front. As I got out, I pulled my coat around me against the cold. I stepped into the house.

It was empty inside. Everything was gone. Someone had pulled out the wooden floors and had taken the iron stove. They had removed the walls.

I quickly went back to the car and climbed in. "Go," I said, shutting the door.

"Okay," Yoshiko said. "You said your aunt and uncle live farther up this road?"

"Yes. About an hour to walk."

Yoshiko started the car, let out the clutch, and the car lurched forward. As we drove away from my home, I regretted stopping here. Seeing the house where I'd grown up reminded me that my youth was dead and so, in all likelihood, were my parents. I swore I'd never return.

We drove the road to my uncle and aunt's house. "This is it," I said. Yoshiko stopped the car by the front gate and turned off the engine.

"We do not have much time," she said.

"I understand," I replied.

The house was in better condition than my parents' house, but it was not as neat and well-kept as it was the last time I'd been here. Roof tiles were askew, and a tarp hung where the carved front door had been. Frozen weeds sprinkled the yard.

And then I saw a woman wrapped in rags, with her back against a persimmon tree. I pushed open the gate and went to her.

"Sookmo?" I said. "Aunt?"

The woman looked up at me. A faded purple scarf framed her face. Her lips were blue from the cold and her eyes were watery and red. She stared at me for several seconds and then said, "You, the cursed one. You have come back."

My aunt looked years beyond her age. Under her rags I saw her body was bent and broken. Her gnarled hands looked like those of an old woman.

"Sookmo, why are you outside in the cold?" I asked, crouching in front of her. "Here, I will take you inside and start a fire."

She recoiled. "I will stay where I am until the spirits take me," she growled.

"Why do you want to die, Sookmo? Where is Uncle? Where are Soo-hee and Jae-hee?"

"Your uncle is dead. Your cousins might as well be."

"Why? Where are they?"

A sad smile spread across my aunt's face. "They went to work in the boot factory in Sinuiju." Her smile slowly twisted into pure pain. "The boot factory . . . ," she whispered.

"Then why do you want to die? Why don't you wait for your daughters until they come back home?"

"They will not come back," she said.

"Why?" I asked. "How do you know?"

My aunt closed her eyes and didn't answer.

"Do you know what happened to my brother?" I asked.

"Your brother," my aunt said as if the words were sour in her mouth. "He joined the Imperial Army. He is a chinilpa." She sighed painfully.

Finally, she asked, "Are you still married to a Japanese man?"

"Yes," I answered.

"Then you are a chinilpa like your brother. The two-headed dragon will curse you."

"Why, Sookmo? Why am I cursed for loving someone?"

"Because the two-headed dragon is Korea," she answered. "He begs you to remember him and not betray him."

"You think I am a traitor. But is love not important, too?"

My aunt spit. "Love. I loved my husband and my daughters, but my love could not save them."

I looked at my aunt and tried to think of what I could do to help her. But it was clear that she wanted to die. "Where is the comb with the two-headed dragon?" I asked. "I want to see it again."

My aunt grinned weakly. "You must have told someone about it. Men came looking for it. They were rebels. They were rough with me, but I did not give it to them. I could not. My grandmother told me I had to pass the comb to my daughters. And so, I did. I gave it to my girls when they left. I did my duty for my country and the spirit of my ancestors. How foolish it seems now."

"What about me, Sookmo?" I asked. "Will the dragon always curse me?"

She turned her red and watery eyes on me. "You are a daughter of Korea. You have a duty to your ancestors and the children of our country. That is why the dragon has two heads. One looks back at our ancestors. The other looks forward to our children. As long as you ignore your duty to them, the two-headed dragon will curse you."

"Sookmo, come to Sinuiju with me," I pleaded. "There are good people at my house. We can make you warm and feed you."

"No!" my aunt said with more force that I thought possible from a dying woman. "My life is done."

My aunt closed her eyes, and her chin fell to her chest. Her breathing was short and shallow. I stayed crouched in front of her for a while. Then, I went to the car and climbed in. Yoshiko was still at the steering wheel.

"Let's go home," I said.

Yoshiko didn't say anything. She started the car and steered it for Sinuiju.

We bounced along the frozen road for miles without talking. I was thankful Yoshiko didn't ask questions about my aunt.

As we drove out of the hills and Sinuiju came into view, I asked Yoshiko, "Is there a boot factory in Sinuiju?"

Yoshiko took a second before she answered. "Why do you ask?" she finally said.

"My aunt said my cousins were sent to work there. If they are in Sinuiju, I want to see them."

Yoshiko went quiet for a long time. "Miyoko . . . Suk-bo," she finally said. "There is no boot factory in Sinuiju. 'Boot factory' is what the Kempei tai call comfort stations."

"Comfort stations?"

"Brothels for the troops."

I took a second to think. "Then they might be in the brothel in Sinuiju with Kiyo," I said.

"No," Yoshiko said. "Comfort stations are at the front lines for the soldiers. You probably will not see your cousins again."

As we drove into Sinuiju, I thought of Soo-hee and Jae-hee. They were still just girls of sixteen and fourteen years old. I couldn't imagine the horrors they were going through.

And I began to wonder if my aunt was right about Japan. The Japanese had done so many evil things. Perhaps marrying a Japanese man was wrong, as my aunt and my father and the rebels had said. Yet in my heart, I still loved Hisashi.

TWENTY-EIGHT

Yoshiko never found a buyer for the house. A few merchants made absurdly low offers that she promptly rejected. It appeared that Japan was losing the war, and no one was willing to pay a reasonable price for a Shinto house that honored the emperor of Japan.

I was glad I could stay. I was there with my son, waiting for my husband to come home. Every day when I awoke, I prayed that Hisashi would walk through the front gate and into my arms. When after months and then years of waiting he didn't come, I began to wonder if he'd been right to tell me I should forget about him. But I could no more abandon him than I could abandon my heart. He'd become part of me and I'd promised to love him for the rest of my life as Mother had told me I should.

My relationship with Young-chul grew strong during this time. Yoshiko was increasingly preoccupied with settling her father's affairs. She would be gone all day—sometimes several days at a time on a trip to Pyongyang or Seoul. And when she was gone, I was alone with my little prince. After I'd been there for several months, Yoshiko agreed that we could tell him I was his mother. I was afraid it would confuse him, but when we told him at dinner one day, he went quiet for a few minutes and then said, "Okay." From then on, he called me "Mother" although he used the Japanese word, "haha," instead of "ummah." He called Yoshiko "Oba," the Japanese word for "aunt." He grew quickly from a toddler into a little man. His shoulders and arms filled out. His hair grew long and shiny. He still looked like his father. Even his mannerisms were Hisashi's—the way he squatted when he talked to someone, the constant look of amusement on his face, how he punctuated his words with his chopsticks when he ate. He climbed trees in the orchard and spent hours collecting insects. He would hide from me in the house and jump out to scare me when I got close. Then he'd laugh and run to hide again. I would tell him jokes and he would laugh aloud, making me laugh with him.

He loved me like a son is supposed to love his mother, and I loved him like only a mother could. Of course, he loved Yoshiko and Fumiko, too, but I was thrilled for what I had with my son. That we were all close to him never became an issue. He was such a fine boy it was natural that we loved him as we did. And he grew in our love as bamboo grows in the warmth of spring.

Young-chul grew sullen the spring before he turned seven. Yoshiko and I tried to understand why. We asked him what was wrong, but he didn't answer. We asked Fumiko, Ai, and Mr. Lee what they thought was happening to Young-chul, but they didn't know. Then we started to notice that he was worse in the mornings when he had to go to school. He'd sulk and complain about having to go to the Japanese school in Sinuiju. Sometimes, he'd pretend to be sick, and Yoshiko would let him stay home. Then, after a short time, he'd run around the grounds playing or beg to go to the city pond with his boat, saying, "I feel better now." Yoshiko and I did our best to encourage him to go to school. Though he was diligent about doing his homework, we concluded there was something going on at his school.

One day when Yoshiko was away, Young-chul and I had a picnic in the orchard behind the house. The peach trees were in bloom, their pink and purple flowers filling the air with a sweet scent. I remembered how Mother had told me that the peach was the fruit of happiness. I wanted to teach my son this and other things about Korea, too. I wanted to tell him the folk stories my mother had told me when I was his age. I wanted to sing traditional songs to him and tell him about our festivals and beliefs. But we lived in a Japanese house at the charity of Yoshiko. And I knew that if I started teaching Young-chul about Korea, my curious son would only want to learn more.

As we ate rice cakes and beans in the shadow of the fruit trees, Young-chul went quiet for a while. Then he said, "Tell me about Father."

It was the first time he'd asked me about Hisashi. I'd expected the question and was prepared to answer it. "He is a good man, kind and gentle," I said. "He is clever and handsome, too. You are a lot like him. You should be proud of him."

Young-chul scratched at the dirt with a stick. "Why did he marry you?"

"We met in the forest outside my village," I answered. "I was picking strawberries and he surprised me and made me drop my basket. He was so nice to me that I liked him right away. I think he liked me, too, because the next time he saw me, he gave me strawberries."

"And then you were married?"

"Yes. Not long after that."

Young-chul stopped scratching the dirt and looked at me. "But you are Korean."

This was a question I was not prepared for. We had insulated Young-chul from the hostility between the Japanese and Koreans. I didn't know he was even aware that I was Korean.

"That is true," I said. "But if two people love each other, what does it matter where they were born? I cannot help that I am Korean any more than your father can help that he is Japanese."

"I wish you weren't Korean," Young-chul said, scratching the ground with his stick again.

"Why do you say that?"

"I do not want to be a *kimchi yarò*," Young-chul said.

"Young-chul!" I exclaimed. "Where did you learn such words?"

"I do not want to talk about it," Young-chul said. "I do not want to have a picnic anymore, either." He threw down his stick and ran to the house. I sat among the peach trees dumbfounded. "Kimchi yarò." I had heard the term before. "Korean bastard." How did my son know these words? Who would have called him that?

School. It had to be at his school. But how would any of his classmates know he was half Korean? How did the word get out?

I had to talk to Yoshiko as soon as she came home. I had to convince her that she should take Young-chul out of the Japanese school. I had to convince her we could no longer ignore his heritage.

That night after Young-chul went to bed, I went to Yoshiko's room. It was much like mine, only she had a working desk with books of her own. I thought she was meditating when I slid open the door and stuck my head in. She sat on a tatami mat with her legs crossed. Before I slid the door closed to leave, she said, "What is it, Miyoko?"

"I'm sorry," I said. "I should not disturb you. We can talk some other time."

"There is not much time to talk," Yoshiko said. "Come in. Say what you have to say."

I told her about the questions Young-chul had asked me in the orchard. I told her how I thought the Japanese boys were bullying him in school. "I think we should tell him what it means to be Korean," I concluded.

Yoshiko didn't move from her position on the mat. "Yes, you should," she replied. "You should teach him about Korea. It is a good time for him to learn. And I will take him out of school."

I was surprised at how quickly Yoshiko agreed. I'd expected her to say that Young-chul should be raised as a Japanese and that he didn't need to know about Korea.

"Why is it a good time?" I asked. "You said we had to be careful about Korean things."

Still sitting on the mat, Yoshiko turned her head to me. "Our navy has been destroyed," she said. "The Germans are all but defeated in Europe. There is talk that when the war ends in Europe, Russia will turn against Japan. We are doomed. It will not be long."

I sat in front of her. "What will happen when Japan is defeated? What will happen to you and this house? What will we do about Masaru?"

"I have to return to Japan. When Japan falls, the Koreans and Chinese will kill the Japanese here. I must get out while I can."

"Yoshiko," I said, "you have been kind to me. I will speak for you."

Yoshiko gave me a half smile. "You will have your own trouble, Miyoko. Remember who you married."

"Maybe they will understand," I said, shaking my head. "I'll tell them I was with the rebels."

"You escaped from them, and for the past years you've been living in a Japanese house. A Shinto house."

"I was here to be with my son! They cannot blame me for loving my son."

"Ah, yes. Your son," Yoshiko said, the smile dropping from her face. "Masaru. Or . . . what is it you named him? Young-chul, your half-Japanese son. Have you thought about how your people will treat Young-chul? No better than the Japanese students at his school, I think."

"Then we will go with you to Japan," I said. "I can bear any hatred the Japanese have for me. They do not have to know that Young-chul . . . Masaru is my son."

"No," Yoshiko said, shaking her head. "Japan is no place for a boy now, even if he is half Japanese. I have decided he must stay here with you. You can live in the house. I will leave the household valuables for you—the silver chopsticks, the gold incense bowl, some jewelry. The ivory carving in the kami dana altar is especially valuable. You must wait here for Hisashi to come home."

Hisashi. I hadn't thought what would happen to my husband when the war was over. He might go to prison or the Russians might shoot him. I didn't even know if he was still alive.

I nodded. "You are right. I should stay here with Young-chul and wait for Hisashi. When will you leave?"

"I do not know. Soon. I will not say goodbye to Masaru when I leave. Tell him I'm on a trip and you don't know when I'm coming back. He will ask about me for a while—months, maybe a year. Eventually, he will stop asking. I have thought a lot about it. This is the best way."

"He will think you left him because he is Korean," I said.

"You must tell him otherwise," Yoshiko replied. "I ask for only one thing," she continued. "I would like to have something of his to remember him."

"How about the toy boat you gave him?" I said. "He does not play with it anymore."

"Yes," Yoshiko said. "It would please me to have it."

For the first time since I'd met her, I saw a tear in Yoshiko's eye. She drew a breath and lifted her chin to try to disguise her sadness. I threw my arms around her. "Thank you for everything you have done," I said.

Yoshiko put an arm around me. "Now then, Miyoko. There is no need for this. What has happened cannot unhappen."

She held me for a few seconds, then gently pushed me away. She'd regained her composure and was the Yoshiko I'd always known. "I will not say goodbye to you when I leave," she declared, "so I shall say it now. Take care, Miyoko . . . Suk-bo. And take care of Young-chul. Promise you will."

"Of course," I said.

She tried to give me her imperturbable smile, but her lip quivered and her eyes betrayed her sadness.

Two days later, she was true to her word and left without saying goodbye as if she was going to take care of another of her father's affairs.

With Yoshiko gone, Fumiko was the one who went into the city to buy provisions and take Young-chul to the city park. I still had to be careful not to venture out. I was afraid of the Japanese soldiers and Koreans who might see me as a chinilpa. When the Germans surrendered in Europe, Fumiko reported there was a feeling in Sinuiju she'd never known. "People everywhere are walking around with their heads up!" she reported. "We are speaking Korean again instead of Japanese. Koreans have started radio broadcasts. We use our real names. I think, someday soon, we will be free!"

And then in August, the news came that the Americans dropped powerful bombs on Japan and they surrendered. The war was over. As a condition of the surrender, the Allies forced Japan to give up Korea. For the first time, I was able to go out into the city with Young-chul. Japanese flags had come down and been replaced by the Korean flags that had been hidden away for years. We watched impromptu celebrations in the streets with singing of traditional songs that people hadn't sung openly for decades. People were drunk with joy. They taunted the Japanese who remained, although they were careful because the soldiers still carried their rifles.

A few days later, the Russians arrived in Sinuiju and disarmed the Japanese soldiers. The Russian soldiers were hard, rough-looking men with stubbly chins and dirty, tattered boots. They scared me almost as much as the Japanese soldiers. The patriotic celebrations stopped, and in hushed talk, many of us worried about the Russians' intentions.

The Russians marched the Japanese soldiers into a prison yard they constructed outside the city. They brought hundreds and then thousands of soldiers there from northern Korea and Manchuria. Ships arrived in Sinuiju to take the prisoners to Japan.

I was anxious to go to the prison yard to look for Hisashi. Before I could, reports came in on the radio and from Fumiko that riots had started. Thirty-five years of rage erupted from the Korean people. And since the Japanese were under the protection of the Russian soldiers, Koreans turned against their own people to unleash their rage. They shouted "Chinilpa!" as they dragged people who'd worked for the Japanese out into the street and beat them. "Chinilpa!" they howled as they threw merchants who'd profited from the occupation off the bridge into the Yalu River.

As mobs marched at night, hunting for anyone who they thought had been a chinilpa, I cowered with Young-chul in my room in the Saito house. I feared that Kiyo would lead them to me and my half-Japanese son. I was afraid that the rebels I'd been with would find me. Old Mr. Lee kept watch at the gate day and night. Young-chul asked questions about what was happening and why we couldn't go into the city anymore. I did my best to answer his questions but I could tell he was troubled.

One night, the mob came. Mr. Lee rushed to my door, followed by Fumiko. Mr. Lee said he heard rioters a few blocks away and that they were marching toward the house. "You must run, Suk-bo!" he said. "They are coming for you and your son."

I was prepared. I'd taken the valuables Yoshiko had given me and packed some clothes and a blanket in a rucksack. Fumiko handed me a sack of food and a skin of water. She cried as she hugged Young-chul and then me.

"What will happen to you?" I asked.

"I will be all right," Fumiko replied. "I'll go back home. Take good care of Young-chul," she cried and then hugged me again. "Go! Quickly!"

I started for the door. Before I left, I said, "Wait." I went to the desk and opened a drawer. I took out the silver hairpin and slipped it inside the rucksack. And from the top of the desk, I took *Les Misérables* and *Romeo and Juliet*.

"Hurry," Mr. Lee said.

I led Young-chul out of the house, through the orchard, and over the back wall. Behind us, torches lit up the night sky, and peopled shouted, "Chinilpa! Chinilpa!" We hurried along streets to the main road leading to the hills. I looked back at the city and saw flames from where we'd come. The mob had set fire to the Saito house.

Seven-year-old Young-chul walked alongside me with his eyes set forward. He seemed angry. We walked until the glow of the fire faded in the distance. Finally, he said, "They came because I'm half Japanese. I am a kimchi yarò." His jaw was tight and anger filled his eyes.

I stopped and made him face me. "That is not why, my son. They were coming for me because I married your father. It had nothing to do with you. Do you understand?"

He turned away and said, "Let me carry the rucksack." I gave it to him and we walked on.

I thought of going up into the hills, back to my house where I'd grown up, but I couldn't bear to see it again. So I stopped before the road began to rise. "Why are we stopping, Haha?" Young-chul asked.

"Ummah," I said. "Call me 'ummah.' That is the Korean word for mother. We are stopping because I have something to do before we go on."

"What is it, Haha . . . Ummah?"

"I want to look for your father among the prisoners."

"Why?" Young-chul asked. "He is Japanese and you are Korean."

"Because I still love him," I replied. "Love is not something that you can just toss away."

Young-chul thought about this for a moment. Then he pointed to a willow tree a little way off the road. "We can hide there until morning."

We went to the tree and spread the blanket. It was a clear night and crickets chirped all around us. And there under the twinkling stars, we tried to sleep.

The next morning, the sun came up bright yellow, promising one of the last hot days of summer. The prison yard was only a mile farther from where we'd stopped. Flies buzzed around our heads as we walked toward the camp. A barbed wire fence enclosed the yard, and there were rows and rows of tents inside. Men in dirty uniforms milled about. Some hung on to the fence looking out. Others sat in small groups. Russian guards patrolled on the outside of the fence.

As much as I hoped to see Hisashi, I was afraid to go farther. I was afraid I might not find him there, or that if I did, he wouldn't want to see me. But I'd yearned to see him for so long, I set my fears aside. I went to the fence as Young-chul followed.

"You there," I said to a group of prisoners. "I am looking for someone."

A Russian guard studied me, and I was afraid he was going to tell me to go away, but he didn't. He just watched as I tried to talk to the prisoners.

"Help me, please," I shouted. "I am looking for Hisashi Saito. Does anyone know him? Is he here?"

A soldier left the group and came to the fence. His uniform was dirty and his face was sunburned. A white crust covered his lips. "Why do you want him?" he asked. His eyes darted back and forth as if he was afraid someone was coming up from behind him.

"This is his son," I said, showing Young-chul to him. "I want him to see his son."

The soldier glanced at Young-chul and then asked, "What did you say the man's name was?"

"Hisashi Saito."

The soldier nodded. "What will you give me if I find him for you?"

"I have some dried meat in my rucksack," I answered.

The soldier's eyes went wide. "Show it to me," he said excitedly. I reached inside the rucksack and took out a scrap of meat Fumiko had given me.

The soldier licked his lips. "Give it to me and I will find Hisashi Saito for you."

I put the meat back into the rucksack. "Find him and I will give you the meat," I replied.

The soldier stared at the rucksack and then at me. "Wait here," he said and hurried into the crowd of soldiers.

Young-chul and I waited for several minutes. Then, the soldier came back, followed by a tall bald man.

"I have not found Hisashi Saito," the soldier said, pointing at the man behind him, "but this man says he knows him."

The bald man stepped forward. "Haru!" I gasped. Mr. Saito's aide stood in front of me wearing a Kempei tai uniform. His uniform was not dirty like the others. His face was clean, too.

From behind Haru the soldier said, "You must pay me. I brought you this man who knows the one you're looking for."

Without taking his eyes from me, Haru said over his shoulder, "Go away."

"But sir," the soldier protested. "She said she would pay me with meat!"

Haru faced the soldier, who took a full step back. "I said, go away."

The soldier gave Haru a quick bow and then ran back to the group he'd been with. "Miyoko," Haru said, facing me again, "I hear you are looking for your husband."

"Yes, Haru. Please, tell me where he is."

"He is not here," Haru said evenly.

"He is alive?" I gasped, bringing my hands to my mouth.

"Yes, he is. But you will not see him again."

"Why? Please tell me."

Haru didn't answer. He inspected Young-chul. "Is this Hisashi's son?"

"Yes," I said. "You knew him as Masaru, but his name is Young-chul."

"Young-chul. I see. So he is fully Korean. We were right about you and Byong-woo."

"No," I exclaimed. "He is Hisashi's son. Please tell me what happened to my husband."

"Hisashi's son." A slow grin spread across Haru's face. "Tell me, Miyoko, do you know what your husband, this boy's father, has been doing for the past years?"

"He worked for Doctor Ishii in Manchuria. But I do not believe the rumors about what they did there."

"Yes, Doctor Ishii. We called his camp Unit 731. And everything you heard about it is true."

"No," I cried. "I do not believe you. You are saying this to hurt me."

"Your husband must have done good work for the doctor," Haru said coolly. "They promoted him to captain. Captain Saito of the Imperial Army. Captain Hisashi Saito, a war criminal."

"Be quiet!" I said. "You are lying! Hisashi worked in a medical camp."

"It does not matter if you believe me," Haru replied. "As I said, you will not see your husband again and your son will never meet his father. Yes, Hisashi was here, but he is no longer. Those suspected of war crimes were sent on the first boat to Japan. I imagine your husband is in prison awaiting trial."

Haru's grin changed into a sneer. "There you go," Haru said. "I've told you what you wanted to know. Now, go away with your bastard son or I will call the guard and tell him you are passing contraband."

I stood at the fence and watched Haru walk away. I was too numb to shout at him.

Young-chul took my arm. "Ummah," he said. "Father is not here and we must go."

In the growing heat of the day, we walked a while until we reached a fork in the road. I pointed for us to turn south instead of up into the hills where my village was. "Where are we going, Ummah?" Young-chul asked.

"Far away from here," I answered.

As we began our journey, I remembered when I first saw Hisashi in the forest behind my house. I tried to image him as a war criminal conducting research on prisoners. It made no sense. It simply was not possible. I had to see him again, talk to him about it. I had to see if the man I loved was gone from me forever.

TWENTY-NINE

Present Day, Los Angeles

"Lemme see if I have this right," Detective Jackson says. He leans his chair back and watches Ms. Yi carefully. He has a pad of paper on his lap and a pen in his hand. "Your husband worked for this Unit 731 during World War Two. Your parents died there, didn't they?"

Ms. Yi keeps her eyes on the table in front of her. "Years later I learned that my parents were killed in Manchuria," she says. "I do not know where they were killed."

"They coulda been sent to Unit 731," Jackson says. "Your husband worked there and that's why you murdered him."

I lean forward. "She's not admitting to anything, Detective. You don't know if the deceased is her husband or, for that matter, if he was murdered."

"What happened to your brother?" Jackson says, ignoring me.

"I discovered he was killed fighting for the Japanese in the Battle of Guadalcanal," Ms. Yi answers.

"And what about this dragon comb?" Jackson asks me. "Her aunt gave it to her daughters, but now you have it? How'd *you* get it?"

"My grandmother gave it to me," I answer.

"Your grandmother?" Exasperated, Jackson shakes his head. "And one more thing," he says, still addressing me. "If this is all true, why's her name Yi and not Saito? I mean, if she married this Hisashi guy, she should be Mrs. Saito, right?"

"No, Detective," I say. "In Korea, it is customary that a married woman keeps her maiden name."

"Is that so?" Jackson says sarcastically. He tosses his pad and pen onto the table. "I don't get it. I need answers. I bet they're gettin' impatient outside."

"I understand, Detective," Ms. Yi says. "There is one more part of my story. Once you hear it, you'll have the answers you need."

"Do you need a break, ma'am?" I ask.

"No," Ms. Yi replies.

"Okay," Jackson interjects. "Let's get on with it. You were saying something about starting a journey."

"Yes, a difficult journey," Ms. Yi says, still staring at the table. "After I left Sinuiju, I made it all the way to Seoul with Young-chul. It took us several months. To get there we had to sell all the valuables Yoshiko had given us. A ride on a truck to Pyongyang cost two silver chopsticks. The cost to cross to the American side was the ivory carving from the kami dana altar. We had to beg for food. We usually slept outside in the cold."

Ms. Yi looks at Detective Jackson. "The journey was difficult, Detective, but once I got to Seoul, it was better. The Japanese were gone, and though we were all still very poor, everyone was optimistic. We had our country back. People were starting businesses. For the first time in my life, it felt like we had a future.

"But then, Korea became the battleground in the cold war between America and the communist nations. Talks between the north and south broke down. The country became divided—the communists in the north led by Kim Il-sung, and the American puppet Syngman Rhee leading the south. Families were separated and both countries put up fences to keep their people from leaving."

Ms. Yi shakes her head. "We did not care about global politics, Detective. All we wanted was to be one nation, to reunite with our loved ones. But then our civil war came, what you call the Korean War. It destroyed everything—two and a half million Koreans died, and our hopes and dreams died with them."

Ms. Yi looks at the table again. Sadness fills her face. "That was the most difficult time of my life."

THIRTY

Seoul, June 1950

"We need more honey," I told Young-chul as I stood over my worktable rolling out sweet rice dough. "And more chestnuts for the *yakgwa*."

It was well before sunrise and Young-chul, now almost twelve years old, was getting ready to go out to buy the ingredients I needed for the sweets I sold in the Namdaemun market. From under his sleeping mat, he'd gathered the money I'd given him from the previous day's sales. "Sugar is easy," he said, pulling on his shoes. "Chestnuts are not so easy. People steal them right off the trees before the farmers can harvest them. If I can find them, they are expensive."

"It does not matter what they cost," I said. "Yakgwa cakes fetch two won more than anything else we sell. I run out of them before noon and could sell more if I had chestnuts."

"I'll get them," Young-chul said confidently. He shouldered his rucksack and slipped out the door.

I smiled to myself as my son ran down the street. He was taller than me now. He was still in his awkward stage, but it was clear that in a few short years, he would grow into his body and be the very image of his handsome father when I'd first met him. He was smart like his father and resourceful, too. He seemed happy, although he often went dark, sometimes for days. I knew why. He was half Japanese in a country where everyone hated the Japanese. And his Japanese side showed. He wasn't tall like a Korean, and his skin was dark like the Japanese. He had Japanese mannerisms, too, like a tendency to look people in the eye instead of diverting his gaze like Koreans did.

We'd been lucky since we'd come to Seoul four years earlier. We lived in a small house not far from the market. It was one room, filled with the pots and cooking utensils I needed to make my confections. It had a stove, a large oak worktable, and a cupboard where I stored ingredients. I loved the house. It was a smaller version of the house I'd grown up in, only it was in the middle of the city instead of surrounded by fields and forests.

I could afford the rent because I was a successful merchant in the Namdaemun market. I sold my confections in a stand on the main street, and everyone said mine were the best. At first, I'd only sold dduk. I made the sweet rice cakes just like Mother had shown me when we made them for the Dano celebration. But I'd always sell them all before noon, so soon, I added other confections like *bukkumi* dumplings with sweet red beans, *dasik* tea cookies and, of course yakgwa. I took care to make them the best I could. I'd pull myself off my mat hours before daylight to make them in the morning so they'd be fresh. I used the best ingredients that Young-chul was always able to find.

After Young-chul left, I finished preparing the confections and packed them into a small one-wheeled cart that Young-chul had found for me when I could no longer carry my wares on my back. It was now light outside, the sun having risen above the mountains in the east. I pushed my cart over the narrow dirt streets, past the low houses of my neighborhood. After several blocks, the streets were wider and cobble-stone. Here were brick buildings, some three stories tall with signs in

Hangul. Up and down the street the people of Seoul were starting their workday. Some swept walks in front of their stores. Others opened awnings with long cranks.

When I got to Namdaemun market, street merchants were laying out their goods on tables and mats. The smell of kimchi hung in the air, and the market stalls held all kinds of merchandise—Western-style shirts as well as traditional hanboks; blue and white and pink stationery; books in Hangul, Chinese, and English; kites and dolls and cheap jewelry; traditional herbs and medicines; foods of all types. When I came to the place where I had my stand, I took the confections and a white cloth out of the cart. I removed the wheel and turned the cart upside down to make a table. I spread out the cloth and arranged my goods in neat groups. Soon, people started to stroll by and inspect my confections.

My customers that day were mostly well-off—women in silk hanboks carrying parasols, and men in suits. As usual, I sold all the yakgwa before midday. There were many working-class and poor at the market. They looked longingly at my confections, but only a few bought them. "It is my husband's birthday," one said. "I can only treat myself once per week," said another.

In the afternoon, a woman dressed in a tattered chima skirt and soiled jeogori blouse led two young children past my stand. The youngest, a barefoot boy, pulled on his mother's hand to go to my stand. "No, Jung-yoo," the mother said, pulling him back. "We cannot have sweets today."

As the boy fell in step with his mother, he looked at me beseechingly. I remembered how much I loved the dduk my mother and I made for the celebrations in my village. I remembered wishing I could have them more than just a few times per year.

"Mother," I called to the woman. "I need your help."

The woman faced me. "I am sorry, but I am poor and cannot afford your treats."

"That is not what I want," I said. "I have made too much dduk today and will not be able to sell it all. I am giving it away. Would you be so kind to take some with you so I do not have to carry it home?"

The woman eyed me suspiciously. "It is okay," I said with a smile. "I understand." The woman nodded and brought her children to my table. "One for each of your children," I said, "and two more for you and your husband. Let the children choose the ones they want."

The children stood wide-eyed over my table and selected their dduk cakes. I took two more and wrapped them in paper and handed them to the mother.

"Thank you," she said with a bow.

"Thank you!" I replied. "Now I do not have to carry so much home."

By the end of the day, I'd sold everything I had and was preparing to leave. It had been a good day and I'd made a handsome profit. As I started to fold the white cloth, a man in a suit and bowler hat came to my stand.

"Anyohaseyo," the man said.

"I am sorry, sir," I replied, "but I have nothing left to sell you. Perhaps you can come back tomorrow?"

"It is my bad luck you have nothing left for me to buy," he said with a pleasant smile. "I hear your confections are the best. But that is not why I am here."

"I see," I replied, looking away. A pang of fear gripped me. I'd heard of men in suits forcing merchants like me to pay them a fee to sell in the market. This man looked like he could be one of them.

"I am Mr. Park with the Namdaemun Merchants Association," he said. "I am here because I want to place an order."

"An order?" I said, stopping the folding.

"Yes. The association wants to hire you to make confections for the summer festival. The festival is next week, and we will need quite a large quantity."

"How much will you need?"

He gave me a number and I set down the white cloth unfolded. "I will need help to make that much," I said. "And I will need to buy a lot of ingredients."

"I am prepared to give you half your fee in advance if you accept." He held out an envelope. "Take it. Use it to hire the help you need and buy your ingredients. My address is in there, too, in case you need to contact me."

"Yes, sir," I said, staring at the envelope. "I accept your order."

"Good. I will come back in a week with a truck to get the confections. I will pay the balance then."

"Thank you, sir," I said.

He nodded at me and winked. "And if our partnership is a success, there will be more opportunities like this for you. Other festivals. Perhaps hotels and restaurants." He tipped his hat and walked away.

I opened the envelope and saw there was a large sum of money inside. I did a quick calculation in my head and realized I'd earn a big profit. And Mr. Park had said there would be more opportunities. I quickly finished folding the white cloth and headed home. If I was successful, in a year or less, I could earn enough to take Young-chul to Japan and find Hisashi.

When I got home, Young-chul was reading a book. "I got the honey and chestnuts," he said without looking up. "I put the leftover money on the table."

I looked at the money. "Why is there so much?" I asked. "I thought you said the chestnuts would be expensive."

He still didn't look up. "They were not as expensive as I thought."

I was his mother and I could tell he was lying. I wanted to ask him if he'd stolen the chestnuts, but I didn't. I was excited about the order from Mr. Park and I'd need the chestnuts. And I'd need Young-chul and his resourcefulness to fill the huge order.

I told Young-chul about Mr. Park, and his eyes lit up. "You can count on me to get everything you need," he said.

"Good," I replied. "Just be careful, my son."

Young-chul somehow got the ingredients I needed, and I hired two neighbors to help me make the confections. I planned to have the four of us work all night before I had to deliver them to Mr. Park. But before that day, war came to Seoul. I'd heard that there'd been clashes along the border with the communists in the north, but I never imagined that the fighting would come to the city.

That morning, rumors spread that the communists were advancing on Seoul. They said President Syngman Rhee had fled to Pusan, and people by the thousands were heading south across the Han River. I was terrified that if Kim Il-sung's soldiers reached Seoul, they would recognize me and shoot me for betraying them.

When the artillery fire started—a concussive booming from the north followed by white explosions within the city—I said, "We must leave!" Young-chul went out to investigate while I huddled inside the house. When he came back, he said, "The streets and bridges are jammed with people. We will not get anywhere. It is safer to stay here."

I'd never told Young-chul that I'd betrayed the rebels. I only told him that I lived with them for a while and then escaped to come back to him. He hadn't asked questions about what I'd done during that time. Now, however, I was in danger. So I told him how I helped make bombs for the rebels, and how I failed to set off a bomb during an important raid. I told him that I'd deserted and if they caught me, they'd shoot me. I didn't tell him about Byong-woo.

Young-chul asked, "How will they know where to find you?"

"Everyone has registered with the government. If the communists take Seoul, they'll look through the records and know where I live."

"Then we need to move," my son said simply. "We'll take food and clothes and go to another house. Everyone is leaving, so we can find an abandoned house. Let's go."

I was amazed how my son knew exactly what to do. It was as if he was much older and experienced than other boys his age. It was the time he spent on the street getting things for my business. Although I felt guilty about making him streetwise, I was relieved that I could depend on his cleverness now.

We quickly gathered food, some clothes, and all our money and stuffed them inside Young-chul's rucksack. We went to the street where the people of Seoul were in panic. They carried sacks heavy with their belongings and dragged children by their hands. They hurried south as the artillery shells fell not far away.

"This way," Young-chul said.

I followed him as we pushed against the crowd, bumping into people who shoved us aside. We turned east and then north again. Soon, we were near Gyeongbok Palace. "There is a wealthy neighborhood just east of here," Young-chul said. "We'll find a good house there."

The streets here were not as crowded, and Young-chul found an abandoned, unlocked house. The house was brick and had a sturdy tile roof. We slipped inside. It was much larger than our one-room house, but not extravagant. It felt like the house of a successful merchant. It had Western-style furniture and, separated from the main room by a sliding shoji wall, a kitchen with an iron stove.

Young-chul dropped his rucksack on the floor and went into the kitchen. "They left food," he said. "Canned peaches, kimchi, and dried pork."

"Is there water?" I asked. "We should fill containers with water."

Young-chul nodded and found several large containers. Though the water came out of the tap in only a dribble, we filled them all up.

We settled into the main room. "Look!" Young-chul said, pointing. "They have a radio!"

There against the wall was a wooden cabinet with a round glass window and knobs on the front. Young-chul went to the radio and turned it on. He rotated a knob and found a channel that was broadcasting. As explosions thumped the city all around us, we sat on the floor and listened to the announcer calmly read reports. He said communist forces were inside Seoul and tens of thousands of refugees were fleeing south. *"The communists are progressing quickly,"* the announcer said. *"The South Korean army is preparing to destroy the Hangang Bridge. Everyone is advised to stay away."*

"There must be thousands of people on that bridge," I said.

Young-chul gave a serious look and nodded. I could see him starting to slip into one of his dark moods again.

The radio went silent two hours later, and soon after that, the bombing stopped. The water stopped running altogether and the lights went out. That night, everything was deathly quiet. Young-chul sat on a sofa with his legs to his chest and said nothing. After a while, I snuffed out the candles we'd found, and we curled up on mats and tried to sleep.

The next day we stayed huddled in the merchant's house. We ate some dried pork and a can of peaches and drank some of the water we'd saved. Young-chul wanted to go outside to see what was happening, but I didn't let him. "We are safe here," I said. "Let's not look for trouble."

We stayed inside the house for two more days. Young-chul never came out of his darkness. He spent hours looking out the window, saying nothing. Then, on the afternoon of the fourth day, we heard a voice coming over a loudspeaker outside. We opened the window and looked out. Slowly rolling down the street was a green army truck with a huge conical loudspeaker on top. "Everyone in this area must go to the Government General building outside Gyeongbok Palace to register with the new government," a voice said over the loudspeaker. "In one week, anyone caught without registration will be arrested." The truck rolled on and repeated the announcement farther down the block.

I pushed the window closed. "What will I do?" I asked Young-chul. "They cannot know who I am."

"Why can't you register under a different name?" he replied. "They won't know."

And so I did. We went to the Government General building—a huge, ugly building the Japanese had erected during their occupation. We waited in line in the lobby where a red flag with a white circle and red star hung from the ceiling. When we got to the desk, I told the male clerk my name was Chun-ja Yi and my son was Sang-ho Pak. When he looked at Young-chul he said, "The boy looks like he is Japanese. Are you giving us your real names?"

Young-chul's jaw went tight and I was afraid he'd say something. "My son's father was Korean and was killed during the Japanese occupation," I said quickly. "I assure you, we are giving you our correct names."

The man grunted and wrote something on a ledger. Then he asked us for an address, and I gave him the address of the house we'd taken over. He wrote it on the ledger next to our names.

"Put your right hands over your hearts," he said. We did and he said, "Do you pledge your complete and everlasting support to the Democratic People's Republic of Korea and to its leader, Chairman Kim Il-sung?"

I remembered Commissar Kim from my time with the rebels. Back then, he'd been a charismatic leader, but I never dreamed he'd become the supreme leader of North Korea. I also knew how brutal he could be. I remembered how he'd left Young-ee to die after the mamushi had bitten her. I remembered how he sent me to be killed by the bomb with the short fuse.

"I do," I said.

Young-chul did not say anything and the clerk glared at him. "What do you say, boy?"

Young-chul glared back at the clerk. "Son," I said quickly, "you must agree."

Young-chul looked at me, then back at the clerk. "I do," he said finally.

The clerk filled out some papers and handed them to us. "You must keep these with you at all times," he said. "If you are caught without them, you will be arrested. Now you may go."

"What will we do for food and work?" I asked.

"What you did before," the clerk answered matter-of-factly. "Everything is the same under the new regime. You are to carry on as if nothing has changed."

I gave him a slight bow, and Young-chul and I went back to the merchant's house.

The clerk was wrong. Nothing was like it was before. The Namdaemun market vendors, most having escaped to the South or afraid to come out with communist soldiers roaming the street, had abandoned the market. The awnings stayed rolled up, and a few had boarded their windows. When I tried to buy food, I learned we had to exchange our money for North Korean won. When I went to the exchange, they gave me only one tenth of what I'd had before. So Young-chul had to find food for us. Eventually, the water and electricity came back on. When we turned on the radio, the only station we could get broadcast propaganda about the virtues of communism and how the great leader, Chairman Kim, was uniting Korea under the Democratic People's Republic. *"We will be one Korea again!"* the reporter said with a little too much enthusiasm.

Everywhere I went I was afraid I'd see someone from the rebel group. Every night, I worried that there would be a knock on my door.

But no one ever came to the merchant's house and, contrary to what the reporter said, Korea never became one.

In September, the Americans invaded west of Seoul at Inchon, and the ensuing battle for Seoul destroyed more of the city. Once the Americans took control, some Koreans who had fled came back. Even so, the city had lost the life it had before the war. We hoped and prayed that the war would end soon so we could rebuild and South Korea would be the way it was. But the radio went off and never came back on, and the Namdaemun market never opened.

Everyone expected the South Korean government and Americans to provide aid. But it was slow in coming, and by the time the daylight grew short and the north winds promised winter, the starving citizens began to panic. Packs of angry, hungry men roamed the city looking for food. Women and children stayed in their houses and stared out of windows with fatalistic eyes.

Eventually, Young-chul and I went back to our house. When we got there, I was relieved to see that it was still standing and that North Korean soldiers had not ransacked it like they had so many others. I still had my pots and cooking utensils, although all the ingredients to make my confections were gone. We had nothing to eat, so Young-chul spent every day searching for food. I wondered if he was in one of the wild packs, but I didn't ask. Half the time he came home empty-handed, so most nights, we went to bed hungry.

One cold November day, I heard the United Nations was passing out food in the square outside of the Government General building. I went there. The line stretched down the block. I took a place in the back behind a woman about my age.

"Is this the line for food?" I asked the woman.

"Yes," she said with a nod, clutching her coat around her. "My brother came home this morning with green cans that had meals inside."

"Good," I said. "We need help."

The woman gave me a look that was both desperate and angry. "Yes, we need help and it could get worse. There is word that the Chinese have entered the war and are winning battles in the north. Pray the war does not come back to Seoul or thousands will starve during the winter." She turned back and said nothing more.

It took over an hour for me to get to the front of the line. There were several military trucks parked in the square guarded by American soldiers holding rifles. Alongside the trucks were makeshift tables made from crates. When I went to a table, a blond American woman with the blue-and-white UN armband over her coat handed me two green cans with English writing on the lid. "This is from the United Nations," she said in broken Korean. "There's food inside. Use the key on the bottom to open the can."

I thanked the lady with a bow and took the cans home.

When I got there, Young-chul took the metal key from the bottom of one of the cans, peeled back a tab on the side, and opened it. Inside were crackers, jam, sugar, and coffee. We hadn't had anything to eat for days, and though the food had a stale, metallic taste, we ate it all. Young-chul wanted to open the other can, but I told him not to. "We do not know when we will have something again. We should save it." We hid the can inside one of my pots.

Every day for several weeks I went to the square outside the Government General building for the food the United Nations gave out. Sometimes they had rice. Sometimes they gave out beans. Most days, they handed out the food in green cans.

Then one day, the trucks weren't there. Everyone held their places in line and waited for the trucks to come. Then, we heard bombs exploding north of the city. We stared at each other. A man came running into the square. "The Chinese are advancing," he said. "The Americans are in full retreat!"

I ran for home as the bombs fell in white flashes to the north. I got to my house and rushed inside. "Young-chul!" I cried out, but he wasn't there. I went back outside. Two low-flying jets roared overhead. They dropped their bombs a mile north, and I saw a white flash as they hit and a few seconds later felt their concussive thuds. Thick black smoke rose from where the bombs fell.

People began to come out of their houses and into the street, but unlike before, there was no panic in them as they moved. Instead, they walked with their heads down and their shoulders slumped forward.

I saw Young-chul coming toward me. "Young-chul!" I called out as another bomb flashed white, closer now. "We have to run!" I said.

"Why?" he asked. "Where will we go? They have not rebuilt the bridges across the river. We are trapped here."

I looked into his face and could see he was in his dark place again. "Young-chul, we have to try."

"It is no use," he said, shaking his head. "I cannot find food anywhere. We are doomed."

A bomb exploded a half mile from where we stood, making the houses around us shudder. The entire neighborhood to our north was on fire. Smoke filled the air, stinging my eyes. People walked faster.

I looked at my son. I had come so close. I'd had a job and was making money. If war had not come, I would have done well and could have gone to Japan to find Hisashi. Now there was nothing but chaos and despair all around. But I had to go on, had to see Hisashi again and tell him that I never stopped loving him. I wanted him to be Young-chul's father. I wanted Young-chul to know Hisashi the way he was before he left me. "No," I said. "I refuse to give up. I will not stop until I see Hisashi again."

"Hisashi?" Young-chul exclaimed. "He abandoned us! And he is Japanese."

I grabbed Young-chul's shoulders and stared into his face. "Do not judge him," I said. "He is a good man and you are his son. We will find him someday, I promise. Now, take us to a place where we will be safe."

Young-chul returned my stare. After a few seconds, his face softened. And as the bombs flashed and the explosions thumped, he nodded and said, "Follow me."

THIRTY-ONE

Young-chul and I survived the war, but after it was over, I could not save him. The four invasions of Seoul had decimated the city. Bombings and firestorms leveled entire neighborhoods. Only brick fireplaces and iron stoves still stood. A fraction of the population remained. The people like us who'd survived were destitute and desperate. For years after the war, suffering and death was common.

We lived miserably in a slum with thousands of others. Our shack was a corrugated tin lean-to with a green army tarp for a door. It was stifling hot in the summer, unbearably cold in the winter, and wet during the rainy season. Raw, foul-smelling sewage ran in the ditch behind us. What remained of the streets were muddy all summer and full of frozen ruts all winter. I had to trek a mile to get water. We often went days without eating. Our clothes were little more than rags.

Young-chul's sullenness before the war grew to anger in the years after. He turned callous and hard. He never asked about his father. He never smiled. He only thought about what he needed to do that day so we could survive. He roamed the street like a wolf hunting prey. I tried to keep him grounded. I tried to talk about a brighter future. I tried to give him hope, although in a city overwhelmed by hopelessness it was difficult to have it myself.

My son was a young man now. He had shiny black hair and big liquid eyes like Hisashi. I believe people hated him because he looked like a Japanese man and they blamed Japan's thirty-five-year occupation for their fate. I suspected that he got into fights.

One bitterly cold day after years of living like this, Young-chul came home with a chicken and a small bag of rice. I was sitting on the frozen ground in our shack with my blanket around me, trying to stay warm. Young-chul put the rice and chicken on the dirt floor without saying anything.

"Where did you get this?" I asked, examining the chicken. This amount of food was rare in the slum, and I couldn't imagine where it came from.

"I'll find some wood for a fire while you pluck it," Young-chul said. He started to leave.

"Young-chul," I said, "tell me where you got this."

"You do not need to know, Ummah," he said over his shoulder. Then he left to find firewood.

That night, we ate chicken for the first time in years. I'd forgotten how good it was to have a full stomach. I said that we should save half the chicken for another meal. Young-chul insisted we eat it all. "I can get more," he said.

"Young-chul," I said after we'd eaten and were wrapped in our blankets, "did you steal the chicken?"

"No," he answered, leaning against the tin wall. "I bought it."

"How did you get the money?"

"I have a job."

"A job? Doing what?"

"I work for some men selling things."

"What kind of things?"

Young-chul eyed me. Then he said, "Opium."

"Young-chul!" I cried, throwing off my blanket and going to him. "It is dangerous to sell opium. The police will arrest you. You might be killed!"

"What would you have me do, Ummah? We need food. We need somewhere better to live."

"I have been without food before," I said. "I've lived in crueler conditions."

"It does not matter," Young-chul said, shaking his head. "It is the only thing I can do."

"Then we will go to Japan," I said. "We will find your father."

"How will we get the money to go to Japan? Anyway, it will be no better there," Young-chul said, his voice straining with anger. "There, I will be a Korean. The Japanese will treat me the same there as the Koreans do here."

"But Japan and Korea are working together now," I countered. "They are helping us rebuild."

"Ha!" Young-chul scoffed. "Do you think the Japanese and Koreans will ever stop hating each other? Do you?"

He glared at me. I didn't want to, but I had to agree he was right.

"They will always hate each other and you know it," he said. "And I, half Japanese and half Korean, will forever be hated by one or the other."

He looked at his hands. "And if I work for these men, we will not starve."

We said nothing more, and after a while, Young-chul pulled his blanket around him and went to sleep. Though my stomach was full for the first time in months, I couldn't sleep. It was the curse of the two-headed dragon. I'd brought the curse on myself and I'd brought it on my son, too. Perhaps, all those years ago, it would have been better to escape to Manchuria as Father wanted instead of marrying Hisashi. But I loved Hisashi and I loved Young-chul. I wouldn't have had either if I'd run away.

But why was Young-chul cursed? I had invited the curse, not him. He didn't deserve it. I needed to do something to help him. I remembered that I still had my silver hairpin. I opened the rucksack and took it out. I stared at the elegant tines, its carved trees and crane. It would fetch a handsome price from a silver merchant in the Itaewon market. But I couldn't sell it. It was the only thing I had that connected me to Hisashi. Anyway, the money would only last for a month or two. Then, Young-chul would have to go back to selling opium.

And so, I couldn't stop my son from his illegal business, and we never went hungry again. Young-chul moved us out of the slum into a tiny second-floor apartment in a part of town the war had not destroyed. He bought mats for the floors and a table where we ate. He bought clothes for us. I constantly worried that he might get killed or arrested. Every day, I made him promise that he'd be careful. Every night I didn't sleep until he came home.

Though we had food and a place to live, Young-chul stayed angry. I sensed that he'd started using opium himself. He was gone for long hours and sometimes stayed out all night. When he did come home, he didn't want to talk. He was always depressed. Some days, he came home with bruises on his face and cuts on his hands and I could tell he'd been fighting again. I tried to think of ways to make money so he could quit his business and get off the street. I tried to find a job, but there were thousands of poor people like me looking for work. So I spent my time in my apartment or walking through the city, trying to think of a way to help my son. I thought about reaching out to Yoshiko for help but I couldn't. I'd promised to take care of Young-chul and I had failed. I didn't want her to see that Young-chul had turned to selling drugs.

One day, there was a knock on my apartment door. My heart sank. I thought it was the police to tell me they'd arrested Young-chul or that someone had killed him. I went to the door and said, "Who is there?"

"It is Shigeru Saito," a man answered.

I cracked open the door. There, standing in front of me with his hat in his hand, was Mr. Saito. He wore a tailored suit and his hair was almost completely gray. He wore glasses now, round with gold-wire rims. There were lines around his eyes that hadn't been there before. Even so, his powerful square frame made him imposing.

"Mr. Saito!" I exclaimed. I was so surprised I didn't think to bow.

"Hello, Miyoko," he replied in his sonorous voice. "I am sorry—Suk-bo. I should call you by your Korean name. May I come in?"

"Of course," I said. I opened the door.

He stepped inside my apartment and looked around. "You should have somewhere more appropriate to live," he said.

"I'm sorry for the condition of my apartment," I said.

"Forgive me," he said with a wave. "I'm sorry I mentioned it." He gave me a smile. "It is a pleasant day. Will you take a walk with me? I sit in meetings all day and do not get to stretch my legs."

"You want me to walk with you?" I said.

"If you would. I have some things to talk to you about."

"About Hisashi?" I asked.

"Let's go outside," Mr. Saito said. "I will tell you everything you need to know."

I quickly put on my shoes and followed Mr. Saito outside. A huge silver car with a chrome hood ornament was parked on the street. A driver with a black hat like Byong-woo used to wear in Sinuiju polished the car with a cloth. A large man dressed in a black suit waited next to the car. As we started to walk, the large man fell in line several steps behind us.

It was, as Mr. Saito said, a lovely day. The sun was shining and the temperature was just right for a walk. Mr. Saito walked with his hands behind his back as if he was inspecting everything he saw. With the bodyguard not far behind us, we walked to a boulevard. Workers were beginning to construct new buildings where old ones had stood before the war. They lugged bricks and glass panels on their backs and climbed on bamboo scaffolding. Trucks carrying lumber rumbled along the street.

"I'm sorry about the bodyguard," Mr. Saito said after we'd walked for a while. "But I am a wealthy Japanese businessman, and Koreans do not like the Japanese."

He continued. "Korea is beginning to recover after your civil war and Japan is helping. I am the head of a bank that is providing loans to your companies. It will take time, but I believe Korea will rebuild."

"That is good, sir," I said.

He looked sideways at me. "It took some effort to find you. And a little money, too."

"I'm sorry," I said, although I wasn't sure what I was apologizing for. "I never expected to see you again."

"No, I suppose you did not. It has been many years. Many apologies for the surprise. I should have written first. But I was in Seoul and I recently learned where you lived. I have to go back to Tokyo in a few days, so I came straightaway."

"Why, sir? Why do you want to see me?" I was anxious to ask him about Hisashi.

Mr. Saito took off his hat and held it at his side as we walked. He kept his eyes forward. "Suk-bo, I have always tried to live my life honorably. My father was a wise man. He told me that the only road to honor is justice. For years, I believed we were doing the honorable thing in Asia and here in Korea. We built roads, constructed dams, laid rail lines. We brought electricity to your country. I truly believed that your people were better off being part of Japan. That is why I wanted you to marry Hisashi."

He shook his head. "I was naïve. Eventually, my eyes were opened. I saw the injustice of our policy. I saw what it did to you and to others. I saw what it did to my son. I remembered what my father had told me about honor. If honor is justice, then there was no honor in what we were doing."

I couldn't wait any longer. "What has happened to Hisashi?" I asked. "Is he alive? Is he well?"

"He is alive, but he is not well," Mr. Saito answered, sadness crossing his face. "What happened to Hisashi is what opened my eyes the most. I was concerned about him before he left for Manchuria. It wasn't hard to see he was troubled. So I used my position as director-general to find out what Doctor Ishii was doing. I was horrified by what I discovered. I thought Doctor Ishii was teaching Hisashi medicine. Instead, he was destroying my son. I no longer believed in the inviolability of the emperor. I finally saw that the state was using Shintoism to justify their crimes. I protested and fell out of favor with the government. I did not care. What we were doing was deplorable and I had to speak out to save my honor."

"What happened to Hisashi after the war?" I asked.

"He was never tried for war crimes. It might have been better for him if he paid for his crimes. He is sick with guilt and I'm afraid he will never get well. I will never forgive myself for what my blindness did to him."

I remembered how sick Hisashi had been when I last saw him before he went to Manchuria. Mr. Saito was saying that Hisashi was still sick all these years later. I wanted to reach out to my husband. I wanted to help him get well. I wanted to make him the man I'd made love to on my wedding night.

"I want to go to him," I said. "I want to help him."

"I am sure you do," Mr. Saito replied. "First, tell me about my grandson. I have dedicated the rest of my life to correcting my mistakes so that I might die with honor. My first son was killed in the war. Yoshiko is not able to have children—that is why she never married. Masaru is my only grandson."

"Masaru," I said. "His Korean name is Young-chul."

"Yes, yes, yes," Mr. Saito said. "I shall call him Young-chul. We should not have taken your names from you."

"I worry about him. He is cursed by his blood. Half Japanese, half Korean. He does not know where he belongs. He cannot find peace in who he is."

"Does he have a job? How do you have money for your apartment?"

I wasn't sure what I should tell my father-in-law about his grandson. I could make up a story that Young-chul had a respectable job and worked hard. But I doubted if I could deceive Mr. Saito. He was a man of wealth and could verify my story. And he'd made the effort to find me and wanted to know about his grandson. He was acting honorably and deserved to know the truth.

"He sells opium," I answered.

Mr. Saito went quiet. I was afraid he was going to scold me for being a bad mother. I was afraid he would take Young-chul away from me.

Finally, Mr. Saito said, "I see. I want to believe that he tried to find some other way to earn money."

"There is not much work here," I said. "But no one would hire him anyway. They can tell he is Japanese."

We came to a construction site that blocked the way, and Mr. Saito pointed us to head back. The bodyguard let us by and continued several paces behind us. "I will help you," he said. "My grandson should know that from this point forward, he does not need to sell drugs. I will set up an account for you at my bank. You will have what you need to live a respectable life."

"Thank you, sir," I said. "But perhaps we could move to Japan. I could be with Hisashi again and help him get well. And Young-chul can start a new life there."

"Hisashi does not live in Japan," Mr. Saito said unhappily. "He hates Japan because of what it did to him—what it made him do. He moved to America. Los Angeles in the state of California. Before he left, he made me promise not to try to find him. Many times, I have been tempted to break that promise. I am a wealthy man and could force him to come home. But I will not break my promise to my son. Still, I am his father and I am concerned about him."

"I am willing to go to America, sir," I said. "I will take Young-chul."

"I am sure he would not want to see you. He is a broken man."

"What can I do?" I pleaded. "I still love Hisashi."

Mr. Saito nodded. "You can take care of his son," he answered. "That is what you can do for your husband."

He was right, of course. If I couldn't help Hisashi directly, then I should help his son. I had to convince Young-chul to stop selling opium. If he was using the drug, I had to get him to stop.

We'd come to my apartment building. The driver stood at the door of the silver car, ready to open it. The bodyguard stood off to the side. Mr. Saito reached inside his suit coat and gave me a business card. On it was the name of a bank and an address in Seoul. "Go to this address and show them this card. Tell them who you are. Someone there will take care of you. I will stay in contact with you. The next time I am in Seoul, I would like to meet my grandson."

"Yes, sir," I said, taking the card. Then I said, "Wait! I have something for you."

As Mr. Saito waited outside, I ran into my apartment and from inside my rucksack I took *Les Misérables* and *Romeo and Juliet*. I ran back to Mr. Saito.

"I took these from your study in Sinuiju," I said, offering the books to him.

Mr. Saito took them and gave me a smile. "Ah," he said, "two of my favorites." He gazed at them admiringly. Then he gave *Romeo and Juliet* back to me. "I will keep *Les Misérables*," he said, "but you should have *Romeo and Juliet*."

"Thank you, sir," I said.

Mr. Saito shook his head. "There is no need to thank me, Suk-bo," he replied. "I am doing this for my own honor, and maybe, in a small way, for the honor of Japan."

Mr. Saito put on his hat and turned to the car. The driver opened the door and Mr. Saito climbed in, followed by his bodyguard. The driver hurried to get behind the wheel, and the big silver car drove off.

The next day I went to the bank, where they treated me like a queen and showed me that Mr. Saito had opened an account for me with a large sum of money. I withdrew some money—more than I'd ever had in my life—and took it to the apartment. I showed it to Young-chul and told him where it came from. I expected him to be thrilled that his grandfather wanted to reconnect with him. I thought he'd be relieved that he didn't need to sell opium anymore.

Young-chul was unmoved. "I do not want his money," he sneered. "Does he think we are beggars, a charity case? He has been gone from me for as long as I can remember. I do not know him. Why should I care?"

"Son," I said, "do not judge him that way. Everything was so confused back then. It was impossible to know what was right. I believe he tried to do the honorable thing. I believe he is doing it now."

Young-chul slumped at the table. "It doesn't matter."

"Why do you say that, Young-chul?" I pleaded. "Why?"

"Because I do not care," he answered.

His eyes were dilated and swam inside his head. His shoulders sagged more than usual and his face was flaccid. He hadn't eaten well in weeks and his cheekbones stuck out. His once shiny hair was tangled and dull.

"Young-chul," I said, "with your grandfather's money, we can get help for you."

"Help," he said, his eyes unfocused. "I have the help I need, and I don't want his charity."

"Perhaps we can use the money to move to America and start over," I said.

"America," he said, lazily shaking his head. "The home of the brave, they call it. I doubt if I will be any more at home there than I am here. No, I do not want to go to America to start over."

He was gone all night. When he came home late the next morning, he had another bruise on his face and a cut lip. He said nothing as I cleaned the cut and applied a cold cloth to his bruise. I didn't ask how he got his injuries. I already knew. He was half Japanese living in Korea, where they hated the people who'd oppressed them for a half century. When I was done, he went to sleep on his mat without eating. He slept all day as I sat at the table overcome with worry for my son.

Young-chul died on a Wednesday in July. I knew why the police were at my apartment when they knocked on the door. Young-chul hadn't come home for three days. I'd roamed the street where he sold his drugs, searching for him. I'd asked people if they'd seen him. No one knew where he was.

Over the previous months, he'd grown more taciturn and withdrawn as if he'd given up on life. I couldn't say or do anything to help him. I'd told him we should move to an apartment in a nicer part of the city where he could escape. He refused. I thought about calling Mr. Saito to have him intervene. But I knew it would only make Young-chul withdraw further.

Standing at my apartment door, the policemen said someone had murdered Young-chul. "Stabbed in the heart," they said. "We think it was a robbery. He was selling drugs." I didn't cry or ask questions, and they didn't ask questions of me, as if they didn't really care about finding the killer. They told me Young-chul's body was at the morgue and that I had to go with them to sign some papers.

I went to the morgue in a police car. There, a man dressed in white showed me Young-chul, but it was like I was floating above the scene and nothing below was real. I signed their papers, and the man in white asked me if I wanted to take the body home for a traditional *kobok* funeral ceremony. I didn't understand why I should have a funeral for this person I didn't know, so I said no. Then he asked me what I wanted to do with Young-chul's body. I said I didn't care. He offered to have the body buried in the community grave for a fee. I agreed. I couldn't understand why he was asking me all these questions. This wasn't my little prince. My Young-chul laughed at my jokes and played hide-and-seek with me in the house in Sinuiju. He wouldn't sell opium. No one would stab him in the heart.

When the man was done with his questions and I had signed his papers, the police took me back to my apartment. I switched off the light and sat in the dark, trying to understand what had just happened. Eventually, all the pieces came together in my mind and I realized Young-chul would never come home again. My son, my little prince, was gone from me forever. Then I cried as only a mother who has lost a child can cry. And there with me, framed by the window, was the two-headed dragon. I didn't mind that it was there. It didn't scare me. I had nothing more it could take from me. It seemed to know that I wasn't afraid of it. It just stayed there watching me, waiting for me.

And when I had cried so hard I could cry no more, the two-headed dragon was no longer with me. In its place was the spirit of a broken man. It was the spirit of my husband, my beloved Hisashi.

THIRTY-TWO

I didn't leave my apartment for two weeks. I slept very little and didn't eat or make tea. Everything reminded me of Young-chul—his clothes, his tea bowl, his sleeping mat. I was so crippled with grief, I did nothing with them. I sat in the dark. Now and then I looked out the window at the people on the street. I couldn't understand how they were able to go on with their lives, what they had to do that was so important. I couldn't see how I would ever be one of them again.

The entire time, Hisashi's ghost was with me. It often stood at the window. Sometimes it was at the table. I never heard it talk. It never touched me. It was like someone you can't see in a dark room yet you know they are there. I didn't know what it wanted from me, and I didn't have the energy to try to understand it.

One morning when I thought I couldn't bear the pain another day, Yoshiko came. She wore a Western-style dress instead of her kimono. Her hair was up as it always was. She told me Mr. Saito had learned Young-chul had died and that she insisted on coming to Seoul to see me. I burst into tears and begged for her forgiveness for not saving Young-chul. She cried, too, and said I shouldn't feel guilty. We hugged. Then, she cleared a space under the window for an altar. We lit a candle so Young-chul's spirit would have light to find its way to the other world. Yoshiko had brought Young-chul's toy boat with her, and she placed it on the altar so his spirit would have something to make it happy. We placed one of his shirts at the altar so his spirit could stay warm. Yoshiko made tea and filled Young-chul's tea bowl. She placed it at the altar so his spirit would have something to drink. We bowed and prayed that Young-chul's spirit would have a safe journey.

Then we talked for hours about the boy we loved. We reminisced about our times with Young-chul in the Saito house. I told Yoshiko about Young-chul after she'd left for Tokyo. We talked about how he died, why he died, and we cried again. We were two mothers—a Korean mother and a Japanese mother—grieving over our child. We shared our pain, and by sharing, it eased a little.

When at last we had nothing more to say about Young-chul, Yoshiko asked, "When did you last eat?"

"I do not know," I answered.

"Take a bath," she said. "You look a mess and we cannot have that. Put on clean clothes. You should get some fresh air."

I didn't want to take a bath, but since it was Yoshiko telling me to do it, I went to the shared bathroom and I bathed. I put on clean clothes. I went back to my apartment where Yoshiko brushed and braided my hair.

I felt better, but I didn't feel like going out and I said so. "You need something to eat," Yoshiko insisted. She took my hand and led me outside. It was a pleasant evening. We walked down the street and then to the boulevard. Yoshiko bought some *japchae* noodles from a street vendor. We took the food to a small park not far from my apartment. We sat on a bench and ate as people strolled by, some holding hands, others with children in tow.

Yoshiko was right, as she always was. The bath, clean clothes, fresh air, and food lifted my spirits a little. I finally saw that though it would take everything I had, it was possible to go on without my prince. Even so, I didn't know what I should do with my life now that Young-chul was gone. I said, "It seems like I have nothing to live for."

Yoshiko looked out at the park. "Yes, you do," she said. "You have two things to live for."

"Two?"

"Your son, our sweet Young-chul, turned to crime and drugs because of bigotry. The Japanese in Sinuiju hated him because he was Korean. The Koreans here in Seoul hated him because he was Japanese. It is heartbreaking—a fine young man killed by hate."

She continued to look out at the park. "To honor him, to give his life meaning, we need to fight against the bigotry that killed him. We need to fight for human rights. My father is dedicated to the cause. He says that to have honor, we must stand up for justice and the welfare of all people. That is why his bank is helping your businesses. I am committed to helping him. You should fight, too."

"How?" I asked. "I do not know what I can do."

"If you are committed to the cause of human rights," Yoshiko said, "you will find a way."

"Yes, I suppose you are right," I replied. "I will try. You said there are two things I should do. What is the other?"

"You know what it is," Yoshiko said, looking at me.

"Hisashi," I said. "I must find him and help him. Your father told me he promised to leave Hisashi alone."

"That is true and we have."

I nodded. "When he left for Manchuria, he told me I had to stop loving him. I refused and I still love him today. He needs to know. I will go to America and find him and show him I always loved him. I will tell him about our son."

Night was upon us and I was exhausted from weeks of grief. We walked back to my apartment without talking. Yoshiko stopped outside my building. She told me she had to go back to Tokyo in the morning. I embraced her and said thank you. She took my hand. She promised she would stay in touch with me and that she and her father would do any-thing for me. She gave me her address and telephone number in Tokyo. She told me to write or call anytime. I thanked her again and bowed to her. She nodded respectfully and walked to the boulevard to hail a taxi.

Over the next several weeks, I started to eat and sleep again. I went out of the apartment for walks to regain my strength. I gave away Young-chul's clothes and sleeping mat, but I kept the altar to him under my window. The ache of losing my prince never left me. After a while, I realized it never would. I would carry the ache with me for the rest of my life and would have to find a way to bear it.

When eventually I felt strong enough, I called Mr. Saito on a pay phone to tell him I wanted to go to America to find Hisashi. He said he'd take care of everything. He asked me when I wanted to go.

"As soon as I can," I answered.

They said the airplane was a DC-4, and I was to sit in the first-class section all the way to Los Angeles. The pretty stewardess in a blue dress showed me to my seat. It was made from leather—the first time I'd ever sat in a leather chair. All the others in first class were men wearing crisp dark suits and carrying expensive briefcases.

I thought it was a little silly to fly to America in an airplane, but Mr. Saito had insisted. "You shall fly first class," he'd said. I didn't know what first class meant, but it sounded expensive. Anyway, I wasn't going to argue with him. I'd never flown in an airplane before, and in my life, I'd never had anything labeled first class.

As I sat in the leather chair, the big airplane roared to life, its huge propellers turning so fast they were a blur. The airplane rumbled down the runway, and just like that, we were airborne. I looked out the win-dow at the city of Seoul. Here and there were construction sites. As

Mr. Saito had said, the city was beginning to rebuild. I saw Mount Bukhansan standing like a soldier guarding the city. After a few minutes, the city gave way to granite-topped mountains and valleys filled with rice paddies in tight geometric patterns. From high above my country, I saw that it was indeed beautiful. This was where I'd grown up. In my youth I'd been happy here. But ever since I'd married Hisashi, my countrymen had rejected me. And they'd rejected my son for being half Japanese and drove him to his death. I was angry at them. Even so, deep in my soul, I was sad to be leaving.

We landed in Tokyo three hours later. The businessmen filed out of the airplane, but the stewardess said I should stay on board. "This airplane goes on to Hawaii," she said. I stayed as a new group of well-dressed men boarded and took their seats. Soon, the airplane was flying again over the Pacific Ocean on its way to Hawaii. We flew into the night. I tried to sleep, but I was too excited. The thrill of flying in a modern airplane to America and the hope of seeing Hisashi again kept me awake all night. I studied a book I bought on how to speak English. I'd heard American soldiers speak the language and I knew a few words. I'd heard that it was difficult to learn, but I was determined.

I changed airplanes in Honolulu and then flew on to California. I was amazed at how long the flight was. I asked the stewardess, "How fast does the airplane go?"

"Over two hundred miles per hour," she answered. I thought she had to be wrong. How could something as big as an airplane move so fast? I shook my head and looked at the blue-gray ocean below.

We landed in Los Angeles in the afternoon. I walked down the airplane stairs and set foot in America. The sun was warm and the sky was blue. A gate attendant led me inside the terminal building and showed me where to pick up my luggage—a large suitcase I had bought in the Itaewon market. There, a man dressed in a chauffeur's uniform met me. "Good day, ma'am," he said in Korean. "I am Sung-ki. I am here to take you to your apartment."

Sung-ki drove me into the city in a tan Ford sedan. I sat in the back as he drove. The road was jammed with cars. They sped along the highway as if they were late to something important. They honked their horns when the traffic stopped. Sung-ki expertly steered the car through the traffic toward an area with many buildings. One was the tallest I'd ever seen. It was white with a peak like a mountaintop. "That is Los Angeles City Hall," Sung-ki said.

I saw palm trees for the first time. I almost laughed aloud at the odd-looking trees with long narrow trunks and fronds like wings high in the air. They swayed gently in the warm breeze.

We went into a residential area. People were everywhere—on the sidewalks, in cars, and staring out windows. Most of them were white people, but some were Asians. "Many Koreans live here, and more are coming every day," Sung-ki explained. "They call this Koreatown. Our civil war displaced so many of our people that thousands are moving to America. That is what I did," he said with a grin.

He stopped in front of a three-story building where Mr. Saito had leased an apartment for me. The driver got my suitcase out of the trunk and carried it inside. A woman stood behind a counter in the lobby. "This is Suk-bo Yi," Sung-ki said.

"Anyohaseyo, Miss Yi," the woman said with a bow. "I am Mrs. Park. I have your apartment ready for you."

Sung-ki gave me my suitcase and bowed. He handed me a business card. "I have been instructed to be available to you to help in any way," he said. "Call the number on this card to reach me."

I took the card and returned his bow. "*Kamsahamnida*," I said. "Thank you."

Mrs. Park showed me to the apartment. It was on the second floor and much larger than the one Young-chul and I had in Seoul. It had its own bathroom, a separate bedroom, and it was furnished. There was a kitchen with a table, and a main room with chairs and a bookshelf.

A box with knobs and a rectangle of gray glass sat against one wall. "What is that?"

"It is a television," Mrs. Park answered. "In America, you must have a television. It is quite the invention. When you have unpacked, I will show you how it works." I'd heard of televisions before, but I'd never seen one. I hadn't expected to have one in my apartment.

Mrs. Park left and I looked out the window at the street. Cars raced by in both directions. All along the street, construction booms raised steel beams high above the ground. It reminded me of the construction going on in Seoul, only this was much more impressive and widespread. I had heard that America had become a world power, and here in Los Angeles, I saw that it was true.

Dozens of people crowded the sidewalks. Some were Asians with black hair, and some wore traditional clothing. I saw they all stepped aside to let the white people by.

As I stood at the window looking at Los Angeles, I thought it might have been a mistake to come here. I was tired from my journey, and a little unsettled at being in such a strange place. I didn't know how to speak English. I didn't know anyone except Hisashi, and I didn't know where he was. I looked at the people on the street again. One of them could be my husband. For the first time in twenty years, I was near where he was. He was somewhere out there, my Hisashi, my beloved, and I was determined to find him.

After I'd unpacked, Mrs. Park showed me how to use the television, and I watched it for a little while. The device was fascinating. There were five channels with different programs on each one. There was a variety show, a movie, someone reading what appeared to be the news. I took out my English book and tried to understand what they were saying. But I was tired from traveling, and in the morning, I had to start trying to find Hisashi. I turned off the television and went to the bedroom.

The bed was high off the floor on a spring frame and had a mattress. I crawled under the blankets and tried to sleep, but the bed was too soft. I got up and pulled the mattress and blankets onto the floor. I pulled the blanket to my chin and fell asleep.

The next day, I started my search for Hisashi. I didn't know where to begin. I walked the streets of Koreatown, but I never saw him. After a week of searching for him on the streets, I concluded that I'd need help to find him in a big city like Los Angeles.

Back at my apartment, I remembered the driver Sung-ki who had picked me up at the airport. I remembered he said he would help me with whatever I needed. I got his card, then went to the lobby and used Mrs. Park's telephone.

"Anyohaseyo," he answered. "You are talking to Sung-ki."

I told him I was the woman he picked up at the airport for Mr. Saito, and I asked him if he could help me with something important.

"Are you at your apartment?" he asked. I told him I was, and he said he'd be right there.

Fifteen minutes later, Sung-ki and I sat in the lobby, and I told him I wanted to find Mr. Saito's son, Hisashi. He listened carefully and asked a few questions. When I was done, he said, "Most Japanese live north of downtown in Little Tokyo. I do not like to go there, but I will see what I can do."

I thanked him and he left. I went to my apartment and studied my English language book.

Three days later, after searching the streets all day for Hisashi, I came into the lobby and Mrs. Park stopped me. "There is a message for you," she said. She gave me a piece of paper. It was a message from Sung-ki. It read, *I have found Hisashi. Call me.*

My hand trembled as I dialed Sung-ki's number. He answered on the second ring and I told him I got his message.

"Hisashi does not live in Little Tokyo," he said. "He lives here, in Koreatown. He works in a restaurant named Silla near where you live." He gave me an address and I wrote it down.

Before I hung up, Sung-ki said, "Miss Yi, I went to the restaurant to be certain it was him. Are you sure you want to see him? I only ask because I don't think he would want to be seen by you."

I started to ask why, but I already knew. "I understand," I said. "Thank you, Sung-ki." I took the address of the Silla restaurant and went to my apartment.

I bathed and put on my nicest dress. I put my hair up and pinned it with the silver hairpin. I looked in the mirror. I was twenty years older than the last time Hisashi had seen me. There were lines on my face that hadn't been there before. My hair wasn't as thick as it once was. I looked like someone who'd been through many hardships. I worried that Hisashi wouldn't like the way I looked.

I left the apartment and headed to the Silla restaurant about six blocks away. The streets and sidewalks were crowded with cars and people going home. The restaurants were filling up. Soon, I was on the right block and my heart beat fast. Every nerve in my body tingled. I saw the sign for the restaurant. It was between a small food market and a furniture store. It had windows to the street so I could see inside. It was nearly full with diners. Two waitresses moved from table to table, taking orders and then disappearing behind swinging doors to the kitchen. I didn't see Hisashi.

I checked the address Sung-ki had given me. I was at the right place. As the waitresses went in and out of the kitchen, I peered into it to see if Hisashi was working there. I didn't have the right angle and couldn't see anyone.

I held my breath and went inside. A young waitress wearing too much makeup said, "Anyohaseyo." She nodded at an open table. "You may sit there," she said in Korean.

I didn't go to the table. The waitress looked at me. "You don't want that table?" she asked. "There is another one close to the kitchen."

"I would like the one near the kitchen, please," I said. The waitress showed me to the table and gave me a menu. It was in Hangul, but I couldn't focus on the words. I looked into the kitchen as the swinging doors opened and closed. I only caught brief glimpses of the people inside, and I couldn't see if one of them was Hisashi.

The waitress came to my table with a pad and pencil in her hand. "What would you like, ma'am?" she asked.

I hadn't read the menu. "Bibimbap," I answered.

"Beef or vegetable?" the waitress asked.

"Vegetable," I said, trying to see into the kitchen as the other waitress went through the doors.

"What do you want to drink?"

"Tea, please. Bori cha."

"Yes, ma'am," the waitress said. She took the menu from me and went into the kitchen to give them my order.

I sat at the table, afraid that Hisashi might come out and see me. I wasn't sure what I'd do if he did. I tried to calm myself, thinking he would probably not recognize me. The waitress came with my tea, and I asked if they had a Korean newspaper to read while I waited for my bibimbap. She got a newspaper from the counter and gave it to me. I pretended to read it as I stole glances into the kitchen.

I heard a plate break in the kitchen. "Ah!" a man's voice said. I could tell by the gruff tone it wasn't Hisashi. "Look what you have done! Stupid *wae-won!*" the man said.

Wae-won—Japanese bastard. I went to the kitchen door. My waitress came to me and said, "Do not worry about that, ma'am. Please sit. It is just our cook yelling at the dishwasher." She gave me a reassuring smile.

"Is your dishwasher Japanese?" I asked.

"Yes, he is. And you know how they are," she said with a look.

My heart stopped. It had to be my husband, Hisashi—a dishwasher in a Korean restaurant.

The waitress delivered my order of bibimbap and I poked at it with my chopsticks. I still couldn't see well enough into the kitchen to see if the dishwasher was Hisashi. But I heard the cook yell at him. "You are worthless," he said. "I should replace you with a good Korean worker." Then, "What are you looking at? Get back to work, you wae-won."

I ate a few bites and drank some tea. The waitress came and said, "You haven't eaten much. Don't you like the bibimbap?"

"It's fine," I said. "I decided I am not hungry. I would like the check, please."

The waitress scribbled something on her pad and gave me the bill. I went to the counter and paid her. Before I left, I asked, "What is your dishwasher's name?"

"Hisashi," she said, and then went back to work.

I left the restaurant and walked the streets of Koreatown for two hours. I was shocked that my husband was a lowly dishwasher. I couldn't understand why he was in Koreatown and not in Little Tokyo. But I had found him! My husband, my beloved Hisashi. I had to talk to him. I had to tell him I still loved him.

I went back to the restaurant just before it closed. I stood in the shadows and watched as the last customers left and the waitress locked the door from inside. She went to the kitchen. Five minutes later, the lights went out and a fat man and the waitresses went out the front door. A man who looked like Hisashi followed them. It was him! Hisashi! My heart beat fast and I thought I would cry. The waitresses went on their way as the fat man locked the door. Hisashi stared at his feet and waited. The fat man poked his chest, scolding him for something. I couldn't hear what he was saying. Then, the fat man shoved Hisashi aside and walked away.

Hisashi started to plod along the sidewalk. He never looked up. I followed him, and the cars, the street, the shops and restaurants all seemed to disappear. The only thing I saw was the back of the man in front of me. For so many years, I'd dreamed of seeing him again. Here he was only a few steps away. I wanted to throw my arms around him and tell him I was here with him. I wanted to tell him he didn't have to be a dishwasher anymore and he could come home with me.

Finally, I couldn't wait any longer. I gathered my courage and went to him. "Hisashi," I said. He kept walking as if he hadn't heard me. I put my hand on his back. "Hisashi, it's me, Suk-bo."

He stopped, but did not face me. He kept his eyes on the sidewalk.

I stepped in front of him. "Hisashi," I said. "Look at me."

He lifted his eyes. His face was as thin as the starving people I knew in the slums of Seoul. His once sparkling eyes were dull and lifeless. His hair was greasy.

I didn't care. I threw my arms around him and hugged him. "Hisashi," I cried, "I have found you."

He didn't return my embrace. I stepped away. I looked at him through my tears. I thought perhaps he didn't recognize me. "Hisashi, it is me, Suk-bo, your wife."

He stepped around me and continued walking with his head down. I followed him. "Don't you remember me? You scared me when I was picking strawberries in the woods behind my house. We were married in Sinuiju. I had a baby named Young-chul while you were in Tokyo." I took the hairpin out of my hair and showed it to him. "You gave me this."

He glanced at the hairpin as he walked. Tears ran down his cheeks.

"I have come all the way to America to find you," I continued. "Your father and sister are concerned about you. We want you to come home." He said nothing, but I could see his chest heave with crying.

"Hisashi," I begged, "say something."

"Please," he pleaded. "Leave me alone." I was stunned. I thought he'd be thrilled to see me after all these years. I'd dreamed that we could be together again, so I could nurse him back to health. We could go to Tokyo where his father and sister would help. I envisioned that someday he'd be well again and it would be like it was before. But he'd said, *Leave me alone*. He was still rejecting me, and though I knew he might do so, and though I thought I was prepared for it, it shattered my heart. And so, I went back to my apartment, crying all the way.

THIRTY-THREE

That night after I stopped crying, I tried to think of a way to reach Hisashi. It would take much more than just talking to him on the street. I pushed away my sadness and gathered my resolve. I would have to spend a long time in Los Angeles—maybe the rest of my life. If that's what it was going to take, then that's what I would do.

The next day I sent a letter to Mr. Saito telling him I'd found Hisashi and planned to stay in Los Angeles indefinitely. He replied saying he'd pay for the apartment and anything else I needed. In the letter was a name of someone to contact for a job.

On yet another sunny day in Los Angeles, I dressed and went to the apartment lobby. I asked Mrs. Park how to get to the address in Mr. Saito's letter. "Three streets down and two to the left," she said. "You can't miss it."

I found the address—a small, two-story building. I went to the blond receptionist and said, "Mr. Fredrik," trying to pronounce the name correctly.

The woman shook her head and said something in English. The only word I understood was "No."

Again, I said, "Mr. Fredrik." The woman rolled her eyes. She lifted a finger, picked up a telephone, and said something to someone on the other end. She hung up and pointed for me to sit in a chair.

A few minutes later, a young man came into the lobby. He wore a suit and glasses with black frames. The receptionist pointed at me and the man came to me. "My name is Peter Kim," he said in Korean. "Can I help you?"

"Yes, sir," I said, standing and bowing. "I am here to see this man." I gave him Mr. Saito's letter. He read it and grinned. "You want to see Fredrik Weinberg," he said. "America is not like Korea. Here they say the given name first and the family name second. Mr. Weinberg is the director of our organization. Come with me. I will take you to him."

As we walked up a flight of stairs, Mr. Kim asked, "Do you speak Japanese? Mr. Weinberg speaks it quite well."

"Yes, I do," I said.

"Good."

We went into an open area where several men and women sat at desks. They talked on telephones or worked on typewriters. None of them were Asian.

Mr. Kim took me to a woman sitting at a desk. She had brown hair and wore a light-green dress. Mr. Kim said something to her in English. The woman studied me as she said something to Mr. Kim.

"This is Carol, Mr. Weinberg's secretary," Mr. Kim said to me. "He is on a call and will see you when he is done." He pointed at a chair. "Sit here and Carol will let you know when Mr. Weinberg is ready."

I waited ten minutes, then twenty. Every so often, I would catch Carol staring at me. Then, she'd give me a condescending smile and look away. Finally, a man's voice came on a box. Carol pushed a button and said something. Then she opened the door to Mr. Weinberg's office. I went in, bowed, and said, "Konnichiwa."

He was a middle-aged man with thick graying hair. He wore a dark wool suit with a vest, white shirt, and a bow tie. He was average height and a little thick around the middle. He nodded to me. "Hello," he said in Japanese. "Please sit."

Mr. Weinstein had a letter in his hand. He studied it and then said, "I have a letter of introduction for you from a Mr. Saito, the president of Yamamoto Bank in Tokyo. His bank is an important donor to our organization. He recommends that I hire you." Mr. Weinstein placed the letter on his desk. He studied me.

"Do you know what we do here, Miss Yi?" he asked.

"No, sir," I answered.

"We are the Worldwide Alliance for Human Rights. We promote the articles set forth in the Universal Declaration of Human Rights. Do you know what that is?"

"No, sir," I said, a little embarrassed.

"It is a declaration adopted by the United Nations after World War Two. It affirms that all humans, regardless of their race, religion, gender, or language have four fundamental freedoms—freedom of speech, freedom of religion, freedom from fear, and freedom from want."

"I see."

"You don't speak English, do you?" Mr. Weinberg asked.

"No, sir," I answered. "I only know Korean, Japanese, and some Chinese."

Mr. Weinberg sighed. "If you don't know English, you can't type or answer the telephone. You can't be a receptionist, either. I'm sorry. I don't know how I can use you."

"I am learning English," I said.

"It will take you a long time to learn it," Mr. Weinberg countered. "In the meantime, I don't have a job for you. I'm sorry."

"I understand," I said with a nod. "Thank you for your time."

As I stood to leave, I remembered what Yoshiko had told me when I'd said I didn't know what I could do to help fight bigotry. *If you are committed, you will find a way.* My son had died because of bigotry. My parents had died fighting for freedom. And my husband was sick because his country had forced him to kill others.

I lifted my chin and faced Mr. Weinberg. "Tell me again, sir," I said. "What are the four fundamental freedoms?"

"Freedom of speech, freedom of religion, freedom from fear, and freedom from want," he replied.

"With all due respect, sir, have you or anyone you loved ever been denied any of these freedoms? Do you know firsthand what you are fighting for?"

He took a second to answer. "My parents were killed by the Nazis in Dachau," he said, finally.

"I'm sorry, sir," I said. "I do not know what happened to my parents. They were probably killed in a prison camp, just like your parents were."

Mr. Weinberg invited me to sit again. He unbuttoned his suit coat and asked me to tell him more. For the next hour he listened as I told my story. I told him what it was like living under Japanese rule, how my parents escaped to Manchuria and died there, how there were times in my life when I had nothing to eat for days and nowhere warm to sleep, how bigotry had killed my son. At the end, I said, "Like you, I know what you are fighting for here, Mr. Weinberg. I know all too well, and I will fight harder for it than anyone."

Mr. Weinberg nodded. "I believe you will," he said. "We don't pay much. But come back tomorrow and you can begin working for us."

Mr. Weinberg gave me an advance on my pay to buy clothes for the office. He also paid for English classes and even set me up with a tutor, who I met with three times per week. I worked hard to learn English, studying late into the night and using it when I went out. I watched television and looked up words and phrases the television people used.

Eventually, I began to understand what they were saying. Although it was different than the Asian languages I knew, in a few months, I was talking to Mr. Weinberg in English most of the time.

At first, I ran errands and learned how an office worked. I helped with anything involving Asia. I did research in documents written in Korean, Chinese, and Japanese. I did interviews and helped Mr. Kim translate them. I made sure I was the first one in the office in the morning, and I was usually the last one to leave. Along with English, I quickly learned how I could help. Mr. Weinberg gave me Japanese, Chinese, and Korean books to read about human rights. I studied them whenever I could.

Every night I went to the Silla restaurant where Hisashi worked. I always wore the silver hairpin, and I always took the table next to the kitchen. I became friends with the waitress who wore too much makeup. She called herself Angel. As it turned out, the food at Silla was quite good. There was everything I remembered from Korea—bulgogi, galbi, japchae, bibimbap, and, of course, kimchi. Over time, I'd ordered everything on the menu, but I never enjoyed the food. I always ate staring through the swinging doors to try to see Hisashi. And when I heard the cook scold Hisashi and call him names, I lost my appetite completely. Angel got used to taking a full plate away. I think she knew I was there for Hisashi. Thankfully, she never once asked me about him.

After I ate, I'd wait outside the restaurant until it closed. When Hisashi was done working, I walked alongside him as he went home to a shabby boardinghouse just west of downtown. I made small talk, saying things like, "The restaurant wasn't busy today," or "I hear it will rain tomorrow," or "It is a good day to be alive."

Hisashi always kept his eyes on the sidewalk. I could tell that my being there was hard for him, but I was determined to reach him. He never said anything until we got to the boardinghouse. Then, without looking up, he'd say, "Please do not do this."

I always replied, "I have to."

This went on for months. I tried to get him to respond by talking about our life in Korea. I reminisced about the time we first met or when he gave me the hairpin. I told him about our son. He never said anything until we got to the boardinghouse.

Then, it was, "Please do not do this."

"I have to."

After I'd been at the Worldwide Alliance for Human Rights for a year, Mr. Weinberg put me in charge of uncovering human rights violations in Asia before and during World War II. I had great passion for the work. After all, I'd lived it. Still, it was almost unbearable to read the reports of inexplicable inhumanity and talk to survivors. There was the rape of Nanking that Byong-woo had told me about—a horrific two-month massacre that murdered hundreds of thousands of Chinese. There was the forced labor of tens of millions of Koreans, Chinese, and Pacific Islanders. There was the torture and murder of rebels.

But it wasn't just the Japanese who committed atrocities. It was other Asian countries, too. There was the imprisonment, torture, and murder of tens of thousands by Kim Il-sung in North Korea. And there was the imprisonment, torture, and murder of tens of thousands by the American puppet Syngman Rhee in South Korea. There was the repression and slaughter of millions of Chinese at the hands of Mao Zedong and the communists. There were wars and atrocities committed in southeast Asia and the subjugation of Tibet by the Chinese. I didn't understand how people could be so inhumane. It seemed sometimes that the entire world had gone mad.

And there was Unit 731. One day when I was at my desk, Mr. Weinberg dropped off a thick envelope from the US State Department marked "Top Secret." I asked him what it was and how he got it.

"Read it," he said. "And don't ask how I got it."

I opened the envelope. A few pages were written in English, but most were in Japanese. I quickly saw that they were documents the Japanese had turned over to the United States after they'd surrendered. They described a research camp the Imperial Army set up after they invaded Manchuria and how the Japanese conducted experiments there. Outwardly, the research was for preventing epidemics and purifying water. However, the real purpose was to develop chemical and germ weapons. They also did experiments on people. Experiments like live vivisection, extreme frostbite, drowning, forced infections, weapons testing. According to the documents, they murdered thousands of Chinese, Filipinos, Indonesians, and Koreans. Doctor Shiro Ishii led the unit.

I immediately thought of my parents. I wondered if the Japanese captured them and sent them to Unit 731. As I sat at my desk, images of the soldiers torturing and killing my mother and father began to form in my mind. I quickly pushed them away. I had to believe the Japanese had killed my parents and didn't capture them, or I wouldn't be able to continue doing my job.

And then I thought of Hisashi. What everyone had said about Unit 731 was true, and Hisashi had worked there. I couldn't deny it anymore. I hadn't heard anything about Unit 731 after the war, so I had questioned if the rumors about it were true. But there it was in the documents in front of me. Doctor Ishii and the Japanese who worked at Unit 731 were war criminals, including Hisashi.

I wondered if I was doing the right thing by continuing to love him. I was angry that he'd abandoned me and Young-chul. Working for Doctor Ishii, he'd committed war crimes—the documents proved it. Perhaps I didn't know him as well as I thought I did. After all, I'd spent only a year with him.

But it didn't make sense. I'd felt his tenderness when we lay together. His mother and Yoshiko had said he was sensitive. And he'd been troubled when he'd come home before going to Manchuria. I wanted to know what had happened to my husband. I wanted to talk to him about it. For months I'd tried in vain to get him to talk to me, but he never did.

As I read through the documents, I wondered why I hadn't heard more about Unit 731 before now. Everyone knew about the Nazi experiments by Doctor Mengele in Auschwitz, but no one knew about Doctor Ishii and Unit 731. I flipped to papers in the back. There were documents translated from Russian that detailed trials and convictions for war crimes committed by the Japanese that the Russians had captured in Unit 731. It accused the Americans of refusing to prosecute the Japanese they had captured—specifically, Doctor Ishii.

I took the pages to Mr. Weinberg's office. "Have you read this?" I asked.

"Yes," he answered.

"Is it true the Americans didn't prosecute Doctor Ishii?"

"Yes."

"Why?" I asked.

A disgusted look crossed Mr. Weinberg's face. "It's simple," he said. "The Americans gave him immunity for his war crimes in exchange for his research. Doctor Ishii lives in Tokyo now, a free man. He never stood trial for torturing and murdering tens of thousands of people."

Now I was disgusted, too. "What can we do?" I asked.

"All we can do is publish this information. The American government will deny it. They'll spin it as Russian propaganda. It could make trouble for us."

"I see," I replied. Typically, I'd express my indignation and tell Mr. Weinberg that I didn't care if we'd get in trouble with the American government, but I had to consider Hisashi. I had told Mr. Weinberg the Japanese had forced my husband to join the Imperial Army and that he had died. I hadn't told him that he had worked for Doctor Ishii. All along, I'd kept secret that my husband was alive and working less than a mile away from the Worldwide Alliance for Human Rights office. I knew I should tell Mr. Weinberg the truth, but I couldn't.

I went back to my desk. Although I knew I should work on publishing the information about Unit 731, I set the papers aside. I told Carol that I had to go outside and get some air. I left the office and didn't come back that day.

That night I went to the Silla restaurant as I always did. I ordered jap-chae and bori cha tea. Angel brought my food, and once again, I didn't eat it. I wondered why Hisashi hadn't refused to work for Doctor Ishii when he learned what they were doing there. I wondered what made him abandon me and throw his life away. I was angry at him.

"You stupid wae-won!" I heard the cook say. Anger swelled inside me, but I wasn't sure what I was angry about. I hated when the cook abused my husband, but I'd never done anything about it before. Now, I thought that Hisashi was getting what he deserved—or at least what he wanted. Whatever it was, I hated it, and I wanted it to stop.

I left the table and pushed open the door to the kitchen. Hisashi was hunched over a sink working on a pile of dishes. The fat cook was at a stove, stirring something in a wok. They both turned when I came in.

"Stop calling him names!" I shouted at the cook.

"But he is Japanese!" the cook replied with a puzzled look.

Angel came into the kitchen and put a hand on my shoulder. Before she could lead me away, I said, "He is my husband."

The cook's eyes went wide and he looked from me to Hisashi and then back at me. Hisashi turned to the sink again.

After a few seconds, Angel said, "Come with me." She led me out of the kitchen, back to my table. All the restaurant customers stared at me.

"Hisashi is your husband?" Angel asked.

"Yes," I answered.

"You married a Japanese?"

"Yes."

Angel looked disappointed. "I don't think you should stay here," she said, glancing at the restaurant patrons. "You do not have to pay today. You never eat much, anyway." She took my plate from the table.

I went to the door. Before I left, Angel said, "You should not come back. I am sorry."

I hesitated, thinking I should give everyone in the restaurant a lecture about bigotry. But I knew it wouldn't do any good. They thought I was a chinilpa and they wouldn't care what I said. So I pushed through the door and left the restaurant.

As usual, I waited for Hisashi to finish work and walked with him to his boardinghouse. I was angry at what had happened in the restaurant. I was angry at what he did at Unit 731 and for not fighting back. Mostly, I was angry at him for leaving me.

When we got to the boardinghouse, my rage spilled out. "Why did you leave me?" I cried. "We were in love! We had a beautiful son. I needed you!"

I'd never talked to him like this before, and I wasn't sure what he'd do. He kept his eyes low and didn't reply.

"Why?" I pleaded. "Why didn't you fight for me?"

"You don't know what they made me do," he said.

I was surprised that he said something. It was the first time he'd said anything except "Please do not do this" at the end of our walks. My anger quickly changed to pity.

"Yes, I do know," I said. "Unit 731."

He looked incredibly sad. "You know?"

"I've read reports about it for my work."

"Then you know why you must leave me alone," he said and started walking again.

I walked with him. "I cannot leave you alone," I said. "I still love you. I will always love you. I just don't understand why you didn't refuse to work for Doctor Ishii. Why, Hisashi? Tell me."

He'd bowed his head and was crying. I put my arm around him and he didn't pull away. I started crying, too.

"It's killing you, isn't it?" I said, holding him. "I want to help. Let me help you."

He pushed away from me. "It will kill you, too," he said. "They kicked you out of the restaurant because you married me. Imagine what they would do to you if they knew what I did."

"I don't care," I said. "Love is a commitment you make every day for the rest of your life."

"A commitment . . . ," he said.

"Yes. I will not leave you, my husband. Come home with me. Let me take care of you."

Hisashi shook his head. "No."

"Then just talk to me. It will help to talk about it."

"No," he repeated.

The look of sadness on Hisashi's face broke my heart. "I'm sorry," he said. "I will not drag you down with me."

As he went into his boardinghouse, I whispered, "I'm sorry, too."

I never again ate at the Silla restaurant, and although I was angry at Hisashi, I walked with him to the boardinghouse every night. He still didn't talk on our walks, but he didn't say "Please do not do this" anymore. I knew I shouldn't push him to talk about Unit 731. I hoped that if I didn't abandon him, he would talk about it someday.

That day arrived on a hot summer night years later. He came out of the restaurant and said, "Let's go to MacArthur Park." The park was out of the way from his boardinghouse, so I knew this was the day he was going to talk.

We found a bench near the park pond. Hisashi looked at his hands and began to tell me his story. He told me how when he got to Tokyo, he immediately regretted taking the position with Doctor Ishii. He'd expected the research to be about how to help people recover from injuries and diseases. He thought he was going to learn a great deal about medicine. Instead, Doctor Ishii's work was on biological warfare. "He *created* diseases so he could study their progression," Hisashi said. "He injured people to see how they would respond. He didn't care about healing them."

He said he wanted to quit right away and go back to me, but they wouldn't let him. Instead, they made him a lieutenant in the army. He didn't dare refuse the commission, but he couldn't work for Doctor Ishii. He asked for a transfer. "I didn't even care if it was somewhere outside the medical corps," Hisashi said. "I only wanted to get out."

They didn't grant him a transfer, and when he objected to what Doctor Ishii was doing, they told him to stay quiet. They threatened to destroy his father's career. "And," Hisashi said, "they threatened me with you."

"Me?" I said, surprised.

Hisashi nodded. "The entire thing about our son being the chauffeur's son and not mine was a ploy by Haru and the Kempei tai. They wanted to destroy my father. They thought he was weak. That's why they gave me the job with Doctor Ishii. That's why they accused you of infidelity. They planned to use you against me and me against my father."

"I thought it was your mother who wanted me arrested," I said.

"Haru tricked her. It was him and the Kempei tai all along."

"They tried to arrest me anyway," I said. "That's why I had to run away."

"Yes, my father wrote to me about that. I wrote and told him it wasn't true about you and Byong-woo. Not long after that incident, Father became disillusioned with Japan and his career was over. As for me, I'd already worked for Doctor Ishii for nearly two years and couldn't get out. It was horrible. If you only knew." Hisashi shook his head.

I knew. I just couldn't imagine how someone as sensitive as Hisashi could be a part of it.

"What will you do now?" I asked.

Hisashi sniffed. "Tonight, I will try to sleep, although most nights I cannot. I will stay here in Koreatown, even though they hate Japanese. It is my punishment for what I did to your people. Tomorrow, I will go to work as a dishwasher at the restaurant."

"Let me help you," I said.

"No," Hisashi replied. "It is my burden and mine alone."

He pushed himself off the bench and headed to the boardinghouse. And in silence, I walked with him.

THIRTY-FOUR

Los Angeles, 1993

A picture of Mr. Weinberg in his three-piece suit and bow tie, shaking hands with President Bill Clinton, made the front page of the *Los Angeles Times*. Mr. Weinberg wore a medal that the president had just given him. The caption read, *Mr. Fredrik Weinberg of Los Angeles receiving the Presidential Citizens Medal for his forty-five years fighting for human rights.*

The article said Mr. Weinberg thanked the hardworking people at the Worldwide Alliance for Human Rights. He explicitly mentioned me. "In particular I want to thank Suk-bo Yi for her tireless work on human rights in Asia," the article quoted him as saying.

Over the years, Mr. Weinberg had built the alliance into one of the world's leading human rights organizations. He regularly met with world leaders and testified before US Congress and the United Nations. With all the money he'd raised, he was able to move the alliance to a new headquarters on Wilshire Boulevard. Sixty employees occupied the entire fifth floor of a new building only a few blocks from our old building.

Upon his return from Washington, Mr. Weinberg, now in his mideighties, announced that he would retire soon. Before he left, he'd asked me when I planned to retire. I was in my seventies now, and I still enjoyed working. I'd become an expert on Asian human rights. I'd read the great literature on human rights—my favorite was *Les Misérables*, which I was finally able to read in English. For the previous fifteen years, I'd been in charge of the Asian sector and now had twenty people in my group. The press quoted me often and I was invited to speak at conferences. I'd had a rewarding career—more so than I ever imagined I would as a young woman in Korea. And though my career never paid much, I didn't need the money.

Ten years earlier, I'd received a letter and a check from Yoshiko. The letter said that Mr. Saito had died. He'd been a successful businessman during his life and had accumulated a large fortune. The letter said that Mr. Saito was proud of me for the work I'd done with the alliance. As a reward, in his will he left some money to me. He asked that I use it for myself and to take care of Hisashi.

I had to sit down when I looked at the check. It was more than I could imagine I'd ever have. I could buy a nice house and move Hisashi into it. I could hire someone full-time to take care of him. But I'd tried for years to get him to accept my help. He never did.

Hisashi was an old man now. The restaurant had fired him twenty years earlier. He roamed the streets of East Los Angeles, homeless and destitute. Every night when I could, I'd buy takeout and search for him to give him something to eat. Sometimes, he took the food. Sometimes, he didn't. I tried to move him into a homeless shelter, but he refused to go. I talked to him, telling him that he had to forgive himself for what he'd done at Unit 731, and that I forgave him for leaving me. It didn't help. He never bathed, and he was rail thin. He slept on park benches or on sidewalks. Korean kids taunted him. His shoes and clothes were tattered, and he refused to take new ones. He didn't talk much, but I never got the sense that he'd lost his mind. He was broken and sad and crippled with guilt.

With Mr. Weinberg retiring, it would have been a good time for me to retire, too. But I had one more thing I wanted to do. In Asia, women were coming forward with stories about how the Imperial Army forced them into brothels during World War II. The Japanese called them comfort women, but in truth, they were sex slaves. Many had died in the brothels—some committed suicide, and many were shot at the end of the war.

The women and some scholars said there had been hundreds of thousands of them. They were Korean, Chinese, Filipino, and even Dutch. The soldiers raped them nearly every day—some for as long as seven years. The Japanese government denied the reports, but I believed them. I remembered the last time I saw my aunt in front of her house outside my village when she told me that my cousins had been forced to work in the boot factory, code for a military brothel. The new information was consistent with her story. I had to contact my cousins to learn more.

In my job, I had access to a lot of information. Although I couldn't locate Soo-hee, it wasn't difficult to find her younger sister, Jae-hee. She lived in Seoul at an address south of the Han River. I wrote a long letter telling her about my work and asking if it was true that she'd been a comfort woman. If so, I asked if she'd be willing to tell me about it. She wrote back and said yes, the Japanese had forced her to work in what they called a "comfort station" and that she was willing to share her story with me. I sent her a letter telling her I was coming to see her, and I scheduled a flight to Seoul.

I'd been back to Seoul several times since I'd moved to America. It always surprised me how much it'd changed since I lived there. They called it "The Miracle on the Han River," and it was. In just a few short decades, Seoul had grown from a poor, backward city nearly destroyed by the Korean War, to a modern metropolis. It seemed like they'd built dozens of new high-rises every time I visited. They were building a modern subway, and new highways crisscrossed the city. I was proud of what my country had accomplished in such a short time. I often wondered what my life would have been like if I'd stayed.

It was a short taxi drive from Gimpo Airport to Jae-hee's apartment in a section of the city that looked like it had been built early in Seoul's rebirth and was starting to decline. Jae-hee lived on the sixth floor of an eight-story building. I took the elevator to the sixth floor and knocked on apartment 627.

Jae-hee opened the door and bowed. Although she was several years younger than me, she looked much older. She was petite, and her hair was nearly all gray. She had a scar on her lip and another above her eyebrow. The lines around her eyes had stories in them.

"You are my sachon, Suk-bo?" she asked.

"I am," I answered. "I am so glad to see you."

She gave me a smile, and I saw she was happy to see me, too. She invited me inside a small apartment with a single window overlooking the street. In front of the window was a table with a hibiscus blossom in a bowl. She invited me to sit and said, "Would you like some tea?"

"Yes, thank you," I answered.

"I drink bori cha," Jae-hee said. "I do not drink coffee. Today young people drink coffee to pretend to be American. I think we should drink bori cha instead."

"I feel the same," I said.

She put a pot of tea on the stove and came to the table. I couldn't believe this woman was the same girl I'd last seen in her home outside my village. She carried herself with dignity and looked intelligent. I sensed she'd had an interesting life. I immediately felt a bond with her.

For the next hour, we reminisced about when we were children and played together. We remembered the holiday festivals we'd had at her house. We talked about our parents and our siblings. We laughed and we cried.

Then, I asked her to tell me about being a comfort woman. "Not many people know about it," she said.

"The world seems to look the other way at what happened in Asia during the war," I said, thinking about Unit 731.

"I have tried to come forward about my experience many times," Jae-hee said, "but people do not want to listen, not even Koreans. I understand. The Japanese deny it because it was a horrible war crime. Koreans are embarrassed about it. Perhaps your work can make it known so it will not happen again."

"That's my job," I replied. "I'll do my best."

For two hours she told me about the comfort station, how the Imperial Army tricked her into going by telling her she was going to work in a boot factory. She told me how they beat and raped her for two years. "Some days it was over thirty times," she said, shaking her head as if she was surprised she survived. "I would have killed myself if not for my *onni*, my sister, Soo-hee. She saved my life."

She told me how Soo-hee had almost died and how they'd been separated at the end of the war. She said Soo-hee was living in North Korea and they hadn't seen each other for fifty years. She told me how she'd fallen in love and had a daughter with a man in North Korea who the communists killed. She escaped to the South and her own people shunned her for being a comfort woman. Although I hadn't suffered the pain and humiliation of rape, our stories were remarkably similar.

"What happened to your daughter?" I asked.

"She died giving birth to my granddaughter."

"I'm sorry," I said. "I know the pain of losing a child."

"I am sorry for you, too," she said.

I did a quick calculation in my head. Her granddaughter had to be young—still a child. Yet, I saw that Jae-hee lived alone. "What happened to your granddaughter?" I asked.

Pain crossed over Jae-hee's face. She tried to put on a brave smile. "I am a poor woman," she said. "I have no means to raise a child. I decided to have her adopted. She lives in America. Her name is Anna Carlson."

I couldn't think of what to say, so I said nothing. We sat in silence for a while. Then I said, "Your mother had a comb. She showed it to me once. It had a two-headed dragon. She said she gave it to you and your sister."

Jae-hee grinned. She reached over the table and lifted the window-sill. Underneath was a hidden compartment. She took out a package of brown cloth tied closed with a string. She opened it, and there was the comb with the two-headed dragon.

It was exactly as I remembered—a gold spine on the back and an ivory inlay of a two-headed dragon.

"May I?" I asked, nodding at the comb.

"Of course," she replied.

I picked up the comb and held it. It was heavy and sturdy in my hand. The gold spine was cool to the touch. I brought it to my face and examined the two-headed dragon. It was truly a work of art how the tiny pieces of ivory made the dragon come alive.

I said, "When your mother showed me this comb, she said the dragon would curse me if I married Hisashi. I married him anyway and there were many times I thought your mother was right and the dragon had cursed me. But I loved my husband. I still do. I believe that loving him has defeated the curse."

I gave the comb to Jae-hee. "My mother told me that the dragon would protect me," she said. "There were times I thought the dragon had abandoned me. But I believe in the two-headed dragon. I must pass it on to Anna someday. I'm not sure how or when, I only know that I will."

"What do you think it stands for, the two-headed dragon?"

"I've thought a lot about that," Jae-hee said. "See how the heads face opposite directions? I used to think one head protected Korea from

Japan in the east and the other from China in the west. But notice this." She showed me the comb. "See how the heads are different? One is round, the other is square. One has whiskers and the other does not. I often wondered why they made it that way. Since the heads come together in one body, I think it's saying that while we look different, we are all the same."

"Yes, I see," I said. "And if that is true, then the dragon would not curse me for marrying a Japanese man."

"No, I do not believe it would," Jae-hee said.

She wrapped the comb inside the cloth and returned it to the compartment under the windowsill. I glanced at my watch. It was late. "I have to go," I said.

"I am pleased that you came," she replied.

We stood and bowed to each other. We promised we'd write often and that I'd visit her when I came back to Korea. "I would like that very much," she said.

I left the apartment and caught a cab to a hotel near the airport.

I would have liked to stay in Seoul for several days to spend more time with my cousin. It would have been interesting to see the new buildings in Seoul, to shop in the Itaewon market, to visit Gyeongbok Palace, Korea's most sacred place. But I was concerned about Hisashi, and I wanted to get back to him.

I took the first flight to LA in the morning. It was a direct flight on a 747 jumbo jet. It would take eleven hours. I remembered the first flight I'd taken to Los Angeles that took almost two days. I smiled to myself at how much the world had changed during my life. I'd gone from a poor country girl picking strawberries in the forest behind my house to flying in jumbo jets halfway around the world.

We were scheduled to land at one o'clock in the morning, so I spent my time writing out what Jae-hee had told me. I made a plan for how I would use the information in my job. Jae-hee was right—people should know what the Japanese had done. I was determined to get the word out. I also wrote down the name of Jae-hee's granddaughter, Anna Carlson.

We landed at LAX, and I took a cab to my new home—a large apartment just west of Koreatown that I paid for with the money Mr. Saito had given me. After the cab dropped me off, I thought about finding Hisashi to see if he was all right. But it was two in the morning and I was tired from my trip, so I went to bed.

I worked all the next day on a paper outlining the alliance's position on the comfort women atrocity. It was brief and to the point. It stated that Japan should accept the responsibility for its military sexual slavery of hundreds of thousands of women and that it should make reparations to the survivors. As support, I included the notes I'd written from Jae-hee's story. I put the position paper in my outbox with a note to Mr. Weinberg asking him to approve it before his last day.

I left work early to look for Hisashi. He was one of a handful of homeless people who'd endured decades of life on the streets of LA. He'd become famous in Koreatown. Everyone knew of him. They called him the crazy Jap-bastard who begged for absolution for his country's crimes.

Usually, I found him in one of three places—Chapman Plaza, where he begged for food; Seoul International Park, where he watched the children play; or in MacArthur Park, where he slept. He wasn't in any of his usual places.

In Chapman Plaza, I asked a street vendor selling pho if he'd seen Hisashi.

"I saw the police arrest him yesterday," the vendor said.

It wasn't the first time they'd arrested Hisashi. A few months earlier, there'd been a call to clean up Los Angeles, and arresting the homeless was an easy way for the police to get the politicians off their backs. After a day or two in the county jail, they'd put Hisashi in a homeless shelter where he'd stay for a few days before going back out on the street.

I caught a cab and went to the Los Angeles County men's central jail. It was an imposing three-story concrete building not far from Chinatown. I went inside to the front desk and asked about Hisashi. The clerk—a large African American woman who never looked up from her monitor—said that they were processing him for a homeless shelter but if I paid a $325 fine and signed some papers, they'd release Hisashi to me. I wrote a check and signed the papers. Forty-five minutes later, I picked up Hisashi at a gate outside.

He had his black plastic bag that he always carried around with his brown blanket and some old clothes inside. His hair was long, tangled, and completely gray. Deep lines streaked his face, permanently darkened from decades in the Southern California sun.

He stood outside the gate, looking at his feet. "I'm sorry," he said.

"Let me help you," I said, as I'd done a thousand times before.

He shook his head. "I will not poison you any more than I already have."

"Then let me put you someplace where they won't arrest you anymore. When your father died, he left me money and said I should use it to help you."

"I dishonored my father," Hisashi said, shaking his head. "I cannot take his charity."

"I do not agree," I replied. "Your father believed that he failed you. That's why he left money for you."

Hisashi took a while to think about what I'd told him. Then he said, "I am very tired."

"Let me take you someplace where you can rest, somewhere off the street where you will be safe."

He looked from the lake to his hands. "Okay," he said.

I caught a cab and had the driver take us to the Angels of Mercy nursing home in a nice neighborhood north of Koreatown. I led Hisashi inside to a lobby with thick carpeting and leather chairs. When I told the receptionist why we were there, she looked at Hisashi and told us to wait. We sat in the chairs as she picked up the phone and made a call. A few minutes later, a woman in a business suit came and introduced herself as Mrs. Dahl. She glanced at Hisashi and pulled me aside.

"This is an exclusive private facility," she whispered. "I think your friend would be better served in a public home."

"No," I said. "I want him here."

"Ma'am," she said, "do you know what this place costs per month?"

"I know exactly what it costs," I answered. "I have researched it."

"Well then, you know that—"

"I will pay for ten years in advance," I said, interrupting her. "And I want him in a private room."

Mrs. Dahl cocked her head. "A private room for ten years? With all due respect, that kind of money . . ."

Before she could finish telling me that I couldn't afford it, I took out my checkbook and wrote a check for ten years for a private room. I gave it to Mrs. Dahl. "Call my bank and verify that the funds are there," I said. "We will wait."

As I sat next to Hisashi, Mrs. Dahl took the check and went to her office. A few minutes later, she came back and gave me a professional smile. "We would be delighted to take your friend," she said. "I can do the intake right away."

And so, Hisashi became a resident of the Angels of Mercy nursing home. Since he had no identification, I registered him as George Adams so no one looking into Japanese war crimes would find him. And since we had no proof that he and I were married, I told Mrs. Dahl that I was only a friend, but I would assume legal custody. Hisashi didn't say a word as they took him in and cleaned him up. They put him in a private room facing downtown Los Angeles.

When the nurses left, Hisashi sat in his room in an upholstered chair and stared out the window. I sat next to him and said, "I love you, Hisashi."

He continued to look out the window. "I'm sorry," he said.

THIRTY-FIVE

It was over a mile from my apartment to the Angels of Mercy nursing home, and every day I put my hair up with the silver hairpin and walked that mile to see my husband. It became more difficult when I reached my nineties and eventually, I had to take a cab.

Over the years, Hisashi grew even more withdrawn. His back was bent and his face was blotched with age spots. The skin on his hands was so thin the veins showed through. He sat all day in his chair, staring out his window as if he was trying to think of a way for salvation. I would take him for a walk in the hall or, on a nice day, outside in the garden. I would talk to him about Korea and Japan and his father and his sister, Yoshiko. I told him about Young-chul, what a sweet boy our son was and how Yoshiko and I had raised him into a fine young man. I would tell him how handsome he was when I first saw him in the forest behind my house. I would say how silly he looked in the mask at the Dano festival at my aunt and uncle's house. I would remind him of our wedding night. Sometimes, he would say, "I remember," or "That was a good time in my life." I had assumed that old age and decades of living on the street would diminish his mind, but it never did. He just didn't seem to want to talk.

Then one day, not long ago, he said, "You have been a good wife. I wish I could have been a good husband."

Surprised, I took his hand. "It is not your fault," I said.

"Yes, it is," he replied. "And I must atone for my sins."

"Atone for your sins . . . ," I said.

"Before I die," he said.

I took a full minute to think about what he was saying. Then I said, "I understand."

This morning when I came in, he was sitting on a chair in his room. Normally, he wore a sweatshirt and sweatpants. Today, he'd dressed in a white shirt and black slacks. His back was straighter than it had been in years.

"You look nice today," I said. "Why are you sitting there? Are you getting ready to go somewhere?"

"Yes," he answered. He went to his dresser and pulled a drawer all the way out. He reached inside the dresser and took out a tanto knife that was hidden in the back. And then, he took out the red scarf he'd bought for me in Sinuiju.

I was stunned. I thought he'd abandoned the scarf eighty years earlier when he abandoned me. Now, he held it out to me. "I tried for so long to make you forget me," he said, "but I could never forget you."

I began to cry. Since the day he told me we couldn't love each other anymore, I'd wondered how he truly felt about me. He'd said then that he'd always loved me, but it seemed that his guilt had crushed his love. I'd come to accept that he would never love me again.

I took the scarf and held it to my cheek as tears ran down my face. "I didn't know," I said.

"I'm sorry," Hisashi replied. "I hoped that if you thought I didn't love you, you would give me up someday and I wouldn't pull you down with me. But all these years you never did, and I never stopped loving you."

I went to him and we embraced. "Oh, Hisashi," I said, "I love you."

"I love you, too," he said.

He stepped back. "You have given me so much. I am sorry, but I need one last thing." He held up the tanto knife. "You are Korean. Before I die of old age, I must atone for my crimes against your people. It is the only way to set my spirit free. I wanted to do it long ago but I couldn't. Help me now do it the right way." He sat again. He held the knife in front of him with both hands. I stared at him for several minutes, not knowing what to do. I had tried so long to save him, but I had failed. Now, he was going to save himself and I knew I shouldn't stop him.

"I am ready," he said.

I wiped the tears from my face. "Okay," I said, "I am ready, too."

I went outside the room and asked an aide for tea and paper and a pen. A few minutes later, she came with a pad of paper, a pen, and a teapot with two teacups. I took them into the room.

I pushed a chair in front of Hisashi, who'd laid the tanto knife across his legs. I set the tea on a table between us. We both bowed to the tea. I took the teapot in both hands and raised it high above our heads. I asked the kami for their blessings. I set the teapot down and bowed to it. Then, I poured tea into a single cup and gave it to Hisashi. He bowed to me and took a sip. Then he gave me the cup. I bowed to him and took a sip. I set the teacup aside.

I gave Hisashi the pen and paper. "Your elegy," I said.

"Yes," he replied. "As they did in the old days."

"As the warriors did," I said.

He nodded, and as I watched, he started writing. He took his time, carefully thinking through each word and phrase. He filled one page, and then two. He stopped and read what he'd written. He scribbled a few changes. Then, he signed it and presented it to me. I accepted it with a nod and folded it inside my dress.

He looked at me and said, "It is time."

I picked up the red scarf and stood behind him. He sat perfectly still as I tied the scarf around his head and let the ends fall down his back. "The scarf will keep us together on your journey to the spirit world," I said.

"Yes, that is good," he replied.

I sat in front of him again. He took the tanto knife from his lap and held it out in front of him. I started to cry again.

His face grew soft and he closed his eyes. "I pray to the spirits of all those I hurt that they accept my humble apology." He opened his eyes and thrust the knife into his stomach.

"Hisashi!" I cried. I desperately wanted to take the knife from him. But then, for the first time in eighty years, he smiled at me, and I saw the young man who I'd first seen in the forest so long ago.

He whispered, "Honor at last." And then he closed his eyes and died.

THIRTY-SIX

We sit in silence for a long time. Ms. Yi wipes tears from her face. I do, too. Finally, Detective Jackson reaches over and shuts off the recorder.

"What did your husband write in those papers?" Jackson finally asks.

Ms. Yi takes the papers out of her dress and gives them to me.

"I should see those," Jackson says with a hand out.

"You will find out what they say soon enough, Detective," Ms. Yi says. I put the papers inside my briefcase without reading them.

Jackson sighs and faces me. "Got anything to say, Counselor?" he asks.

"She's innocent," I answer. "You have to let her go."

"Tell you what," Jackson says. "The prints on the knife should be back from the lab. If hers aren't on it, I'll tell the DA it was a suicide."

I tap on the table. "If her prints are on the knife, it doesn't prove she killed him."

"It is okay, Anna," Ms. Yi interjects. "I never touched the tanto knife."

Jackson leaves and I'm alone with Ms. Yi. She gives me a tired smile. "You must read what Hisashi wrote," she says.

I take Hisashi's papers out of my briefcase. They are in Japanese, but I know Japanese and I read it through twice. It is his confession of his war crimes and a hope that his final act of contrition—his seppuku—will save his soul. It is a plea for an end to racism.

"This proves your innocence," I say.

"Yes, but I believe Hisashi wanted to make it public. People should know about Unit 731. Do you think you can have it published?"

I nod to myself and say, "There are reporters outside who'd love to get their hands on this. I'll take care of it." I put the papers back inside my briefcase.

"Thank you," Ms. Yi says. "That is why I needed you here. Also, I wanted to see the comb one last time."

I take the comb out of my briefcase, unwrap it from the brown cloth, and place it on the table in front of Ms. Yi. She picks it up. "For so long I thought I was cursed by the two-headed dragon," she says, gazing at it. "Then I came to believe that my love for Hisashi conquered the curse. Now, I do not believe there was ever a curse from the dragon. A dragon doesn't curse people. The thing that curses us is ourselves."

Ms. Yi continues to stare at the comb. "Your grandmother, Jae-hee, told me something. She said this comb was made for Queen Min, the last queen of Korea. Is it true?"

"Yes, it is, ma'am," I say. "Your cousin and I are direct descendants of the queen."

She smiles. "That would make me the queen's relative, too."

"Yes, it would," I reply.

She gives me the comb. She reaches behind her head and takes out the silver hairpin. She sets it on the table and gazes at it sadly. I notice she hasn't drunk her tea. "Would you like your tea warmed up while we wait?" I ask.

"No," she replies. She takes the teacup in both hands and looks at it. "Since our wedding night when Hisashi was so gentle and kind, I have committed myself to loving him. For more than eighty years I dreamed of being with him, the way we were back then. But he was not the same man after he went to Tokyo. Now, today, he has atoned for his sins and his spirit is free. I knew this day would come. He is my Hisashi again and I don't want to wait to be with him."

She gives me a sad smile and then drinks all her tea. She sets the cup on the table and I notice a small vial next to it. Gradually, I realize what's happening, but don't move to stop it. She smiles at me, perfectly content. Her eyes cloud over and her head nods. She closes her eyes and gently lays her head on the table.

After Ms. Yi draws her last breath, I see her spirit soar high. It flies over the Pacific Ocean and on to Korea. It goes to her village outside of Sinuiju. She sees Hisashi waiting for her behind her house. He is a young man, handsome in his loose white shirt and black slacks. His hair glistens, and his liquid eyes sparkle. She is a young woman, pretty and petite, dressed in a blue-and-yellow hanbok. She goes to him. He takes her hand and they run into the forest. They pick strawberries and put them in her bamboo basket. When the basket is full, they find a sunny place in the forest and lie on the cool grass. There, they make tender love.

After, he lies on his back with his hands behind his head, gazing at the sky. She lies facing him, running a finger over his chest. A flock of red-crowned cranes glides overhead. A water deer steps lightly in the forest beyond. Time stands still. They are at peace, and joy fills their hearts.

"I love you, Hisashi," she says.

"I love you, too, Suk-bo," he replies.

AUTHOR'S NOTE

On January 27, 1945, the 322nd Rifle Division of the Soviet Red Army liberated the Nazi concentration camp at Auschwitz. There, they discovered that along with a mass extermination program, the Nazis had conducted experiments on prisoners. The experiments included radiation exposure, forced diseases, freezing, drowning, and biological weapons testing. Thousands died horrifying deaths. Thousands more suffered painful, permanent disabilities and mental distress. The program was led by Dr. Josef Mengele, the "Angel of Death," who after the war, escaped to Argentina and lived in hiding for thirty-five years before he died in 1979. He never paid for his crimes.

In 1939 near the city of Harbin, Manchuria, the Japanese Imperial Army set up Unit 731, a camp used to conduct human experimentation exactly like what the Nazis did in Auschwitz. The Japanese called their subjects *maruta*, Japanese for "logs" because they told outsiders that Unit 731 was a sawmill. And like Auschwitz, thousands of innocent people died horrible deaths, and thousands more were scarred for life. The program was led by Dr. Shiro Ishii, who escaped to Japan after the war and died in Tokyo in 1979. Like Dr. Mengele, he never paid for his crimes.

Most Americans know about Dr. Mengele and his horrifying experiments at Auschwitz. On the other hand, most Americans—like me before I did the research for this book—have never heard of Dr. Ishii and Unit 731.

There's a reason. The Russians captured the research from Auschwitz, which gave them valuable information for waging war. The Americans were worried about what the Russians had in Mengele's research, so much so that when they arrested Dr. Ishii after the war in US-occupied Japan, they struck a deal with him. They gave him immunity for his war crimes in exchange for his research. And to prevent moral outrage in the age of McCarthyism, the Americans withheld from the public information about Unit 731 and the agreement with Dr. Ishii.

The three books in this series—*Daughters of the Dragon*, Jae-hee's story about sexual slavery; *The Dragon Queen*, the story of Queen Min and imperial exploitation; and this book about wartime atrocities—expose atrocities committed by the Japanese. Lest we, the victors in World War II, assume righteous indignation against the Japanese (and Nazis), consider this from historian Richard Drayton:

> *After 1945, we borrowed many fascist methods. Nuremberg only punished a handful of the guilty; most walked free with our help. In 1946, Project Paperclip secretly brought more than 1,000 Nazi scientists to the US . . . Other experiments at mind control via drugs and surgery were folded into the CIA's Project Bluebird. Japan's Dr Shiro Ishii, who had experimented with prisoners in Manchuria, came to Maryland to advise on bio-weapons. Within a decade of British troops liberating Bergen-Belsen, they were running their own concentration camps in Kenya to crush the Mau Mau. The Gestapo's torture techniques were borrowed by the French in Algeria,*

and then disseminated by the Americans to Latin American dictatorships in the 60s and 70s.[1]

Human experimentation, sexual slavery, oppression, political murder, and other atrocities occur when one race, religion, or nation feels they are superior—in other words, when they practice bigotry. I hope that the books in the Dragon trilogy have helped readers think about how we treat each other. I know for certain that writing them has given me a lot to think about.

William Andrews

---

1   The Guardian, May 9, 2005

ACKNOWLEDGMENTS

A book like this is never a solo effort. I owe a debt of gratitude to my friends and family who have supported me over the years. A special shout-out to the extraordinary people at Lake Union Publishing who have helped make this book all it could be. And, of course, an extra special thank-you to my researcher, first editor, sounding board, encourager, and love of my life, my wife, Nancy.

SELECTED BIBLIOGRAPHY

This is a work of fiction. As such, I took some liberties with history for dramatic purposes. Nevertheless, I did my best to portray the lives and times of Koreans during the twentieth century.

If you want to learn more about Korea, the fascinating and often tragic history of the Land of the Morning Calm, below is a bibliography of books I found useful.

On Korean History

Breen, Michael. *The Koreans: Who They Are, What They Want, Where Their Future Lies.* New York: Thomas Dunne Books, 2004.

Cumings, Bruce. *Korea's Place in the Sun: A Modern History.* New York: W. W. Norton & Company, 2005.

Eckert, Carter J., Ki-baik Lee, Young Ick Lew, Michael Robinson, and Edward W. Wagner. *Korea Old and New—A History.* Cambridge: Korea Institute, Harvard University, 1990.

Oberdorfer, Don. *The Two Koreas: A Contemporary History*. New York: Basic Books, 2001.

Pratt, Keith. *Everlasting Flower: A History of Korea*. London: Reaktion Books, 2006.

Seth, Michael J. *A Concise History of Korea: From Antiquity to the Present*. Lanham, MD: Rowman & Littlefield, 2006.

One last thing. I'd like to ask readers to please go to their online retailer and write a review of this book. Or, send me an email at bill@williamandrewsbooks.com. It's the only way I can get feedback from my readers!

ABOUT THE AUTHOR

For more than thirty years, William Andrews was a copywriter and a marketing/brand executive with several Fortune 500 companies. For fifteen years, he ran his own advertising agency. At night and on weekends (and sometimes during the workday), William wrote fiction. His novels include *The Dirty Truth* and *The Essential Truth*, the latter of which won the Mayhaven Award for Fiction. *The Spirit of the Dragon* is William's third novel in his trilogy about Korea, following *The Dragon Queen* and *Daughters of the Dragon*. He lives in Minneapolis with his wife, an inner-city schoolteacher. For more information, visit www.williamandrewsbooks.com.